Praise for Lynn Michaels and
MOTHER OF THE BRIDE

"Throw the rice and cut the cake! *Mother of the Bride* is a winner!"
—JULIE GARWOOD

"This humorous romantic comedy warms the heart with its zany yet believable characters and snappy dialog . . . Michaels's keen sense of comic timing and oddball characters never fail to entertain."
—*Publishers Weekly*

"*Mother of the Bride* is filled to the brim with wonderfully eccentric characters, layered emotions and downright hilarious antics."
—*Romantic Times* (Gold Medal, Top Pick)

Praise for
RETURN ENGAGEMENT

"This heart-warming story wraps itself around you and draws you into a different world. Ms. Michaels has done it again!"
—*Rendezvous*

"With whacky characters, a wonderful small-town atmosphere, and a love story that won't quit, Michaels's romance will keep readers completely engaged."
—*Booklist*

Also by Lynn Michaels
Published by Ballantine Books

MOTHER OF THE BRIDE
RETURN ENGAGEMENT

Honeymoon Suite

A Novel

Lynn Michaels

BALLANTINE BOOKS • NEW YORK

Honeymoon Suite is a work of fiction. Names, characters, places, and incidents are the products of the author's imagination or are used fictitiously. Any resemblance to actual events, locales, or persons, living or dead, is entirely coincidental.

An Ivy Books Mass Market Original

Copyright © 2005 by Lynne Smith

All rights reserved. Published in the United States by Ivy Books, an imprint of The Random House Publishing Group, a division of Random House, Inc., New York.

Ivy Books and colophon are trademarks of Random House, Inc.

ISBN 0-345-47600-X

Printed in the United States of America

Ballantine Books website address: www.ballantinebooks.com

OPM 9 8 7 6 5 4 3 2 1

For my dad, Del,
who, alas, does not own a bank.

My nephew James,
who really does look like Sir Paul but can't sing a lick.
Take care of yourself, JP.

For the real Rocky the tuxedo cat.

And for Benjamin and Lucas,
who took less time to be born than this book.

Honeymoon Suite

Chapter One

**Outlook Farm
Kansas City, Missouri
Summer 1988**

It was Saturday. Dory Lambert's favorite day of the week. On Saturday, Chase McKay, the chauffeur's son, washed the cars.

One by one he'd drive them out of the garage, fan them on the tarmac and take off his shirt. It was the high point of fourteen-year-old Dory's dumb, boring, stupid, pointless week.

The Rolls, the Bentley and Daddy's grand old Packard touring car. The Town Car that Daddy occasionally drove himself. Mother's Volvo, her sister Jilly's 1957 Thunderbird hardtop convertible, the Chevy station wagon and the van that Wallace the butler used for errands.

It was a lot of hosing, sponging, wiping and polishing so Chase started early. No later than seven A.M., Dory would plunk herself with a book on the round bench under the massive old elm tree that grew by the garage. Close enough that she could see Chase and he could pretend she wasn't there. He was awfully good at that.

She'd lie on the bench reading till Chase started to get tired, till the scowl that made her heart twist curled the corner of his mouth. When he upended the red plastic milk crate that held the sponges and chamois cloths, sat down

on it and lit a cigarette, Dory would put her book aside,
sidle up to him and say, "I'll give you a hand, Chase."

"Are you trying to get me in trouble?" He'd squint at her
through a curl of smoke. "Go away, squirt."

"You won't get in trouble," she'd say. "Nobody cares
what I do."

Dory didn't say because she wasn't beautiful like Jilly,
but it was true. Chase would flip his cigarette away, throw
a sponge at her and go back to work. Dory would chase the
sponge down, pick it up and start scrubbing. Chase would
scowl for a while, then he'd smile. He'd flip soapsuds at her
when they met at the bucket. Next thing Dory knew, she'd
have a bucket of her own. Chase would go to the spigot
and fill one for her, drop down on his heels beside her and
show her how to get the road gunk off the chrome fenders.
The brush of his arm against hers made her stomach flutter.

At some point in the morning Jilly would walk by with her
friends. In boots and jodhpurs on their way to the stables,
in white pleated skirts swinging tennis rackets, or pastel
shorts and matching sun visors on their way to the nine-
hole golf course. Dory could feel the spring that would
tighten in Chase and turn him around half a second before
Jilly appeared with her friends.

Jilly was blond, leggy—"coltish," Mother called her in
those days before her figure filled out—and gorgeous. She
and her friends never stopped, but their eyes would slide
toward Chase. He'd turn around and stand there, let them
look at him as they walked past, his naked, blond-haired
chest sweaty with soap. The blue eyes that met and held his
longest were Jilly's. When they were gone, Chase would
turn back to Dory and pick up where he'd left off showing
her how to get just the right buff on the bumper of the
Rolls.

When they finished the cars they'd drink a Coke on the
bench under the elm tree and Dory would tell Chase about
her stupid, dumb, boring, pointless week. How did French
people learn French? Her ballet teacher said she danced
like a cow. The new uniform she had to wear to school in

the fall made her look like a penguin. She did not want to go to London with Mother and Jilly. She wanted to stay home with Daddy and Aunt Ping but Mother said she had to go to London.

"You got a rough life, squirt." Chase would give her a look that was part scowl, part amused smile. "I don't know how you stand it."

I look forward to Saturdays, Dory wanted to tell him. Doing something that has a point, a purpose, achieves a goal. I look forward to being with you. Dory wondered later what would've happened if she'd said that to Chase, if it would've changed anything. Nope, she concluded. Chase was nineteen, Jilly was seventeen and she was a fourteen-year-old squirt.

Chase lived over the garage with his father, Charles McKay, Daddy's chauffeur. It was a really big garage, climate controlled to protect Daddy's cars, especially his treasured old Pack. The apartment above it was more like a penthouse than a garret.

"Awfully nice digs for the chauffeur," one of Jilly's friends said on a Saturday night when they were all staying over.

They were on the balcony outside Jilly's bedroom. In their peignoirs and painted toenails, with Daddy's binoculars so they could spy on Chase. Dory had wormed her way in. She always did and Jilly always let her. When one of her friends said, "Do we always have to have the brat with us?" Jilly's eyes would flash. "She's not a brat," she'd say. "She's my baby sister." Dory worshipped Jilly.

When her snippy friend made that comment about the garage, Jilly said, "Daddy's very good to our servants. Mother tells him he's an idiot but he tells Mother if you want people to take care of you, you'd better take care of them. Daddy treats our servants like family."

One Saturday night that summer it was just Dory and Jilly and Jilly's best friend Marilyn on the balcony. They caught Chase in the binoculars as he slid outside onto the flat part of the garage roof in jeans and nothing else, leaned his elbows on the parapet and lit a cigarette. Dory saw the red flare in the darkness as he inhaled.

"God he is *sooo* gorgeous," Marilyn said and all three of them sighed. Then Marilyn swung around on the chaise they'd drawn up to the brick balustrade and tipped her head to one side. "Sooo," she said to Jilly. "Have you let him kiss you yet?"

"*Mar*-i-lyn." Jilly flicked her eyes at Dory.

Kissing? Dory's heart seized. When was *this* going on?

The next night when Jill snuck out of the house Dory followed her. She bumped into a stone bench and knocked over a birdbath, but Jilly zipped through the ornamental garden like a bat with radar. Chase waited for her by the stables. Dory saw the flash of his white T-shirt when he stepped out of the darkness. Jilly flew to him, threw her arms around him. Chase lifted her off her feet.

Dory clung to the corner of the garage. When Chase took Jilly's hand and drew her into the long, low horse barn where Mother kept her Arabs and her saddlebreds, Dory followed. Chase had left the cross-planked doors ajar. If Eddie the head groom walked the stable yard, and he did sometimes at night, he'd investigate. Because she loved Chase, Dory eased the doors shut behind her and sank into a ball of misery against the wall near the tack room door.

Moonlight glowed through the skylights. Chase had his shirt off. Jilly's blouse was unbuttoned. Chase had her backed against the wall between two stalls. He was kissing Jilly and squeezing her breasts through the white lace cups of her bra. Jilly was making noises like it hurt. Dory's heart tore down the middle. She didn't know which one of them to yell at first—*Stop hurting my sister! Stop kissing Chase!*

"No." Jilly lifted Chase's hand from her breast and slipped it between her legs. "There. Oh yes. There."

Dory's mouth fell open. Where had Jilly learned *that*?

The barn doors swung open, the lights blazed on and there stood Daddy and Charles McKay in their pajamas and bathrobes. Chase jumped away from Jilly, but Daddy and Charles had seen his hand on Jilly's breast, the other between her legs. Both men looked like they'd been punched in the stomach.

"Chase," Charles said. "How could you do such a thing?"

"It wasn't Chase," Dory said. "Jill put his hand between her legs."

"Jesus, Mary and Saint Joseph!" Daddy shouted, first at Dory, then at Jilly. "In front of your sister!"

Jilly yanked her blouse over her breasts and burst into tears.

Daddy snatched off his leather slipper. He'd never hit Dory or Jilly with it. He'd pitch it at Aunt Ping's cat, Tobias, when he jumped into his leather chair in the library, but when he took off his slipper and started waving it around you knew you were in trouble.

Daddy flung out his hand, pointed his slipper at the house and thundered *"Go!"* at Jilly. She went, clutching her blouse and sobbing.

"We'll discuss this is the morning, Charles," Daddy said to his chauffeur, then swung a glare and his slipper on Dory. "You too. *Go!*"

Dory wanted to look at Chase but didn't dare. She ran out of the barn, one jump ahead of Daddy's slipper.

Mother and Aunt Ping were awake. Aunt Ping slept like Tobias, like a cat. The birdbath Dory knocked over was right outside her window on the ground floor of the south wing. She'd seen Dory hopping one-footed through the garden and went upstairs to waken Mother and Daddy.

Daddy yelled. Mother lectured them on appropriate behavior for young ladies named Lambert, which did *not* include making out with the chauffeur's son or snooping on your sister. Daddy yelled some more. Aunt Ping sat in a pink-gilt Louis XIV armchair in the front parlor with Tobias in her lap, her head bowed as she stroked his gray fur.

Dory's head hurt by the time Daddy and Mother finished. She stumbled upstairs, fell face-first on her bed and slept until eleven o'clock the next morning, when she yawned downstairs to the breakfast room. Aunt Ping came in and sat beside her while she drank her milk-laced coffee. She told her Chase was gone, did her best to make Dory believe this had been planned all along. That Daddy would pay for Chase to go to college.

"It's June, Aunt Ping," Dory said. "School starts in September."

"There was an opening for summer semester. Chase had to leave right away to take advantage of it."

"Is Charles gone? Did Daddy get rid of him, too?"

"Dory." Aunt Ping looked shocked. "What a thing to say."

"This is because of Jilly, because of what happened last night."

"Really, Dory, it isn't. It only looks that way."

"If it looks like a duck and it quacks like a duck, then it's a duck, Aunt Ping," Dory said and stomped out of the breakfast room.

When Daddy came home from the bank that evening, Dory let herself into the library without knocking. He blinked at her, surprised, from his leather chair, a cigar in one hand, a whiskey sour in the other.

"How can you say you treat our servants like family and then send Chase away because he kissed Jilly?" she demanded.

"It wasn't my idea," Daddy replied. "Charles thought it was best."

"Are you going to pay for Chase to go to college?"

"Yes. It was part of the arrangement Charles and I made when he came to work for us."

Almost twenty years ago, Dory knew, when Chase was just a baby. After Charles' wife died and Daddy and Mother were first married. Dory left the library and the house and climbed the stairs to the garage apartment.

"Why did you think it was best to send Chase away?" she asked when Charles McKay opened the door.

"Go back to the house, Miss Dory. That's where you belong."

Charles said it gently and closed the door in her face.

Mother came to her room that evening. She came to Jilly's room almost every night. They'd sit on Jilly's bed and giggle like girls, but Mother rarely opened the adjoining door to Dory's room. No one had to tell her why; Dory knew. She was small and dark like Daddy and Aunt Ping. Mother said she looked like a gypsy.

Dory was lying on her bed, her hands clasped between her barely there breasts, squinting at the shadows thrown on the ceiling by the long summer twilight sifting through the sheers on the balcony doors. She could *almost* see Chase's face in the swirls of light and dark, then Mother spoke and the pattern scattered.

"Jill and I are leaving for London tomorrow. You're staying home. You're being punished for spying on your sister."

Dory pushed up on her elbows. "What's Jill's punishment for putting Chase's hand between her legs and getting him sent away?"

Mother's eyes turned to blue icicles. "Do not annoy your father about Chase. What's done is done and that's the end of it."

Dory thought it was the end of her life. She didn't miss going to London to visit Mother's widowed sister Deirdre and their divorced cousin Diana. All the aunts did was whine about how poor they were until Mother gave them money. Which Dory didn't understand since Deirdre had inherited the Darwood family manse—an ivy-covered rock pile in Dorset—and the London town house the cousins shared was crammed to the rafters with antiques. Dory thought her life was over because Chase was gone.

She hardly ate, though no one but Aunt Ping noticed. She cried herself to sleep every night, trying so hard to build Chase's face in the shadows on her ceiling that she gave herself a headache that wouldn't go away. She blamed Jill. She hated her sister, refused to go down for dinner the night she and Mother came home from London.

At bedtime Jill crept into Dory's room, picked her up from her pillow crying and throwing her fists and hugged her. "Oh, Dory. I'm so sorry. I miss him, too." They cried together, fell asleep together in Dory's bed, and in the morning they were friends again.

Until Dory met James Darwood, Aunt Diana's son, at breakfast. The story was that Aunt Diana had his name legally changed after her divorce so there'd be a Darwood to inherit the family estate. On Dory's past trips to England with Mother and Jill, James had been away at boarding school, then at Eton, then at Oxford.

He was twenty-two years old and had blue eyes, about three rows of eyelashes and long brown hair he wore in a ponytail at the nape of his neck.

Mother glowed watching James eat his weight in Cook's buttermilk pancakes. Jilly's eyes sparkled. Daddy couldn't understand a word he said. Tobias laid his ears back and hissed at James from Aunt Ping's lap.

"Silly puss," he said mildly but Dory didn't like the glint in his eyes when he smiled at the cat. Or the sneer she heard in his voice as she trailed Jilly and James out of the dining room. "Aunt Ping. What kind of name is that? She obviously isn't Chinese."

"Her name is Margaret," Jill said. "Daddy couldn't say her nickname Peggy when he was small. He called her Ping and it just sort of stuck. Even the servants call her Miss Ping."

"Miss Ping," James said. "Miss Ping Pong Ball."

Dory expected Jill to slug him, but she laughed. Her goofy, aren't-you-the-cutest-boy laugh that sounded to Dory like she was gargling.

From that moment on she despised James, but Jilly took him everywhere with her. To dances at Mother and Daddy's club in her little red T-bird, shopping on the Country Club Plaza. They rode Mother's horses, swam in the Olympic-size marble pool, played tennis, shot golf. All the things Jill used to do with Dory when her friends weren't around.

There was something scaly about James, something that

made Dory's skin crawl. She couldn't explain it and no one would listen to her when she tried, even Aunt Ping. When Dory begged her to read the I Ching, Aunt Ping took the black and red lacquered box that held the Chinese fortune-telling yarrow sticks out of Dory's hands and smoothed her hair.

"This isn't about James, is it?" she said. "This is about Chase."

"No, Aunt Ping. This is about James," Dory said firmly. "Even Tobias thinks he's creepy. He hisses every time he sees him."

"Tobias is a cat, Dory. James is a new person in his territory. He'll warm up to him. So will you, if you give yourself a chance."

Mother wanted Daddy to give James a job at the bank.

"For God's sake, Drusilla," he said, loud enough that Dory could hear him through the library doors. "Isn't it enough that I support your sister and your cousin, that I paid for James to attend his fancy schools? Now I have to give the little bastard a job?"

Dory smiled; she thought Daddy was referring to James' personality, not his parentage.

"You know how grateful Deirdre and Diana are," Mother said. "You're a saint to them, Del. A saint."

"I'm a meal ticket to them," Daddy said bluntly.

"Don't be a stick, darling. James has experience. He worked two years for Woolwich Bank. A fine, rock solid firm, you've always said."

Woolwich had sacked James for pilfering the till, but that didn't come out until it was too late. Aunt Diana slept with one of the managers to keep it hushed up and James walked away whistling with a reference.

"I don't like the way he looks at Dory," Daddy said and Dory blinked, startled, outside the library doors.

"Oh, Del. You're imagining things." Mother laughed. "As if anyone would notice Dory next to Jill."

"I don't like that, either. He and Jill are cousins, for God's sake. Second, third—I don't give a damn. This isn't

England and it isn't Arkansas, either. I expect you to put a stop to it, Drusilla."

"A harmless flirtation," Mother cooed.

Daddy stopped grumbling, started purring like Tobias and the next day James Darwood had a job at Lambert Bank and Trust.

All of Jill's stupid friends thought James was to-die-for handsome. At the next sleepover they took turns painting each other's toenails and sighing over James. Dory wanted to scream. Six weeks ago they'd all been sighing over Chase.

"James looks like Paul McCartney," Marilyn said.

"No, he doesn't," Dory said. "Paul McCartney is old."

"I meant when he was young, you little dork. When he was a Beatle," Marilyn said and pushed Dory's face into her pillow.

When Marilyn finally let her up, gasping for air, Jill just smiled. Like she had the day they'd all gone swimming and James held Dory's head underwater till her lungs nearly burst.

Dory ran out of the house and flung herself sobbing on the round bench under the elm tree. Charles McKay found her there in the middle of the night. Wallace locked the house at eleven, so Charles took her up to his apartment over the garage. He made her tea and toast; when she finished, a bed on the squishy, scratched-up leather sofa that used to be Daddy's library couch and let her read the letters Chase had written to him.

Chase was at Cornell University in New York, taking classes in architectural design and mechanical drawing. The food in the dorm sucked. He'd found a part-time job, stocking shelves at night in a grocery store. He'd written Mr. Lambert to thank him for this opportunity to make something of himself. Dory read that and frowned; Daddy hadn't said a word about hearing from Chase.

She looked up from the letter at Charles. "I didn't know Chase wanted to be an architect."

"He's always wanted to be an architect," Charles replied and handed her a thick, spiral-bound pad of graph paper filled with sketches of houses and buildings and meticulously drawn blueprints.

Of course she hadn't known Chase wanted to be an architect. All she'd ever done was talk about herself. Dory felt her face burn and gave the notebook back to Charles. He said good night, left the lamp on beside her, Chase's letters in her quilt-covered lap and went to bed.

"*I miss you, Dad,*" Chase had written to Charles three weeks ago. "*I miss a lot of things about Outlook that I never thought I would. Friday night poker games with you and Wallace and Henry and Eddie. I'm glad Tom took my place. Tell Esme I can't wait for the box of cookies. My mouth is watering just thinking about her snickerdoodles.*"

Wallace was the butler, Henry Daddy's valet. Tom managed the vast stretches of Outlook that were still a working farm. Dory had no idea that Esme was Cook's name till she read Chase's letters. She didn't know that Tom had four grandchildren, either, or that Mrs. Grant, the housekeeper, had lost her husband in Vietnam, that he was listed as MIA but Mrs. Grant still hoped that someday he'd come home.

Dory felt so ashamed that she didn't know these things, that she'd never bothered to look beyond the end of her own spoiled, selfish nose, that she almost threw up. She fell asleep with tears in her eyes and a plan forming in her head. She thought it out as carefully as Chase had drawn all those blueprints in his notebook. When Daddy called her into the library on July 14, the day before she turned fifteen, and asked what she wanted for her birthday, Dory was ready for him.

"A job," she said and Del Lambert blinked at her.

"A what?"

"A job," Dory repeated. "At the bank."

"Why do you want a job at the bank?"

"I don't especially but I'm too young to be hired anyplace else, so it's the bank or nothing."

"But, Dory. School starts in six weeks."

"I'll work till then. I'll work school vacations and Saturdays. You can pay me cash under the table like you pay the fruit pickers who help Tom harvest the strawberries and the apples."

Daddy's jaw dropped. "How do you know about that?"

Dory smiled. *Thank you, Chase.* "I pay attention."

Daddy dismissed her and summoned Mother to the library. Dory listened through the ornate brass keyhole. It was so big she could see through it, but she didn't peek.

"Now I understand why Dory's been spending so much time with the servants," Mother said. "Why she's taken to calling Cook 'Esme.' Her plebian roots are showing."

Mother's great-grandfather was a marquis, Daddy's a corporal in the Union cavalry, mustered out at the end of the Civil War with a lame horse and twenty-seven cents he'd parlayed into the funds he'd needed to build Lambert Bank and Trust, and Outlook Farm.

"What's wrong with working and earning a living?" Daddy snapped. "Maybe Deirdre and Diana should give it a go, as you Brits say."

"Don't be cross, darling," Mother cooed. "It's perfectly natural for children to rebel at this age. If Dory wants a job, give her a job. She'll tire of it soon enough."

"That's what you think," Dory muttered and took herself to bed.

Dory began her career at Lambert's in the mail room. It was the lowliest, most rinky-dink job her father could think of, Dory was sure, but she loved it. She spent her first week wandering around with her mail cart like a rat lost in a maze. But she loved that, too, learning her way around Lambert's cavernous main branch in downtown Kansas City, a twelve-story granite behemoth crouched atop the bluffs above the Missouri River bottoms on the far north end of Walnut Street.

She refused to be chauffeured to work with Daddy and James. She rode the bus every day to and from Lambert's, glaring out the back window at Charles trailing the bus in the Rolls.

She borrowed two weeks' bus fare and lunch money from Daddy and promptly repaid him with interest from her first pay packet.

"Look here, Drusilla," he said proudly. "We've raised a banker."

Mother rolled her eyes. Dory kept hers peeled on James.

Only the best tellers, the most accurate and most experienced, were allowed to serve Lambert's customers in the crimson-carpeted main lobby on Walnut. They sat behind frosted glass windows on tall stools with padded leather seats and backs. James was scrunched on a plain wooden stool at a tiny window with no glass at all in the garden level lobby on the Baltimore Street side of the building.

Dory couldn't keep from smirking the first time she saw him.

"Make all the faces you like, pug," James said. He called her pug because she reminded him of a yappy little dog. "This is only temporary. I'll be in the main lobby before you know it."

"Not without three years' experience you won't," Dory snapped.

"Smart little mutt, aren't you?" James grinned. "But I'm family and nepotism begins at home."

"Really? Is that why I'm pushing a mail cart and you're stuck down here in the basement?"

"Not for long, pug." James winked. "You hide and watch."

"That's exactly what I plan to do," Dory said.

Every Labor Day, Daddy hosted a daylong picnic at Outlook for all of Lambert's employees, all six hundred and thirty-seven of them from the bank's eight branches, plus their families, and all the servants. Mother hated "the help and their brats running tame all over the place," but since Outlook belonged to Aunt Ping, who was the eldest, and

Daddy refused to end the tradition begun by his great-grandfather, Mother had no choice but to grit her teeth and try to act gracious.

Aunt Ping sat on Lambert's board of directors with Daddy. Her primary duty was planning the Labor Day picnic. She was so pleased when Dory offered to help that she blushed.

Though the event was catered there was still a huge amount of organizing and detail checking. Listening to Aunt Ping wring the best possible price out of vendors on the phone made Dory's jaw drop. Mother never quibbled; she simply whipped out a credit card.

"How do you think Nicholas Lambert turned a lame horse and twenty-seven cents into Lambert Bank and Trust?" Aunt Ping said. "He wheeled, he dealed and he haggled."

She taught Dory how to haggle, too. How to write checks and keep a single-entry ledger, how to figure percentages and unit prices on a calculator. Dory loved it. She loved algebra and geometry in school, too, but this was way more fun than solving problems on the board for Sister Immaculata. This had a practical application.

It was hotter than the Fourth of July on Labor Day, the air so humid Dory swore she could drink it if only she had a straw. The sun glared down on Outlook from a hazy white sky, but the tents Aunt Ping had arranged for were the size of circus big tops with perforated panels for ventilation and big fans that blew over steel tubs of ice packed with sodas to keep everyone cool.

Dory stood in the tent closest to the golf course, gnawing on a turkey leg and watching James and Jill shove aluminum cans of Coke and Dr Pepper into one of the tubs. James slipped a handful of ice chips down the front of Jill's bright yellow tank top. She yelped and hopped around, flapping her tank top and giving James an eyeful of her cleavage and her white lace bra. James' nostrils flared.

Dory looked around but didn't see Daddy or Aunt Ping. When James caught Jill's fingers and led her out of the tent,

Dory tossed her turkey leg in a trash can and followed. She followed James and Jill most of the afternoon, keeping herself hidden in the crowds of Lambert's employees and their running, shrieking kids.

She trailed them from the driving range, where Daddy was handing out cash prizes for the longest drives, to the tennis courts, where Aunt Ping sat in a straw coolie hat in the judge's chair supervising the mixed doubles tournament. When James changed into swim trunks and Jill a hot pink bikini, Dory hid and watched them swim. Jill didn't bother to dry off afterward, just tugged her tank top over her bikini. It took five seconds for the yellow cotton to soak up the water and make dark wet circles around her nipples. James almost drooled. Jill smiled.

So did Dory, peering between the fronds of the ferns and palms growing around the waterfall at the deep end of the pool. "Gotcha," she muttered, though she wasn't sure which one of them she had.

When they turned away from the sunburned adults and children splashing in the pool, Dory darted out of her hiding place, slipped in a wet spot and fell. She shot to her feet and raced after James and Jill, so intent on keeping them in sight she hardly felt the throb in her tailbone.

She didn't realize the sky had turned as gray as Tobias' fur until she heard a rumble and glanced up at the black clouds boiling across Outlook from the southwest. Lightning cracked, thunder boomed and the rain exploded in an ice-cold sheet that swept through the ornamental garden adjacent to the pool like a curtain of needles.

The rain snatched Dory's breath and flattened her hair over her eyes. She raked it back, darted and dodged around people running for cover toward the house and the tents. James and Jill ran toward Mother's horse barn. Dory stopped with her hands pressed to her head to keep her hair out of her face and saw them just as James tugged Jilly inside and pulled the cross-planked door shut.

Dory ran toward the golf course and the clubhouse

Daddy had built to entertain his friends. Hailstones pelted her head and her back, lightning flashed all around her and thunder echoed in her ears. Daddy and Aunt Ping blinked and turned pale in the center of a group of Lambert's vice presidents when she burst into the clubhouse soaked and muddy and sobbing with cold.

Aunt Ping followed when Dory grabbed Daddy's arm, yanked him outside, pointed at the barn through the blinding rain and panted, out of breath and her heart thudding in her throat, "Jill and James."

"Jesus, Mary and Saint Joseph!" Daddy shouted and dove at a run out from under the clubhouse eaves.

Aunt Ping clapped the coolie hat on Dory's head to protect her from the hail and they followed Daddy across the puddled lawn. A limb on the elm tree cracked like a pistol shot and fell on the round bench, breaking a big chunk out of it as Daddy yanked open the barn door. Mother's horses wheeled and trumpeted in their stalls.

Only one stall had the top door shut. Aunt Ping hit the lights as Daddy flung it open. Dory stood on her tiptoes beside him and saw James with his pants off lying in the straw on top of bare-breasted Jill.

James looked over his shoulder at Daddy and said, "Bugger."

Mother slapped James but threatened to pack up and go back to England if Daddy fired him, so James was transferred to the farthest of the suburban branches and put to work in the mail room.

Daddy threw him out of the house, gave him five thousand dollars to get himself a place to live and a car and told him if he ever set foot on Outlook again he'd tie his dick in a knot. Dory had no idea her father knew words like dick, but she grinned hearing him say it through the keyhole in the library door.

She was on the front porch the next morning, sitting on a white iron settee with Tobias in her lap, when a taxicab pulled up beneath the portico and Wallace shut the door behind James. He put down his monogrammed leather suitcases, turned and looked at Dory.

"Clever little pug, aren't you?"

Dory stroked Tobias' ears. "Lot more clever than you."

"Cleverer, pug. Jesus. You Americans butcher the English language every time you open your mouths."

"I hate you," Dory said.

"I hate you, too, pug." James smiled. "I hate your mother, I hate my mother, but most of all I hate your old man."

"You're a bastard little prick," Dory said, quoting part of the tirade she'd heard Daddy give Mother last night.

"But I'm a clever little bastard prick." James leaned close to her. Tobias hissed and spat and jumped out of Dory's lap. "A lot cleverer than you, pug. I'll get even. You watch. I will."

He picked up his suitcases, got in the cab and drove away. When Dory stood up, she realized her knees were shaking and that Tobias had left a bloody scratch on the inside of her left elbow.

Jill was sent to a convent school in St. Louis founded by an order of nuns that ran it like a prison camp. She left the morning of Dory's first day as a high school sophomore. When she opened the door between their bedrooms, Dory was standing at the full-length mirror in her new uniform. She saw Jill's face in the glass and turned around.

"Do I look like a penguin?" she asked.

"No," Jill said. "You look totally sharp."

She smiled but her mouth trembled. Dory blinked at the tears in her eyes. Jill threw herself across the room and hugged her.

"I'm going to miss you, squirt," she said and Dory felt her heart twist. This was the first time in weeks she'd thought of Chase.

"You'll be home at Christmas," she said and Jill sobbed again.

In the driveway, Charles honked the horn on the Rolls.

Mother knocked on Jill's bedroom door. "Jillian," she said. "It's time to go."

"Shit." Jill backed away and scrubbed her eyes with her hands. "This is the worst day of my life, I swear to God."

"Mine, too," Dory murmured once Jill was gone.

And so it was until September 8, 1994.

Chapter Two

The Kansas City Star, September 8, 1994:

FRAUD CHARGES ROCK KANSAS CITY'S OLDEST BANK

Charges of wire fraud are expected to be filed today in U.S. District Court against Lambert Bank and Trust Co., Inc., and its brokerage division, Lambert Securities.

The charges stem from a $34.6 million wire transfer from Lambert Securities on Friday, September 2 to the First National Bank of Belize. Within an hour of the wire's receipt, the funds were withdrawn and so far have not been recovered.

The transaction was approved by James Darwood, supervisor of Lambert Securities wire room. Mr. Darwood approved the transfer on September 2, before he left Lambert Securities' office on the Country Club Plaza for a scheduled two-week vacation. Attempts to contact him at his hotel on Maui failed and his whereabouts at this time are unknown.

"I doubt he was ever in Hawaii," said U.S. Attorney Marshall Phillips. "Wherever he is, he has almost $35 million of other people's money in his pocket."

When asked if Lambert Bank's president and chairman of the board Del Lambert would also be named in the indictment, Phillips said, "We'll make that decision once we've interviewed Mr. Lambert."

An anonymous source close to the investigation said "it doesn't look good" that Lambert has been out of the country since September 1, the day before the wire transfer was made.

"The intimation that Del Lambert is in any way involved in this is preposterous," said Clifford Niles, a Lambert vice president. "The fact that he and his wife are presently cruising the Caribbean is pure coincidence. This is their wedding anniversary. Besides, Del is on his way home even as we speak."

"No he isn't," Aunt Ping said. "I told him not to come home."

"You what?" Dory let the newspaper fall on the breakfast room table. Her hands were shaking. Her insides, too, but her voice was even. "That is *not* going to look good, Aunt Ping."

"I don't care what it looks like. Your father isn't a thief."

"I can't think of a better way to look like one than to refuse to come home and talk to the U.S. attorney. That man means business."

"Of course he means business," Aunt Ping said. "James vanished with thirty-five million dollars of Lambert investors' money. The FBI can't find him. When they give up looking, they'll want someone to hang this on. The individuals and mutual funds that trusted Lambert Securities with their money will want someone to hold responsible. Who do you think that will be?"

"The president of the bank," Dory said, her stomach sinking. "The chairman of the board."

"Precisely." Aunt Ping gave a sharp little nod. "That's why I told your father not to come home."

The big black headline FRAUD CHARGES ROCK KANSAS CITY'S OLDEST BANK pulled at Dory's gaze like a four-car pileup she knew she shouldn't look at but couldn't look away from. She forced herself to turn her head and look out the window.

It wasn't raining as hard as it had been in Columbia at six o'clock when she'd rolled out of bed to make her eight thirty economics class. She'd punched on the TV while she made coffee, heard the anchor on the early morning newscast say, "The investigation of financial wrongdoing involving Lambert Bank and Trust, one of Kansas City's most respected financial institutions, looks like it's headed toward indictments and possible arrests. Details follow this short break."

Dory dropped the glass carafe. It didn't break but water spewed all over the kitchen floor. She mopped it up while she listened to the details, every shocking, ugly one of them, then she'd yanked Jill out of bed, out from under her latest shackup. She'd kicked him and his pants out the front door of the condo Daddy bought them so they could attend the University of Missouri in style, told Jill what had happened and threw water in her face when she started screaming.

When she stopped, they'd jumped into their clothes and Dory's green Saturn. She'd driven the two hundred miles from Columbia to Outlook in a deluge. Now it was eleven A.M., it was only drizzling, and here the three of them sat, Dory, Jill and Aunt Ping, in the breakfast room adjacent to the family kitchen where Aunt Ping occasionally cooked pasta and Mother had never touched so much as a teakettle.

"I'm almost afraid to ask," Dory said. "But how did James get to be wire room supervisor?"

"Your mother," Aunt Ping said between her teeth.

"Why am I not surprised?" Dory slid her elbows on the table and covered her face with her hands. "Where is Daddy?"

"Throwing Drusilla overboard, I hope." Aunt Ping sighed. "I don't know where he is. I told him not to tell me. If I honestly don't know I'll be telling the truth when the FBI calls me in to take a lie detector test."

"What?" Jill blinked. "Why would you have to take a lie detector?"

"We may all have to, Jill. James is family, don't forget."

"Daddy should have fired him," Jill said.

"Daddy should've *killed* him," Dory said.

"This is all my fault!" Jill wailed and burst into tears.

"It's my fault," Dory said. "I ratted on you and James."

"It's no one's *fault*," Aunt Ping said. "Your mother was stupid, your father was weak and I was blind. James is a thief. Probably a sociopath."

"Don't forget bastard little prick," Dory said. "What have you heard from Aunt Diana?"

"Nothing. I sent a telegram and told her and Deirdre not to contact any of us in any way. We might need them."

"For what?" Dory snorted. "Why did you send a telegram? Why didn't you call or e-mail?"

"Phone records and e-mails are easy to trace," Aunt Ping said. "Hopefully the FBI won't think to check Western Union."

"Aunt Ping." Jill's bottom lip trembled. "You're scaring me."

At one o'clock that afternoon, Charles stopped the Rolls beneath the front portico with its ivy-twined brick pillars, got out and opened the rear door for Francis Singleton Cooper—Coop for short—the best criminal attorney money could buy. Because Aunt Ping was Margaret Lambert and owned Outlook Farm, he'd flown to Kansas City from New York to meet with her.

The word *criminal* filled Dory with dread, but she sat on a settee in the front parlor with Jill to hear what Coop had to say. Aunt Ping told him the whole story. He asked if she knew where Daddy was.

"Somewhere in the Caribbean," Aunt Ping said. "I've spoken to Del once. I told him not to tell me precisely where he is. I also told him it would probably be best if we didn't speak again until this is settled."

"Excellent," Coop said. "Keep it that way."

He asked about the *Drusilla*, the oceangoing yacht Daddy had purchased because Mother refused to sail around the Caribbean for her anniversary on a boat that wasn't hers. Coop wanted to know if the *Drusilla* had satellite TV, a satellite phone, a shortwave radio? How long could she stay at sea fully provisioned?

That Aunt Ping knew the answers to all these questions made Dory clench her fingers together till her knuckles turned white.

"I know Marshall Phillips. We clerked together," Coop said. "I'll call him in the morning, set up an appointment. Have you spoken with him?"

"Briefly on Tuesday, at the Lambert Securities office," Aunt Ping said. "I made it a point to be there when he arrived with the FBI."

"Were you deposed?" Coop asked.

"Mr. Phillips indicated I might be," Aunt Ping said. "But at that time he saw no reason to take my written statement."

All of a sudden Dory saw why, too. Today Aunt Ping was Margaret Lambert. She wore a blue Chanel suit with Grandmother Lambert's triple rope of perfectly matched pearls. Usually she "wafted about," as Mother phrased it, in silk trousers and layers of scarves with Tobias under one arm and chunky amber bracelets on her wrists.

Coop wrote in a leather notebook and muttered a word that sounded like "sloppy." Dory thought it was damned clever of Aunt Ping.

"You'll hear from Marshall." Coop shut his notebook and smiled. "Probably tomorrow once he's seen me. I'll be in touch afterward."

"Come for lunch." Aunt Ping rose from the pink-gilt Louis XIV chair. "Cook serves at one."

"Young ladies." Coop glanced at Dory and Jill. "I expect Marshall will want to talk to you as well."

Jill made a gurgling sound. Dory grabbed her elbow, yanked her into the family kitchen, cranked on the cold tap and splashed her in the face. Jill sucked a breath, jerked out of Dory's grasp and glared at her.

"Will you stop trying to drown me?"

"You were about to start screaming."

"I was not. I was about to start crying."

Jill grabbed a dish towel. Before she could bury her face in it and howl, Dory snatched it away and gripped Jill's arms because she couldn't reach her shoulders. She wasn't fourteen anymore but she was still a squirt. Jill was four inches taller.

"No screaming. No crying. That won't help."

"Nothing will help!" Jill wailed. "Daddy and Mother are *fugitives*!"

Dory turned on the cold tap again. Jill's tears snapped off like a light switch.

"Daddy and Mother are not fugitives. They're on a cruise."

"Then what was all that crap about radios and provisions?"

"I don't know," Dory lied. "Make tea and I'll go find out."

"Uh." Jill glanced at the stove. "How do I do that again?"

Jill wasn't brainless, just useless. Twenty-three and in her fifth year of a four-year fashion merchandising course. Dory was twenty-one, thanks to summer school on track to have her business degree in the spring, and determined that Jill was *not* going to turn into Mother.

"Water in the kettle, kettle on the burner. Turn on the gas," Dory said. "That's the step you keep forgetting. Rinse the pot with hot water, put the tea bags in the pot. Make sure you take them out of the envelopes this time. When the water boils, pour it in the pot. When steam comes out of the spout and the kettle whistles? That's boil."

"Right." Jill snapped her fingers. "Got it."

Dory had a headache and a knot in her stomach. She wheeled out of the kitchen, through the breakfast room, the little dining room and into the corridor toward the front of the house. She was stunned and still shaky, so worried about her father she could barely think. She even felt sorry for her stupid, *stupid* Mother. She'd be mad as hell once the shock wore off. She'd wait till then to decide how she'd kill James.

If the FBI didn't find him, she would. If it took the rest of her life, Dory vowed, if she had to consult a psychic, hire an army of detectives, turn over every rock on the planet with her own two hands, she'd find him. Then it would be *her* turn to get even.

Two windows stretched from the floor to the ceiling on both sides of the huge front doors in the foyer. Aunt Ping stood at the left-hand window, her fingers curled against the trunk of a thirty-foot potted palm tree, watching the Rolls with Charles at the wheel and Coop in the back sweep away down the curved front drive. Tobias crouched at her feet.

When Dory dropped to the floor with her back against the window, Tobias got up stiffly and stepped into her lap, laid his chin on her knee and sighed. Dory stroked his ears and looked up at Aunt Ping.

"Daddy kicked James out on Labor Day, September 5, 1988," she said. "James pulled this on Friday, September 2, the beginning of the Labor Day weekend. That's almost six years to the day."

"Yes, Dory. I know." Aunt Ping sounded tired. "I caught the irony."

"I was on the front porch that morning. I wanted to make sure James left. He told me he hated his mother. He said he hated my mother, too." The knot in Dory's stomach had dissolved in a pool of acid, which was a good sign. Anger always gave her heartburn. "Most of all, he said he hated Daddy. I'll get even, he told me. You watch. I will."

"I'm glad you didn't say that in front of Jill," Aunt Ping said and sighed. This was twice she'd sighed. Aunt Ping never sighed.

"Did Tobias enjoy 'wafting about' Lambert Securities with you?"

"He did, yes." Aunt Ping smiled a little, sat down on the floor with her feet tucked under her and stroked Tobias. "The old boy doesn't get out much these days."

Tobias was almost eighteen; his gray muzzle was speckled white with age. He closed his eyes and purred at Aunt Ping's touch.

"Unless he sent the wire himself," Dory said, "I figure

James had at least one accomplice. Maybe two. Have you found them yet?"

"He had one. Marilyn Vanderpool."

"*Marilyn?* Jilly's Marilyn?"

She hadn't been Jilly's Marilyn since Jill was sent to convent school. They'd drifted apart with the separation; still Dory couldn't have been more surprised if Aunt Ping said Elvis was James' accomplice.

"Jilly's Marilyn." Aunt Ping nodded. "She's an MBA candidate at Stanford. She was interning with Lambert Securities for the summer. September 2 was her last day. James approved the wire transfer that morning and left, supposedly to catch a plane to Honolulu. Marilyn sent the wire and left at half past three for a dentist's appointment. She was supposed to fly to Banff to meet her parents and tour the Canadian Rockies, but she called them, said she'd had a root canal and begged off. No one has seen her since. Her mother is frantic."

"Oh, no." Dory shut her eyes and let the back of her head thunk against the window. "I am not telling Jill."

"Gina Vanderpool is my dearest friend," Aunt Ping said. "For her sake I chose not to make Marilyn's part in this public."

"So the FBI is looking for Marilyn, too?"

"Yes." Aunt Ping smoothed her palms on her skirt and sighed again. "The FBI discovered that James chartered a jet that morning to fly him to Belize. Marilyn sent the wire at three fifteen. At three thirty Belize time—Belize is an hour behind us—James was there to withdraw the funds. As James was walking out of the First National Bank of Belize, Marilyn was leaving Lambert Securities for her dental appointment."

"How did the FBI find *that* out?" Dory was amazed. "In my financial law class last semester we studied mutual legal assistance treaties. Belize refuses to sign any of the MLATs."

"The FBI didn't find out. I did. I sent an investigator to Belize with James' photograph and several thousand dollars."

"You *did* tell the FBI, didn't you? And Marshall Phillips?"

"Of course I did." Aunt Ping smiled. "I at least want to *look* like I'm cooperating till I find a way to keep your father's neck out of the noose."

Dory was sure Aunt Ping's plan to save Daddy would be brilliant. Unfortunately, she never got to see it in action because Mother's gallbladder shot craps on the way back to Galveston.

Daddy thought about what Aunt Ping said, listened to Coop's advice on the shortwave, decided to hell with both of them and told the *Drusilla*'s captain to turn the goddamn boat around and haul ass for the U.S.A. No snarky little English bastard was going to ruin his bank and his reputation and live to tell about it.

The *Drusilla* was plowing up the coast of Mexico, out of the Caribbean and into the Gulf of Mexico when Mother started vomiting. When her fever spiked at 104, the captain made for Cancún.

Once Mother was out of surgery, Daddy raised Coop on the shortwave and told him what had happened. Coop called Marshall Phillips.

"I suppose," the U.S. attorney said, "you expect me to believe this."

Coop said, "I can produce the medical records."

"You could pull a rabbit out of a hat," Phillips replied, "if you thought it would get your client off the hook."

"The woman's gallbladder nearly ruptured, Marsh. She was damn lucky they got her ashore when they did. Del Lambert was on his way back to Kansas City. He will be again as soon as his wife recovers."

"Uh huh," Phillips said, nonplussed. "Tell me again how the Lamberts conveniently ended up on Isla Rica. A privately owned island with no mutual legal assistance or extradition treaties with the United States."

"It's not sinister, Marsh. It's simple. Del Lambert went to school with Bernard Grayson. They were planning to put in to Isla Rica at the end of their cruise. Del called Grayson from Cancún. He offered his villa for Drusilla's convalescence."

"And how long will her convalescence take?"

"I don't know. The surgery was dicey. There's a lot of infection."

"Here we go," Phillips said. "The old stall-aroo."

"I'm not stalling, Marsh. Neither is Lambert. This was a medical emergency. He's faxing me the surgeon's reports. I'll fax them to you."

"Fax them to the Tooth Fairy," Phillips said and hung up.

Coop related the conversation to Aunt Ping over lunch at Outlook on Friday. Dory heard it while she and Aunt Ping drank tea in her suite in the south wing at four o'clock. Aunt Ping had talked Jill out of going shopping so she'd gone riding instead. That was Jill. Perfectly happy so long as she was spending money or she had something between her legs.

"Fax them to the Tooth Fairy," Dory repeated, a chill brushing up the back of her neck. "That sounds ominous."

"Very ominous," Aunt Ping said. "I'm planning to spend the day at Lambert's on Monday."

"I'll go with you," Dory said.

"I'd rather you stay here and keep Jill with you," Aunt Ping said. "I don't think it's wise for any of us to be out and about just now."

The front gates of Outlook were closed. Dory had nearly crashed her Saturn into them in the rain yesterday, sending the herd of reporters gathered at the gates scurrying toward their satellite trucks. Dory had never seen the gates closed during the day, only at night.

"Why did I hear about this on the news, Aunt Ping?"

"I was hoping you wouldn't hear about it period," she said. "Or by the time you did it would all be settled and your father would be safe."

"If the worst should happen," Dory said, the Tooth Fairy shiver crawling up her back again, "you won't be able to protect Jill and me."

"Yes, I *will,* young lady," Aunt Ping said fiercely. "Oh, *yes* I will."

At 10:13 A.M. Monday morning, Marshall Phillips pushed through the big glass front doors of Lambert's downtown branch with a horde of FBI agents and a search warrant for Del Lambert's office.

Aunt Ping and Coop were waiting for him, sitting on Daddy's leather sofa, drinking coffee. While Coop read the search warrant, Aunt Ping ordered more cups, served everyone coffee, and the search began.

In Daddy's file cabinets the FBI found dull, boring banking papers; on his desk, invitations to golf tournaments. Behind the Jackson Pollock on the wall behind the desk, they found Daddy's safe. Marshall Phillips asked if Aunt Ping knew the combination. She said yes and opened the safe, supremely confident that Phillips would find nothing.

What the U.S. attorney found was a "Happy wedding anniversary" card. The cream-colored envelope was unaddressed. The card was signed by James with a handwritten P.S.: "In case the plan goes awry, Uncle Del, I thought you should have this—" Beneath that he'd written the account number from the First National Bank of Belize.

Aunt Ping almost fainted. The investigator she'd sent to Belize had discovered the account number, which she'd turned over to the FBI.

"The dumbest criminal on earth would be smart enough not to leave such an incriminating piece of evidence in his own safe," Coop argued. "Anyone with the combination could've put the card in there."

"Including Del Lambert," Phillips said.

Four people knew the combination: Daddy, Mother, Aunt Ping and Anita Sawyer, Daddy's secretary for the past seventeen years.

According to the log Anita kept in her desk, the last person to open the safe was Mother, the day before she and Daddy left on their cruise.

"Mrs. Lambert," Anita told Marshall Phillips, "said she

had the dearest, sweetest surprise she wanted to leave for her husband."

"I'd say thirty-five million is pretty sweet," said one of the FBI guys.

"I'm sure Drusilla meant the anniversary card," Aunt Ping said. "My brother and James have been estranged for several years."

"If it was just a card," Phillips said to Aunt Ping, "why did Mrs. Lambert put it in the safe?"

"My guess is because James told her to put it in there."

Aunt Ping guessed right. Daddy confirmed it to Coop on the shortwave. James asked Mother to put the card in the safe. She'd done it without question or opening the card to read what James had written.

"I told your brother he should smother his wife while she's still bedridden. Before she can fuck up anything else," Coop said furiously to Aunt Ping. "I'm not sure he heard me. There was a lot of static."

"I told him the same thing after their honeymoon," Aunt Ping said.

She sounded exhausted. She looked absolutely shattered, curled in Daddy's chair with Tobias in her arms. Aunt Ping and Anita Sawyer had spent the day in the federal courthouse six blocks from Lambert's being questioned by the FBI and taking lie detector tests.

Aunt Ping had left the house at seven fifteen that morning. It was now ten thirty P.M. and Dory was on her knees snooping through the keyhole because she hadn't been invited to join her aunt and Coop in the library.

"Is all this as bad as it looks?" Aunt Ping asked Coop.

"Yes," he said. "Here are the facts Marshall Phillips has so far. Fact one: A year ago Del Lambert put his wife's nephew James Darwood in charge of Lambert Securities' wire room. Marsh doesn't know and he won't care that your brother's wife made Del's life a living hell until he gave her nephew the promotion. Fact two: Del and Drusilla Lambert bought a yacht and sailed off into the Caribbean the day before James pulled the heist in Belize, which is in the Caribbean. Fact three: This morning Marsh found an anniversary card from Darwood in the safe in Del Lambert's office, put there by his wife, with the account number from the bank in Belize written inside."

"Oh no," Dory moaned. Her forehead thunked against the library door. By the time Coop opened it, she'd scrambled to her feet.

"Hi, Mr. Cooper," she said. "Isn't this all circumstantial evidence?"

"Yes," Coop said. "But I can't say I blame Marsh for thinking it's all hokum. It defies belief that your mother was stupid enough to put a card from someone she knows hates her husband in his office safe."

"I'm sure Drusilla hasn't the first clue that James can't abide her and Del," Aunt Ping said. "She reminds me of the Wicked Queen in Snow White, spending her days gazing into a mirror that tells her she's the fairest in the land. Drusilla has lived in my house for almost thirty years and has no idea that I despise her."

"That's the good news." Coop sat down on the leather sofa and jerked the knot out of his silk tie. "The feds can't take Outlook."

Dory scampered around the rolled arm of the sofa to look at Coop. "You say that like they can take everything else. Can they?"

"Oh yes. If I were Marsh I'd file the paperwork to freeze Del Lambert's assets first thing tomorrow."

"Mr. Phillips needn't take such a drastic step," Aunt Ping said. "Lambert Securities intends to make full restitution to our investors."

"Marsh isn't interested in restitution," Coop said. "He will be down the road because the government still has egg on its face from the savings and loan debacle, but right now what Marsh wants is to make it impossible for Del Lambert to stay on Isla Rica. If he can't afford to buy a loaf of bread, Marsh figures that will bring him in."

"It won't," Aunt Ping said. "Not now that Drusilla is involved. Del will do whatever it takes to protect her."

"Darwood's a clever little psychopath," Coop said. "He made sure the finger points equally at Del and Drusilla."

"What d'you mean the finger points equally at Daddy and Mother?" Dory asked. "Are you telling us that the FBI is going to stop looking for James? I don't see how they can do that when James approved the transfer and James walked out of the bank in Belize with the money."

"And from there he vanished as James Darwood," Coop replied. "That means he had a new identity waiting for him. Belize is not a signatory to any of the mutual legal assistance treaties. The FBI will play hell trying to get information out of anyone in Belize."

"My brother is worth two hundred and sixty million dollars," Aunt Ping said. "Surely Mr. Phillips must consider that Del has no motive to steal. Especially from his own bank."

"People do the damnedest things for the damnedest reasons, Miss Lambert. Of course Marsh has considered motive. Still, he has a pile of evidence—circumstantial, but pretty incriminating—and a boss in Washington screaming for someone's head. Marsh can't find Darwood but he knows Del Lambert is in Isla Rica. He can't go after him because the island is privately owned and it doesn't sit in international waters, but he can and he will do everything legally possible to force him to return to Kansas City."

"If Daddy and Mother came home tomorrow," Dory said, "what do you think would happen?"

"I think your father would be arrested and charged with wire fraud. Your mother, possibly, as an accomplice. I'd have them out on bail in a blink, but the actual arrest is what you want to avoid. It never looks good to a jury that your client wore handcuffs, even for twenty minutes."

"Then they can't come home, can they?" Dory asked.

"If I were Del Lambert," Coop said. "I'd pray that Darwood screws up and gets caught before my wife recovers from gallbladder surgery."

*   *   *

That night, Tobias died in his sleep.

Aunt Ping wrapped him in a silk Hermès scarf, fetched a spade from the potting shed and buried Tobias beneath her bedroom window.

Wallace told Dory as he poured her coffee in the breakfast room.

"Miss Ping took her morning tea in her suite," he murmured, "and asked that she not be disturbed today."

"Then don't tell my sister," Dory said. "Thank you, Wallace."

She dumped half the cream pitcher in her cup, chugged her coffee in two swallows and hurried out of the house, into the garage and her little green Saturn. It was a six-mile drive along Outlook's immaculately paved private roads to the farm manager's office in the big white barn that housed most of the tractors and farm machinery. Tom came outside to meet her, a tall, lanky man in faded jeans and a plaid shirt.

"Morning, Miss Dory." He touched the bill of his John Deere cap. "Everything okay up at the house?"

Tom looked worried, his long face craggier than usual. Dory didn't blame him. She was petrified.

"Everything's fine," she lied. "Tobias died, Tom. I need a cat. Any kittens around that are ready to be weaned?"

"I always got litters underfoot, Miss Dory, but these is just cats. Not a single pedigree Russian Blue among 'em."

"I don't have time to shop for a purebred," Dory said. And probably no money to buy one, either. Thirty-five million dollars. Holy God.

"Whelp." Tom was from Oklahoma, where a lot of words came out with a *p* tagged on the end. "Let's go have us a look-see."

The farm cats nested in the hay barn, in the loft where Tom built them a nursery out of stacked and staggered bales. The big doors creaked when he opened them. Sunshine spilled inside, lighting the straw bales stacked on the scarred wooden floor like Rumplestiltskin's gold. Dory smelled fresh-cut clover, inhaled dust and sneezed.

"Hey, Queenie! Belle! Susie Q!" Tom thumped a hay hook hung over a nail against the wall. "Fetch them young-ins down here!"

The youngins came on their own down the open-planked staircase from the loft in a multicolored tumble of furry little bodies, bright eyes and tiny mews. Dory laughed for the first time in days, dropped to the floor and let the kittens scramble into her lap and claw their way up her arms. The mother cats, a gray tabby, an orange tiger and a gray and tan tortoiseshell sat on the steps. Tom went down on his heels; his cap tipped back and a smile fanned the creases in his face.

A brown kitten the color of a Hershey bar perched on Dory's left knee. Its cupped little bat ears looked like they'd been dipped in dark chocolate. It cocked its head to one side and blinked aqua-blue eyes.

"Oh my," Dory said. "Where did you come from?"

"Think old Belle," Tom said, "found herself a high-class fella."

Dory thought she'd found Aunt Ping a cat.

Jill was on the terrace above the pool, arms folded and pacing when Dory came up the flagstone steps from the ornamental garden carrying a perforated egg crate with a lid. Jill had on jeans, a cashmere sweater the color of champagne and diamonds in her ears.

"Where've you been?" she demanded. "Aunt Ping won't come out of her room and Wallace won't tell me why. Cliff Niles called. He said something's frozen or something's in the freezer. I told him to call his wife. Coop called but Aunt Ping won't come to the phone. What's going on?"

"Tobias died," Dory said. "Aunt Ping buried him this morning."

"Oh no." Jill's eyes filled with tears. Big gorgeous tears that only made her eyes look even more like sapphires. "Poor Aunt Ping."

The egg crate mewed and Jill blinked. Then she grinned, lifted the lid and squealed. The kittens dove for the corner and glared at her.

"How come there's two?" Jill asked.

"I picked the brown one. The black and white one jumped on my leg and wouldn't let go so I brought them both. Aunt Ping can choose."

"She'll love it!" Jill slapped the lid on the crate and snatched it out of Dory's hands. *Hey!* she thought, but let it go and followed Jill into the house. Outside the double doors of Aunt Ping's suite, Jill wheeled and shoved the crate at Dory. "What am I doing? This is your idea."

"Let's make it our idea," Dory said and opened the doors.

The drapes were drawn over the windows in the sitting room, the adjacent library and music room and Aunt Ping's bedroom, the marble floors a dull, veined glow where they weren't covered with ornate rugs. Aunt Ping was a hump of padded silk covers in the center of the Chippendale-style bed commissioned by Nicholas Lambert for his bride.

Jill climbed the handmade steps on the left side of the bed and placed the egg crate near the foot. Dory climbed the steps on the right and lifted the lid. The kittens scrambled out and jumped on Aunt Ping. She rolled over, pushed the bedclothes off her head and sat up, blinking at the kittens clinging by their claws to the silk coverlet.

"*Ohhh,*" Aunt Ping breathed. "Look at you two."

She scooped the kittens up gently, one in each hand, and lifted them to her face. The black and white one swung like Tarzan off her left thumb. The brown one raised a tiny paw and boffed her on the nose.

Aunt Ping laughed, her eyes damp and shiny. "Where on earth did you find a Tonkinese kitten?"

"In the hay barn," Dory said. "She's one of Belle's litter."

"What's a Tonkinese?" Jill asked.

"A Burmese, Siamese cross," Aunt Ping said.

"Tom," Dory said, "thinks Belle found herself a fancy man."

"And a tuxedo cat." Aunt Ping smiled. "How adorable."

The black kitten had a white chest, four white paws and a white-tipped tail. It scrambled onto Dory's knee and mewed. She plucked it off, turned it around and gave it a push back up the bed toward Aunt Ping.

"Thank you, girls." She gathered the kittens into the pool of silken covers between her knees and smiled first at Jill, then at Dory, a soft, teary-eyed smile. "I'm so touched that you thought of me."

"Well, Aunt Ping, you're just not you without a cat," Jill said. "Which one are you going to keep?"

"Both." She picked up the kittens and kicked back the covers. "Come along, little kit-cats. You need litter boxes, food bowls and water dishes." Aunt Ping swung her legs over the side of the bed and sniffed the kittens. "And a bath. You smell like the barn."

"Count me out." Jill held her hands up. "I learned with Tobias."

Aunt Ping laughed and slid out of the big, high bed. When her bare feet touched the floor, the iron band around Dory's chest let go. She hadn't drawn a deep breath since Wallace told her Tobias had died.

"Coop called, Aunt Ping," Jill said. "He needs to speak with you right away. So does Cliff Niles. He said it was urgent, though why something that's frozen in the freezer is urgent, I don't know."

Aunt Ping stopped halfway to the bathroom with the kittens. "I'll ring them shortly. If they call again, let Wallace answer the phone."

"Okay," Jill said with a cheerful shrug and headed for the door.

"I'm fine, Dory, really," Aunt Ping said when she was gone. "I was only going to grieve for today. You needn't worry."

"I'm not worried," Dory said quickly. "I'm just—" Her voice cracked and she sucked a breath. "I'm scared, Aunt Ping. What about all the people who work for Lambert's, who depend on the bank for their jobs? What's going to happen to them?"

"Nothing, if I can help it." Aunt Ping put the kittens on the floor and faced Dory with her chin lifted, her shoulders squared and her long French braid of dark hair hanging down her back. "There's been a wobble in customer confidence, but the board feels that if I issue a press release stating that we intend to make full restitution the bank will be fine."

"Do we have thirty-five million dollars, Aunt Ping?"

"Yes," she said and sighed. "How much we'll have left once we've made restitution will depend entirely on Marshall Phillips."

The United States attorney had no idea what one small woman trailing silk scarves and cat hair could do to defend her brother and her nieces. He found out when he went after Del Lambert's assets.

The first person the Lambert Securities internal auditors notified when they discovered the 34.6-million-dollar discrepancy on September second was Margaret Lambert. Aunt Ping took the call at ten P.M. that evening and moved like the wind to protect everything she could.

Daddy was a fool for Mother but not about money. Phillips couldn't touch Jill and Dory's trust funds, ten million each, their education funds or the condo in Columbia. Daddy's beloved Packard, all the cars and Mother's jewelry, her furs and her horses, all the sculpture and paintings by old and modern masters displayed at Lambert's eight branches. Every item he'd inherited or accumulated were all in Margaret Lambert's name.

Marshall Phillips almost had an aneurysm. The veins in his forehead were still pulsing when he came to Outlook to see Aunt Ping.

"You were smart not to touch the cash and the securities. I'll give you that," he said to her. "The continued assistance of the United States government in finding James Darwood? You can forget it."

"I already have, Mr. Phillips," Aunt Ping replied coolly. "Your lack of interest in pursuing him since you searched my brother's office has made it clear to me that as far as you're concerned you have your man."

"I have *one* of them. I have Del Lambert on Isla Rica."

"He's not the man you want. You want James Darwood."

"I'd have him if I could find him. In the meantime, I'll concentrate on your brother. And you, Miss Lambert. I'll be watching you." Marshall Phillips turned toward Dory and Jill sitting on the settee. "And I'll be watching you two, as well. I'll be watching the whole lot of you. Good day."

He glared at them all, even Coop standing by the marble fireplace, and wheeled out of the parlor. Wallace met him at the arched doorway and followed him toward the foyer.

"What did he mean?" Jill asked Coop. "Are we going to have FBI agents following us around?"

"For a while," he said. "Till Marsh cools off."

"Great, Aunt Ping," Dory said. "Piss off the Justice Department."

"It couldn't be helped," Aunt Ping said to her, then to Coop, "I suppose that could've been much worse."

"And likely will be until Marsh calms down. Till then, Del and Drusilla's best course, if Bernard Grayson will have them, is to stay on Isla Rica, though you never heard me say that. Yours is to have no contact with them. None at all." Coop swept all three of them, Aunt Ping, Jill and Dory with a stern glance. "It will be difficult, but Marsh may have people listening as well as watching. God knows what could put them in jeopardy. I've already explained this to Del. He isn't happy about it."

"Does Mr. Phillips," Jill asked, "stay mad for a long time?"

Coop nodded. "He's been known to."

When Coop left, Aunt Ping made tea in the family kitchen. Dory sliced half a loaf of Esme's date nut bread and put it on a plate on the breakfast room table. Jill sat down, Aunt Ping and then Dory, all three of them staring at Daddy's empty chair and Mother's beside it.

Aunt Ping rang for Wallace and asked him please to remove the chairs. Once the chairs were gone she looked at Jill, then Dory.

"We'll put them back when your parents come home," she said. "Till then, it's just the three of us."

Chapter Three

Dory and Jill survived being tailed around the University of Missouri campus in Columbia by making a game of it. Spot the FBI Guy. By Christmas, 1994 Dory swore she could smell the agents by their aftershave. Jill tormented them by lounging around their room in her underwear with the blinds up.

"I have to do *something*," she said when Dory complained. "I can't keep a boyfriend. They get hauled in for questioning."

"Jill," Dory said wearily. "Buy a vibrator."

"Oooh," she breathed huskily. "What a great idea."

Dory bought her a box of C batteries for Christmas. It was all she could afford. Every cent of Aunt Ping's fortune and Jill's trust went to repay the investors. Even so, Lambert Securities went belly up. Aunt Ping and Cliff Niles, newly appointed president and chairman of the board, found jobs at the bank for everyone from the brokerage division.

Dory sold the condo, moved to a dorm and cashed her trust to keep Outlook afloat and finance the Catch the Bastard Little Prick Fund. Aunt Ping was positive that one of the eight private detectives she'd hired would find James by the time Dory and Jill received their bachelor's degrees in May 1995. They didn't.

Dory stayed in Columbia to find a cheap place to live before she started her MBA program in September. She settled on a two-room apartment with a leaky toilet and off-street parking for the Saturn. Jill went home to Outlook and got a job as a buyer for Hall's, one of the swankiest stores on the Country Club Plaza where names like Gucci graced shop doors. She was canned in a month, by Saks in a week, Abercrombie and Fitch, then Nordstrom.

"Did you know I'm color-blind?" she said indignantly to Dory. "I see primary colors and jewel tones just fine, the ophthalmologist said. It's tints and pastels I can't distinguish. No wonder it took me five years to get a degree in fashion merchandising!"

By Christmas 1995 Jill had been fired by every major retailer in Kansas City. She was totally depressed, but there was no money to send her shopping to cheer her up. There wasn't much money for anything.

Dory went home for Christmas and one afternoon up to Charles' apartment over the garage to let him beat the socks off her at cribbage. He told her while they were having cocoa and cinnamon toast that Chase had his degree in architecture and a job with a firm in New York City.

"Kudos to Chase." Dory licked cocoa foam off her lip and smiled. Her heart didn't bang anymore when Charles mentioned Chase; it just ached like an old bruise. "I'll bet you're one proud papa."

"Very proud. He went to school straight through, never skipped a semester, always had a job and graduated with honors."

Dory had two jobs, tutoring undergrads in math and a weekend job at a bookstore. Two salaries paid her rent and put gas in the Saturn so she wasn't hitting Aunt Ping up for money all the time.

"Chase called last night." Charles put down his cocoa mug and looked at Dory soberly over the toast plate. "He wants me to retire and move to New York. I told him no."

"Maybe you should reconsider." Dory's stomach unclenched. For a second there, she'd thought Charles was going to tell her Chase was getting married. "If we don't find James soon and turn him in to Marshall Phillips so he'll unfreeze the family funds, things could get dicey."

"I'm not drawing a salary. Neither are Wallace, Esme, Henry and Peter, Eddie, Tom and Esther, but don't tell Miss Ping I told you."

"I can't believe she agreed to that." Dory was stunned. "Aunt Ping would rather do without herself than see someone else go without."

"We stopped cashing our checks. When she called us up to the house to ask why, we reminded her that the eight of us have been at Outlook for thirty years or better. This is our home as much as it is hers. We intend to do all we can to help until things improve."

Dory leaned across Charles' kitchen table and kissed him. Tom blushed when she drove down to his office and kissed him. Eddie grinned. Esme and Esther Grant hugged her. She found Henry in the greenhouse with Peter. No one needed a valet, but Peter always needed help with the gardens. They both hugged and kissed her. Wallace raised an eyebrow when she puckered up so Dory settled for a handshake.

She didn't tell Aunt Ping she knew the senior staff had waived their salaries, but before she went back to Columbia she asked Charles why he'd told her. He said, "Because you look so worried all the time."

Charles didn't know the half of it. Dory missed her father so much it hurt, her mother not at all. She felt guilty, but at last she'd stopped grinding her teeth at night. Instead she had nightmares about Daddy wandering the beach like Robinson Crusoe or begging on the streets like the pauper Marshall Phillips had made of him. She dreamed phone conversations with him, schemed ways she could sneak across the border into Mexico and from there to Isla Rica. Envisioned being hauled away in chains by the FBI for taking food to her parents.

In high school working had been fun because she didn't have to work. Now she needed to work to take the pressure off Aunt Ping and she was terrified. She lived in constant panic that she'd be late or get sick and wouldn't be able to cover the rent. She missed having Jill in Columbia to talk to, but at last, guys started to notice her. She had dates and a few sleepovers, but mostly she was alone and sad and poor. Her only comfort was the tuxedo cat. The little black and white female jumped into the Saturn when Dory left Outlook the day after New Year's and refused to come out from under the seat. Dory named her Rocky because she never gave up.

In March of 1996 Dory and Rocky went home for spring break. She and Aunt Ping and Jill were finishing lunch on Wednesday when Cliff Niles came to Outlook. Lambert's president and chairman of the board had a big smile on his face and a letter from Daddy in his pocket.

Dear Ping, dearest Jill, my darling Dory,

This letter comes to you via the kindness of Mike Austin, a fellow school chum of Bernie and me. He's taking a risk carrying it to Cliff Niles, so please read it and then burn it. Let's don't drag anyone else into this mess. Coop would say I'm taking a risk even writing it, but Coop doesn't need to know everything, if you get my drift, Ping.

Your mother and I miss you all terribly, but we're managing. If we have to be stuck someplace till who in hell knows when, then I guess being stuck in paradise isn't all bad. Bernie is the soul of kindness to let us stay.

I hear from Coop occasionally. He's a genius at getting messages through, must've worked for the CIA. He assures me that you and the girls are fine, Ping. That's the only thing that's making this bearable for Drusilla and me, knowing that you're there to look after Jill and Dory.

Don't worry. We're coping. We love you. Take care of yourselves.

Del

"The letter carrier, Mike Austin," Aunt Ping said to Cliff Niles. "I trust you did something very nice for him."

"Yes, Margaret." He nodded and smiled. "I did."

"Thank you." She smiled and passed the letter to Dory and Jill.

They read it again while Aunt Ping saw Cliff out. When she came back into the breakfast room, Dory looked at her and frowned.

"This reads like Daddy has no idea that you have a small army of private detectives scouring the earth for James. Why is that?"

"Coop and I discussed it. Your father is an idiot about your mother but not about money." Aunt Ping sat down and warmed her tea from the pot. "Del knows we made restitution. He knows we could afford that. He doesn't know how much Marshall Phillips froze in the way of cash and assets. If he did, he'd fly back to Kansas City and let himself be arrested to keep Outlook from going bankrupt."

"Aunt Ping!" Jill's eyes flew open. "Are we out of money?"

"No, Jill." Aunt Ping smiled and patted her hand. Then she picked up the letter, rang for Wallace and said to him when he came, "Would you please light a fire in the parlor?"

Dory memorized the letter before it went up in flames. She was lying in bed that night reading it in her head when Jill came into her room, switched on the lamp and sat down on the bed beside her.

"If Daddy doesn't know we're trying to find James," she said, "he could think that he and Mother will be stuck on Isla Rica forever."

Jill had come to this conclusion a lot quicker than Dory expected. She wasn't stupid, but Jill and logic didn't have much in common. Dory shoved her pillows against the headboard, sat up and took Jill's hand.

"If we don't find James, if we *never* find James, Daddy and Mother *will* be stuck on Isla Rica forever."

"I was afraid you were going to say that." Jill linked her fingers through Dory's and squeezed. "You and I could move to Isla Rica."

"You and me and yes we could, but Aunt Ping won't leave Outlook and how can we leave Aunt Ping with things in such a mess?"

"Dory. Tell me the truth. Are we bankrupt?"

"No," Dory said. *But we're getting there,* she thought. "Outlook has forty rooms. The monthly electric bill comes with three zeros."

"Why is this taking so long?" Jill flung herself off the bed and threw her arms out. "How come not a single one of those damn detectives Aunt Ping is paying can find James?"

"He keeps changing his name. They tracked the identity he picked up in Belize to Buenos Aires where he changed it. That second name they followed as far as the Philippines where they lost it and James obviously changed it again. He's smart and he had a long time to plan this."

"If we're running out of money, won't James, too? Eventually?"

"That's the hope. Identities as perfect as the ones he's using go for twenty to thirty thousand, so James has spent at least sixty grand already just on fake documents. Plus plane tickets and hotels and for all we know plastic surgery to change his appearance."

"I don't think he'd do that." Jill sat down on Dory's bed again and pursed her lips. "He really gets off on looking like Paul McCartney."

"But he doesn't want to get caught, Jilly."

Jill shuddered. "I can't believe I let that creep *touch* me."

Dory put her arms around her sister.

"I know we've only been poor for a couple of years, but I hate it." Jill laid her head on Dory's shoulder and sighed. "I was born to be rich."

Casseroles, which Mother forbade, began to appear on Great-grandmother Lambert's Haviland china. Born in Provence, Esme was a wizard with sauces, a genius with leftovers.

Dory interned the summer of 1996 at the accounting firm of Perth and Blye. Cliff Niles offered her a spot at Lambert's downtown branch, but she declined. "I think my FBI watchdogs might make my coworkers a tad nervous," she said. The truth was she didn't think she could bear seeing Cliff in Daddy's office.

Tom planted a truck garden the size of three football fields. Peter devoted half of one greenhouse to vegetable seedlings. Mrs. Grant and Esme canned all summer long. Peas and beans, beets and carrots. Tomatoes, zucchini, yellow squash and pumpkin. They made pickles out of cucumbers and peppers, just like Peter Piper.

On weekends Dory helped Jill work the produce stand Tom built in front of the orchard, across the road from the front gates. Dory kept the cash box. Jill waited on customers in shorts and a bikini top. Men in general, the FBI guys in particular, were their best customers.

A lot of Lambert's employees bought Tom's produce. So did most of Daddy and Mother's friends. The first time Bill Westerbrook, one of Daddy's golf buddies, tried to slip Dory an extra one-hundred-dollar bill for a dozen tomatoes, she refused. The second time, Jill nipped Ben Franklin out of his fingers and gave him a dazzling "Thank you."

"Jill!" Dory cried, appalled. "That hundred bucks is charity!"

"No it isn't," Jill replied. "It's take-this-so-I-don't-feel-guilty-about-dropping-you-because-you're-not-rich-anymore-and-I-still-am money."

Dory opened her mouth but nothing came out. She was stunned that Jill had seen through Westerbrook and she hadn't.

That night she went to bed sunburned and depressed. She lay on her back with the balcony doors open, staring at the shadows the moonlight threw on the ceiling, remembering what Chase had said to her that long ago Saturday morning. *You got a rough life, squirt. I don't know how you stand it.*

"Oh boy, Chase." Dory sighed. "If you could see me now."

By December 1996, two years and three months after James got even with Daddy, Dory's trust was mostly gone, spent on the Bastard Little Prick Squad, a few business ventures begun by Aunt Ping that had yet to show a profit, and maintaining Outlook. The place ate money like Dory ate Tums when she was angry.

In addition to the truck garden, Tom raised and slaughtered a few head of Angus cattle, six dozen hens for their eggs and roast chicken, and still the food bill for Aunt Ping and Jill and twenty-three servants would choke a horse. Yet it took all twenty-three of those people to keep Outlook from falling down around their ears.

On Dory's way home to Outlook for Christmas, she had a flat. The two FBI guys tailing her stopped and changed the tire.

"I haven't seen a G-man in weeks, but they've started following me again," she told Aunt Ping and Jill at supper. "I asked why and they said because it's Christmas. A lot of fugitives get homesick on the holidays, so they're hoping Daddy and Mother will phone home."

"Damn it." Aunt Ping slapped her fork on the table, startling Jill and making Dory jump. Aunt Ping never swore. "If Marshall Phillips invested half the time and manpower he spends watching us on finding James he'd have him behind bars by now."

The next day Dory found a sheet of Aunt Ping's monogrammed notepaper on the bread box in the family kitchen. At the top she'd written *Paintings,* beneath that, *"Small Monet, North Branch, $2.7 million. Call gallery."* Dory picked it up and went looking for Aunt Ping. She found her in the music room with her harp on her shoulder and the Tonkinese cat, Coco, named for her color and Aunt Ping's favorite designer, at her feet.

"What does this mean, Aunt Ping?" Dory handed her the note. "Are we down to a lame horse and twenty-seven cents?"

"Not quite." Aunt Ping placed the harp on its stand. "Insurance and real estate taxes are due—" Both those bills, Dory knew, came with five zeros. "—Christmas bonuses for staff and retainers for the investigators."

"How many paintings have you sold?"

"The Monet will be the third."

"We can't give up the search. We've got to find James to clear Daddy. I'll quit school, donate what's left of that money and—"

"You will *not*," Aunt Ping cut her off. "You're five months shy of having your MBA, which might—" She smiled. "—come in handy."

"Let me see your ledgers. Maybe I can come up with something."

Dory was buried in Outlook's account books when Jill came into her room later that afternoon. Rocky stretched out of a nap on the foot of the bed and touched noses with Jill when she bent to scratch her ears. Jill smelled like Joy and looked like a *Vogue* model in a winter white sweater and pants that made her hair glow like platinum.

"I had the best lunch," she said, settling on the corner of the desk with Rocky purring in her arms. "Jed Walling took me to the club and fed me Peking duck. Wasn't that sweet?"

"Adorable." Dory glared at the Excel spreadsheet on her laptop.

"What are you doing?" Jill peeked over the top of the screen.

"Looking for money. You wouldn't happen to have three or four million you don't know what to do with, would you?"

"No. But I've got almost thirty thousand and this."

Jill stuck her right hand in Dory's face. So close to her nose she had to take off her computer glasses to see the diamond and sapphire tennis bracelet on her wrist. The stones were so big Dory had to blink to bring them in focus.

"Holy crap! Where did you get that?"

"Jed gave it to me." Jill smiled. "So I'll sleep with him."

"Jill!" Dory shot to her feet, startling Rocky out of Jill's arms and under the bed. "What are you doing?"

"Till the produce stand opens next summer I'm contributing," Jill fired back, her eyes as hard and glittering as the sapphires in the bracelet. "The only way I can."

"You're sleeping with men and taking presents from them?"

"No! I'm not sleeping with them! I'm taking presents they give me so I *will* sleep with them, only I *don't,* so I'm not a wh—"

"Don't say that word." Dory clapped a hand over her mouth. "Don't even think it. Just stop. Please. You don't have to do this."

Jill shoved her hand away and pushed off the desk. "You're smart, Dory. You're in grad school and you work two jobs. I'm not smart. I can't tell teal from aqua. Computers baffle me, which means I can't even run a cash register. This face and this body are the only assets I have. What am I supposed to do? Not use them? Let you and Aunt Ping carry the whole load while I just stand around like—like Mother?"

Jill burst into tears. Dory stood on the small footstool she kept under her desk so her feet wouldn't dangle and hugged her. Rocky came out from under the bed and wound around Jill's ankles.

"Maybe we can find you a job where all you have to do is look gorgeous," Dory said. "Like modeling."

"I tried that." Jill sniffed. "I'm too fat."

"How can you be too fat?" Dory held Jill by her shoulders. "You're five-eight and you wear a size six."

"They said I should be a size two."

"I should be Madonna, then we wouldn't have to sweat the gas bill. You've been selling the presents, haven't you?"

"Yes." Jill sniffled. "Only now I can't think of a thirty-thousand-dollar lie Aunt Ping will believe."

"Oh, boy," Dory said. "Neither can I."

Dory received her MBA with a specialty in finance in June 1997.

The FBI attended the ceremony, just in case her parents decided to risk leaving Isla Rica in disguise to see her graduate. The same two agents who'd changed the flat for her at Christmas. Dory gave them a jaunty salute from the stage that made them grin.

"Look. They gave me a present," she said to Coop at her graduation party. He'd come to see Aunt Ping and tagged along to the ceremony, riding with her in the Rolls to Columbia and back to Outlook. He admired the gold ballpoint pen in its slim box, gave it back to Dory and said, "Very thoughtful."

"I know they're sitting in their car by the front gates," she said. "I'd invite them in for cake but they'd get in trouble, wouldn't they?"

"Oh yes." Coop laughed. "They pushed it with the pen."

"They're nice guys, really, just doing their job," Dory said. "I think I'm going to miss them when they're gone. If they ever leave."

She and Coop were sitting on the terrace drinking punch from Baccarat crystal cups. The French doors were open, letting a breeze scented by blooming lilies and roses into the ballroom. Dory couldn't remember the last time they'd used the ballroom or taken the Holland cloth off the grand piano, but now laughter and music drifted outside.

For a change everyone was having a good time. Aunt Ping and Jill, Wallace and Charles, Esme and Mrs. Grant, Eddie, Peter and Henry, Tom and his wife and the rest of the servants. Dory's whole family.

"I can't believe Daddy is still on Marshall Phillips' radar screen."

"It might help if Miss Lambert would scale back on the search for James. Keeping as many investigators as she has turning over rocks all over the planet only gives Marsh the idea that she's on to something. Not to mention that it's costing her a fortune she doesn't have anymore."

"I don't mean to be rude," Dory said, "but so are you."

"I've been pro bono for the last two years." Coop smiled. "I like you and your family, Dory. Your hearts are in the right place, even if what little money you have left isn't."

"Do you think we should give up on finding James altogether?"

"No, but I'd cut down to no more than two investigators. It's been almost three years. It's going to take more than skill and manpower to find him now. It's going to take luck or a mistake on Darwood's part."

"I'm guessing you told Aunt Ping this but she wasn't receptive so that's why you're telling me."

"Correct. I'm hoping she'll listen to a newly minted MBA."

Aunt Ping did not, which didn't surprise Dory. What Aunt Ping did listen to was her advice that she give up all the side businesses she'd started but the latest, the Happy Spirit Wine and Feng Shui Shop.

A funky, kitschy little store on a narrow tree-shaded side street in Westport, named for Westport Landing, the original pioneer settlement. Westport was the Funky Kitschy Capital of Kansas City, crammed to the gills with college kids, artsy types, new age devotees and hippies old enough to collect Social Security.

The Happy Spirit was a huge hit, a fun little shop that mixed Aunt Ping's knowledge of wines and her love of all things Chinese. Especially feng shui, the art of living in harmony with your environment. At the Happy Spirit you could buy books and kits to help you balance your life, an array of great wines to enhance the new you or drown your disappointment if you couldn't get your yin and your yang together.

Dory loved working weekends at the Happy Spirit. Jill worked weekdays with a cashier to keep track of the till. The energy and the oddball clientele made Dory's spirit happy after forty deadly dull hours at Perth and Blye. She made great money but her heart wasn't in accounting. Her heart was in banking, but her conscience wouldn't let her go near Lambert's till the wrong that had been done was made right.

On the whole 1997 wasn't a bad year. Dory's salary, profits from the Happy Spirit and a check for seventy-five thousand dollars paid the taxes and insurance on Outlook and kept the two-man Bastard Little Prick Squad afloat.

The seventy-five grand came from Chase: repayment of the sum Del Lambert spent on his college education. Aunt Ping showed Dory the note from Chase that accompanied the check.

> *Dear Miss Ping,*
>   *I know it's not customary to repay gifts, but I hope you'll accept this and put it to use bringing Mr. and Mrs. Lambert home to Outlook.*
>   *Sincerely,*
>   *Chase McKay*

His penmanship had improved since Dory had read his early letters home to Charles. Her heart skipped, but only a little.

"Pretty smooth for a guy who used to throw sponges at me."

"What do you think I should do with the check?" Aunt Ping asked.

"Cash it," Dory said and Aunt Ping did.

Just before Thanksgiving 1997, she sold a Renoir to cover maintenance on the house and the grounds, pay the servants—Charles and the rest of the senior staff were accepting half their salaries now—and fund the farm through the growing season.

"We're getting rich again, aren't we?" Jill asked hopefully.

"No, Jilly," Dory said. "We're getting barely solvent."

Once the paintings, sculptures and other assets Aunt Ping saved from Marshall Phillips were gone, then what? That's what kept Dory awake nights. Jill gave her the Sleep with Me Gift fund to invest, but that would take years to grow into anything useful.

Dory advised selling Daddy's coin and stamp collections, worth two million each, and at least some of Mother's horses. The feed and vet bills were astronomical, but Aunt Ping refused.

"Aunt Ping," Dory reminded her. "These things belong to you."

"In name only," she replied. "I'm holding them in trust."

With a solid, unwavering belief that James would be found and Daddy and Mother could come home. That was Dory's hope, too, but it was fading like Tinkerbell, growing dimmer by the day.

Mother's older sister Deirdre arrived unannounced at Outlook in April of 1998. On Palm Sunday, a week ahead of the Easter Bunny.

Dory and Jill and Aunt Ping had just come home from mass, were sitting down to a cup of tea in the breakfast room when Wallace appeared and said, "Miss Deirdre Darwood to see you, ma'am."

Aunt Ping's brown eyes took a startled leap. "Is she alone?"

"Except for her luggage, ma'am, yes."

"Keep her bags in the foyer, Wallace. I'll see her in the parlor."

"Yes, ma'am." He nodded and left.

"Deirdre hasn't been to Outlook in ten years," Jill said.

"Do you think she knows where James is?" Dory asked. "Do you think she's come to tell us?"

"No," Aunt Ping said. "I think she wants something."

Dory thought so, too. She hoped it wasn't money because it was Lent. She'd sworn off murder for Lent.

"I don't know where James is," Deirdre said when Aunt Ping came into the parlor with Dory and Jill. "I'd tell you if I did."

She stood by the marble fireplace in mango-colored slacks, a print blouse and beige sweater. The hyacinths and daffodils planted in clusters on the three-acre front lawn were poking their pastel and yellow heads through two inches of half-melted snow that had fallen in an unseasonable cold snap. Deirdre looked brown as a nut. Like she'd just come off the beach. Say a beach in the Caribbean.

"I believe you, Deirdre." Aunt Ping waved toward a rose brocade wing chair separated from the pink-gilt Louis chair by a round table. "Would you care for tea?"

"Yes, please, Margaret. Tea would be lovely, thank you."

Deirdre sank into the wing chair like her knees were about to give. Aunt Ping sat in the Louis chair, Dory next to Jill on the settee, her stomach in a knot.

Esme brought the tea on a trolley with a plate of hot cross buns, which Deirdre declined. She drank two cups of tea, put her cup and saucer on the round table and folded her hands on her knees.

"I've so much to tell you," she said. "I don't where to start."

"How about with your suntan?" Dory asked. "Where'd you get it?"

"Isla Rica," Deirdre said, turning in her chair. "I've just come from Drusilla and Del."

"How's Daddy?" Jill vaulted over the table in front of the settee. "Are he and Mother all right? Do they have enough to eat?"

"Your parents are fine, Jillian, doing very well. Del sold the yacht, made a two-million-dollar profit and opened a bank for the native population and the small expatriate community on the island." Deirdre drew three paper photo envelopes out of her handbag. "I brought snaps."

Jill grabbed one packet, Dory another, Aunt Ping the third.

"Isn't that the most lovely villa?" Deirdre was on her feet—all four of them were—pointing over their shoulders as they flipped through the photos. "It's tucked into the hillside, has a spectacular view of the harbor. Things are ever so much cheaper there. You can live like a king."

Daddy and Mother were, that's for sure. Their villa looked like Versailles with a red tile roof, surrounded by tropical gardens the size of the Amazon basin that were dotted with fountains big enough to pass for public monuments. Dory stared, her stomach churning, at a photo of Mother in silk capris and Daddy in a print shirt, cruising a blue bay in a sporty little boat and waving at the camera.

" 'Scuse me." Jill shoved the photos in her hands at Dory and raced out of the parlor, her face pale, her mouth trembling.

"Do you see, Dory?" Deirdre said. "How well your parents look?"

"Yes," she said numbly. "I can see."

Mother in Versace, Daddy in Armani dancing under the stars amid flowers and crystal and flaming torches. They had a Mercedes and a Rolls, about a billion brown servants in sparkling white uniforms. In short, they had the same life they'd always had, only in a warmer climate and they didn't have to pay the IRS.

Aunt Ping looked like she'd been shot through the heart. Daddy had a bank and a speedboat. *A speedboat!* Aunt Ping had white streaks in her dark hair and worry lines on her forehead.

"How did you get here?" Dory put the photos back in their sleeves and gave them to Deirdre. "Were you followed?"

"You mean by the coppers, don't you? No. No one followed. I came in a taxi and I watched the whole way from the airport to make sure."

Deirdre sat down and put the photos back in her bag.

Aunt Ping sat in the pink Louis chair and patted the seat for Dory to join her.

"My dear Jeremy worked for the London *Times*." Deirdre referred to her husband who had been dead so long she'd taken back her maiden name. "I still have friends there, so I've been able to keep track of all you've been through these past three years. I wasn't needed on Isla Rica. I thought I might be here."

"Gee, thanks," Dory said. "But unless you brought a suitcase full of money I don't think there's a damn thing you can do for us."

"Dory," Aunt Ping said sharply. "Deirdre is our guest."

"No, no, Margaret. It's quite all right. I brought a check."

Deirdre dipped into her purse again and handed Dory a check.

"I'm not good with pounds," she said. "How much is this?"

"Eight million, three hundred and twelve thousand dollars."

"Holy crap," Dory said. "What did you do? Sell the family manse?"

"I couldn't. It's entailed. I sold the London house and its contents. Diana found herself a viscount and eloped with him to Aruba. I sold out and went to Isla Rica to find Drusilla. I believed she was in dire straits and this was my chance to come to her aid for a change. Well. As you saw for yourselves, Drusilla and Del are doing just fine."

"Aunt Ping," Jill said from the doorway. She looked steadier and not quite so pale. "Wallace says there's a taxi out front."

"Oh dear." Deirdre glanced at her watch. "They're early."

Aunt Ping arched an eyebrow. "They, Deirdre?"

"Last May, Marilyn Vanderpool came to see Diana and me. She was very ill. That's why she risked coming to London. She found our address in James' things before he left her in Singapore four years ago."

"Marilyn?" Jill said and went pale again. "My Marilyn?"

"I'm sorry, Jillian," Deirdre said gently. "She died at Christmas."

Jill buried her face in her hands. Dory went to her and hugged her.

"Diana ran off with her viscount on Boxing Day. She was never meant to be a mother, let alone a grandmother," Deirdre said. "That's who's in the taxi, Margaret. Marilyn's son and his nanny."

"I assume," Aunt Ping said, "this is James' child as well?"

"Yes. We weren't welcome on Isla Rica. I'll understand if we're not welcome here, but I'd be so grateful if you could help me locate Marilyn's family. My letters were returned and the telephone is disconnected."

"Marilyn's parents moved to Canada," Aunt Ping said. "Who made you unwelcome on Isla Rica, Deirdre? Your sister or my brother?"

"Oh, it wasn't Del. He was kindness itself, as he's always been."

"So it was Mother." Dory turned to face Deirdre. "The woman who brought James to Outlook, badgered Daddy to hire him at the bank, badgered him again till he put James in charge of the wire room. The idiot who helped James frame Daddy, who's living like a queen on Isla Rica while Aunt Ping is selling everything that isn't nailed down." Dory heard the shrill in her voice and took a breath. "My mother wouldn't let a little kid who just lost *his* mother through the door?"

"Yes, Dory," Deirdre said. "I believe that about sums it up."

"Jill," Aunt Ping said, "tell Wallace to pay the taxi driver."

Dory, Aunt Ping and Jill waited in the foyer to meet Marilyn's son.

He was three and a half, Deirdre said, he'd be four in December. He came up the brick steps ahead of Deirdre and his nurse. A slim little boy, with red-blond hair and

Marilyn's hazel eyes, buttoned into a tweed coat that just reached the cuffs of his knee-length shorts.

He almost swallowed his bottom lip when he saw Wallace, so tall and austere in his black coat with his silver hair and clipped mustache. When Wallace winked, he giggled and stepped inside the house. Deirdre leaned forward and murmured in his ear.

"Hello, Aunt Margaret." He held out his hand. "I'm Jamie."

"Hello, Jamie." She took his hand. "Call me Aunt Ping."

"Auntie Ping," he said and Dory's heart nearly stopped at the flash of James she saw in his quick little grin. "Oh, I like that name."

"Jamie," Aunt Ping said. "This is Jill."

"Don't cry," Dory hissed, noticing her sister's lip was trembling as she leaned forward to shake his hand and say, "Hello, Jamie."

"Hello, Jill," he said and there it was again, this time in the faint British clip in his voice, a hint of James. "You're really pretty."

"Why *thank* you, Jamie," Jill gushed. "This is my sister, Dory."

This is a motherless little boy, Dory told herself as she bent down on one knee. He hasn't a clue that his father is a bastard little prick.

Dory forced herself to smile. "Hi, Jamie."

"I like you, Dory," he said. "You're small like me."

Then he put his arms around her neck, his head on her shoulder and that was it. That's all it took to break the vow she'd made when she lost Chase, that she'd never love anyone ever again. Dory felt it snap like a dead twig in her heart. She straightened and lifted Jamie with her.

"Hey, squirt." Dory jostled him and he popped bright-eyed off her shoulder. "Do you like snickerdoodles?"

Gina Vanderpool came from Vancouver on Tuesday to meet her grandson. Jamie sat on her lap in the rose brocade wing chair in the parlor, let her hold his face in her hands and gaze at her daughter's eyes. She didn't cry; she'd done most of that on the phone with Aunt Ping.

When Gina put him down, Jamie climbed up on Dory's knees, wrapped his arms around her neck and clung to her, shivering like a little monkey. Gina smiled at her, dipped her chin and wiped her eyes.

"Dory," Aunt Ping said. "Would you take Jamie outside to play?"

"Hey, squirt. Ever ridden in a golf cart?" Jamie shook his head. "Would you like to?"

"Yes, please." Jamie glanced at Deirdre. "May I, Auntie Deirdre?"

"You may," she said. "But let Dory drive."

Jill went with them. Dory managed to get his tweed coat buttoned over his sweater and jeans, his cap on with the earflaps down, but it took both of them to get his hands into his mittens. Esme handed him a snickerdoodle as they passed through the kitchen.

When Jill opened the back door, Jamie took off yelling and waving his arms like he'd been shot out of a cannon. Dory laughed, her breath puffing on the chilly air and ran after him, zipping her nylon parka and tugging a knit cap over her ears.

He was the perfect little passenger in the golf cart, sat quietly with his seat belt on. The second his feet touched ground he was off like a heat-seeking missile, his target—trouble. He stampeded the milk cows, frightened the hens off their nests in a flurry of feathers that sent Jill into a sneezing frenzy, climbed the monster John Deere in the main barn and had to be rescued by Tom.

"You two." Tom grinned at Dory and Jill. "Look like you been drug backwards through a knothole."

"Kittens!" Jamie squealed, bolting for the steps as he caught sight of the furry little faces peering down from the loft.

Tom caught him, tied a rope securely but not too tightly under his arms, said, "Git up," and let Jamie tow him up the stairs.

"Shit." Jill collapsed on a straw bale, her face dirty and chicken feathers stuck in her hair. "I hope Gina takes him back to Vancouver."

Dory didn't, but she figured Gina would. Deirdre had shown them Jamie's birth certificate, the rest of his papers. Gina Vanderpool was his grandmother. She had every moral and legal right to Jamie.

He fell asleep in the golf cart on their way back to the house. When Dory unbelted him and lifted him out, Jamie blinked at her sleepily.

"Do you think Grandmummy will let me stay here?"

"I think Grandmummy will do the very best thing she can think of to take the very best care of you."

"Then she'll let me stay here," Jamie said and grinned.

Oh boy, Dory thought. She left Jamie in the kitchen to drink cocoa with Esme, took off her jacket, finger-combed her hair and went back to the parlor. Jill was already there, her face washed and the feathers brushed out of her hair. She did not look happy.

"The best place for Jamie right now is here," Gina Vanderpool said. She didn't look happy, either. "He's had enough sadness and upheaval. I won't put him through any more. He's been with Deirdre for nearly a year and obviously feels quite at home at Outlook."

Dory glanced at Aunt Ping. She nodded. Deirdre was smiling and teary-eyed. Dory sat down, so surprised she couldn't stand up.

"Jamie's with Esme," she said to Gina. "If you'd like to tell him."

"I told you," Jamie said to Dory when she put him to bed that night in the cot in her bedroom. "I told you Grandmummy would let me stay."

Dory rumpled his hair. "You know everything, huh, squirt?"

Jamie's grin faded. "I know Grandmummy Diana doesn't like me."

"I've known your grandmummy Diana my whole life

and you know what?" Dory leaned down and whispered, "She doesn't like anybody."

Jamie's eyes widened. "Not even you?"

"Not even me. Not Jill. Not Auntie Ping or Auntie Deirdre."

"Well." Jamie sat up, puffed out his thin little chest and folded his arms. "I like you all very much. But I like you best."

She laughed. "Right. 'Cause I'm a squirt like you."

"You're pretty like Mummy." Jamie's bottom lip trembled. "And you love me like she did."

"Oh, Jamie." Dory tugged Marilyn's son out from under the covers and onto her lap, wrapped her arms around him and somehow managed to push her voice around the lump in her throat. "No one will ever love you like your mummy, but I'll try. I promise I'll try."

"Dory." Jamie rocked her awake by the shoulder at five-fifteen A.M. "Dory, I have to go pee-pee."

"Okay." She struggled half dead out of her bed. "Okay."

The bathroom was marble, the toilet raised on a dais, and it scared Jamie. He wouldn't go near it by himself. Dory took him to pee-pee, but forget going back to bed. He was hungry. Down to the kitchen for tea and toast in the half dark. Esme wasn't even up yet. Then back upstairs for jumping on the bed, throwing pillows and general devilment. Once she was awake, Dory loved every second of it.

By six thirty they were both dressed and Jamie was hungry again. Back to the kitchen for microwave oatmeal, a banana and orange juice. Esme put a kiss on his head and said, "Good morning, *mon petite*."

"What's that mean?" Jamie asked on their way upstairs again.

"It's French for squirt," Dory said.

"No it isn't. It means little."

Where the heck has this kid been for three and a half years, Dory wondered. "Then why'd you ask, Mr. Know Everything?"

"I just wanted to see if you knew." He skipped off the stairs and turned a circle looking at all the doors up and down the second floor hallway. "Can I see all the rooms? How many are there?"

"Forty total," Dory said. "Twenty-eight are bedrooms."

"That's not many. Mummy and I stayed in bigger hotels."

"This isn't a hotel, Jamie. It's our home."

"It could be a hotel, though, couldn't it?"

"Well, I suppose it could, if—" Dory blinked, a slow, ooh-wait-a-minute shiver crawling through her. *If we wanted,* she thought.

A hotel? Outlook?

Jamie ran ahead, chattering, opening doors, darting into rooms, darting out. Dory followed him, thinking, shutting doors. Opening them again, looking around, sizing things up.

Outlook. A hotel. She shut the door and smiled.

"You've had one Twinkie too many with Jamie, haven't you?" Jill asked. "Outlook is our home!"

It was Friday afternoon. Dory had spent two days thinking, planning and writing a proposal. Jill gaped at her across the table in the little dining room. Aunt Ping looked stunned. Deirdre looked interested.

"No, Jill, and yes, Jill. Outlook is our home. Do you want to keep it or do you want to lose it?" Dory passed out copies of the spreadsheet she'd created. "I used Aunt Ping's ledgers to come up with these numbers. We only have so many paintings and pieces of art we can sell. At its present rate of consumption, Outlook will eat itself alive in five years."

Dory waited, laser pointer in hand, drape-covered easel behind her. The sketches and blueprints she made were rank amateur stuff—Jamie helped her color the borders on her charts—but it would give them the idea. Aunt Ping read the spreadsheet and looked up at her.

"I thought we'd have more time." *More time,* said the look on her face, *to find James.*

"We're out of time, Aunt Ping. If we don't find a way to make Outlook pay for itself we're going to lose it. To taxes or sell it ourselves, either way it will be gone because we can't afford to maintain it."

"A hotel?" Aunt Ping cocked her head. "What kind of hotel?"

"Ladies." Dory flipped the drape off the easel and clicked on her pointer. "I give you—The Outlook Inn."

Chapter Four

**The Outlook Inn
Present Day**

From *Condé Nast Traveller* magazine:

A DESTINATION NOT FOR EVERYONE

Only the ultra rich need apply. No nationwide, toll-free reservation line here. Send your application for accommodations on twenty-pound watermark stationery—preferably monogrammed in gold leaf, with your family crest if you have one—to The Outlook Inn, 16700 Outlook Lane, Kansas City, Missouri 64146.

That's the way it works at the Outlook Inn. You don't reserve a room—you request one. If you're descended from royalty, your forebears rowed the boat that towed the *Mayflower* ashore, or your money is so old it explodes in the sun like a vampire, your request will likely be accepted.

Once it's been vetted, of course, by the prospective guest committee chaired by Margaret Lambert, whose brainchild it was to turn her family estate into the Outlook Inn.

"In eighteenth century England, the nobility did not stay at hotels when they traveled. They stayed at the homes of other aristocrats," Miss Lambert explains. "That's the idea behind the Outlook Inn. For our guests, staying here is like staying in their own home."

It is if home happens to be a forty-room mansion with a ballroom, two dining rooms and a library, a game room, a music room, two parlors and thirty-two bathrooms. All with marble floors, twenty-foot ceilings and crown molding crafted of mahogany harvested by hand and machete from the jungles of Burma before the sun set on the British Empire.

The house, listed on the National Registry of Historic Places, is a three-and-one-half-story Southern Colonial built of rose brick in 1875 by banking magnet Nicholas Lambert, Margaret Lambert's great-grandfather. From its brick-pillared front entrance to its elegant rafters, the house contains furnishings, paintings and works of art most museums would kill for. Every room, even the bathrooms, has a working bell pull.

The grounds encompass two whole sections of rolling, wooded countryside. That's two square miles or 1,280 acres of stunning gardens, an outdoor pool with waterfall, an indoor pool with its own pool house, stables and bridle paths, tennis courts and a 9-hole golf course with an adjacent clubhouse where casual but elegant luncheons are served.

Each guest room has a fireplace and its own bathroom, some a sitting room and private terrace. The most requested room at the Outlook Inn is the Honeymoon Suite. Miss Lambert asked us not to photograph it or describe it in this article. We agreed but take our word for it—it would be worth a trip down the aisle to spend a night in this room.

Bring your Ferrari if you like. There's a twenty-car, climate-controlled garage to protect its custom paint job. But leave the servants at home. The Outlook has a staff of thirty-five that includes a butler, a housekeeper, a French chef, a maid for each of the twenty-five guest rooms and two chauffeurs to motor you around Kansas City in a vintage Bentley or Rolls-Royce.

The article went on, but Chase McKay had read enough. He closed the magazine and tossed it on the burgundy leather seat beside him. He thought he'd thrown the damn thing away, but he'd found it just now when he'd opened his briefcase.

He wanted to rip the article to shreds, but one did not

make confetti in the backseat of a Rolls-Royce. The same Rolls mentioned in the article, a mint 1977 Silver Shadow the color of old pewter, the one Chase had washed and polished more times than he cared to remember.

His father had sent him the copy of *Condé Nast Traveller*. Two weeks after Chase sent him the issue of *Architectural Digest* with his picture on the cover. A real tit for tat if Chase had ever seen one.

He should've said no when Miss Ping offered to send the Rolls to pick him up at KCI, but he'd still been pissed about *Condé Nast* so he'd jumped at it. Taken it as an acknowledgment that Miss Ping no longer viewed him as the chauffeur's son but as an equal.

It would've been better—no, it would've been *perfect*—if the offer had come from Del Lambert, but that poor schmuck was still on the lam, still stuck in Isla Rica. Which left Chase stuck in the back of the Rolls feeling like a jerk for taking advantage of Miss Ping's graciousness.

At least his father wasn't driving him. That was something.

The kid behind the wheel, weaving the Rolls in and out of traffic on southbound I-435 in time to the hip-hop music that Chase could hear leaking out of the headphones clapped over his ears, had said his name was Diego. He looked like Julio Iglesias' kid, what's-his-name, and he looked to be all of twenty-two if he was a day.

Charles was at Outlook, recuperating from the heart attack he'd suffered two months ago. Good thing. He'd have another one watching the way this kid drove.

Chase had been in Toronto closing the deal on the design and construction of a medical park when the call about his father came on his cell phone. He'd left the conference room to talk to Dory Lambert, his own chest seizing as he listened to her tell him what had happened.

Charles had suffered the attack behind the wheel of the Rolls, en route from Outlook to the Fairmont Hotel on the Country Club Plaza to deliver Miss Ping to a charity tea. He stopped the car in the sweeping hotel drive, got out to open the door and fainted. Miss Ping shouted at the door-man to call 911, had a bellman help her load Charles into the Rolls and drove him herself, tires squealing and horn blaring, the six blocks to St. Luke's Hospital in two min-utes and thirty seconds flat.

Miss Ping who didn't drive, who carried a Missouri state identification card instead of a driver's license in her Italian leather wallet.

"You're a fine young man, Chase McKay," she'd said to him the morning he was sent away from Outlook. "Go make yourself into the best architect my brother's money can buy."

She'd given him a tin of Esme's snickerdoodles for the trip. He'd opened it on the plane, found an envelope inside that held twenty brand-new one-hundred-dollar bills and a note from Miss Ping that suggested he buy himself an Ivy League wardrobe.

Chase invested the money instead, made a series of lucky picks in the futures market and graduated from Cornell with three quarters of a million dollars. He'd sent Miss Ping a check for seventy-five thousand dollars to pay for his education, kept investing the rest and saving his salary until he had enough experience to leave the firm that hired him out of Cornell.

That was five years ago. Now McKay Design and Devel-opment had offices in midtown Manhattan, L.A. and Dal-las, three hundred twenty-two employees and a net worth of 570 million dollars.

He owed a good chunk of his success to Miss Ping, and quite possibly his father's life. And still, Chase thought with a scowl, he'd been a bonehead about the Rolls.

He should have rented a car—and he should *not* have let his father talk him out of flying straight from Toronto to Kansas City.

"There's nothing you can do here and plenty you need to do up there," he'd told Chase on the phone, his voice breathy. "Stick to your original plan and come see me in April for my birthday."

It was April and on Sunday his father would turn sixty-five. He couldn't tell Chase he wasn't old enough to retire anymore, especially now that he'd had a heart attack. A mild one, thank God—Dory Lambert had FedEx-ed the EKG, the echocardiogram and the angioplasty results to a cardiologist in New York for a second opinion—but the heart attack was the silver bullet in Chase's arsenal.

His cover story was McKay Design and Development's first project in the Kansas City metropolitan area, an up-scale shopping mall in Lee's Summit. Chase didn't need to be here, but overseeing the job was a reason to stick around for as long as it took to convince Charles that it was time to hang up his driving gloves.

"I can't retire," he told Chase whenever he brought up the subject. "Miss Ping needs me. She needs all of us."

It was hard to argue with the truth. Nonetheless, Chase had hopes that Dory Lambert would be sympathetic to his cause.

He'd heard the quaver of worry in her voice when she'd called to tell him about Charles. She and the old man were pals; she played cribbage with him and poker on Friday nights if they were short. She was hell on wheels at five-card stud. His father's letters, and in the past couple of years the e-mails he wrote on the PC that Chase had bought him, and Dory taught him to use, were full of things Miss Dory said and did.

Turning Outlook into a hotel to save it was Dory Lambert's idea, but you never heard it from her. In print or TV interviews, Miss Ping was the spokesperson. The Outlook Inn was her brainstorm, her creation.

The Dory Lambert that Chase had gotten to know via e-mail and text messages over the last two months was a far, modest cry from the pudgy, homely brat who'd done nothing but piss and moan and whine to him when she was fourteen about how awful it was to be rich and pampered.

You take my life, you spoiled little twit, Chase had wanted to say to her, and I'll take yours. Now he had Dory

Lambert's life, her former, privileged, pots of money life. He wouldn't rub her nose in it, but he'd use her affection for his father and her concern for his health to pry Charles away from Outlook once and for all.

He'd take his time, get the lay of the land. He'd be charming, persuasive, and if all else failed he'd dangle his checkbook. He had no ax to grind with the Lamberts, but facts were facts. They needed money and he had piles of it. He'd give them whatever they wanted, money enough to close the hotel and keep Outlook afloat for the rest of Miss Ping's life if that's what it took. All they had to do was help him convince his father that it was time to retire.

The Rolls made a sharp swerve into the passing lane. An air horn blared and Chase glanced out the back window at the chrome-toothed grille of an eighteen-wheeler damn near skinning the back bumper. He raised a hand to the trucker high up in his cab, unclipped his seat belt, leaned over the front seat and yanked the headphones off Diego's ears.

"Ow!" The kid grabbed his right ear. "Hey, man!"

"This isn't a lowrider." Chase met his glare in the rearview mirror. "Pay attention or pull over and let me drive."

"I had plenty of room."

"Not from back here you didn't."

"*Hombre blanco estupido,*" the kid said under his breath.

"Stupid white man," Chase replied. "I speak Spanish."

"My luck," the kid said sourly to Chase's reflection. "I s'pose you're gonna tell Mr. Charles and Miss Ping."

"Keep your foot off the gas, your eyes on the road and I won't."

The kid thought about it. Checked his mirrors, signaled, and settled the Rolls into the middle lane at a discreet sixty-two miles per hour. The trucker flicked his lights and the big rig roared past.

Diego set the cruise control and eyed Chase. "This okay?"

"Peachy." Chase sat back in the seat. "Keep it right there."

The kid grumbled something, clapped his hands on the wheel at two and ten o'clock and fixed his gaze on the road. Chase refastened his seat belt with a smile Diego couldn't see, took a file labeled SUMMIT CREST PROJECT out of his briefcase, opened it and flipped on his PDA.

The file was perfectly organized. Calculator tapes that looked like they'd been ironed, spreadsheets creased to fit inside the folder with military precision. Copies of permits precisely stapled. The crew lists and contact sheets for the two dozen subcontractors on the project in perfectly typed alphabetical order.

The few Post-its were color-coded in order of importance. Yellow meant FYI, green ASAP and pink FMA for Five Minutes Ago. His PA, Sylvia, had an accounting degree from Penn State and an obsessive-compulsive streak Chase relied on to keep his butt off the black leather stool at the drafting table in the living room of his apartment above Central Park. He had a PC with a mainframe-size memory that could take the specs he fed it and render blueprints for the designs that were constantly sketching themselves in his head, but Chase preferred to draw them by hand rather than rely on AutoCAD. He could spend hours, days at his drafting table if it weren't for Sylvia. He paid her a CEO's salary to keep him on task and his ass off that stool and smiled every month when he signed her payroll check.

There were two yellow, one green and zero pink Post-its in the Summit Crest folder. God love Sylvia. Chase could count on the fingers of one hand the times in the past five years that she'd sent him a pink one. Chase pushed MEMO on his PDA and wrote, "Bonus for Sylvia."

Take care of the help. He'd learned that from Del Lambert. From Jill Lambert, Chase had learned not to think with his heart.

It had been years since he'd wondered what might've happened if Dory hadn't knocked over the birdbath that woke Miss Ping. What could've happened if he'd had his way with Jill without a condom.

He respected women, revered them—he'd learned that from Miss Ping—he was kind and gentle, attentive and lavish, but he never, ever let a woman get in the way of his good sense.

Del Lambert had and look what happened. Lambert's the bank had recovered, but Lamberts the family—Miss Ping, Jill and Dory—were still paying for his lapse in judgment. According to Charles, Del and Her Ladyship—the name the servants called Drusilla behind her back—were living the high life in Isla Rica. If you called never seeing your children and never being able to go home again living high.

Chase felt bad for Miss Ping. He had to hand it to Dory for coming up with a way to save Outlook. Of Jill Lambert, the girl he thought he'd die if he didn't have when he was nineteen, he rarely thought at all. The train wreck of Del Lambert's life had been very instructive.

A spear point of sunlight glared off the PDA screen. Chase blinked and looked up. Over the guardrail whipping past the right side of the Rolls, he saw the Missouri River, a wide, sluggish ribbon of water dragging itself past the dingy levees that protected the surrounding industrial park from its seasonal floods. He could see snags in the channel, a sandbar and a string of tarpaulin-covered barges drawn up to the bank because the water level was too low to navigate.

The mild weather was a lucky break for Chase. The Summit Crest project was ahead of schedule, but the warm, dry winter after last year's scorching summer and parched autumn was bad news for Outlook. Tom's fields were bone dry, his steers underweight. Charles had written Chase about it. All Charles ever wrote about was Outlook.

Outlook and Miss Dory, but that was going to change. Without a fight, Chase hoped, but he was ready for one if his charm and his bank balance failed to persuade his father and the Lamberts. The old man was stubborn, but so was Chase. When he left Outlook his father was going with him. Period.

In the distance he could see the skyline of downtown Kansas City etched against the pale April sky. There were some great old buildings down there, especially along Baltimore Street. He wondered how many were still standing. He knew that Union Station, site of a gangland shooting in Al Capone's day and the Liberty Memorial, the only monument to World War I in the entire country, had finally been given face-lifts. He itched to see them and the new federal courthouse built into the bluffs overlooking the river, but not today.

Chase focused on his PDA and the latest price quotes for materials and labor on the Summit Crest project. The next time he glanced up, the Rolls was sweeping off I-470 south onto the Outlook Road exit ramp.

This stretch of interstate was all new since he'd left Kansas City. Chase looked around and scowled. No landmarks to recognize, only dull stretches of empty field that looked as foreign as the face of Mars. He had no idea where he was. It was disconcerting as hell.

At the end of the ramp Diego made a left over the interstate and steered the Rolls through a right-hand curve where the four-lane road widened out to accommodate the overpass narrowed back to two lanes. Two lanes that were familiar to Chase. Twenty miles of blacktop that crested big hills and dipped through hollows as it veered steadily east and south, until the trees gave way to a spear-tipped iron fence spaced with posts built of rose brick with white enameled cement caps.

Chase knew exactly where he was now. The jump he felt in his pulse and the clench in his stomach didn't surprise him. He'd expected it. He'd spent the first nineteen years of his life at Outlook, the last sixteen as far away from it as he could get without crossing an ocean.

The purposeless kid so besotted with Jill Lambert that he would've spent the rest of his life washing cars just for a chance to grope her in the barn was long gone. So was a lot of the open space that used to surround Outlook. Across the road a housing development fanned out in cul-de-sacs with shake-shingled roofs and privacy fences that enclosed in-ground swimming pools. In the far distance he could see a strip of road lined with one-story commercial buildings, the wink of a stoplight changing and beyond that more shake-shingled roofs.

Diego braked at a four-way stop and made a left. The street sign said this was Outlook Lane. Through the bars of the fence, Chase saw a cluster of Tom's Black Angus steers pulling hay out of a big round bale. Another knot of them stood in a giant mud puddle Chase guessed would be a pond if it ever decided to rain again.

He shut off his PDA, closed the Summit Crest file and put them back in his briefcase with *Condé Nast Traveller*. The day he left Outlook with his father he'd throw the magazine away.

The road veered away from the march of black iron and brick posts, crossed a bridge with weathered guardrails that looked like sliced-in-half wagon wheels, bore to the left for another mile, then swooped to the right to make the uphill swing around the front of Outlook.

The fence reappeared on the right above the steep culvert edging the road; the orchard on the left side behind a stone wall overhung with stooped and gnarled fruit trees. Chase couldn't remember how big the orchard was, how many acres, but if you wandered off the tractor paths you could get lost among the apple, peach, pear and cherry trees.

The trees that soared inside Outlook's black iron fence were older than the house. A couple of them, a burr oak here in front and the elm by the garage, were state champions. Peter's pride and joy. Through the forest of winter-bare branches, Chase could see Outlook's rose brick chimneys, all eight of them capped white like the fence posts, drifting pale smoke toward the paler sky. His pulse kicked again and he scowled, turned his head away and caught Diego watching him avidly in the rearview mirror.

His dark-eyed gaze jumped back to the road. How long, Chase wondered, had he been spying on him? And who had put him up to it? His money was on Esme and Esther Grant, his surrogate mothers.

"What do you do at Outlook?" Chase asked.

"Whatever I'm told." Diego flashed him a cocky grin in the mirror. "Mostly help Mr. Wallace. You know, man, with luggage and stuff."

Chase was glad. Wallace was no spring chicken. Hell, most of the staff was older than gunpowder. They should all retire. But none would, any more than his father would, so long as Miss Ping needed them.

The Rolls purred over the crest of the hill, swirling a wake of moldy yellow leaves out of the culvert. Chase saw them in the rearview mirror, on his left the produce stand Tom had built at the front of the orchard, and Diego watching him again. This time he didn't glance away.

"Mr. Charles says you're building a shopping mall," Diego said. "You looking to hire people?"

"Maybe." So much for loyalty, Chase thought. "You want a job?"

"Me? No way. My cousin Beni."

"Is he legal?"

"Legal as *you*." Diego glared at him, insulted, in the mirror. "Me and Beni? We are Chicano. American. Born in L.A., man."

"Then he's got a nice, legal birth certificate, doesn't he?"

"Yeah. So do I. You wanna see it?"

"No. So long as you've got a driver's license, I'm happy."

"You are one *stupid hombre* if you think Miss Ping would let me touch this car if—" Diego glanced in the mirror, saw Chase grinning and huffed a pissed-off-but-trying-not-to-laugh breath. "That was low, man."

"You asked for it. Catch me later and I'll give you the name of my foreman. He's the man Beni needs to see."

"Thanks." Diego nodded in the mirror. "I'll do it."

The front gates of Outlook loomed just ahead. Tall, black iron barricades flanked by rose brick walls and white-capped gateposts hung with carriage lamps the size of buffalo heads. Diego pressed the remote clipped to the sun visor and the gates swung inward to admit the Rolls.

For a quarter mile the drive ran straight and flat between towering oaks. It split where the terraces began and climbed up the hill in two loops that rejoined in front of the house. Diego bore to the right, guiding the Rolls past daffodils and hyacinths in vivid bloom. Forsythia with long yellow canes lined the terrace walls. Waterfalls splashed from the rocks into pools where Miss Ping kept Chinese goldfish. She'd nearly skinned Chase alive the summer he was ten and he caught three of her prize six-pounders with the fishing pole Del Lambert gave him for Christmas.

Very picturesque, the front drive. Plenty wide enough, not as steep as it looked from the bottom, but still tricky. His father could wind the Rolls with its long nose and wide wheelbase through the curves without touching the brake, but Diego kept skimming the edge with the whitewalls. There'd be hell to pay if Peter found tire tracks in the grass.

Chase would've used the north gate. It was a short, straight shot to the garage. No terraces and no killer blind spots, he thought, just as the Rolls reached the top of the middle terrace and the blind spot there filled suddenly with a boy wearing jeans, a red windbreaker, pads and a helmet, airborne on a neon purple skateboard.

Chase caught a flash of a small, white, horrified face before the kid twisted in midair and Diego wrenched the steering wheel. The Rolls careened nose-first into a lawn statue of Artemis, snapping the gilt-edged bow in her hands. The kid went sailing into an azalea hedge.

Chase was out of the Rolls and over the hedge before the azaleas stopped quivering, Diego half a step behind him. The stupid-ass kid was sprawled on his back, eyes closed, arms flung out, face ashen.

"Jesus Christo," Diego moaned. "Is he dead?"

"If he is, it's his own damn fault."

"Bite me." The kid's eyes blinked open. Glassy, hazel and belligerent. "I'm not dead."

Chase leaned over him. "Are you hurt?"

"I don't think so." The kid moved his arms, then his legs, turned his head from side to side. "Nah. I'm okay."

"Good." Chase grabbed a fistful of his windbreaker, hauled him to his feet and pinched his thumb and index finger under the kid's nose. "You came that close to being a bug splat on the windshield."

"Well, I'm not, am I?" The kid sneered. "You want to let me go?"

Chase wanted to pop him but released him. "What's your name?"

"Jamie Lambert. Who'er you?"

Ah. The Demon Spawn. He'd heard about this kid from his father.

"Chase McKay."

"Oh, yeah. Chuck's kid. Dory said you were coming."

"My father's name," Chase said between his teeth, "is Charles."

"Whatever." Jamie fished his board out of the azaleas, stepped over them and walked up to the Rolls. He eyed the crumpled fender and broken headlight and grinned. "Somebody's name is gonna be mud when Aunt Ping sees this. You got a lotta 'splaining to do, Diego."

"*Poco* punky." Little punk, Diego snarled in Spanish and started toward Jamie.

"Let me." Chase put out a hand to stop him. "You could get fired."

"Artemis! Oh no!" A shrill voice wailed. "You've broken Artemis!"

Chase recognized Peter's voice, the gnash of an engine changing gears, glanced behind and saw a John Deere lawn tractor towing a trailer piled with tools chugging full tilt up the drive. Peter manned the wheel in denim coveralls and jacket, a yellow knit cap over his ears.

"Her bow! My God!" he howled. "You broke her bow!"

The tractor squealed to a stop and Peter hopped off, a small man who moved like a hummingbird and looked like a lawn ornament. One of those round-bellied, apple-cheeked gnomes. He dashed up to Artemis, tilted halfway off her pedestal by the collision with the Rolls, bent and snatched up the golden arrow broken out of her bow.

"I should shove this up your nose!" Peter shook the arrow at Jamie. He slouched with his board under one arm, a kiss-mine look on his face. "This statue is priceless! She was cast in 1922 from a one-piece mold and you broke her! You broke Artemis, you little heathen!"

"I don't drive. I didn't break her." Jamie hooked a thumb over his shoulder. "Diego broke her, you silly old swish."

"Hey," Chase barked. "That's enough out of you."

He started toward Jamie, but Peter threw up a hand like a traffic cop. "No, Chase. Lovely to see you, but I can handle this little monster."

"If you keep calling me names," Jamie said, "I'll tell Dory."

"Let me write them down so you can give her a list."

"Stuff it. I'm outta here." Jamie swung away toward the house.

"I think not." Peter grabbed the back of his windbreaker and spun him around toward Chase. "If you wouldn't mind, dear boy."

"Glad to." He corralled Jamie in a loose half nelson. The kid dropped his board, wrapped his hands around Chase's arm and glared up at him. "I'm warning you. I know karate. I'm a second degree brown belt."

Chase smiled. "Take your best shot, Bruce Lee."

The kid twisted and grunted, trying to hook Chase's ankle with one foot, then both feet, till he exhausted himself and hung like a stretched-out rubber band from Chase's forearm. "This is child abuse," he panted, out of breath. "Let me go or I'll call the hotline."

"I'll loan you my cell." Chase tightened his grip. "Now shut up."

Peter whipped out a walkie-talkie and spoke into the mouthpiece. "Lurch, this is Twinkletoes. We have a situation on the second terrace. Artemis is down. Suspect in custody—the Bad Seed. I repeat—suspect in custody is the Bad Seed. Alert Mama San Three. The scene is secure. Await you here. Twinkletoes out."

"What in hell," Chase asked, "was that?"

"Just having a little fun with the FBI." Peter winked and tucked the walkie-talkie in his overalls. "They eavesdrop on our conversations. Lurch is Wallace. Mama San Three is Dory."

"I didn't see the feds on the road today," Diego said. "If they're hanging around they must be parked in the orchard again."

Chase frowned. "The FBI is still watching Outlook?"

"Hardly twenty-four-seven, dear boy. Not anymore. They like to surprise us. Dory came up with our little code. It's made it ever so much easier to bear the G-men and their pop-in, drive-by snooping runs."

"Ten years of being hounded by the FBI," Chase said. "That can't be good for business."

"The agents are very discreet. Dory had a word with them when we opened the Outlook Inn. Our guests really never notice them. One doesn't unless one knows what to look for. And where."

Like the orchard, Chase thought, watching Diego sidle up to the Rolls. He took a peek at the ruined front end and cringed.

"It was the kid or the statue." Chase half dragged, half carried Jamie across the drive to stand beside Diego and the Rolls. "Too bad you can't ask for a do-over."

"Hey!" Jamie punched him in the wrist. Right on the bone with his knuckles, hard enough to smart. "You can let me go now."

"No, he can*not*." Peter turned away from the trailer and the arrow he'd wrapped in an old towel. "You aren't skating out of this one."

Jamie crossed his eyes and stuck out his tongue. Peter made the same face right back at him. Chase wanted to laugh, but didn't.

A four-seat electric golf cart glided over the crest of the

terrace. Chase recognized Wallace behind the wheel, a red muffler wound around his neck above his starched white shirtfront and shiny black coat.

The woman beside him Chase wouldn't have recognized if he'd fallen over her. The only thing that hadn't changed about Dory Lambert was the color of her hair. And her height, Chase noted, as Wallace stopped the cart and she swung out of it.

She was still a squirt. A perfectly coordinated squirt in cinnamon trousers, a cream-colored, cowl-neck sweater and a short camel hair coat with gold, French knot buttons like her earrings. Chase had never seen her wear anything that matched.

"I didn't break Artemis!" Jamie declared, struggling to wrench free. "Diego hit her with the Rolls, Peter called me names and this gorilla won't let me go!"

"Thank you for the summation, Jamie." Dory picked up his skateboard from the edge of the drive and held it in both hands. "First of all, you're grounded. Second, you aren't supposed to be on the front terraces with this, are you?"

"Look, I was only—"

"Are you?" Dory repeated.

"No," he said sullenly. "But I was only—"

"Jumping *off* the terrace," Dory cut in. "Which you are strictly *forbidden* to do, just as the Rolls was coming *up* the drive. Correct?"

"Well, yeah, but it's not my fault that Diego freaked out and ran off the road and hit Artemis. Peter called me a monster and a little heathen."

"Thank God you were alive to hear him call you a monster and a little heathen. Wallace." Dory passed the skateboard to the butler, who stood beside her. "Lock this in the luggage room for the next week."

"Dory! *C'mon!*" Jamie howled. "I've got an X-games tournament next month and I gotta practice!"

"Make that two weeks," Dory said to Wallace. To Jamie she said, "One more word and it will be three."

"All right, all right," the kid groused. "Can the gorilla let me go?"

"Yes," she said and smiled. Her teeth were straight, perfect and very white. The last time Chase had seen her she'd had enough metal in her mouth to fashion a new grille for the Rolls. "Hello, Chase."

"Hello, Dory." He nodded. He wanted to smile at her but wasn't sure he could without grinning and saying something stupid like, "Well, look at *you*!" which he figured would go over like a lead balloon.

"Hey." Jamie belted him again. "She said you can let me go."

"Right." Chase lifted his arm. Jamie sprang away from him, spun around and pushed at the helmet that was sliding off his head full of red hair. "Thanks for nothing, King Kong."

"Jamie," Dory said sharply. "Get in the golf cart."

"Be sure you buckle up, Evel Knievel," Chase told him.

"Bite me," Jamie said under his breath and stomped away.

"What about the Rolls, Miss Dory?" Diego asked. "You trust me to drive it around to the garage?"

"This wasn't your fault, Diego. I'm just glad you didn't hurt Jamie." She smiled at the kid sulking in the golf cart. " 'Cause now I get to."

"Go ahead." Jamie scowled. "Take turns picking on me."

"It's Thursday," Chase said to Dory. "Why isn't he in school?"

"He's suspended. Shocking, I know." She smiled again—whatever her braces cost they'd been worth every penny—tucked a strand of chin-length dark hair behind her ear and faced Diego. "I called our insurance agent. He's sending an adjuster right away." If your name was Lambert and you owned a Rolls-Royce, Chase thought, insurance companies did things like that. "You and Chase go with Wallace. I'll wait with the Rolls."

"I'll wait with you," Chase blurted.

Dory glanced at him and blinked. She looked as surprised as he was to hear him make the offer. "That's very sweet, but your father and Aunt Ping are waiting to have lunch with you."

"Better get myself up to the house, then," Chase said. Damn it, he thought. "I'll see you later?"

"Oh, I'm sure." She smiled like she could care less whether she saw him later and turned away.

Chase wanted to laugh. Served him right for all the sponges he'd thrown at her. All the times he'd told her to bug off when she was a homely, pudgy squirt with a crush on him the size of the one he'd had on Jill. He caught Wallace looking at him with one silver eyebrow raised over his all-seeing, all-knowing blue eyes and wiped the grin off his face.

He leaned into the Rolls for his briefcase, slid into the suede blazer he'd taken off at the airport and followed Diego with his suitcase to the golf cart. Jamie slouched in the back, his arms jammed together, his head turned away. Diego got in beside him, Chase up front with Wallace.

"Welcome to the Outlook Inn, sir," he said.

"Thanks." Chase glanced at Wallace, puzzled by his formal tone.

The butler turned the golf cart toward the house, gave a small roll of his eyes and a nudge of his head. Chase looked over his shoulder at Jamie. The kid was staring at him, boring holes in his back with a fearsome glare.

He and the Bad Seed, Chase guessed, were not going to be pals.

The second the golf cart disappeared over the terrace Dory's lungs remembered how to breathe. The only organ in her body that hadn't shut down at her first glimpse of Chase was her heart. It was still banging in her throat, where it had jumped to the second she'd laid eyes on him. Her stupid, silly, go-ahead-and-break-me-again-oh-*please* heart.

"Ninny!" Peter snatched the yellow knit cap off his shaved head and smacked her with it. "He wanted to wait for the adjuster with you!"

"No, he didn't." Dory took the keys to the Rolls, which Diego had given her, out of her coat pocket. "He was just being polite."

"Who cares? It was an opportunity to be alone with him!" Peter gave her another slap with his hat.

"You don't have to hit me, Peter. I got the message. I'm a ninny."

And she was freezing in the damp, chilly air. Dory slid behind the wheel, started the engine and slammed the door in Peter's face. Before she could find the button that tripped the power locks, he'd darted around the Rolls and jumped in beside her.

"Hit me again," Dory warned, "and you'll eat that hat."

"If you don't want my help," he said indignantly, "you should never have told me that you love Chase."

"I told you I loved him when I was fourteen, Peter. I'm not fourteen anymore."

She only felt like she was fourteen. It was ridiculous. She'd seen hundreds of pictures of Chase, taken in front of buildings he'd designed, snapshots from father and son vacations. She'd viewed them all coolly and calmly, helped Charles put them in scrapbooks. Her pulse never flickered, her heart never jumped. Not once. Even a beefcake pic of Chase in tropical print trunks on a South Carolina beach didn't faze her.

Nothing about him fazed her till Wallace drove the golf cart over the terrace and she'd seen him standing in the drive with one arm lassoing Jamie, wearing tailored tan slacks, a heather green sweater over a striped beige shirt— and the scowl. The soulful James Dean scowl that used to turn her knees to goo.

Her knees still felt like Jell-O, her stomach like she'd swallowed a handful of butterflies. She felt awful, sick. Flushed, pale, giddy, witless—like Dory the dopey, fourteen-year-old dweeb. She hoped to God that Chase hadn't noticed.

"He couldn't take his eyes off you," Peter said. "He kept staring."

Dory's heart stopped banging and she glanced at her watch. If the adjuster got a move on she'd have a two-hour window to stick her head in the oven before Esme had to make dinner.

"The last time Chase saw me," Dory said, pointing at her mouth, "I looked like a walking scrap heap."

"You *were* a pretty ugly little duckling," Peter agreed, then he grinned and threw his arms wide. "But now you're a swan!"

Chapter Five

Chase couldn't get over Dory Lambert. She hadn't turned into a swan exactly. More like a nice little mallard. He hadn't expected her not to change. He didn't know what he'd expected. Maybe that's why he was sitting at the desk in his father's living room above the garage, thinking about her when he should be reading the fifty-four e-mails on his laptop.

His father was not a happy camper. Miss Ping had put him in a ground floor suite in the north wing and told him he was staying there till his cardiologist said he could climb stairs. He'd bitched about it to Chase after lunch.

"I want to go back to my apartment. I'm not comfortable here."

"Come on, Dad. Miss Ping brought your bed down." Chase waved toward the bedroom that adjoined the sitting room. "You're ensconced in your favorite chair. You have your computer, your books, your cribbage board and maid service. Looks pretty comfortable to me."

"Well, it's not," Charles grumped. He looked pale and tired. "I want to go home. Bossy damn woman won't let me."

When Charles fell asleep, the bossy damn woman served Chase tea. In the breakfast room, at a round oak table in a sun-flooded bay, joined to Esme's brick-floored domain by a smaller galley kitchen.

"We reserve the front rooms for the use of our guests,"

Miss Ping said. "I hope you don't mind having your tea here."

"Not at all," Chase lied. Now he knew how his father felt. These were the family quarters. He didn't belong here. He wasn't the help, but he wasn't family, either. He felt awkward and ill at ease.

The two cats curled on the padded window seat staring at him seemed to know it. One, marked like a Siamese, had aqua eyes and a coat that looked dusted with cocoa. The black and white one watched him with big oval emerald eyes.

"I suppose Dad naps a lot," Chase said, turning his attention from the cats to Miss Ping, "because of the heart attack."

"Not entirely." She smiled. "Mostly he naps because he's sixty-five."

Yeah, Chase thought, grinning inside. *I know.*

Esme served them shortbread and Earl Grey in paper-thin china cups. Chase carried the tea tray back to her, got a kiss for his trouble and a hug from Esther Grant, then let Miss Ping give him the tour. The cats padded along behind, silent and watchful.

Chase supposed Miss Ping wanted to show him the changes they'd made to turn the house into the Outlook Inn because he was an architect and he loved the old place. She'd caught him peeking in a window when he was eight, gave him a glass of lemonade and spent two hours showing him all the rooms and telling him every story she knew about Outlook.

The changes were minimal and confined to the first floor, mostly a matter of closing off rooms. Chase was relieved. When his father told him Miss Ping was turning Outlook into a hotel he'd had visions of magnificently wainscoted and plastered walls being taken out with a sledge.

The mahogany pocket doors between the front parlor and the foyer bore a tasteful brass plate that read OFFICES—PRIVATE. Dory, whose official title was manager, shared the space with Anita Sawyer, Del Lambert's former secretary, and Jill, who was coordinator of public relations.

"Even though we're taking in boarders these days," Miss Ping said wryly, "we still receive a number of invitations to charity functions and society dos. Jill attends. She travels a good deal, which she loves—she's away now, in California—and she is utterly brilliant at drumming up business for the Outlook Inn."

The perfect job, Chase thought, for a social butterfly.

The giant palm trees still stood watch at the front doors, their bathtub-sized containers surrounded by smaller thatch palms, ferns and blooming tropicals. From his days of being Peter's slave in the greenhouse Chase recognized bromeliads, Amazon lilies and a bird of paradise.

The foyer still looked as humongous to him as it had when he was a kid. So vast he hardly noticed the reception desk, a baroque sideboard rescued from the attics, Miss Ping said, so ornate and ugly Chase figured it must be priceless. It stood to the left of the staircase that lifted from the rose marble floor to the gallery, where two more curved staircases at each end climbed to the second floor.

A middle-aged couple appeared on the gallery; the woman swathed in mink that matched her champagne hair, the man in a navy wool suit sporting a stickpin with a sapphire so big Chase blinked.

"The Morgensterns," Miss Ping murmured to him. "Excuse me."

She moved forward to greet them, a gracious smile on her face, her hand extended. Her hairstyle, an elaborately pinned chignon, hadn't changed in sixteen years. As she stepped away from him, Chase noticed white roots at the nape of her neck and realized she colored her hair.

Hell, he thought with a jolt. *Dad is sixty-five. How old is Miss Ping?*

"Pssst. Chase," hissed a low voice. "You're staring, dear boy."

He glanced behind him and saw Henry, Del Lambert's valet, now concierge for the Outlook Inn, grinning at him from the desk that used to dominate the library when it was Del Lambert's private sanctum. It sat to the right of the stairs, a huge slab of walnut almost invisible beneath the overhang of the gallery. Henry looked like a munchkin behind it.

Chase eased away from Miss Ping and the Morgensterns. Henry came around the desk and shook his hand.

"Pop in for a nightcap. Say around ten?"

"Love to, thanks," Chase said.

"Grand." Henry nodded at the Morgensterns and said from the side of his mouth, "Zoe and Felix. Wonderful people. Off to the ballet this evening." He plucked a white envelope off the desk. "They come three times a year to visit the grandkids. Stay two weeks each trip and drop twenty-five hundred a night to stay in Del and Her Ladyship's suite."

"Yow," Chase said under his breath.

"Yow-*za*." Henry wagged his shoe-polish black eyebrows and sailed away to give Felix Morgenstern his ballet tickets.

Chase drifted away from the desk to watch the dignified half bow Wallace made to the Morgensterns as he swept the front doors open and preceded them down the brick steps. The Bentley, a vintage, deep blue 1988 Mulsanne S, waited beneath the portico. Diego, in a dark suit and tie, held open the rear door. He nodded to the Morgensterns, tucked them in and closed the door. Chase hoped he'd ditched his headphones.

His father slept through dinner, so Chase dined with Miss Ping and her guests in the little dining room. It was half the size of the main dining room, which meant it was only huge rather than gigantic. Chase hoped to see Dory, dreaded seeing Jamie, but Deirdre Darwood came in without him and Dory never showed.

He met a couple from Topeka, Kansas, who owned half the natural gas rights in the state, a cattle baron from Wyoming who'd spent the day advising Tom on his steers.

And Miss Fairview. A rail-thin woman who lived on the income from shares of AT&T and Standard Oil her grandfather bought after the Great Depression. She was a frequent and persnickety guest, Esther Grant told him later.

There was no ordering from the menu at the Outlook Inn. Esme was a Cordon Bleu graduate, not a short order cook. She served rack of lamb, new potatoes with rosemary, asparagus, a salad that looked like cactus needles but melted in your mouth under a raspberry vinaigrette.

Miss Ping selected the wine from Outlook's cellar. Wallace served it in crystal goblets purchased in France on the eve of World War I.

"My grandmother, Matilda Lambert," Miss Ping said, "wrapped each piece in one of her petticoats and packed them carefully in her suitcases. She hired four extra maids in Paris, assigned each one a valise full of crystal to hand carry onto the boat, then the train, and last the carriage. All the way from France to Outlook."

Everyone smiled but Miss Fairview. Chase eyed his goblet. Damn thing looked like it would break if he blew on it. His hand shook just thinking about picking it up. He'd already noticed that Wallace trembled. Except when he poured; then he was steady as a rock.

After dinner the gents invited him for a brandy in the billiard room. Chase accepted, hanging around in case Dory appeared, but she didn't. He finished his game of nine ball, said good night and dawdled his way toward the north wing. He wandered into the back parlor, where Miss Fairview looked up from her book and glared at him. His last stop and his last chance to find Dory was the music room.

He heard a harp and a piano playing, so softly he thought someone was listening to a CD. Till he stepped into the room. Deirdre Darwood glanced up at him from the keyboard of the Steinway baby grand piano and Miss Ping's fingers stilled on the strings of her harp. The cat that looked Siamese sat at her feet, its dark pointed ears pitched toward him.

"Hello, Chase," Miss Ping said. "Don't tell me you're lost."

"Uh, no. Sorry to disturb you. I was just—" *Oh, grow up,* he told himself. *You aren't nineteen anymore.* "I'm looking for Dory. I didn't have much chance to talk to her earlier."

"It's past eight." Miss Ping stood her harp on its stand. "I'm sure she's gone home by now."

"Home?" Chase said blankly.

"Dory and Jill moved into the guesthouse when we opened Outlook," she explained. "So we'd have more guest rooms."

"Jamie went with her," Deirdre added. "He stays with Dory when Jill isn't home."

"While he's grounded and suspended from school?" Chase held up a hand. "Sorry. None of my business."

"Jamie is a redhead," Deirdre said. "His pediatrician says that in twenty years of practice he's seen only one red-headed child that didn't need to be kept on a leash."

"A leash is good." Chase nodded. "How about a cage?"

"We've considered both." Miss Ping smiled. "But Tom assures us that Jamie is a perfectly normal ten-year-old boy. He should know. He and Marjorie have eight grandsons."

"Sounds like an expert opinion to me. Sorry for the interruption." Chase backed out of the room. "I should say good night to Dad."

His father was sitting in his chair in his robe and pajamas, white socks and leather slippers, the black and white cat curled on the ottoman next to his feet. His glasses sat on his nose, a book in his lap. He looked up but he didn't look happy when Chase came through the door.

"You're awake. Great." *Christ.* Chase's gut clenched. He looked gray as gravel, like he hadn't closed his eyes in two months. "How 'bout I sweet-talk Esme out of some grub for you?"

"I had soup in the kitchen with Jamie and Dory." Charles took off his glasses and frowned. "She doesn't treat me like a feeble old man."

"You're not feeble, Dad. You're just sick."

"I'm not sick. I had a heart attack." Charles slapped his book shut. "I'm gonna have another one if that bossy damn woman doesn't let me out of here. I don't belong here. I never did, but she won't listen."

"I'm listening, Dad." The cat jumped off the ottoman as Chase sat down on it. "Come on now. Take it easy."

"Oh, for God's sake! You're as bad as she is!"

Charles swung out of his chair, out of the room and slammed the door. Chase waited a minute to give them both a chance to cool off, then got up and opened the bedroom door. His father sat on the side of the bed, his fists digging into the mattress.

"Okay, Dad. I'll take you back to your apartment, but here's the deal. You aren't cleared for stairs yet, so I'm carrying you."

"You can't carry me up those stairs."

"Do you want to try it or do you want to sit there and complain?"

"I'll get my jacket and my toothbrush."

Chase thought he might have a heart attack, or give himself a hernia, but he managed to haul his father up the garage stairs. On his back, his elbows hooked under his knees, the way Charles used to carry him when he was a kid.

He made his father a bed on the scuffed old leather couch that used to belong to Del Lambert and tucked Charles into it with a quilt wrapped around him. That was forty-five minutes ago. His father was asleep and he was still staring at his unread e-mail.

Chase heard a snort, bent his elbow on the back of the desk chair and looked at Charles, his head thrown back on the pillow tucked against the arm of the couch, his mouth half-open and snoring. Chase crossed the living room, sat on the coffee table—gently, so it wouldn't creak—and watched his father. Damned if he didn't look better. His face had some color and the lines pinched around his mouth were gone.

He'd seen his father last at Thanksgiving. He'd flown him to New York, had him picked up in a Rolls so he could ride in the back for a change, and took him to dinner at Tavern on the Green because he'd always wanted to go there. He'd looked great, his hair more silver than blond, but other than that, he no more looked like a man pushing sixty-five than Chase did. He'd stayed a week, slept like a log in the guest room, walked all over midtown while Chase worked, hiked through Central Park every day without a huff or a puff.

Now he looked like someone had let the air out of him. Wallace, whose hair had been silver for as long as Chase could remember, looked younger than Charles did. Who the hell had shanghaied his strong-as-an-ox father and replaced him with this crabby, petulant old man?

Charles stirred, opened his eyes, saw Chase and smiled.

"Why don't you sleep in my bed, Dad?" He nodded at the loft above the living room and kitchen. "I'll get you up the steps."

"No. We've both had enough stairs for one day." Charles pulled the quilt up to his chin. "I'm fine here."

"Henry invited me for a drink. Will you be okay?"

"I'll be out like a light—" Charles yawned. "—in two seconds."

And he was, head back on the arm of the couch, mouth open and snoring again, before Chase plucked his suede blazer off the back of a kitchen chair, slid into it and opened the door.

The carriage lamps spaced along the brick wall that enclosed the flat part of the garage roof came on automatically at dusk. Mist hung around them; chilly enough that Chase could see his breath. He shut the door and reached in his pocket for his cigarettes. He let himself have five a day. He lit his fourth one and sat on the wall to smoke it.

They didn't used to be, but now the grounds were lit at night. To keep the guests from wandering out to smell the roses in the dark and breaking their necks, Chase guessed. From the garage roof the paths that wound through the garden and the flagstone walks between the house and the outbuildings glimmered like runways beckoning a 747.

He finished his cigarette; fieldstripped the butt to throw away later and went down the stairs.

It was a five-minute walk along the pea gravel path that bisected the stretch of greensward below the ornamental garden. A few trees along the way were lit by strings of clear miniature Christmas lights. He could just imagine how Peter must've howled about hanging those.

The path forked under a twinkling little pin oak where it connected with the road, an offshoot of the front drive that came around the house and ran straight to the golf course and clubhouse. The road was lit, too, along its edges by tiny white lights bubbled in plastic strips. Flexible, easy to roll out and dirt cheap at Wal-Mart.

The gardener's cottage lay to the right, the guesthouse to the left, both two-storied and built of stone. The dark shadow of the greenhouses loomed behind the roof of the gardener's cottage, the glass panes picking up here and there a gleam of moonlight. The living room lamps glowed at the windows. Chase saw a figure move behind the sheer curtains. Henry or Peter watching for him. He glanced at the guesthouse. It had to be ten or better but light still spilled through the downstairs windows.

"Sorry, fellas," Chase murmured. "Gimme a rain check."

He followed the road and then the driveway that led to the two-car garage attached to the guesthouse by a breeze-way glassed in for the winter. A stone wall enclosed the front patio. Carriage lamps flickered at the corners and on both sides of the black iron gate that swung open without squeaking when he touched it.

Another carriage lamp glowed beside the red-painted front door. A fountain wrapped in plastic sat in the middle of a dry pool. Tubs of witch hazel perched on the cement steps that led up to the porch. He brushed one with his sleeve, sprinkling faded white petals on the toes of his shoes. He rang the bell, heard it chime inside and waited.

A curtain twitched. Chase glanced at the window and saw Jamie's pale face peering back at him through the glass.

Dory was in the kitchen scrubbing the counters. When the doorbell rang she glanced at the microwave—quarter past ten. It wasn't unusual for Henry or Peter to come by this late. If the door wasn't locked, and it wasn't so far as Dory knew, they pranced right in like they owned the place. It drove Jill nuts, which is precisely why they did it.

"Jamie!" Dory shouted over the blare of Tom Petty and the Heartbreakers on MTV. "Who is it?"

She heard him hit mute, the couch springs squeak as he rolled up on his knees and looked out the window. "Nobody I want to see."

"*Jamie!*" Dory bellowed in a warning tone.

"Okay, okay! It's what's-his-name—Chance—Chuck's kid."

"His name is *Chase*." Dory's pulse jumped. Had something happened to Charles? No. Chase would've called 911 first and then Aunt Ping. "Tell him I'll be out in a minute."

What was she thinking to wear jeans and a bleach-stained sweatshirt to clean the kitchen? She should've put on white gloves and the Dior gown she'd worn to make her debut to society at the Jewel Ball.

Well, crap. Dory drained the sink, wiped her hands and hurried out of the kitchen, through the small dining room, up the three carpeted steps to the living room and stopped. Jamie sprawled on the couch with one leg hooked over the back.

"Where is he?" she asked. "Where's Chase?"

"On the patio." Jamie thumbed at the front door. "You told me to tell him you'd be out in a minute."

"I meant out of the kitchen." *And you know it!* Dory wanted to yell, but yelling at Jamie did no good. She pointed at the stairs. "Good night. You should be in bed anyway. You're running a fever."

"Oh wow. A whole one hundred point five. I could have convulsions any second." Jamie rolled his eyes and shut off the TV, rolled off the couch and headed up the stairs.

"Brush your teeth!" Dory called after him, then drew a deep breath and crossed the living room.

Chase leaned against the wall, his head down, his arms and ankles crossed. He glanced up when she opened the door and smiled, his hair gleaming like dark silver in the mist hanging around the carriage light.

"Hi," he said. "Is it too late to drop by?"

"Have you had measles?" Dory asked.

"I don't know," Chase replied. "I don't remember."

"Jamie has rubella, the three-day, mild kind. He was exposed at school and he broke out after his shower. I called the pediatrician. If you've had measles, you can come in. If you haven't, you could catch them and spread them. They're not like mumps, but the doctor says they can make an adult feel like real crap for a few days."

"I've probably had them," Chase said. "But I'm not sure about Dad, so I probably shouldn't chance it."

Be smart, Dory, she told herself. *You managed to avoid him all day. Say, "Good plan. Good night," and shut the door.*

"I've had measles," she said. "Just a second. I'll come out."

Dory pulled her camel hair coat off a hanger and shrugged into it, made a swing away from the closet, then a dash across the living room and caught Jamie creeping down the stairs. "Gotcha!"

He dropped onto a step, laughing. "A guy's gotta try."

"Go to bed," she said. "Or a guy's gonna get a swat on the butt."

"I'm going." He grinned and turned up the stairs. "G'night, Dory."

He wouldn't come down again. That was the rule. Caught on the stairs and the game was over. Dory trusted Jamie and she loved him, which was the only reason she didn't kill him for being such a little pill.

"Will he be okay?" Chase pushed off the wall when she stepped outside. "He won't burn the house down while you're out here?"

"Oh, he'd love to hear you say that, so don't let him. We have enough trouble keeping him in school and out of detention."

"What did he do to get kicked out for two weeks?"

"He put a whoopie cushion on Sister Mary Tereza's chair. Nuns never look before they sit down. Poor woman almost wet her habit."

Chase laughed. "I'm sorry. It's not funny. It's one hell of a picture, but it's not funny."

"Oh, but it is. The school surveillance camera caught Sister Mary Tereza on tape. Sister Immaculata played it for me. She was my algebra teacher, now she's the principal." Dory sighed. "If I could get my hands on that cassette I'd make a fortune on the Internet."

Chase laughed again and Dory smiled. She'd never make his blood burn and yearn. She'd known that in the driveway this afternoon when he'd looked at her like he wanted to pinch her cheek she was just so darned cute, but at least she could make him laugh.

"I'd say," Chase grinned, "that he's lucky he wasn't expelled."

"Sister Immaculata told him the same thing. He's on her Watch List, which let me tell you, is not a happy place to be."

Oh, but it was nice to be out here with Chase. Even though she was freezing already and her nose felt drippy. Mist clung to her eyelashes and her teeth wanted to chatter. Jill would shiver—Jill would fake a shiver—just to see if he'd put his arm around her, but that was Jill.

"How would you know about Sister Immaculata's Watch List?"

"She says she created it just for me. Some claim to fame, huh?"

"There's always the Outlook Inn. Dad says it was your idea."

"Technically, no. Technically, it was Jamie's idea."

"Entrepreneur and holy terror. A hellion of many talents."

"He has an IQ of one hundred and fifty-seven. Aunt Ping and Deirdre had him tested. That explains a lot about Jamie."

"So does the fact that he has, what? Four mothers?" Chase tipped his head at her. "You, Miss Ping, Deirdre and Jill."

"He has five mothers. Add Esme and Esther and subtract Jill. She and Jamie do not get along."

"He and I didn't exactly hit it off, either."

Dory grinned at him. "He called you Chance."

"He doesn't call Dad 'Chuck' to his face, does he?"

"He did." Dory held up her index finger. "Once."

"Speaking of Dad, I left a note for Miss Ping, but I thought I should tell someone else that I sprang him out of the big house tonight."

"You what?" Dory said with a laugh.

"I took him back to his apartment. He didn't climb the stairs—I carried him. He's asleep, snoring like a freight train on the couch."

Dory's mouth fell open. "You carried him up those stairs?"

"He looked ready to chew his foot off. I would've carried him up Mount Everest to get that trapped animal gleam out of his eyes."

"I'm glad. Aunt Ping won't be, but I am." She glanced at Chase and saw that he'd raised an eyebrow. "I am. Really. He's been miserable in the house. I tried to tell Aunt Ping, but—" Dory sighed and shrugged. "She's Aunt Ping. The Great and Powerful."

"He looks better already. He's got some color in his face and he's sleeping like a baby." Chase smiled. "Except for the snoring part. I'm surprised you can't hear him clear over here."

"As loud as Jamie plays the TV? Smart as a whip, that boy, but deaf as a post."

"So." Chase leaned back against the wall. Dory stood in front of him, her hands stuffed in her pockets to keep warm. "What do you like to talk about besides Jamie?"

"Sorry." She wrinkled her nose and sniffed to keep it from running. "Guess you don't want to see his baby pictures."

"Not tonight." Chase straightened. "You're cold. I should go."

"Don't even think about it!" Peter's shrill voice rang out of the darkness. "We've got you surrounded!"

"What the—?" Chase glanced over his shoulder.

Dory leaned around him and saw Peter and Henry, bundled in caps and coats, coming up the flagged path from the gardener's cottage. Hand in hand and grinning, they pushed through the gate into the muted glow of the mist-hung carriage lamps.

"And we're armed." Henry swung a wicker picnic basket and a five-gallon stainless steel pump thermos onto the wall next to Chase. "With hot cocoa, graham crackers, Hershey bars and marshmallows."

"And wood." Peter plucked a small, gnarled apple branch out of his canvas carry bag and waved it at Dory. "What do you think? I say at least twenty lashes for this lout—" He bonked Chase on the head with the stick. "—for even thinking he could stand us up and live to tell about it."

"You stood Peter up?" she said to Chase.

"No, I stood Henry up." Chase shot her a grin and ducked another blow from Peter. "He invited me for a nightcap."

"Yes, and you accepted." Peter flailed him on the sleeve with the stick. "Then we find you over here, you naughty boy. One, two—" The apple branch snapped in half on three. "Now look what you've done." Peter held up the stub. "You broke my twig."

Chase was laughing, Peter grinning; Dory struck dumb that Chase had stiffed Henry and Peter to see *her,* to talk to *her,* to— Wait a minute. Get a grip. He'd wanted to tell someone besides Aunt Ping that he'd sprung Charles out of the big house. That's all it was.

Dory sighed. Henry filled a Styrofoam cup and passed it to her.

"For the spotted wonder," he said, nodding at the second floor.

She looked up and saw Jamie at the window, leaning his elbow on the sill and his chin on his hand. He wiggled his fingers at her.

"Thanks, Henry. I'll be right back."

Jamie met her on the stairs, plunked down on a step in his plaid sleep pants and sweatshirt and scratched his throat. She'd put cortisone cream on the rash after his shower but the bumps were still there.

Dory passed him the cup. "Don't scratch."

"It itches." Jamie took a sip of cocoa. "Tell Henry thanks for this. He's a nice guy. I don't know what he sees in that old crank Peter."

"You know what they say, squirt." Dory wrapped her arms around the newel post and batted her lashes at him. "Love is blind."

"Oh, funny." Jamie flushed and smirked, drank some more cocoa and eyed her soberly. "You like old Chad, don't you?"

"His name is Chase and yes, I like him. I grew up with him."

Jamie made a face. "He doesn't like me."

"After the way you behaved today? Gee, I wonder why."

"You're gonna make me apologize to him, aren't you?"

"Yes. And to Peter for breaking Artemis and Diego for scaring him half to death."

"Maybe I'll get measles on my tongue and it'll swell up so bad I won't be able to talk."

"I wouldn't count on it if I were you, but if that happens you can write them notes of apology." Dory pushed off the newel post. "Don't forget to brush your teeth."

On her way outside she stopped in the downstairs bathroom to blow her nose, wash her hands and stuff Kleenex in her pocket. She thought about grabbing a couple news-papers, too, but Peter already had a fire going in the copper fire bowl he'd given her for Christmas.

Chase stood next to it toasting marshmallows on a long, crooked stick. He shot her a flame-lit smile that made her heart flutter.

"I'm still Peter's slave," he said. "Some things never change."

"Tell me about it," Dory replied. *Stop that,* she told her stupid, silly heart and turned to help Henry unwrap Her-shey bars for the s'mores.

Chapter Six

His father was awake and dressed when Chase came down from the loft at six o'clock the next morning. He sat on the couch in khaki trousers, a plaid shirt and rust-red sweater, a cup of coffee—decaf, Chase hoped—on the table in front of him. His toothbrush protruded from the breast pocket of his navy poplin jacket.

"Going somewhere?" Chase asked around a yawn.

"Back to my prison cell." Charles slapped his hands on his knees and stood up. "You can't keep hauling me up those stairs."

"Wait a minute, Dad. I've been thinking. Doesn't Tom have a cherry picker for the orchard?"

"Oh, no." Charles laughed. "Till I can climb the stairs on my own, I've no business being up here. My cardiologist won't even discuss stairs till I finish this medication I'm on and I take a stress test." He sighed and frowned. "Three weeks from today."

"That's not too long." But it ought to be just about long enough, Chase thought, to make his case. "I'll get dressed and go with you in case there's a problem with the bossy damn woman."

"All right." Charles grinned and sat down. "I'll wait."

Chase headed for the shower, peeling off his T-shirt on the way. It smelled like smoke and he could still taste scorched Hershey bars and burnt stick on his tongue.

"That's the fun part of eating s'mores," Dory had said to him last night. "Flossing bark out of your teeth."

She'd told him she'd joined the Girl Scouts when she was nine just so she could eat s'mores till she puked. Chase had almost choked on the one in his mouth when she said that, but managed to swallow before she'd described the camp-out she'd attended with Her Ladyship.

"The rest of the girls and their mothers showed up with sleeping bags," she said. "Mother and I arrived in a fifty-foot Winnebago driven by your father. Killed the whole back-to-nature thing dead on the spot."

While he buzzed his electric razor over his face Chase smiled, remembering how she'd pantomimed driving a stake with a mallet. A regular little comedienne, Dory Lambert, still refusing to take credit for the Outlook Inn. Now it was Jamie's idea. Right. A four-year-old kid.

He had two appointments today; lunch with his friend Curtis Rowe, equipment manager for their high school football team, now a United States congressman, and a consult with Dr. Eric Woods, his father's cardiologist. The rest of the day was his.

The old man had it right, Chase decided. Khaki trousers with a hunter green and maroon check shirt, a tan V-neck pullover and a tie he could tuck in the pocket of his suede blazer ought to cover all the bases.

Charles was pacing by the door when he came down from the loft. Chase eyed his empty coffee cup suspiciously but said nothing.

"Thanks for last night, son," Charles said as they walked to the house. "That's the first decent night's sleep I've had in two months."

"Anytime, Dad." Chase put his arm around his father. "Anytime."

Dory stood at the bay window in the breakfast room. When she saw Chase and Charles coming up the walk from the ornamental garden, she breathed a sigh of relief. When Chase put his arm around Charles she caught her bottom lip between her teeth. You had to love a man who said he'd carry his father up Mount Everest. Too bad he didn't love her.

"Here they come." Dory turned to face Aunt Ping across the oak table. "I told you Chase would bring him back. I told you Charles was sensible. He needed a break and you need to stop babying him."

"Do I?" Aunt Ping said and raised an eyebrow.

She never raised her voice, but when the eyebrow went up you were cooked. When she'd tried before to talk to Aunt Ping, the eyebrow had defeated her, but this time Dory held her ground. If Chase could carry Charles up the garage stairs, she could brace Aunt Ping.

"If you keep treating him like an invalid you'll make him one."

"I am merely following his cardiologist's orders."

"Dr. Woods said no stairs and no lifting. No driving and no stress. He did not say tie him to his chair and make sure he never lifts a finger. You won't even let Charles play poker, Aunt Ping."

"On the contrary. I have repeatedly offered the billiard room."

"And Charles and Peter, Henry and Tom and Eddie declined, didn't they?" Aunt Ping didn't reply, just pressed her lips together. "Offering the billiard room is like Queen Elizabeth offering Buckingham Palace. They wouldn't be comfortable here. Charles *isn't* comfortable here."

"Why am I hearing this from you?" Aunt Ping demanded.

"What's Charles supposed to say? 'I don't mean to sound ungrateful, Miss Ping, but you're driving me batty'? He'd never say that to you."

"I suppose not," Aunt Ping replied. Grudgingly, but the eyebrow slid down a notch.

Dory didn't mean to sound ungrateful, either. If it weren't for Aunt Ping, God knew what would've happened to her and Jill, but facts were facts. Charles' recovery was not going well and Aunt Ping wasn't helping.

Lately Dory wondered if it wasn't time Charles retired.

He was sixty-five, which made Aunt Ping sixty-two and Dory a basket case.

The trust Dory had designed with Cliff Niles to fund Outlook in perpetuity needed at least ten more years of major cash infusions and damn shrewd investing to even come close to keeping the wolf away from the door. It was doable at the rates they charged. Dory thought they should wear masks at the reception desk and greet everyone who checked in with a cheerful "Stick 'em up." But did Aunt Ping have ten more years of being the perfect, gracious hostess in her?

The fall and winter months weren't bad. Occupancy was light—though Jill was working her tail off, traveling like a gypsy to increase it—but from Easter to Labor Day Outlook was full most of the time. Some nights Aunt Ping went straight to bed after dinner. She never said a word, but Dory saw how pale and drawn she looked, could imagine how wearing it must be for her to have Outlook packed to the attics with strangers. On those days Dory thought that if she could get her hands on her father she'd make him eat his goddamn speedboat.

"All right, Dory," Aunt Ping said. "What do you want me to do?"

"Leave Charles alone. That's all. Let him do what he feels like doing when he feels like doing it. Don't make Esther wait on him hand and foot. Let Chase do it. I've got a hunch that's why he's here."

"I seriously doubt that." Aunt Ping's eyebrow went up again. "I'm more inclined to think Chase has come to force Charles to retire."

"Good luck to him." Dory thought exactly the same thing, but till Chase declared his intentions, she intended to play dumb. "I can't see anyone forcing Charles to do anything. Not even Chase."

"Oh, I think his bank balance could be very persuasive."

So did Dory. The profile she'd read in *Fortune* magazine on McKay Design and Development had left her mouth hanging open.

If Charles did retire, she almost hoped he wouldn't collect his pension. It was a miserly thing to hope—Nicholas Lambert would be so proud—but Charles could live like a nabob and employ his own staff of servants on Chase's pocket change alone. If he didn't claim it, Charles' portion of the servants' pension fund could mean a great deal to Wallace or Esme, neither of whom had a filthy stinking rich son to help support them in their decrepitude.

Dory had established the servants' fund first, ahead of the trust for Outlook, funded it by selling a Picasso with Aunt Ping's blessing and combining it with Jill's Sleep with Me Gift money. With Cliff Niles' help she'd made the fund bulletproof and seventy-five percent employer funded along with first-rate medical and disability insurance.

Take care of the help. She'd learned that from her father. Cover your ass at all times, she'd learned from Marshall Phillips.

When he was ten years old Chase thought Outlook was the biggest house in the world. He'd seen bigger ones since, designed and built a few himself, but Outlook's dimensions—nearly the length of two football fields and damn near as deep as one—were still impressive.

The kitchen was the size of a barn; the floor made of rose brick. So was the interior wall that held a giant Aga gas stove and four built-in ovens. At that end of the kitchen Esme cooked. At the other she fed the staff. In between there was space enough to play tennis.

The exterior walls were half brick topped with white-painted windows. The wooden countertops had been bleached so many times they gleamed like old bones. Bowls and plates striped and glazed in rainbow colors gleamed inside cabinets with glass doors. Esme's cookware hung from copper ceiling racks.

The kitchen usually smelled like the herbs Peter grew in the greenhouse and that Esme hung in clumps in the pantry to dry. This morning it stank like calamine lotion. The source was Jamie, perched on a stool at the end of one counter with a mug of tea and a plate of cinnamon toast.

He glanced at the door and scowled when Chase came through it with Charles from the glassed-in back porch. Chase wanted to grin at the pink streaks on the kid's throat and the spots on his face that looked like he'd sprouted a million new freckles overnight, but scowled back at him.

"What'er you doing here? I thought you were infectious."

"Relax, son," Charles said. "I've had the measles."

"I'm not infectious. I'm contagious." Jamie held his hand out for Chase to shake. "Put 'er there, Chester old pal."

"Jamie." Esme popped him with a wooden spoon. "You are rude."

"Ow." The kid rubbed his head. *"Il est un dopant."*

"Êtes ainsi vous—so are you." Chase glanced over his shoulder and saw Dory coming across the tennis court from the galley kitchen that connected to the breakfast room where Miss Ping had served him tea. "If you're going to call Chase a dope do it in English."

"Okay." Jamie looked him square in the eye. "You're a dope."

Chase had a feeling a laugh wasn't the reaction Jamie was hoping for, so he snarled back at him, "Takes one to call one."

Sure enough, the kid almost grinned.

"What are you doing here, mister?" Dory put her hands on her hips and frowned at Jamie. "I told you to stay in the guesthouse today."

"It's boring over there all by myself."

"Do your schoolwork. Read a book. Vacuum the popcorn you spilled last night out of the couch cushions. Unload the dishwasher while you're at it." Dory pointed at the door. "Now go and do *not* come back."

"I have measles, not bubonic plague," Jamie griped, but slid off the stool and flipped Chase a wave. "See you, Chet."

Chase nodded to him. "Later, Jimmy."

The kid flashed him a grin and slammed the door. Dory gave Chase a what-was-that-about look and wheeled on Esme.

"*Je sais, je sais,*" she said in French. "I shouldn't have let him in."

"I know, I know doesn't help, Esme," Dory replied. "If I tell Jamie to do something, but you let him do as he pleases—or Deirdre does, or Aunt Ping or Esther—then it's no wonder he never minds anyone."

"But he is ill, *mon petite*. His throat is very sore."

"He ate cinnamon toast with a sore throat?" Dory nudged Jamie's plate full of crumbs. "I don't think so. He conned you."

"You are too hard," Esme shot back. "Jamie is just a little boy."

"He's a spoiled little brat. I should know. I used to be one."

Chase grinned remembering the pampered little pain in the ass that used to follow him around, but Dory didn't see. She had her back to him, arguing with Esme in English and French, her hands spread on the counter, Esme shaking her spoon under Dory's nose.

"Here we go again," Chase's father said under his breath. "If she isn't going at it with Esme about Jamie, it's Esther or Deirdre or Miss Ping."

He shook his head, picked up a thick white mug from the end of the counter and held it under the spigot of a sterling silver coffee urn.

"Charles! *Non!*" Esme cocked her spoon. "That is not the decaf!"

"Keep your skirt on. This isn't for me," Charles said, but he took a healthy swig before he passed the mug to Chase with a wink.

Jamie had five mothers. His father, Chase thought, had five nurses. No wonder he'd looked ready to chew his foot off. When Dory turned away from the counter, Charles held out his wrists.

"Put the cuffs on. Take me back and chain me to my chair."

"Not me." Dory waved a hand. "You're free as a bird."

Charles blinked. "I'm what?"

"Free to do as you please. So long—" Dory held up one finger "—as you stay within the perimeters Dr. Woods gave you."

"No stairs, no driving, no stress." Charles smiled. "What did you do? Tell Miss Ping I threatened to quit?"

"Not at all." Dory shot Esme a look that said are-you-listening? "I merely pointed out the pitfalls of treating like a baby someone who *isn't*."

"Out." Esme leveled her spoon at Dory, then at Chase and Charles. "All of you—*allez*. I have breakfast for eight to serve in an hour." Her spoon flicked the air. "*Vite, vite.*"

English translation: Scram on the double. Chase had heard it a million times when he was a kid. Dory and his father headed for the breakfast room. Chase waited till Esme put her spoon down and asked while he rinsed his coffee cup, "Do I get my snickerdoodles today?"

"After luncheon I will bake them. We will have them with our tea."

"I might not be back in time for tea."

"The snickerdoodles will wait."

"You won't sneak some over to the spoiled little brat?"

Esme gave him one of her maybe-yes, maybe-no shrugs, a twinkle in her sharp brown eyes. "Who can say?"

Chase put a kiss on her head. Like Miss Ping, her hairstyle hadn't changed in sixteen years, a coronet of braids that were mostly silver now.

"Don't get caught," he said and hiked across the tennis court to the breakfast room.

His father sat at the table. Dory leaned on the wainscoted wall, her hands folded behind her, her trim ankles crossed above a pair of two-tone suede flats, half sage green like her trousers and half cream like her turtleneck sweater set. Holy cow. Two days in a row everything matched.

He didn't notice her walkie-talkie till it beeped and she plucked it off her waistband. Awful tiny waist for someone who used to be such a pudge. All those s'mores, Chase thought, as she glanced at him.

"Wallace says your foreman is here to pick you up."

Chase looked at his watch. Seven-thirty. "Right on time."

"Since I'm a free man I think I'll check out the garage," Charles said. "See how many of my tools Diego's lost or put in the wrong place."

The Rolls. Chase glanced at Dory, saw the uh-oh look in her brown eyes. His father took such pride in the Rolls you'd think it belonged to him. He wouldn't let Chase back it out of the garage till he was eighteen.

"Now don't be upset, Charles," Dory said, and his father scowled. "The Rolls isn't here. There was a *tiny* little collision with Artemis."

"Those damn headphones!" His father's ears reddened, a sure sign that he was losing his temper. "I *told* Diego watch the curves, but he can't hear me for the damn headphones! I'm gonna break 'em, I swear."

"It wasn't negligence, Dad," Chase said. "Jamie was skateboarding on the drive. It was hit Artemis or make a hood ornament out of the kid."

"Oh." His father's ears went from crimson to pink. "How bad is it?"

"Headlight, the grille and the right front fender," Chase said.

Charles winced. "You sent it to McPherson?" he asked Dory.

"Yes, Charles." She nodded. "The Rolls went to McPherson."

"I'll have Tom drive me over there. I can *ride* in a car, can't I?"

Dory held her hands up. "Fine with me."

"See you later, son." Charles gave him a clap on the shoulder and headed for the back door.

"Go easy on Diego," Chase called after him.

His father gave him an over-the-shoulder wave and pulled the door shut behind him. Chase turned toward Dory.

"From crabby invalid to a man on a mission," he said to her. "I don't know what you said to Miss Ping, but thank you."

"I gave her the same speech I gave Esme," Dory said, clipping her walkie-talkie on her waistband. "We'll see how long it lasts."

"Since I'm headed that way, I'll walk you to your office."

"Since you're headed that way, I'll let you."

Chase pushed open the servant's door that led into the corridor that ran up the middle of the house to the foyer. Dory went through it. His legs were twice as long as hers, but he had to hurry to catch up.

"Why the rush? Where's the fire?"

"At my desk." She shot him a grin but kept up her race-walk pace. "We have a prospective guest committee meeting at one o'clock and I have a dozen applications to review."

"Damn clever idea, that committee. Who came up with it?"

"Deirdre. And it is brilliant. Really adds to Outlook's cachet."

"Glad to see you finally conquered French."

"I took your advice. I asked Esme for help."

"So now she's teaching Jamie to mouth off in two languages."

"He came to us speaking French. He was sly about it at first, only dropped a word here and there. Esme alerted us that he was fluent."

"Where did he learn French?"

"The Orient most likely. That's the conclusion of the linguist we consulted. Jamie's mother—Marilyn Vanderpool, Jill's friend—was pretty vague with Deirdre about where she and Jamie had been living. He remembers his mother and staying in hotels but that's about all. Aunt Ping sent the Bastard Little Prick Squad to Saigon, Bangkok and Singapore but James' trail was too old. They found zip."

"What's the Bastard Little Prick Squad?"

"Daddy called James a bastard little prick. I call the investigators Aunt Ping hired to find him the Bastard Little Prick Squad."

"Peter told me you devised the code names for the walkie-talkies."

"If you can't have a little fun with the FBI—" Dory glanced him a sideways smile. "—what's the point of getting up in the morning?"

"Hope the agents hiding in the orchard have a sense of humor."

"I've known most of them for ten years. They're almost friends."

"And Marshall Phillips? Do you have a code name for him?"

"Sure." Dory grinned. "Uncle Scrooge."

The backside of the new federal courthouse, built against the bluff at the intersection of Walnut Street and Admiral Boulevard, faced north where the Missouri River meandered through the West Bottoms. A solid wall of curved glass overlooked the old River Quay section, an area of rehabbed warehouses with pricey lofts and refurbished brick buildings that housed art galleries and studios.

Chase stood at the window in the lobby outside Congressman Curtis Rowe's office on the eighth floor, admiring the view and waiting for Curt to finish a conference call to D.C. and take him to lunch.

Short, stocky Curt was already losing his curly brown hair. An overabundance of testosterone, he liked to boast. He was up for election in November to a second term from the ninth district, which included Outlook. Chase figured he was a shoo-in.

He'd checked into the building twenty minutes ago, left his cell phone and pager at the security checkpoint and showed his ID to the guards. He turned the token they'd given him to reclaim the items in his fingers and watched a diesel locomotive pull a string of flatcars through the maze of rail lines crisscrossing the riverbanks.

He heard the elevator ping and the doors slide open behind him. A moment later a man appeared beside him. Chase glanced at him. Tall, lanky, salt and pepper hair. Rumpled gray suit, loosened blue tie at his wind- and sun-reddened throat. A golfer in his spare time. Maybe a sailor.

"An amazing view," he said. "I imagine I can see all the way to Iowa from my office." He smiled and offered his hand. "Marshall Phillips."

Uncle Scrooge. The United States Attorney.

"Chase McKay." He shook his hand. "But you know who I am."

"I keep tabs. How's your father?"

"He's fine." Chase bristled. "Can I help you?"

"Me? No. But you could be very helpful to the Lambert family."

"By snitching for the FBI?" Chase shook his head. "I doubt Miss Ping would consider that being helpful."

"Jill Lambert might. I understand you two were an item once."

"We were a couple of horny teenagers once. Am I being followed?"

"You're a person of interest in an ongoing investigation."

Phillips shrugged. Trying, Chase thought, to look affable.

"I'm a person of none of your business," he said. "The son of Margaret Lambert's chauffeur. I'm here to visit my father. Period. If you're listening to my conversations and having me tailed, I suggest you stop."

"Calm down, Mr. McKay. There's no need to get huffy."

"I'm not the least bit huffy. I'm a businessman, not an old lady and two young women who you've been intimidating for the past ten years. Back off or I'll call my attorneys. I keep six on retainer."

"Is one of them Francis Singleton Cooper?"

"No. One of them is his son. He came highly recommended."

"Stonewalling won't help Del Lambert or his family."

Chase wondered if punching Phillips in the nose would. "When's the last time you looked for James Darwood? Now that would be helpful."

"If you change your mind," Phillips offered his card, "call me."

He walked to the elevator, pushed the up arrow and turned around like he had something to say. Chase could hardly wait to hear Uncle Scrooge's parting shot, but Curt saved him by popping out of his office.

"Sorry, Chase. That was Senator—" He broke off when he saw Phillips, shrugged into his suit coat and smiled. "Hello, Marshall."

"Congressman." Phillips nodded. The elevator opened and he stepped into the car. "Enjoy your lunch."

"How does he know we're going to lunch?" Curt said when the doors shut. "How did he know you're in the building?"

"I think the FBI followed me from Outlook." Chase drew a deep breath through his nose to calm the pounding in his temples. "Peter says they park in the orchard and listen to their walkie-talkie conversations. They must've picked up the call I made to you on my cell."

"You should've waited downstairs." Curt frowned. "Or in the car."

"I wanted to see the building. If I hadn't today, I've got a hunch I would've pretty damn soon." Chase showed him Marshall Phillips' card. "Did you know I'm a person of interest in an ongoing investigation?"

"Is that so?" Curt gave him the look he'd used in high school on tackles twice his size. Wise guys who abused their shoulder pads, just before he showed them how he'd made the All State Wrestling Team. "I'll bet I can fix that."

"Don't make it a priority." Chase tucked the card in his jacket pocket. "Coop Junior might enjoy giving Uncle Scrooge a call."

Curt took him to the Savoy Grill where the specialty was seafood. They both ordered and made short work of Kansas City strip steaks.

"Where are you headed this afternoon?" Curt asked.

"Two o'clock consult with Dad's cardiologist, Dr. Eric Woods."

"I've heard he's good. His office is on the Plaza."

The Country Club Plaza, built in the Spanish style along the banks of Brush Creek. The ultra-rich kept multimillion-dollar condos in stately old buildings that overlooked shops like Gucci. Statuary bloomed on the sidewalks and fountains splashed on every corner. The Fairmont Hotel, where his father had suffered the heart attack, had a lovely artificial waterfall out front and a view of St. Luke's Hospital. On its hill above the Plaza was where Miss Ping had driven him in the Rolls.

"While you're in that neck of the woods," Curt said, "you should swing through Westport and visit the Happy Spirit."

"That sounds familiar," Chase said. "What is it?"

"The only business venture besides turning Outlook into a hotel that's made Miss Ping a few bucks." Curt squeezed a lemon wedge into his iced tea. "The Happy Spirit Wine and Feng Shui Shop."

"That's right." Chase nodded. "Dad told me about it."

"The wine selection is excellent. The feng shui stuff is fun, but the clientele is the real kick. And the manager, Gary Somebody. A real nut."

"If the FBI is following me and I can't lose them on the Plaza." Chase grinned. "I should be able to shake 'em in Westport."

"Why do you call Marshall 'Uncle Scrooge'?"

"I don't. Dory does." Chase told him about the code, that Wallace was Lurch and Peter was Twinkletoes.

Curt laughed. "Boy am I sorry I blew it with her."

"You and Dory?" Chase said, surprised. "When was this?"

"Never, which only proves I'm an idiot." Curt shook his head and took a swig of his iced tea. "Miss Ping was very supportive during my first campaign. She talked me up to her friends and held a fund raiser at Outlook. Dory worked evenings in my campaign headquarters. Jill helped with public relations. I didn't think she knew I was alive. She set up meet-and-greet lunches and raised a ton of money. We got pretty chummy."

"Uh oh," Chase said, wishing he'd ordered a beer.

"It was nothing like that." Curt waved a hand. "In my head, yes. In reality, no. I sent Jill flowers after the election. I sent Miss Ping roses. Couple months after I took my seat in Congress, Jill came to D.C. We had dinner. I'd told her on the phone that I'd been appointed to the Justice Department Oversight Committee. She wanted Marshall off their backs and the assets he'd frozen returned."

"You didn't see it coming?" Chase asked. He'd seen it, the second Curt told him Jill volunteered her PR skills.

"Honestly? No. It's not like Jill's clairvoyant. No way could she have known I'd get justice. Even I had no clue which committees I'd get."

"You're an attorney, Curt. How many years did you put in with the city prosecutor's office? I'd say it was a good bet on Jill's part."

"I don't know about good. Hopeful, maybe." Curt shrugged. "It's the way of the world, sure as hell the way of politics. I told Jill I didn't have that kind of clout, that I could and I would gladly talk to Marshall but that's all I could do. After that, our weekly phone calls tapered off to e-mails once or twice a month."

"You sent Dory flowers, too, didn't you?" Chase asked.

"Nope." Curt winced. "My first day in Washington I received a candy bouquet made of Pixy Stix and cherry Tootsie Pops, my favorite. The card was signed Margaret, Jill and Dory Lambert, but it was a funny card, and that's Dory. Once I got over my Jill Lambert Rowe First Lady fantasy I remembered that bouquet and felt like a damn fool.

"I came home for the holiday recess. Miss Ping invited me to lunch. Jill wasn't there. Maybe that's why, I don't know, but I took one look at Dory and it was like I'd never seen her before. I asked her out, but she said no. Four times. No big surprise since I'd done everything I could think of to prove to her that I'm a shallow clod who can't see past a gorgeous face and a great body."

"Well, sure you did. You're a man." Chase grinned and raised his iced tea. "It's what we do."

"There you go." Curt clinked his glass against his, grinned back at him and they ordered dessert.

The five members of the prospective guest committee convened their monthly meeting arranged around a wormwood library table that Del Lambert had kicked up to the attics. Dory had it brought down and placed in the curve of the big bay window in her office, the former front parlor, and used it as a conference table.

A silver bowl of tulips and daisies sat in the center. Peter had spent three hours arranging each bloom just so; Esther polished the bowl till the tendinitis in her elbow flared. All to keep Georgette Parrish, renowned etiquette columnist and flaming fussbudget, from blowing a gasket.

By virtue of her marriage for the second time to bestselling, jet-setting spy novelist Fletcher Parrish, Georgette hobnobbed with all the Beautiful People in all the Beautiful Places, which made her an incredible asset to the committee. She was also Aunt Ping's oldest friend.

She drove Deirdre to drink and Dory straight to the Tums.

Aunt Ping sat at the end of the table nearest the pocket doors with Georgette; Dory at the other end with Anita Sawyer, dutifully taking notes in shorthand as she had for Del Lambert for seventeen years. Deirdre sat beside Anita with a cordial glass and a crystal decanter of sherry.

Jill attended via speakerphone. Meetings bored her silly. While Anita read the result of the vote they'd just taken on the last of the twelve applications, Dory thought she could hear Jill filing her nails.

"Thanks, Anita," Dory said. "Does anyone have anything else?"

"I do," Aunt Ping said. "We voted last month to accept the Patrick application, but do we really want to let show people through the door?"

"Yes!" Jill shouted, so loudly the speakerphone gave a squawk of feedback. "Noah Patrick and Lindsay Varner are a huge feather in Outlook's cap. Every hotel in Kansas City wanted them, threw in every perk they could think of to get them. They're not the Rolling Stones, Aunt Ping. They're married. They have children. They're coming to Kansas City to perform *The Music Man* at Starlight Theatre. They're due to check in next week. You can't renege on their reservation at this late date."

"I beg your pardon, Jillian," Aunt Ping said frostily. "Outlook *still* belongs to me. I have the final say on this committee."

"Of course you do," Dory said quickly, before Aunt Ping's eyebrow could shoot up. "I think what Jill means is—"

"Oh for heaven's sake, Peg." Georgette overrode Dory with a curt, I'll-handle-this wave. "Cydney and Gus vouched for them. I vouched for them. What more do you want?"

"A little peace and quiet in my own home!" Aunt Ping slapped her hands against the table and pushed to her feet. "And do *not* call me Peg!"

She whirled, overturning her chair with a thump, and pushed the doors open with such force that they ricocheted out of their pockets. Aunt Ping gave them another mighty shove and fled.

"Margaret!" Deirdre leapt to her feet and knocked over the sherry.

Georgette yelped and jumped clear of the amber flood gushing across the table. Anita grabbed the Kleenex box and started mopping.

"Dory!" Jill's voice shrilled out of the phone. "What's happened?"

"I'll call you back!" Dory shouted. "Meeting adjourned!"

She raced for the foyer, dodging Georgette and the chair, met Diego in the doorway and almost smacked into him. "Which way did she go?"

"This way. Mr. Wallace followed her." Diego caught Dory's arm and pulled her into a run. "I never seen a old lady move so fast."

The chair behind Henry's desk was spinning on its swivel. The phone in Esther's office swung by its cord over the edge of her writing table. She and Henry, and Esme and Wallace huddled in a knot at the big windows in the glassed-in porch adjacent to the kitchen.

"Where is she?" Dory asked, wedging herself between them.

"There." Wallace pointed at Aunt Ping buzzing down the drive in one of the golf carts they kept parked near the house, the flowered red-silk jacket she wore with a tunic and trousers billowing around her.

"Esther. Make tea." Dory pulled on a hooded gray sweatshirt with a zipper, snatched Aunt Ping's green corduroy gardening jacket off a hook and yanked open the back door. "I'll go get her."

Aunt Ping had taken the white cart. Dory pulled the plug on the blue one, leaped in and turned the key, backed it away from the charging station, cut the wheel toward the drive and punched the pedal.

Top speed in the carts was fifteen miles per hour. Her car would be faster but if Aunt Ping made it past the golf course where the road forked three ways Dory could lose her. She nearly did rounding the clubhouse, which partially blocked her view of the juncture, but she caught a glimpse of red disappearing into the trees around the first curve in the left-hand branch, the most twisted stretch of road on Outlook.

In a dozen places the South Drive split and wound through the grounds and the rest of the gardens. Dory pushed the

pedal—God knew why, it was already on the floor—
hunched over the wheel with her fanny in the air and drove
like a jockey riding the neck of a horse. Like it would actually help her go faster, but she was desperate.

As Aunt Ping must've been to bolt out of the house.

In search of a little peace and quiet, Dory thought, and
sat back on the seat. Maybe she should let her go, let her
get whatever possessed her to shout at Georgette out of her
system. But it was cloudy and cold; forty degrees, tops. The
wind felt damp and smelled like wet dirt. It rattled through
the mostly bare trees lining the drive and made Dory shiver.

Okay. She wouldn't drag Aunt Ping back to bedlam.
She'd find her, make her put on her coat, and then she'd
leave her alone. Dory fished a Kleenex from the pocket of
her gray warm-up jacket, wiped her drippy nose and drove
on, wondering where along the South Drive Aunt Ping
would most likely go to find peace and quiet.

The Lily Pond, she decided, where the Chinese carp win-
tering in the aquarium in the pool house lived in summer
and Peter and Aunt Ping indulged their passion for water
plants. It was gorgeous in June, with willows skimming the
pond and the pale, velvety lilies blooming on their pads. It
wouldn't look like much now but it was quiet and sheltered
with benches, a gazebo and a curved bridge over the still
green water.

Aunt Ping loved the Lily Pond. And Dory knew a short-
cut.

A walking trail that sliced through the trees, ran parallel
with the bridle path in places and skirted the green on the
sixth hole. Dory ignored the NO CARTS PLEASE sign and
made a left off the road.

The trail was surfaced with pea gravel, bone dry after
weeks of no rain. The tires spun up tiny stones that pinged
off the undercarriage. The racket startled a deer, a young
buck, out of a thicket on Dory's right.

He sprang onto the trail right in front of her, almost in
her lap—close enough that she could see the little velvet
nubs where his antlers would be this fall. The cart had no

brake, just the one pedal that served both functions. Before she could take her foot off it, the deer leaped the split rail fence on her left and bounded away up the bridle path.

Dory pressed a hand to her throat and swallowed her heart.

Maybe she'd walk from here. She was almost there, anyway. The Lily Pond lay just beyond the next curve in the trail. Dory turned the cart off and picked up Aunt Ping's jacket.

With the head start she had, Dory expected Aunt Ping might beat her to the Lily Pond. She didn't see the white cart when she rounded the curve; she saw one of the yellow ones from the golf course and Charles sitting on a bench at the edge of the water. Leaning on his hands with his back to her, knees crossed, one foot swinging in a slow, lazy motion. A few yards ahead of her the trees fell away, giving her an angled but clear view of the pond, the smaller road that branched off South Drive and came down the hill past the trail to the Lily Pond. She could see Charles but even if he turned around he couldn't see her.

If Aunt Ping came this way and found Charles parked on her favorite bench, would she seek peace and quiet elsewhere? Dory couldn't tell him Aunt Ping had run away—no stress, said the cardiologist—but she could ask if he'd seen her. And if Charles asked why she was looking for her? What was she doing with her coat?

Well, crap. That wouldn't work.

Wondering what she could say to Charles that wouldn't alarm him, Dory started toward him. She heard the hum of a golf cart, glanced at the road and saw a flash of white, a wink of red through the bare hardwood branches. Aunt Ping making a beeline for the Lily Pond.

Dory stopped, expecting Aunt Ping would, too, when she saw Charles, but the white cart shot past the trail. Charles heard it, turned and leaped to his feet. Aunt Ping stopped the cart and jumped out running. Charles came around the bench and caught her in his arms.

Dory's mouth fell open. What was this? What was she seeing?

When Charles took Aunt Ping's face in his hands and kissed her on the mouth, Dory knew. She scrambled off the trail and threw herself backward against a gnarly barked oak, her face scalding.

How had she never seen this? Now that she had, Dory realized it had been there all her life, right under her nose. Did Chase know? Did anyone else? Did everyone else and she was the last to find out?

Aunt Ping and Charles—Charles and Aunt Ping!

Her walkie-talkie beeped. Dory ripped it off her waistband and shut it off, her heart pounding. Sound had a tendency to carry out here. Had Aunt Ping and Charles heard it? Dory held her breath and rolled around the tree on one shoulder.

Didn't look like it. They sat on the bench, Aunt Ping wrapped in Charles' jacket, his arm around her, her head on his shoulder. When Aunt Ping raised her face Charles kissed her again.

Dory shrank behind the tree, let her head thunk against it and listened to her heartbeat slow. Well. This explained a lot.

She crept away from the tree and back to the cart, climbed onto the seat and turned on her walkie-talkie. It beeped almost instantly.

"Lurch to Mama San Three," Wallace said. "Search and rescue mission underway. Repeat. Search and rescue underway. Mr. Green Jeans—" that was Tom—"and Man-O'-War—" Eddie, the head groom—"in charge of sweep teams."

Sweep teams! Dory envisioned Eddie and his grooms and Tom and his farmhands fanning out across Outlook, whacking sticks against the ground like beaters in an Indian tiger hunt. If every single one of them knew about Aunt Ping and Charles, no prob. If they didn't . . .

"Negative, Lurch," Dory responded. "Cancel search and rescue. Repeat. Cancel search and rescue. Mama San Three out."

Dory turned off her walkie-talkie. Aunt Ping and Charles. Holy crap. She turned the key in the ignition and drove back to the house in a daze, parked the cart, plugged it in and turned around. Wallace stood on the small, flagged patio outside the back porch door.

"I couldn't find her," she said. "I'm sure she's fine. She knows every inch of Outlook. The more I looked for her the more I thought as upset as she is, maybe we should give her some space. You know. Some *privacy.*"

Dory emphasized the word. Hinting, hoping Wallace would react in some way. Hah. He looked at her with all the animation of a stone wall.

"As you wish," he said and opened the door.

Dory went past him, hung up her jacket and Aunt Ping's coat, went into the kitchen and told Esme the same thing, word for word, while she washed her hands at the sink. Esme shrugged and slid a tray of snickerdoodles into the oven.

Dory's do-you-know-what-I-know emphasis on *privacy* drew the same nonplussed response from Esther and Henry. Had the aliens come while she was gone? Had they abducted Aunt Ping's devoted, worried staff and replaced them with I-know-nothing clones?

Her last shot was Diego. Low man on the staff totem pole, but he was bright, quick-witted and to Jamie's dismay, excellent at connecting dots. But Diego had left in the Bentley with the Morgensterns.

Hmmm. Maybe Deirdre. Dory went looking for her aunt and found her in the last place she expected. Sitting at her desk, listening to someone on the phone. When Dory came through the pocket doors into the office, Deirdre almost wilted with relief.

"She's just come in now. Yes, this second. One moment." Deirdre pressed hold and put the handset on the base. "It's Gary. He's frantic. Something about someone refusing to leave the Happy Spirit."

The aliens, Dory hoped, making a last stop to pick Gary up on their way home. "Where's Anita?"

"Gary called earlier. Amber didn't show up for her shift and he was out of ones. Anita offered to go to the bank for him. I told her to take the rest of the day off." Deirdre rose from Dory's chair as she came around the desk. "He's just rung again and as I say, he's frantic."

Dory sat down and lifted the receiver. "What's wrong, Gary?"

"He's *here*." The muffled hiss in her ear sounded like Gary was in the office with his hand cupped around the mouthpiece. "He's been here almost an hour. He looked at the wines. Fine. I can deal with that. Now he's looking at the books. He's sitting out there reading. I told you putting chairs in the store was a mistake."

"Who, Gary? Who's there?"

"Do I have to spell it out for you? *McKay!*"

"Jill loves you, Gary." Only God in heaven knew why. "Chase is not a threat to you."

"He keeps talking to me, asking me things. Do we stock such and such a wine? Can I order So and So's book?"

"You're the only one there. Who else is he supposed to ask?"

"You," Gary said. "When you get here."

"I'm not coming down there."

"Fine. Have it your way. I'll call the police."

"You can't call the police. Chase is not a nuisance."

"He's a spear through my heart!" Gary's voice cracked. "The first man Jill loved! I can't take any more! I'm breaking out in hives!"

"Oh, for God's sake!" Dory spat disgustedly. "Would you please tell me how on earth you got into the FBI?"

"My uncle. He's a senator." Gary drew a breath. "Are you coming?"

"All right." Dory sighed, her stomach a burning pit of acid. "I'll be there as soon as I can."

"Thank you, Dory. Make it quick," he said and hung up.

Chapter Seven

"**W**hy does Gary have to be an undercover FBI agent?" Jill had sobbed to Dory on the below zero night in February that he'd confessed to her. "Why can't he be the cute little dweeb I thought he was?"

That's certainly what Gary looked like, certainly how he behaved, and precisely how he'd slipped under the Lambert family radar. The day after Jill told her about Gary, Dory drove down to the Happy Spirit and had a little finger-in-the-chest chat with him. Her finger in his chest.

"Phillips thinks you're communicating with your parents," Gary told her. "He's convinced you're doing it from the Happy Spirit."

"Is the store bugged? Are the phones tapped?" Dory demanded. "Has the FBI hacked into the computer?"

"If Phillips had electronic surveillance on this place I wouldn't be here. He tried for a court order, but the judge called it a vendetta."

"What exactly do you tell Phillips?"

"I report comings and goings. Yours, Jill's and Miss Lambert's. I tell him when you're here, how long you stay, what you say and what you do. Miss Lambert doesn't come in much and you're only here twice a month to do the books and the payroll."

But when Jill wasn't traveling she spent a lot of time at the Happy Spirit. The store was a solid success, a fixture now in Westport and popular enough to draw the custom of the rich folk who lived on the Plaza and along Ward Parkway. Jill sold them their most expensive wines by the semitruckload and gathered up business cards like confetti.

"Does Phillips know about you and Jill?" Dory asked Gary.

"Of course not." He looked insulted. "We're very careful."

"What if the FBI is following *you*, Gary?"

"Jill and I never leave the store. There's a futon in the office."

That was more information than Dory wanted. "Did Marshall Phillips suggest that you sleep with her?"

"No! Dory!" Gary cried, shocked. "I love Jill, not the FBI."

"Prove it. Quit the Bureau."

"Much as I'd like to, much as I hate sneaking around with Jill, if you want to raise Phillips' suspicions, that's the way to do it. He's suspicious enough already, totally obsessed with nailing your father."

"That's yesterday's news, Gary. Tell me something I don't know."

"Okay. Every agent who works this case sympathizes with you and your family. We don't know how Phillips keeps justifying the expense of the surveillance. We suspect he has the ear of someone very influential in Washington. He's convinced this person that you're in contact with your parents and that he'll catch you at it eventually. If he can charge one of you as an accessory after the fact in the commission of a felony, he thinks your father will come tearing out of Isla Rica to save you."

"More old news, Gary. Coop explained all that to us years ago."

"The guys in the orchard? Half the time their sets are turned off."

"I know that, too. You're fired, Gary. Get out."

"Dory, wait." He'd caught her arm as she'd turned toward the door. "We've been told on the QT to expect deep cuts when the new budget comes down in July. Frasier. The agent in charge. You know him?"

"Yes." He'd changed the flat for Dory that long-ago Christmas, had given her the gold pen when she'd received her MBA.

"He's ninety-nine percent sure this investigation will be the first to go. He's put off retiring so he can be the one to tell you. Phillips has heard the scuttlebutt and he's not stupid. He can feel the ax. This is not the time to provoke him. If you can me, he'll pull out all the stops."

"If we're so close to being home free, why did you tell Jill?"

"I love her. Lying to her was eating me alive."

"You could be lying to me. Why should I trust you?"

"Because I love Jill. C'mon, Dory. I'm on your side."

"You're an undercover FBI agent but you're on our side? How can that be, Gary? How can you serve two masters?"

"It's only a few months. I can do it. I can handle it."

"Let him try," Coop said an hour later, when Dory called him from Sister Immaculata's office, on the safest, most secure phone line this side of heaven. "You're better off keeping Gary where you can watch him than cutting him loose. Will he tell you if Marsh decides to go for broke?"

"He says he will, but how can I trust him?"

"You can't completely. If Marsh catches wind of his affair with Jill he can kiss any future he may hope to have with the Bureau or the Justice Department good-bye. Gary knows that. What has Jill told him? Anything about what the Bastard Little Prick Squad is up to?"

"She swears she's told him nothing. She also swears he's never asked questions about Daddy and Mother. I'm not sure I believe that."

"How long has this been going on between Jill and Gary?"

"Since last September sixteenth. Gary's first day at the Happy Spirit was September fifteenth, so maybe Jill's right. Or maybe Gary seducing her, then confessing to her is all part of an elaborate, last ditch scam on Uncle Scrooge's part to arrest us all before the plug gets pulled."

"I'd take Gary's warning not to provoke Marsh seriously, Dory."

"Gary says he's obsessed. The judge who denied his request for electronic surveillance on the Happy Spirit called it a vendetta."

"I agree it's obsessive. But a vendetta? Absolutely not. Marsh doesn't break laws, he upholds them. I'm sure he believes he's acting in the people's best interest. No prosecutor likes to lose."

The next day Dory returned to the Happy Spirit with Tom Gordon, the computer and electronic security expert who checked the phones at Outlook twice a month to make sure they weren't bugged. He wore a plumber's uniform, swept the store and pronounced it free of listening devices and hidden cameras. Dory paid him and he left.

"I told you the store wasn't bugged." Gary looked like he was about to cry. "You didn't believe me."

"Of course I didn't believe you. You work for the FBI. You'll be seeing more of Gordy, by the way. He'll be dropping in now and then to make sure the store stays clean. And he won't call ahead."

"I'm under a lot of pressure here, Dory," Gary snapped. "It isn't easy working both sides of the street and you aren't helping."

"Don't talk to me about pressure, Gary. Aunt Ping and Jill and I have lived for ten years with the FBI breathing down our necks. Jill loves you so I'll give you a chance to show me why she trusts you. One chance. Just one." Dory held up her index finger. "The day Gordy's bug finder goes off or I see men in black creeping around the Happy Spirit, I'll be on the six o'clock news screaming FBI harassment. I'll be prepared to name names and take my chances with Marshall Phillips. If you can't handle that, tell me now."

"No problem." Gary licked his lips. "I can handle it."

*   *   *

Obviously he couldn't. Barely two months had passed and Gary was breaking out in hives. Over Chase, for heaven's sake.

Every time Jill went out of town Gary had a meltdown. Dory had better things to do than fight her way through Friday afternoon traffic to calm him down. Especially with Aunt Ping still missing. Charles, too, and if anybody put that together before she got back to Outlook . . .

Her cell phone rang. Dory grabbed it, hoping it was Gary calling to tell her Chase had left the Happy Spirit. She'd have to knock him in the head—only in the direst emergency was he to call her cell—and still she hoped. But it was a wrong number. Crap.

At Broadway and Westport Road she pulled into the left turn lane, waited for the light to change and rubbed her stomach. The fistful of Tums she'd eaten before she left Outlook had capped the volcano of acid shooting up her throat but now she felt like she'd swallowed a boulder. Might be time to fill the prescription for Prevacid in her purse.

"While you still have an esophagus," the doctor advised as he'd written out the scrip. "Cut down on the stress, too."

"I'll put that on my to-do list," Dory told him.

Right behind raise twenty million dollars for the Outlook trust, keep Jamie out of juvenile hall and manage the Outlook Inn. Pay the bills, do the books, the taxes and the payroll for the hotel and the Happy Spirit. Keep an eye on Deirdre as well as Aunt Ping 'cause she was no kid, either. Monitor the two-man Bastard Little Prick Squad's expenses. Remind Esther to remind Wallace to wear the compression socks for his varicose veins. Consult with Tom on the farm budget; with Peter about the gardens and the golf course; with Eddie about the horses, their feed, vet and farrier bills. Acknowledge birthdays and anniversaries of everyone on staff. Make sure—

A horn blared behind her. Dory started and blinked, saw the cars ahead of her streaming off Broadway onto Westport Road and punched the gas. Her little green Saturn and the guy in the red pickup who had honked at her barely made it through the intersection on the arrow.

Dory thought about parking behind the Happy Spirit and using her key to the back door, but she wanted this to look like a casual drop-in, not a planned bum's rush. That meant the front door.

The parking gods smiled and opened a space for her in the only public, unmetered lot on Westport Road. She picked up the folder full of last month's store receipts—her cover story—locked the car and started walking the block and a half to the Happy Spirit, huddling into her coat against the chill in the damp but not humid enough to rain air.

It had been a while since she'd reviewed her to-do list. Now that she had, Dory realized she'd assumed most of the duties that used to be Aunt Ping's. She thought she was helping, taking some of the load off; giving Aunt Ping time now that they had a few extra bucks, to entertain her friends and work for the charities she'd always supported.

Perhaps Aunt Ping didn't see it that way. She'd reminded Jill that Outlook was hers, but Dory thought that was just pique. Shouting at Georgette was long overdue. Running out of the house over the Patrick application didn't seem likely. But Aunt Ping suspected Chase had come to Outlook to force Charles to retire. If she feared she might lose the man she loved, that made sense to Dory. That added up to a ripsnorting, door-banging, give-me-some-peace-and-quiet tantrum.

If the problem was Chase, the solution was Chase had to go.

Out of the Happy Spirit, then out of Kansas City. *If* he intended to take his father with him. Dory decided she should find that out first, make sure Aunt Ping wasn't over-reacting, that neither one of them was jumping to a wrong conclusion.

Dory turned the corner onto Pennsylvania, a narrow, brick-paved side street twisting downhill to the Happy Spirit.

She saw the sign hung above the door, a woodcut painted Chinese red in the shape of a bagua, the eight-point feng shui compass, felt her pulse jump and hoped Aunt Ping was right about Chase.

If he stayed he'd break her heart again. Without trying, without even knowing, but she'd be damned if he'd break Aunt Ping's.

In college Chase had studied a little feng shui, taken a couple of elective courses in the Chinese discipline of living in harmony with your environment. Seemed right up an architect's alley.

The Happy Spirit carried a broad range of books on feng shui, from the serious to the silly and everything in between. After his washout interview with his father's cardiologist, he'd gotten a much-needed kick out of browsing through them, but he'd been here close to an hour. It was almost four, nearly five in New York. Sylvia would expect to hear from him before the end of the day. She wouldn't leave the office till she did.

Now if he could just get out of this chair. It hadn't looked all that comfortable but its pale blue leather cushions were soft as kid. Between the chair, the peaceful, mostly green and blue color scheme and the murmur of a small fountain in one corner he'd nearly nodded off twice.

Gary, the guy Curt said was a nut, had vanished into the back of the store. He'd thought Curt meant nut as in ha-ha-funny, but Gary was a call-your-shrink-while-you're-back-there-buddy kind of nut. A totally jarring note to the Zen-like calm of the Happy Spirit.

Chase approved of the décor. Natural wood shelves to hold books and bottles of wine in diamond-shaped racks against the raw brick walls of the building, the spring green carpet and blue chairs. Touches of red and yellow, purple, black and white in the appropriate areas of the bagua, crystals hung strategically to keep the chi or the energy in the store circulating. He wanted to meet, and maybe hire, the designer.

But first he had to get out of this chair.

"One, two, three." Chase gripped the wooden arms and pushed to his feet, saw a shadow flicker past the miniblinds on the front window.

A second later the red-painted door opened and Dory Lambert stepped into the Happy Spirit. She didn't see him till she shut the door and turned around. Then she blinked, obviously surprised, and tucked the manila folder she carried in the curve of her arm.

"Chase. Hi. I didn't expect to see you here."

"I was in the neighborhood," he said. On the Plaza, he thought, having my ass chewed by my father's cardiologist. The memory made him want to scowl, but he smiled and gave the store an appreciative, one-handed sweep. "Very nice."

"Be sure you tell Aunt Ping." Dory laid her purse and the folder on the top of a glass-fronted case that held tiny brass cymbals and bells. "Next to the Outlook Inn, the Happy Spirit is the best idea she ever had."

Was it coincidence or Providence that Dory was standing in the Helpful Places and People area of the bagua? Chase decided to call it Providence. Dr. Eric Woods had told him to mind his own damn business and go back to New York. That left Plan B—Dory Lambert.

It was time to be charming. When she reached for the French knot buttons on her camel coat, he stepped forward and helped her out of it.

"I was thinking about grabbing a beer, maybe some dinner." Chase smiled. "Would you like to join me?"

Dory blinked at him. Chase heard a clack, glanced over his shoulder and saw Gary's head stuck through the variegated strings of beads hung in the doorway between the front of the store and the back.

"Miss Lambert," he said. "May I see you in the office?"

His head vanished and the beads swung together.

Chase turned to Dory. "He's been back there the whole time I've been here. Is he phobic?"

"Possibly." She picked up her purse and the folder. "I

need to double-check a couple of last month's receipts with Gary before I can close the books on March."

Sylvia would approve. It's what a good little MBA did.

"I'll wait. I need to call my office, anyway."

"Great. Then I'd love to join you. I'll be just a few minutes."

"Take your time."

Chase watched her cross the store. She had mud on her left heel. Was it raining? He walked to the window and looked through the blind. Nope. Sidewalk was dry. He glanced back at Dory and saw a hand—Gary's hand—reach past the beads and yank her through them.

Dory let Gary keep her wrist till he'd dragged her into the office. When he shut the door she wrenched free, tossed her purse and the folder on the desk and gave him a shove.

"Don't ever do that again. I'll deck you."

"I'm sorry, Dory. I didn't hurt you, did I?" Gary's hands fluttered around her. "I'm sorry. I'm just so upset."

He was sweating and he had a big red welt on his neck.

"Crap," Dory said. "You really are breaking out in hives."

"I told you I was! Did you think I was making it up?"

"Sit." Dory pushed him into the desk chair. "I'll be right back."

She opened the door, wheeled into the hall toward the front of the store and almost smacked into Chase. He caught her shoulders to keep her from plowing nose-first into his chest. Darn it.

"Everything okay?" He looked past the top of her head at the office, a hawklike glint in his narrowed eyes.

"Yes. Fine. Gary's allergies are acting up." Dory wished she could stand here forever with Chase's hands on her shoulders. Big, warm, strong hands that made her knees quiver. "Could you help me?"

"Sure." He stepped aside and followed her through the curtain.

"I need that." Dory pointed at a giant aloe plant sitting on a wide shelf above and behind the sales counter.

She'd need a ladder, but Chase lifted it down easily. Dory broke off a long, fat leaf, said, "Thanks," and hurried back to the office.

Gary was scratching the welt on his neck. Another one was coming up on his chin. The tops of his ears were red.

"Stop that." Dory smacked his hand, squeezed aloe on her finger and smeared his neck and his chin. "Take off your shirt."

Gary pulled his blue polo over his head and slumped in the chair, his narrow shoulders prickled with gooseflesh. He looked miserable and totally goofy with his sandy, moussed-to-the-max hair standing on end.

"There's one." Dory globbed aloe on a small hive on his collarbone. "Let's see your back."

He twisted sideways in the chair. It had to be love, Dory thought as she doctored a hive on his chicken wing shoulder blade. It couldn't be lust. Gary could model for the Before photo in a Gold's Gym ad. Cute enough to remind her of Mark Hamill in his Luke Skywalker days. Except for his glasses, which he managed to hopelessly entangle in his shirt as he pulled it back over his head.

"If you're the future of the FBI," Dory said, "God help us."

"Very funny." Gary wrestled with the sleeves caught on his elbows, his voice muffled by the fabric. "Give me a hand, will you?"

"Hold still." Dory sighed.

She moved in to get a grip on the shirt. Gary gave a mighty heave to free himself and fell out of the chair. Dory tried to scramble out of the way and tromped on his left ankle. The shirt stifled his yelp of pain.

"Oh, good grief." Dory dropped to her knees, pushed the leg of his jeans up, his blue sock down and stared, horrified, at the tattoo on his calf—a red heart with *Jill* stitched in flowery script in the middle.

Gary yanked his leg out of her grasp and sat up. Dory ripped the shirt off his head and threw it at him.

"Are you *insane*? You have *Jill* tattooed on your calf!"

"That's why it's on my calf. No one ever sees it."

"*I* saw it! Listen, Billy Bob. Maybe it's slipped your mind, but you're in the FBI. That little doodle is *incriminating evidence*!"

"I'm resigning in July, Dory. That's only three months."

"You're resigning if the budget gets cut. What if it doesn't?"

"Jesus Christ." Gary yanked his shirt on and glared at her. "Could you just *once* have a little faith?"

"I can't afford faith. I haven't been able to afford much of anything since Marshall Phillips came into my life." Dory pushed to her feet and grabbed her purse off the desk. "I'm leaving now with Chase."

She stopped in the bathroom first, washed her hands and watched her last suspicion that Gary's clueless bumbling was a clever ruse go down the drain with the aloe. The tattoo pretty much clinched the fact that he wasn't pretending—he really was a helpless, hapless putz.

Dory leaned on the sink and looked at her face in the mirror. Her mascara had flaked and she didn't have her makeup bag. Swell. She dampened a square of toilet paper, dabbed her nose and beneath her eye, plucked at her hair with her fingers and wished she had a toothbrush.

When she opened the door, Gary was standing in the hall. His shoulders slumped, hands in his pockets. His mat of moussed hair flared like wings above his ears.

"Thanks, Dory. I feel better." The hive on his chin was gone, the one on his neck didn't look quite as angry. "Thank you for coming."

"Brew yourself a cup of catnip tea," she said gently. How could you stay mad at such a poor, clueless dweeb? "It should help, but if it doesn't, don't stay open till eight. Close the store and go home."

"About my doodle. I'll buy some really big Band-Aids. Okay?"

"Great idea, Gary." Dory patted his shoulder. "Good thinking."

Now if he only had a light saber.

Westport sprawled above the Plaza like a gypsy caravan camped outside the castle of the king. A bohemian hodge-podge of bars and boutiques housed in old brick buildings crammed between fast-food joints, avant-garde shops and more bars.

The only one Chase knew was Kelly's, the first saloon built in Kansas City, but the big, square building was packed with college kids. So many he and Dory could barely squeeze through the door.

"Doesn't anybody go to class on Friday afternoon?" He leaned close to her ear so she could hear him above the crack of billiard balls, shouts and laughter and music so loud he couldn't make out the song.

"Did you?" Dory laughed. "C'mon. I know a place."

A quiet, classy establishment around the corner on Broadway that smelled like beef sizzling on a grill. Brass lamps lit the tables. A Tiffany fixture hung above the bar. Chase fit just fine into one of the bloodred leather booths. Dory sat across from him, her chin almost on the table.

Chase grinned. "Would you like a phone book to sit on?"

"No thanks." She tucked her right foot under her fanny, boosting herself high enough that she could fold her arms on the table. "Do not," she warned, "call me squirt."

"I wouldn't dream of it." Chase laughed and signaled the waitress.

He ordered a Bud Lite in the bottle, Dory a cosmopolitan.

"What is Gary allergic to?" he asked. "Work?"

"He's actually a very good manager. A little flaky but—" Her cell phone rang. She drew it out of her purse, checked the number on the LED screen and answered with a crisp, "Mama San Three."

It was Wallace. Chase wasn't trying to listen, but he could hear the butler's overloud and garbled voice. His cell phone was the same. Either he couldn't hear at all or the damn thing broadcast like a bullhorn.

Wallace said something Chase didn't quite catch till he repeated it: "The eagle has returned to the nest." He didn't notice that Dory had tensed up till he saw her features relax as she glanced at him.

"I'm with King Kong," she said. "Yesterday? The drive-way?"

Wallace chuckled. So did Chase. Jamie had called him King Kong.

"Thanks for the update. Mama San Three out." Dory ended the call and put the phone back in her purse.

"Why don't you carry a combination cell phone and walkie-talkie?" Chase said. "It would be more cost effec-tive."

"I'd love to save the money, but keeping the cell phones separate makes it just a teensy more difficult for the FBI to track us and snoop."

"Do they have wiretaps on the house phones?"

"No. Phillips tries from time to time, but Aunt Ping knows every judge on every circuit in Kansas City and Jackson County. Uncle Scrooge can't seem to find one who'll let him bug Margaret Lambert's telephones. To be sure, we keep a security guy on retainer. He comes in twice a month and makes sure every phone in Outlook is bug free."

Chase doubted the *we*. He thought it was probably all Dory.

She'd come out of the back of the Happy Spirit with a cheerful let's-go smile but a harried glint in her eyes. It van-ished by the time they'd walked to Kelly's. She'd teased him, made him laugh about calling her squirt. She didn't look harried anymore, but her isn't-this-fun sparkle was gone. She seemed distracted, like she was thinking about something else. Chase decided not to tell her that he'd met Marshall Phillips.

The waitress came with their drinks. His Bud was ice-cold, the bottle frosty. Dory's cosmopolitan arrived in a margarita glass, a pretty pink drink with a lime wedge on the rim, loaded with enough vodka and triple sec that Chase could smell it.

"Be glad I'm not a lush. I love these things." She grinned at him and lifted the glass with both hands. "Salute."

"Your health." Chase touched his bottle to her glass and took a pull on his beer. "I had lunch with Curt today."

"I haven't seen him since Christmas. How is he?" Dory squeezed the lime into her drink. "Still mooning around about Jill?"

"I wouldn't say that." Chase shrugged and took another swig of Bud Lite. "He talked about you. I think he'd like to hear from you."

"You *what*?" She glared at him; lips pursed like a nail gun ready to fire and impale him to the back of the booth.

"It was just my impression. He spoke very highly of you."

"And well he should," Dory snapped. "I worked my fanny off on his campaign. So did Jill. Anita and Deirdre, too."

She lifted her glass to take another swallow, her head turned just enough that the lamplight caught on something in her hair.

"Hold still." He reached across the table and tugged it out, laid it on his palm and showed it to her. A small sprig of evergreen.

"Huh," she said, nonplussed. "Wonder where that came from."

The same place as the mud on her shoe, Chase bet. He hadn't seen a single pine or evergreen in Westport, but there were tons of them, whole forests of them on Outlook. Why would she go clomping around the grounds in suede flats?

And why did he care? What was it to him? He'd paid his debt to the Lambert family. He was sorry for their trouble, but it wasn't his problem. His problem was a bullheaded old man who saw no reason why he should retire and a boneheaded cardiologist who agreed with him.

"What did Wallace mean by the eagle has returned to the nest?"

"Hmm?" Dory glanced up from pulling lime pulp off the rind. "Oh, nothing." She waved a hand. "It's just one of our code phrases."

"So I'm King Kong, huh?"

"I think Frank Lloyd Wright would be a little obvious, don't you?"

"So what if it's obvious? Lurch isn't exactly subtle."

"We do *try* not to involve innocent bystanders."

"What's my dad's code name?"

Dory grinned. "Kato."

"The Green Hornet's chauffeur," Chase said and laughed.

"See? That's the whole idea." Dory pointed a finger at him. "If the feds are laughing, they're not listening."

"But aren't they recording?"

"Probably. Unless they're laughing too hard to push the buttons."

"You are one smart little squirt." Chase winked. "Squirt."

"Don't call me squirt." She took a big slug of her cosmopolitan. "We change names every so often and everyone has input when we do."

"To keep the feds listening to the wrong thing."

"Exactly. Plus it's just fun to jerk their chain."

She told him that at present Tom was Mr. Green Jeans, Eddie was Man-O'-War and Deirdre Darwood was Mary Poppins.

"Jill, of course," she finished, "is always Barbie."

"What else would she be?" Chase said and they laughed. "Did the prospective guest committee meeting go well?"

"We had a couple tussles, but we usually do. Imagine a room full of opinionated women, none of them shy about speaking up." She raised her drink and took a swallow. "How was your day?"

"The morning was productive. I toured the job site, had a word with my foreman, Buck, about Diego's cousin Beni.

I think we have a spot for him on one of the framing crews."

"How nice of you." Dory beamed at him. "Beni is a terrific kid. As hard a worker as Diego. He pitches in at Outlook when we need extra help. We just can't afford him full-time."

"Okay." Chase drew a check mark in the air. "That's his reference."

She flushed, flattered, exactly as he'd intended. "You had lunch with Curt," she said. "Did he pick you up?"

"I leased an Expedition. The dealer delivered it to the job site. Has all the bells and whistles. Should do me just fine while I'm here."

"Ah." Dory nodded. "How long are you planning to stay?"

It was the perfect opening. He'd planned to take his time and be subtle about this, but Woods had been a total bust. Chase had every expectation that following the EKG three weeks from today, the cardiologist would clear his father for stairs. He'd as much as said so. Once Charles was ensconced in his comfy little nest above the garage, he wouldn't be able to budge him out of it with a stick of dynamite.

Chase smiled, a friendly, we're-just-having-a-conversation-here smile. "That depends on how long it takes me to convince Dad to retire."

Dory took her elbows off the table and sat straight up in the booth. "Aunt Ping said that's why you'd come."

"Considering the heart attack I think it's time, don't you?"

"It doesn't matter what I think. What does Charles think?"

"I haven't discussed it with Dad yet. I wanted to talk to his cardiologist first. I spoke with Dr. Woods this afternoon."

"I've talked to him, too. Charles gave his permission."

"Then you know why I'm talking to you."

"No, I don't," she said flatly. "Why are you talking to me?"

"You were there, Dory. You saw Dad blow his stack about the Rolls. A ding in the fender and a scrape on the grille and he goes through the roof. I don't think he can handle the job stress anymore."

"We hired Diego to take some of the load off Charles."

"And how's that working out?"

"It isn't at the moment. Charles hasn't been able to train him. He'd just gotten serious about it when he had the heart attack."

"That doesn't surprise me. I've seen Diego drive. Artemis wasn't his fault. He deserves credit for not hitting Jamie. I'm not sure how he missed him, so clearly he has potential, but he's a kid and he's flighty. I can understand why Diego driving the Rolls makes Dad nuts."

"I didn't say that," Dory said sharply. "Did I say that?"

"You don't have to say it, I know my dad. I couldn't back the Rolls out of the garage till I was eighteen. Thank God he's not as possessive about the Packard or the Bentley or he'd have another heart attack."

"We sold the Packard." She didn't say, "Because we had to"; her nearly clenched teeth said it for her.

"Have you considered hiring someone a little older? Someone with more mechanical and driving experience?"

"Chauffeurs don't grow on trees and they don't come cheap. Quite frankly, Diego is all we can afford. Is that what you want to hear?"

"Want to, no, but it's what I suspected. I also suspect Dad doesn't want to train Diego. He doesn't want to train anybody. Does he?"

"Just spit it out, Chase." Dory plunked her clasped together hands on the table between them. "What do you want?"

"I want my dad to enjoy the rest of his life. I don't want to peel his cold, dead fingers off the steering wheel of Miss Ping's Rolls-Royce."

Chase saw her clasped hands tighten. "I won't let that happen."

"How can you stop it? You wrangled him a parole and

what's the first thing he did? Had Tom drive him to McPherson's. He refuses to see the heart attack as a warning to slow down because he doesn't want to see it. He has no intention of slowing down."

"You've been trying for years to talk Charles into retiring. What makes you think he'll listen to you this time?"

"I'm not sure he will, but I'm hoping he'll listen to you."

She sat back against the booth and dropped her hands in her lap. "That's not what I expected you to say."

"You're fond of Dad. I know you want what's best for him."

"The person who should decide what's best for Charles is Charles."

"I don't agree. Dory. I need your help."

"I can't help you, Chase." She shook her head. "I'm sorry. I won't."

"Will you think about it? I know what I'm asking isn't easy."

"Easy?" She gave a short laugh. "You have no idea."

There it was again, the harried glint in her eyes. Chase saw it as she glanced away from him toward the bar. He should back off and give her a chance to think about it, but he only had three weeks.

"I believe I do, Dory," he said kindly. "I know these last ten years have been rough on your family. I can afford to take care of Dad. I can also afford to compensate Miss Ping for the loss of a valuable employee."

She snapped her head around, her face white. "What did you say?" Her voice held a lethal edge. "Did you just offer me *money*?"

"Yes," Chase said, wishing he hadn't. It was the wrong move, the worst possible move. "Baldly and by the look on your face—" Like she wanted to reach across the table and rip his throat out. "—very badly."

"Thanks for the drink." Dory scooped up her coat and her purse and scooted toward the end of the booth.

Chase beat her to her feet. He reached for her coat but she jerked away from him and flung herself into it.

"I apologize, Dory. I didn't mean to offend you."

"Too late." She hooked her purse over her shoulder and glared at him. "I'm not going to tell Charles or Aunt Ping that we had this conversation. I'm going to pretend it never happened. Good night."

Chapter Eight

The cosmopolitan was a mistake. Dory's throat was in flames.

She stopped at Walgreen's and filled her prescription, bought a bottle of water and took a Prevacid. It helped a little. The pharmacist told her it would take at least a week to totally calm her acid reflux.

It was seven-fifteen when she left the drugstore. Pitch-dark, the roads leading to Outlook were draped in fog. Thin, clingy wisps drifted like wraiths across the nose of her little green Saturn. Halos the size of Saturn's rings hung around the carriage lamps on the front gates. Dory parked the car on the edge of the drive, got out and balled her hands into fists. Then she drew a deep breath and ran around the trees in the park screaming at the top of her lungs.

Fog shimmered around the lights staked at the base of the pin oaks and the flower beds. The grass was slick with dew. Dory almost hoped she'd smack face-first into a tree—anything to take away the pain where her heart used to be—but she managed to stay on her feet until she ran out of breath to scream with.

"Feel better?" Chase asked.

Dory wheeled around toward the drive. Chase was leaning against a burgundy red Expedition, the one with all the bells and whistles. He'd parked it behind her Saturn, between two of the black-domed Malibu lights that lit the edges of the drive. It was very like—No. It was *exactly* like the one she'd seen in her mirror, turning behind her into Walgreen's parking lot.

"No." She crooked her finger at him. "Come here and lean over so I can punch you in the eye. Then I might feel better."

"If it'll help." He pushed off the truck and started toward her.

"Oh, go away." Dory gave him a push-off wave and spun away.

"Dad is all I have," Chase said behind her. She heard him following her, his footsteps swishing through the wet, heavy grass. "I love him."

"I know you do." Dory walked faster. "That's why I'm not going to tell him you're a pompous, arrogant, condescending ass."

"I deserve that. Now come on. We've always been friends."

"No we have not." Dory turned around. "I was a sawed-off little pain in your ass, which you told me at least five or six times a day."

"Well." He smiled and shrugged. "You're still short."

"You're still an ass." Dory wheeled and marched away.

"You look as silly running around down here shrieking like a banshee as you did when you were a kid."

"I only did this when I was mad at my mother."

"But why down here? I could never figure that out. You were too far away from the house for Her Ladyship to hear you."

"I wanted a policeman to hear me. I thought if I told him I was adopted he'd take me away to an orphanage. Then she'd be sorry."

"Can you forget that I offered you money?"

"Relax, rich boy." Dory snorted. "It was verbal, no witnesses, you didn't name a figure. I'm not going to sue you for breach or bribe."

"The thought that you would never entered my head."

"Bull hockey. Rich people are the biggest skinflints on

the planet. I should know." Dory whirled around, so furious she slipped and almost fell. "You didn't even buy me dinner, you cheap jerk!"

Chase just looked at her. The lawn lights were dim as fireflies under the trees, the fog so thick it hung like gauze. Dory felt like she was breathing through a wet paper towel. She reached for a Kleenex, felt the change from Walgreen's in her pocket and threw it at him.

"That's for my drink," she said.

The quarters made a dull plop. The ten-dollar bill wilted on contact with the soggy ground. Chase glanced at the money, then at her, his mouth twisted in the soulful, heart-in-his-eyes scowl that used to make the heart she'd had until an hour ago catch in her throat.

"You've got me all wrong, Dory."

"No, Chase. For the first time in my life I've got you *right*."

This time when she turned away he didn't follow her. She turned back when she heard him start the Expedition, saw the murky spear of its headlights stabbing uphill toward the house and dripping wet plunked herself down on an iron bench, her throat aching and her eyes brimming.

She would not cry. She hadn't shed a single tear over any of this mess since the day Tobias died. Crying wouldn't solve anything—getting rid of Chase wouldn't, either, but it was a great place to start.

Dory headed for the car, brushing the back of her coat and searching the ground for the money. There was no wind to blow it away, but she couldn't find it. Chase must've picked it up. Cheap jerk.

Her suede flats were soaked, stretched out and flapping on her feet like Olive Oyl shoes. Damn it. She loved these flats. She'd had them forever, not quite as long as her green Saturn but close.

The driver's door creaked when she opened it. Then it clunked. Dory jumped, snapped her head around and realized it wasn't the door making eerie, Frankenstein-movie noises in the dark and the fog. It was the gates, swinging shut automatically on their five-minute delay.

She could've sworn she'd pushed the remote to close them, but obviously she hadn't—look at the bozo that had followed her home.

Stepping into the sitting room of Aunt Ping's suite in the south wing was like stepping into a Chinese temple. Everything was Chinese. The rugs woven of silk, the furniture red or black trimmed with gold or painted with scenes of white cranes flying over green rice fields.

Aunt Ping was curled in a red chaise lounge, wrapped in her chenille bathrobe under an afghan that Deirdre had knitted. Coco slept in her lap. A tea tray sat on the table beside the chaise.

"You're all wet," she said to Dory. "Is it raining at last?"

"No. Just really foggy." Dory moved a black lacquer chair from the desk to the table and sat down. "Why did you run out of the meeting?"

"I don't know." Aunt Ping lowered her gaze and stroked Coco's head. The Tonkinese cat twitched an ear in her sleep and started to purr. "I just—felt trapped. I've apologized to everyone for my behavior."

"If you want to close the Outlook Inn, just say the word."

Aunt Ping raised her chin and her eyebrow. "And do what? Go back to selling tomatoes on the side of the road?"

"Sometimes I feel like I forced you into this."

"Of course you did and thank God. I would've lost Outlook by now if you hadn't. You were absolutely correct."

"But you hate having the house full of strangers."

"I don't hate it, Dory. It's simply that taking in boarders is not what I planned to do with the rest of my life."

She said it with a wry smile but a resigned, this-is-my-fate-and-I-accept-it edge in her voice. Dory was glad she didn't have a heart anymore. It would've cracked right down the middle.

"You didn't plan on turning Outlook into a hotel. You didn't plan on James or Jamie, losing Daddy or saving Jill and me from God knows what. I realize that. And I realized today when you ran out of the house that I've never once said thank you." The tears Dory swore she wouldn't shed filled and burned her eyes. She blinked them away and managed to smile without her mouth trembling. "Thank you, Aunt Ping."

"Dory. Are you all right?" She turned Coco and the afghan out of her lap, sat up on the side of the chaise and took her hands. "You're freezing. How did you soak yourself through?"

"The car was making a funny noise. I got out to check it."

"You love that car but it's ancient. I think it's time to replace it."

"It was just a rock in the tire." Dory squeezed her warm hands. "I have an idea. Why don't you move into the guesthouse and let Jill and me take this suite? I think most of your furniture will fit. You wouldn't be so accessible for every little thing and you'd have your privacy back."

She'd also be closer to Charles, but Dory didn't say that. Aunt Ping made a soft moue and brushed her cheek with one hand.

"I've worried you, haven't I? I'm so very sorry."

"How about a cruise? Wouldn't you love to loll in a deck chair for a week or two?" While I get rid of Chase, Dory thought, so you don't have to live in terror that he'll take Charles away from you. "We can afford to send you and Deirdre. She loves to sail and I think it's time she got back a bit of her investment in the Outlook Inn, don't you?"

"I think you should get out of your wet things and into a hot bath. I behaved like a silly, spoiled old woman today. It will not happen again, I assure you. I give you my word along with my apology for troubling you."

Trouble? Dory thought. You ain't seen trouble. Yet.

"We'll talk about the cruise tomorrow." Dory let go of

Aunt Ping's hands and grinned. "I had no idea you could drive a golf cart."

"Nor did I." She laughed. "It was quite fun. I may do it again."

She'd driven the Rolls the day Charles had his heart attack. Now she'd driven a golf cart. What else could Aunt Ping do? What else had she done that Dory didn't know about?

"I think you absolutely should," she said. "Crank that cart up to fifteen miles per hour and feel the wind in your eyelashes."

Aunt Ping laughed. Dory kissed her forehead, moved the chair back to the desk and turned toward the door. "Good night, Aunt Ping."

"Dory," she said. "Did someone follow me today? When I brought the white cart back, I laid my hand on the blue one. It felt warm."

Oh crap. Dory froze with her back to Aunt Ping. Had she asked Wallace? What had he told her?

"I did." She turned with her hand on the doorknob. "I followed you as far as the golf course. Then I decided to give you some peace and quiet and went back to the house."

"Ah. I wondered." Aunt Ping didn't curl up on the chaise; it seemed to Dory like she wilted onto it with relief. "Sleep well, Dory."

The quickest way to get rid of Chase would be to tell Aunt Ping he'd offered her money. He'd be thrown off Outlook, but Charles would find out and either be furious or heartbroken, so that wouldn't work.

Aunt Ping didn't know that Gary was an FBI agent. Neither did anyone else. It was just Jill and Dory's little secret.

Dory didn't like secrets, but she kept Gary's because Aunt Ping would kill him. The same thing could happen to Chase if Aunt Ping found out about the bribe—strangled with an Hermès scarf.

Dory fell asleep picturing it in her head, a smile on her face.

She woke with a jolt when Jamie screamed. She shot up in bed, blinking in the sunlight pouring through her bedroom windows and caught Jamie as he leaped on her in a tangle of bony arms and legs, a dribble of milk on his chin and the blue sweatshirt he'd slept in.

"Hide me!" His eyes were wide, his face pasty beneath his freckles and the measles rash. "She's back!"

"*Dor-ry!*" Jill bellowed from downstairs.

"Go to your room and lock the door," Dory told Jamie.

He dashed across the hall, holding on to his plaid sleep pants so they wouldn't fall off, and slammed the door. Dory ran for the stairs and started down them just as Jill started up. She stopped on the third step from the bottom, Dory on the second step from the top.

"Why is the monster here?" Jill demanded. "He's supposed to be gone when I get back."

"Why are *you* here? I wasn't expecting you till tomorrow."

"I left you a message. You were supposed to call me last night. When you didn't I called Wallace. He told me Aunt Ping ran away so I caught the first flight home. What's going on?"

"Start the coffee. I'll be down in a minute."

"Make it snappy," Jill said and wheeled away from the stairs.

Dory turned down the hall, her heart thudding from being jolted awake. Jamie opened his bedroom door and stuck his head into the hall. "Is she coming after me?"

"No. She's making coffee."

Dory had forgotten to check messages and call her sister but she'd remembered to fill the coffee drip machine on her way to bed. She always did and Jill knew it. All she had to do was push the red button, but it could take her ten minutes to find it.

"Do I have to go back to the house?" Jamie asked.

"You have measles. You can't go back to the house."

"Cool." He grinned, shut the door and locked it.

Dory went to the bathroom and washed her hands, raked her hair out of her face and groaned at the time on her clock radio. Seven twenty. It was Saturday, her one day to sleep late. In the off-season Esther covered the office and the front desk so she could.

Her stomach still felt lumpy. Dory rubbed it, muttered, "C'mon, Prevacid," pulled a yellow robe over her green pajamas, stuck her feet in pink terrycloth mules and went downstairs.

Jill's red suitcase sat just inside the front door on the stone floor at the foot of the stairs. Cartoons blared out of the TV in the living room and a bowl of Apple Jacks sat on the coffee table in a puddle of spilled milk. Jill had come through the door and scared the crap out of Jamie. Dory picked up the bowl and gave the table a wipe with her sleeve.

The combination kitchen and breakfast room ran across the back of the guesthouse. Plaid rugs scattered the flagged floor. Dory winced in the sunlight spilling through the diamond-paned windows on the outside stone wall. Jill had opened the top of the Dutch door that led out onto the enclosed back patio. Dory shivered in the cold and shut it.

Jill turned away from the kitchen counter. She'd spent at least half the night getting here, yet her hair looked like she'd just pinned it up on top of her head. Her skin glowed, her blue linen slacks and silk blouse held nary a wrinkle. Dory had a pillow crease in her left cheek. Her eyes felt full of sand, her mouth like she hadn't brushed her teeth in a week.

"What," Jill demanded, "is Jamie doing here?"

"He has measles." Dory put the bowl in the sink and rinsed it.

"Okay," Jill said when she turned around. "So why is he here?"

"Zoe Morgenstern can't remember if she's had measles."

"She's old enough to remember the Alamo!" Jill shoved

her hands on her hips. "What do you mean she can't remember the measles?"

"Well, she can't, so Jamie has to stay here till Zoe and Felix leave."

"Shit," Jill said disgustedly. "When will that be?"

"They're booked through Wednesday."

"Wednesday! *Dory!*" Jill cried like it was her fault. "I've been gone two weeks! I want to sleep in my own bed!"

"Go sleep with Gary on the futon. Take some sandpaper with you," Dory said between her teeth. "*And get rid of that tattoo on his leg!*"

"Oh hell." Jill winced. "How did you see that?"

"Gary broke out in hives because Chase was in the Happy Spirit. He called him a spear through his heart. What did you tell him about Chase?"

"Just the usual stuff to make him jealous and hot for me."

"*Un-*tell him." Dory gave her a one-finger push on the shoulder. "I had to put aloe on his hives and drag Chase out of the Happy Spirit."

"I suppose you want me to break up with Gary."

"What? Do something sensible? God forbid!"

Dory glared at her. Jill glared back, then she blinked and bit her lip, threw her arms around Dory and hugged her.

"Oh, honey. Chase still doesn't know you're alive, does he?"

"Of course he knows I'm alive." He just doesn't care, Dory thought, and pushed Jill away. "He came here to convince Charles to retire. He told me last night."

"Who does he think he is? Charles can't retire. Aunt Ping won't drive with anyone else. Is that why she ran away?"

"She says she felt trapped. She doesn't know positively why Chase came, but she suspects. We talked about it yesterday morning."

"Has Chase had the measles?"

"He isn't sure," Dory said. "He can't remember."

"Invite him to lunch." Jill smiled. "Let the monster make him a peanut butter and jelly sandwich."

*   *   *

"I can't believe Dory." Jill rolled away from Gary and sat up on the side of the futon. Naked and sated but still in a snit. "I gave her the perfect way to get rid of Chase, but no. It's too mean to expose him to the measles. Like it would be *our* fault if he got sick and died."

When Gary didn't answer, she glanced at him over her shoulder. He stared at her with a furrow between his eyebrows. "What?"

"Whose fault do you think it would be, Jill?"

"His, of course, if he was dumb enough to eat the sandwich."

Gary clapped a hand over his eyes. "Yikes."

Jill frowned. She hated when Gary did that, smacked himself and said "Yikes." Like she was stupid, which she wasn't. She was simply unafraid to say what she really thought. That she'd *l-o-o-v-e* to see Chase McKay, Mr. Hoity-Toity Big Shot, all speckled up and sicker than a dog. It was the truth. Why should she lie about it or be all namby-pamby?

Like Dory, the little dummy. Did she really think Jill hadn't seen the wistful five-second flash of oh-what-I-wouldn't-give-to-see-that in her eyes? She should know better. So should Gary.

Jill straddled him. Gary's eyes sprang open. He growled, clutched her hips and pushed inside of her. She let him have two thrusts, then gripped his shoulders and pinned him flat against the futon beneath her.

"Now that I have your attention," she said.

"Oh God, Jill," he said raggedly. "Not now."

"You have to help me think of a way to get rid of Chase."

"*Right now?*" Gary's eyes bugged. "While we're making love?"

"Do you want to finish this?" Jill leaned over him, brushing her nipples close to his lips. "Think of a way."

She slid off him and scooped her clothes off the floor.

"One that doesn't involve disease or death so Dory will go for it."

Gary clapped his hands over his eyes but didn't say yikes. He groaned. Jill smiled and took her clothes into the bathroom.

Tight, low-slung jeans, a white ribbed crop top that showed her perfect navel and the taut, flat tummy she killed herself with crunches to maintain. No bra so she'd bounce, a short red leather jacket and matching stiletto-heeled boots. She'd paid four hundred dollars for the eighteen-hundred-dollar ensemble in a designer outlet. She called it her upscale slut outfit. She pulled her hair into an off-center ponytail so it would swing along with her hips and she was ready to jump-start Gary's brain.

The man had a law degree, another one in criminal investigation procedures. He was an undercover FBI agent. She loved Gary but it was time he earned his keep for the Lambert family.

He'd folded up the futon and reopened the Happy Spirit. Jill swept through the beaded curtain with her red leather backpack and saw him ringing up a sale, an el cheapo pair of small brass cymbals, for a petite older woman in a pastel tweed coat and a hot pink beret.

Gary looked sullen. The customer looked loaded. Her tiny, wrinkled fingers blazed with enough diamonds to buy Aunt Ping a new Rolls. Jill dumped her bag in a chair and moved in with a smile.

Twenty minutes later Mrs. Hazel Pronger left the Happy Spirit with 850 dollars' worth of feng shui enhancements for her top floor apartment in the majestic old building her son Seymour owned on the Country Club Plaza. She paid with a gold American Express card, signed up and wrote a check for 250 dollars to attend the next feng shui class given by one of Aunt Ping's nutty friends. Jill carried her packages out to the hired car waiting for her. Hazel gave her a kiss on the cheek and a ten-dollar tip.

"You're merciless," Gary said when she came back into the store.

"Most people just want some attention, Gary. Hazel told me about her grandchildren. She doesn't see them much. They live in New Jersey. Most of her friends have died. She can come to the Happy Spirit, drink green tea and eat ginger cookies with the rest of the class. Learn how to play mah-jongg and make new friends. How is that merciless?"

"All right. I've thought about it. Just tell McKay to blow."

"Can't. It might upset Charles." Jill leaned toward him over the counter. Her nipples were hard. She watched Gary's gaze drop to her breasts. He whimpered. "Keep Charles and lose Chase. Keep thinking."

"How about my sanity?" Gary asked. "Do you care if I keep that?"

"Nope." Jill popped her lips at him in an air-blown kiss. "Get your head out of your pants and apply it to the problem."

"You've got Diego. Why do you need Charles?"

"Aunt Ping won't get in a car with anyone else."

"Is that all? I thought he was her paramour."

"Don't be insulting." Jill gave him a push in the head. "If you ever want to use your dick with me again, stop thinking with it."

"You really are merciless," Gary said, his voice hoarse.

"When it comes to Aunt Ping and Dory, you bet I am." Jill picked up her bag and flung it over her shoulder. "Don't call me till you have a way to get rid of Chase."

Chase sat on the garage roof wall in jeans and a gray sweatshirt, a navy and red McKay Design and Development baseball cap turned backwards on his head, his father's field glasses trained on the guesthouse.

He was sure he looked as dopey as Jill and Dory used to when they'd spied on him through Del Lambert's binoculars. If Eddie or Tom came up the stairs, he was bird watching.

He'd found out from Esther when he'd shown up in Dory's office at nine thirty that she didn't work on Saturdays. He'd hiked over to the guesthouse and rang the bell but no one answered the door.

Esther gave him the phone number. He dialed it on his cell, got the answering machine and left a message. He'd leaned for a minute against the patio wall staring at the guesthouse, then went back to the big house and loaded his father in the Expedition, took him to breakfast and told him what he'd said to Dory.

The old man laughed so hard he'd had a coughing fit. It was not the reaction Chase expected. He'd expected him to hit the roof.

"Still watching for the lynch mob?" Charles asked.

Chase lowered the binoculars. His father stepped out onto the roof, shut the door and grinned. Chase had carried him up the stairs again as penance for being a pompous, arrogant, condescending ass.

"I'm glad one of us thinks this is funny," he said.

"I'm gonna tell you this now 'cause it's too late." Charles zipped his navy poplin jacket and sat down on the wall by the steps. "You should've confessed to Miss Ping. She would've kicked your butt off Outlook and because you're my son, I would've had to go with you."

"Start packing." Chase stood up. "I'll be right back."

"Go tell her." Charles shrugged. "But I'm not going with you now."

"You were never going with me." Chase scowled and sat down. "I don't know what made me think I could talk you into retiring."

"You didn't think you could." His father's eyes crinkled up at the corners. "That's why you tried to drag Dory into it."

"I thought she shared my view that your heart attack was a warning to slow down."

"It was a blockage, son, not the big one. Woods cleaned it out and I feel great." Charles bent his elbows and fisted his hands. "Fit as ever."

"Two days ago," Chase reminded him, "you looked like hell."

"Two days ago I was a prisoner. I'm free now and I feel fine."

Charles drew his sunglasses out of his breast pocket and put them on, leaned back on his hands and turned his face up to the sun.

The roof was a great place to get a tan. In high school Chase would stake himself out up here so he'd look like he'd spent the summer at the pool rather than washing cars and slaving for Peter. His dad would wait till he was half asleep to nail him with a squirt gun filled with ice water.

Chase would roar to his feet, pissed as hell, and shag the old man down the stairs and around the elm tree. He could run like a deer and he had some NFL moves on him. He'd dodge around the tree, nailing him till the gun was empty, then he'd go for the hose. That's when Chase would catch him. They'd end up wrestling and laughing, then his dad would pop him one on the ass, just to remind him that he still could.

Charles drew a breath and let it go in a deep sigh, his mostly silver hair ruffling in the breeze. Chase sat gazing at him, a lump in his throat.

"I wish you'd at least think about New York, Dad. You love it."

"I don't want to live there." Charles lowered his head and slid his sunglasses down his nose. "I'm not going to retire and I'm not leaving Outlook. I've lived half my life here. This is my home."

"It isn't mine, Dad. Not anymore. I live in New York."

"Live where you want, son. I don't expect you to give up your life for me. What made you think I'd be willing to give mine up for you?"

"I never thought you'd be willing." Chase raised the binoculars and focused on the guesthouse. "That's why I tried to enlist Dory."

"Look where that got you. Are the flowers still there?"

"Yes. On the porch where the delivery guy left them." Two hundred dollars worth of pink roses in a crystal vase the size of a vat, their tops wrapped in a green tissue paper cone to protect them. Chase put the glasses down and looked at his father. He'd taken off his shades and crossed one leg over the other. "Miss Ping could still give me the boot."

"Dory won't tell her." Charles shook his head. "She doesn't tell her anything that she thinks will upset her. I'm amazed you told me."

"I didn't plan to, but I thought about it and decided that if I was going to hear, 'Get out,' I wanted to hear it from you. Not Miss Ping."

"If you'd talked to me first, you wouldn't be in this pickle with Dory. In the future, Mr. President of My Own Company, it wouldn't hurt you to consider the possibility that you don't know everything."

"Thank you, Dad," Chase said dryly. "I've had that lecture."

"Pompous, arrogant, condescending ass." Charles grinned. "Hits it right on the head, doesn't she?"

"I think she would have if she'd had a ladder."

Charles laughed. Chase frowned at the guesthouse, a good quarter of a mile away from the garage. Without the binoculars all he could see was the red-tiled roof through the leafing out trees. It was two o'clock in the afternoon. He hadn't seen a single stir of life from the place all day.

"I expected you to blow a gasket over the money I offered Dory."

"See there? You don't know everything."

Chase glanced at his father. He was grinning again.

"I don't understand why you think this is funny."

"Lighten up, son. It's over and there's no real harm done."

"No real harm? I haven't taken one misstep in my business or my personal life since I left Outlook. I've only been here two days and I've offended Dory and blown my campaign to convince you to retire."

"That's what's funny. Watching you stub your toes."

"I hope you'll be able to keep laughing if Dory changes

her mind and Miss Ping throws me bodily out the front gates."

"That's the thing *I* don't understand." Charles cocked his head at him. "For sixteen years you did everything you could think of to avoid coming back here. Now you're worried about being kicked out."

"It wasn't fun the first time. I'd rather not repeat the experience."

"I think you're safe till my birthday party tomorrow. After that—" Charles shrugged, his eyes twinkling. "—all bets are off."

"I've had enough of this." Chase put the binoculars down and rose off the wall. "I'm going over there and ring the bell again."

"Mind the upstairs windows and water balloons."

"I'll do that. You stay here and keep cracking jokes, Jay Leno."

His father laughed. Chase went past him and down the stairs, cut across the lawn between the garage and the path below the ornamental garden. He wanted to jog but made himself walk, gritting his teeth at the crunch of pea gravel beneath the soles of his running shoes.

Being kicked off Outlook was the least of his worries. What to do about his reckless streak troubled him more. He'd thought he had it gagged and bound so tightly it could never break free, but last night it had busted through his carefully tied knots of discipline and self-control. Two things he hadn't had a lick of in his nature till his father and Del Lambert caught him with Jill.

He didn't like to be thwarted. That was part of why he'd jumped the gun with Dory. Woods, the idiot, who thought he knew Charles McKay better than his own son because he had M.D. after his name. Impulsive people didn't like to be stymied. That's what made them impulsive and their instincts unreliable. He'd learned that in Her Ladyship's horse barn.

"Look," he wanted to tell Dory. "I'm sorry about last night, but I can't help myself. I think it's Outlook. I seem to be reverting, turning back into the reckless, selfish jerk I used to be. I don't know why it's happening, but there it is."

He didn't expect her to understand—he didn't understand it completely himself—he expected her to tell him to bend down so she could punch him in the eye.

If it would make her feel better, he'd do it. If Dory didn't answer the door, he'd park his fanny on the steps with the roses and wait.

She didn't answer the door. Chase sat down on the top step and turned his cap around to keep the sun out of his eyes.

He'd pissed her off but good. And hurt her feelings. In spite of the fog, he'd seen it in her eyes when she'd spun around under the trees and glared at him. The shimmer of how-could-you tears. Must've been the last little smidgen of the crush she'd had on him.

That bothered him, too. He didn't like to hurt people.

"Why don't you just stab me in the heart?" Peter said.

Chase looked up from the toes of his shoes. Peter leaned on the patio wall, in his coveralls and a green plaid shirt, his yellow stocking cap on his head, a glare fixed on the tissue-wrapped bouquet.

"It's April. Do you have three dozen roses in the greenhouse?"

"Roses?" Peter said suspiciously. "Are those for Jill?"

"No, they're not for Jill. They're for Dory." Chase stood up and turned around, cupped his hands around his mouth and yelled at the house, "If she ever bothers to open the door!"

"Oh, my. What did you do, dear boy?"

"You don't want to know and I don't want to tell you."

"If you'd like to deliver those in person, you might try the ballroom. Dory and Jill and Deirdre are decorating for Charles' party tomorrow."

"Jill?" Chase picked up the bouquet. "I thought she wasn't here."

"She came home this morning." Peter opened the gate for him. "What color roses?"

"Pink," Chase said, struggling with the giant arrangement.

"Bad choice." Peter made a face. "Dory likes yellow."

Hell, Chase thought. "I ordered pink," he said, turning sideways through the gate with the roses. "So pink will have to do."

Dory thought it was going to be difficult if not downright impossible for Aunt Ping to top the Grim Reaper theme she'd come up with for Wallace's last who-knew-how-many-birthdays party in January.

"Why does one dance in one's socks at a sock hop?" Deirdre asked.

"So one does not damage the gymnasium floor," Dory replied, "and piss off the basketball team."

"Ah." Deirdre nodded. "What's basketball?"

Diego grinned at Dory and explained the game while he leveled the Wurlitzer jukebox he'd brought down on a dolly from the attics in the elevator that Aunt Ping's father had added to Outlook in 1942 so baby Margaret's nanny didn't have to bump her pram down the stairs.

The Wurlitzer was Aunt Ping's fifteenth birthday present. It was a beaut. The Rolls-Royce of jukeboxes. When Diego plugged it in the whole front of it lit up like a neon Christmas tree.

"Chi-wawa." He grinned at Dory. "What else you s'pose Miss Ping has in the attics?"

"I don't know, but if she's got the crown jewels up there I'd wish she'd hurry up and find them."

"How lovely of Margaret to provide us all with costumes." Deirdre turned a circle on a red swivel stool at Aunt Ping's soda fountain, the other half of her fifteenth birthday present. Tom and Eddie had brought it up to the house yesterday afternoon from its storage spot in one of the barns. "I quite like my doodle skirt."

"Aunt Deirdre," Dory said, "it's called a poodle skirt."

"Mine is the most lovely shade of pink. What color is yours, dear?"

"I wouldn't be caught dead in a poodle skirt. I'd look like a top."

"This is gonna be one *fabuloso* party." Diego hopped onto a stool next to Deirdre and nodded at the rented chrome and red Formica tables arranged around the soda fountain to look like a malt shop. "I can't wait to see Mr. Charles in a black leather biker jacket."

"What's your costume, Diego?" Deirdre asked.

"It's a surprise, Mrs. Deirdre." He wagged his eyebrows at her. "You wait. I'm gonna knock your socks off."

Dory sat at one of the tables stuffing paper-wrapped straws into a glass dispenser with a chrome top. She smiled and ducked her head so she wouldn't blab. Diego's uncle in L.A., Beni's father, played in a mariachi band. He'd sent Diego one of his costumes so he could come as the Cisco Kid, the Mexican cowboy hero of the campy old '50s TV show. Dory bet him five bucks he couldn't get through the ballroom doors with the flying saucer-size sombrero on his head.

All the guests were invited. Miss Fairview sniffed at her invitation, but Dory bet she'd come just to show off her prune face. The Morgensterns were coming as Mr. and Mrs. Howell, the filthy rich castaways from *Gilligan's Island*. It was a '60s show, but who else could Zoe and Felix be? Buck Madison, a cattle rancher from Casper, Wyoming, whom Tom depended on for advice on his Angus steers, was coming as Gene Autry. Simple, he'd said, 'cause he already had the wardrobe. Olaf and Charlotte Ericson, who owned most of the natural gas wells in Kansas and could give Zoe and Felix a run for their money to be Mr. and Mrs. Howell, were coming as Ozzie and Harriet Nelson.

Esme was in the kitchen making patties for cheeseburgers. Wallace had volunteered to be the soda jerk. Dory could hardly wait to see him out of his black coat and with a white fly-boy cap cocked at a jaunty angle on his regal silver head.

The guys with the canisters of compressed gas to run the fountain and dry ice to keep the ice cream frozen should be here soon. Then Diego would relieve Wallace at the front door so he could practice. Dory planned to hang around and eat the flops. She'd already filled the syrup dispensers and sent Jill to Hy-Vee for bananas, strawberries and pineapple for banana splits. She'd called on her cell phone to ask how to spell maraschino. Like she couldn't just look on the shelf till she found a jar of small red cherries with stems, but that was Jill.

Diego was right. Aunt Ping had outdone herself. It was going to be a *fabuloso* party. The quiver of excitement that Dory felt in her stomach was a nice change from acid reflux.

The middle bank of French doors on the far wall of the ballroom stood open to the terrace, its flagged stone surface glittering in the bright afternoon sun. The white chiffon panels on the doors stirred in an almost-warm breeze. It was April twentieth. High time for spring to arrive.

The day that had gotten off to such a crappy start was turning out okay. So Dory thought until Chase came through the French doors carrying some big huge thing wrapped in green tissue paper.

It wasn't his head, more's the pity. That was still on his shoulders, his hair covered by a navy ball cap with the initials MDD on the front, which probably didn't stand for Mega-Dumb Doofus.

For a second Dory didn't see expensive jeans, a designer sweatshirt and leather running shoes. She saw faded Levi's and a white T-shirt, unruly blond hair and sunburned arms. But just for a second, till she blinked. Then the boy she'd loved vanished and the conceited ass she despised was striding toward her across the ballroom.

Dory wheeled out of her chair to suggest to Diego that they crank up the jukebox and saw him scurrying out of the ballroom with Deirdre.

"I'll get you, Cisco," she muttered and turned to face Chase.

"These are for you." He plunked the big thing on the table and tore off the tissue paper. "They've been on your porch since eleven o'clock."

Dory blinked at the giant bouquet of roses. "I hate pink," she said.

"Peter told me. Still, these are for you. From me. I'm sorry."

"Could you possibly sound any *less* sorry?"

"You want me on my knees? Want to punch me in the eye?" Chase pushed his hat back, springing a thatch of pale gold hair over his forehead. "How 'bout on my knees so you can reach to punch me in the eye?"

"I want you gone, but Charles would go with you."

"Dad's not going anywhere. I told him what I said to you. He won't retire and he won't leave Outlook. Happy?"

"Ecstatic," Dory said between her teeth. "When are you leaving?"

"Unless you're throwing me out I'd like to stay till—"

"Excuse me?" Jill said. "You there—excuse me."

Dory and Chase turned away from each other, the vase of roses and the torn tissue paper on the table between them. Jill came briskly across the marble floor from the terrace. She'd exchanged the top half of her slut outfit for a blue oxford cloth shirt with the sleeves rolled up, her red boots for white Reeboks and still she was stunning. Tall and lithe in her skintight jeans with the face of a movie star. Or maybe a goddess.

A second before she turned her head, Dory heard Chase catch his breath. And felt, like she always had, the spring that tightened in him at the sight of Jill. Sure enough. When she glanced at him he looked like he'd been whacked between the eyes with a two-by-four.

"We don't accept deliveries in the ballroom." Jill opened the tiny bag hung by a spaghetti strap on her shoulder and fished out a five-dollar bill. "In future, flowers come to the front door, okay?"

She offered Chase the money. He didn't take it. He didn't

move. He just stood staring at Jill, almost but not quite slack-jawed.

"Thanks." Dory plucked the five out of her sister's fingers.

"Hey." Chase snapped his head toward her. "That's my five bucks."

"Bull hockey, rich boy. You took my ten last night."

"Rich boy? He took your—*Chase*!" Jill squealed, her eyes flying open. "Oh my God! I didn't recognize you!"

She laughed and threw her arms around his neck. He caught her around the waist, laughed with her and swung her off her feet.

What had Chase said to her Thursday night? *Some things never change,* Dory remembered, and felt her stomach clench.

She stuffed the five in her pocket and headed for the French doors. She had about an acre of marble floor to cross to reach the terrace but she didn't run, she walked. Behind her she heard Jill say, "The hat totally threw me! I thought you were a delivery boy!"

"There," Chase said. "Is that better?"

Took off his ball cap, Dory thought, half a second before Jill said, "God, no! Now you have hat hair!"

Chase laughed. Jill laughed. Loud, giddy, goofy laughs like they were oh so funny, oh so witty. Like they couldn't take their eyes off each other. Neither one of them noticed that she was leaving.

Jamie hated math. He had a flare for languages. He'd picked up Spanish from Diego. He watched artsy foreign films on Bravo and knew enough Italian to get his face smacked in Rome, said Eddie, who spoke it with his parents, but math was beyond Jamie. He despised it.

"If you'd just learn percentages," Dory told him. "Sister Immaculata would take you off the Watch List."

"I hate percentages." Jamie tossed his pencil inside his math book and closed it. "Why do I have to learn them? I can run a calculator."

"What will you do when you're president of Lambert

Bank and Trust and the electricity goes off? So does your calculator."

"No it doesn't," Jamie said. "It's solar powered."

"What if it's a cloudy day?"

"I'll shine a flashlight on the solar cell."

"What if the batteries in your flashlight are dead?"

"I'll walk two blocks to Walgreen's and buy more."

"What if the power is out all over town and neither you nor the clerk in Walgreen's can figure percentages without a calculator? How do you compute the tax so she can sell you the batteries? And don't—" Dory warned him, "—say some guy comes in behind you to buy batteries and he knows how to figure percentages."

"Okay." Jamie slapped open his math book, picked up his pencil and tapped the eraser against his temple. "Let me try this again."

"That's my boy." Dory pushed out of her chair and tousled his red hair. Jamie slanted her a frown. "I'll warm up the chicken soup."

"Why can't I have a cheeseburger and fries?"

"Because you're sick and Esme made the soup for you."

Jamie made a face at her. Dory made one back and went into the kitchen. She wasn't expecting Jill. Though it was nearly four thousand square feet, the guesthouse wasn't big enough for her and Jamie. Still, she'd thought Jill would come for her suitcase and clean clothes before she moved into Outlook till Zoe and Felix checked out on Wednesday.

She hadn't seen Jill since she'd walked out of the ballroom. Almost four hours ago Dory noted by the Kliban Cat clock hung on the stone wall by the Dutch door in the breakfast room. She had no idea where Jill was. *And I don't care,* Dory told herself. *So help me Hannah I don't.*

She poured herself a glass of water. Lots of H_2O with the Prevacid, the pharmacist said, then she pulled the top off a can of cat food. Tuna, Rocky's favorite, and boom, there she was. Winding around Dory's ankles, risen from her coma on the chair next to Jamie at the first whiff of albacore. Dory filled Rocky's dish, then almost jumped onto the counter with her when Jamie screamed and came flying into the kitchen.

"Math book!" Dory caught him by the elbow and spun him around.

He raced back to the dining room, gave another shriek, then tore past Dory with his schoolwork, across the kitchen and up the backstairs. Rocky's emerald eyes were huge, her tail bushed out like a bottlebrush.

Jill strolled into the kitchen and grinned. "I love doing that."

"Enjoy it while you can, Elpaba."

"Who's Elpaba?"

"The Wicked Witch of the West."

"Little shit." Jill's gaze narrowed at the backstairs. "Damn it." She snapped her fingers. "I forgot your roses."

"Huh." Dory said. "Imagine that."

She picked up her glass of water and walked into her den. At the far end of the kitchen past the laundry room, tucked behind the stairs and sunken like the dining room, three steps down from a hallway that led to the breezeway and the garage. The walls were stone like the rest of the house, the freestanding bookshelves and the mantel hewn from a giant hickory that had fallen when Aunt Ping and Daddy were children.

Dory put her glass on a soapstone coaster on the desk and shook the mouse to clear the James Dean screen saver from her PC monitor. She reached for her glasses just as Jill leaned over the front of the desk and snatched them up.

"What's with the five bucks? And the ten that Chase took from you?"

"Ask him." Dory held her hand out. "My glasses, please."

"I did ask him. He said it was a private joke."

"A *joke*! He thought it was a *joke*?"

"Apparently." Jill frowned. "What did he say to you?"

Don't tell her, Dory told herself. *Do not tell Jill. You'll regret it if you do,* but she was so angry and so hurt she wanted Jill to be angry and hurt, too. Misery with no one to share it was—well, misery.

"I should've punched him in the eye when I had the chance! That pompous, arrogant, condescending ass! He offered me money if I'd help him convince Charles to retire!"

"You are *kidding* me!" Jill shrieked, bug-eyed. "How much?"

"*Jill!*" Dory cried, appalled.

"Sor-ry." She winced. "What did he say to you *exactly*?"

"He said—" Dory sucked air into her lungs. "I can afford to take care of Dad. I can also afford to compensate Miss Ping for the loss of a valuable employee."

"*That son of a bitch!*" Jill shrilled at a decibel that would crack glass. "Does he think we lost our pride when we lost our money?"

"We didn't *lose* our money. Marshall Phillips took it." *And you're sleeping with one of his minions,* Dory thought, but didn't say so.

Jill narrowed her eyes. "What are we going to do to get even?"

"We aren't getting even. We're getting rid of Chase." Dory spread her hands on the desk. "I was on the verge of kicking him off Outlook after the party tomorrow when you pranced in and tried to tip him, and his brain fell out on the floor."

"It didn't fall on the floor, honey." Jill smiled. "Give me three days."

"What for?" Dory asked warily.

Jill leaned over the desk and put a kiss on her head. "To grind Chase McKay under my heel like a cockroach."

"Oooh," Dory breathed. "I like the way you think, Elpaba."

"I'll start tonight." Jill grinned. "He's taking me to dinner."

Chapter Nine

Operation Cockroach, Phase One
20:00 Hours
Coordinates: Mother and Daddy's Club

By the time Chase picked her up at eight o'clock Jill was starving. If Dory hadn't given her a handful of oyster crackers while she warmed Jamie's chicken soup, she would've eaten every last Starlight mint on the snack bar in the back of the long, white Lincoln limousine.

She hadn't been to the club since Jed Walling brought her here for Peking duck and gave her the diamond and sapphire bracelet so she'd sleep with him. The Lambert family membership was one of the first things to go in the fire sale of their lives, but the maître d' remembered her and bowed. He almost hurt himself kowtowing to Chase.

"Well, you're a big deal," Jill said, once they were seated in a round booth with plush seats and a high back scalloped like a conch shell that overlooked a torch-lit lagoon. "A lot bigger than Daddy used to be."

"It's business." Chase shrugged modestly. "Two senior board members are major investors in the Summit Crest Mall project."

"Lucky for us," Jill replied. "We got the best table."

She could see her reflection in the window behind Chase, the teardrop diamond flashing in the scooped neck of her very little black dress. Dory called it her little black T-shirt.

She'd sold all her jewelry, but Aunt Ping insisted that she keep this two-carat pendant, her twenty-first birthday gift from Daddy. The only jewelry Dory had from their father was her sweet sixteen ruby locket.

"You look very beautiful tonight," Chase said.

"Thank you." Jill smiled and managed not to yawn.

This was the third time he'd told her she looked beautiful. God, she hoped she could stay awake. She didn't sleep on planes and she'd boinked Gary four times during his lunch hour. Chase was as handsome as sin, but dull as beige. A total flatliner. At seventeen, she'd been entranced by the bulge in his jeans, but now she had Gary. What in hell did Dory see in this zero?

Even zero was a number, she said, which made no sense to Jill. But Dory loved numbers, so maybe that was it. She loved Gary. Once she'd annihilated Chase McKay for insulting her family and hurting her baby sister she could get back to their lumpy futon and counting the days till the budget cuts in July. Time to get started.

Jill spread her right hand on the brushed suede seat and leaned toward Chase. The bodice of her dress sloped off her shoulder, pushing her breasts up to fill the gap in her low neckline. Chase's gaze dipped to her cleavage, then jerked back to her face.

"You don't look beautiful. You look gorgeous."

Four times. A sizzling conversationalist.

"You're much handsomer without the baseball cap."

Chase grinned. "You really didn't recognize me?"

"I truly didn't," Jill lied, widening her eyes. That's the story she's sticking to, even with Dory. "But I did think, *ooh*—" She pursed her lips and shivered, which made her jiggle and Chase's gaze drop again. "I wish he'd brought me flowers."

He raised his eyes, a bit slower this time. "Do you like pink roses?"

Jill brushed her bare arm against the sleeve of his flawlessly tailored navy blue suit. "I love pink roses."

Chase's nostrils flared. "I'll remember that."

By the time they finished dinner he could barely remember how to chew. She fed him lobster dipped in butter, ran her fingers up and down her breadsticks, licked chocolate mousse off her top lip. His eyes glazed, his hand trembled as he poured cream in his coffee. His palm cupped around her elbow as they left the club felt just a teensy bit damp.

He opened the moon roof in the limo and suggested a drive.

"That's so romantic, but I'm so tired." Jill let one of the yawns she'd been fighting all evening overcome her. "I was on a plane half the night and I have to get up early to wash my car."

Chase blinked. "You wash your own car?"

She tucked her hand around his arm and gazed up at him through her lashes. "I've become *very* accomplished since you left Outlook."

He made a noise in his throat. "I'd be glad to wash your car."

"That's sweet, but I wouldn't dream of asking you."

"You didn't ask. I volunteered."

"Tell you what," Jill offered. "You can watch."

"What time?" he asked, a rasp in his voice.

"Seven-thirty." She smiled. "I'll honk."

Operation Cockroach, Phase Two
07:30 Hours
Coordinates: Outlook, the driveway

Jill didn't have to honk. Chase was waiting for her.

He'd opened one of the overhead doors and stood inside the garage in jeans and a plaid shirt. The sleeves rolled up, a bucket of sponges in one hand and the hose in a neat coil at his feet.

He waved at her. She smiled and shut off the engine of her red '57 T-bird. Thanks to Charles the little convertible looked and ran like new. Jill slid out from behind the wheel and stepped away from the door.

In a paper-thin white bikini that accented the tan she'd

picked up in L.A., her nipples huge and hard from the early morning chill.

The bucket hit the driveway. Chase's jaw nearly followed.

"Jesus Christ, Jill," he said hoarsely. "Will you marry me?"

"Not until you wash my car." She crooked her finger at him and said seductively, "Now bring that hose over here and let's get started."

Dory completely forgot that Congressman Rowe was invited to Charles' party till he came through the ballroom doors wearing a brown suit, a buttoned-down yellow shirt and a striped tie.

"Who're you s'posed to be, son?" Buck/Gene Autry asked him.

"A politician," Curt replied, deadpan.

"Great get-up." Buck clapped him on the back.

Curt walked past Dory four times and didn't recognize her. Home free, she thought, till she turned away from the soda fountain with a chocolate phosphate in her hand— humming along with "Rock Around the Clock" on the jukebox—and almost smacked into him.

"Dory?" He tipped his head to one side. "Is that you?"

She waggled her white-gloved fingers. "Hi, Curt."

"Clarabell the Clown, right?"

"How'd you guess? I look like a Kewpie doll in her pajamas."

"Now that you mention it." He eyed her baggy, pink and blue zebra-striped jumpsuit. "That's exactly what you look like."

"I had to improvise the hair." Dory shook the red string mop on her head. "The wig that came with the costume was way too big."

"Your nose is cute." Curt wrinkled his at the giant red bulb in the middle of her face.

"Squeeze it," she said. "Go ahead. Give it a squeeze."

He did and her nose honked. Curt laughed.

"See?" Dory grinned. "It's a giant squeaky toy."

"Great schnoz, Clarabell. Where's Howdy Doody?"

"Dancing with Jill." Dory nodded at the center of the ballroom.

Chase was dressed like James Dean. Rolled-up jeans and a white T-shirt, black leather biker jacket and slicked-back hair. His arms and legs jerked in spasms like a marionette with broken strings. About two beats off the music and the rest of the dancers.

"You're his friend," Dory said. "You should tell him he can't dance."

"He never could. Herman Munster has a better sense of rhythm." Curt shook his head watching Chase, then he glanced at Jill in her white chiffon halter dress and platinum Marilyn Monroe wig, the dazzling smile on her face aimed at Chase. "Okay. Now I get it." Curt turned toward Dory. "He was fine Friday. When did this hit him?"

"Yesterday." She sucked a mouthful of phosphate through a straw so she wouldn't smear her red greasepaint mouth. "The second he laid eyes on Jill."

Curt looked at Chase again, shook his head again. "I know that vacant, glassy-eyed expression. I used to see it in my shaving mirror."

"Hard to believe, isn't it, that the president of a Fortune 500 company has no idea he's making a fool of himself."

"You mean on the dance floor or salivating over Jill?"

"Both," Dory said and Curt laughed.

So did she till "Rock Around the Clock" ended and "Tears of a Clown" began. Then her breath caught on a tiny sob in her throat.

Curt offered his hand and a tentative smile. "Care to dance?"

"I'd love to dance. Let me take off my feet."

Dory left her flat, floppy Clarabell shoes and her phosphate behind the soda fountain, took Curt's hand and followed him into the throng of dancers. If she'd learned nothing else from Uncle Scrooge she'd learned that you'd better figure out a way to be happy no matter where, when or how you found yourself 'cause nobody else was going to do it for you.

So Dory enjoyed the party. She danced with Curt and the birthday boy, who was dressed like Chase and told her he was James Dean Sr. Eddie came as Eddie Arcaro, the great jockey of the '50s, in riding boots and orange silks. He was a head shorter than Esther was in her pencil thin gray skirt and yellow sweater, but boy, could they dance.

Esme was a short-order cook, a white fly-boy cap like Wallace's on her head, mustard and ketchup and grease stains on her apron. Everyone cheered when she came in pushing a trolley piled with cheeseburgers and homemade French fries.

Peter and Henry were supposed to be beatniks. They looked like burnt marshmallows stuck on toothpicks in black leggings, turtlenecks and berets. Deirdre twirled on the dance floor every chance she got to make her poodle skirt flare and show off her four pastel net petticoats.

Diego looked *fabuloso*. Black bolero jacket stamped with silver and sequins, black pants and boots and silver spurs, a ruffled shirt and red sash. He looked like Tyrone Power and had Anita swooning like Linda Darnell in *Zorro* even though she was old enough to be his grandmother.

But Aunt Ping stole the show as Carmen Miranda.

A slit-up-the-front tropical print skirt and red platform shoes, flouncy white blouse that showed a bit of collarbone, chunky bracelets up to the elbow and the fruit-piled headdress that Deirdre said looked like a trifle without the bowl. Curt said it looked like Marge Simpson's hair run amok in the produce department.

Diego bowed to Aunt Ping, swept his Flying-Nun-sized sombrero at her feet and led her out to dance the samba. She didn't just keep up with him, she hoochie-coochied Diego off his feet.

Dory's mouth fell open. Where and when had Aunt Ping learned to samba like she was born in Brazil?

She watched Charles watch Aunt Ping, but the grin on his face wasn't any bigger than anyone else's. Aunt Ping didn't flick so much as an eyelash at him. At the end of the dance she bowed with Diego to whistles and applause and let him escort her off the floor. Charles turned away to talk to Tom and Buck, probably about the steers.

"Wow," Curt said beside her. "They're good, those two."

"Tell me about it," Dory replied. *Years of practice,* she thought. She wondered how many, how long she'd been in a coma and hadn't noticed.

As arranged, Zoe and Felix as Mr. and Mrs. Howell stayed till four o'clock. They waved to Dory on their way out of the ballroom; she waved back and slipped outside onto the terrace to call Jamie on her cell phone.

"Coast is clear," she said. "The Morgensterns just left."

"Did you save me a cheeseburger and fries?"

"I did and Wallace is making you a chocolate milk shake."

"Cool. I'm on my way."

"Don't run. You'll sweat and start itching again."

"Okay, okay." Dory could hear Jamie rolling his eyes. "I'll walk."

She flipped her phone shut and dropped it in her pocket, felt a paper-wrapped straw she'd slipped in there and plucked it out. She tore the end off as she turned toward the French doors to go back inside—just as Chase stepped outside, shaking a cigarette out of his pack.

"Cute costume, squirt." He lit up and squinted at her through the smoke like she was still a pudgy, homely, fourteen-year-old dweeb. "Jill says your nose honks."

Dory blew the paper off the straw. Right in his face. It caught him in the corner of the eye, made him blink and wheel away. Dory honked her nose at him and went inside.

He wouldn't buy *her* dinner but he'd take Jill to the club in a limo. She hoped she'd put his eye out, then worried that she had. Till he stepped into the ballroom and scanned the crowd with a bloodshot eye and a scowl on his face that morphed into a brain-in-his-pants grin when Jill sashayed up to him and trailed a finger down his chest.

"I can't watch this," Dory said under her breath.

"It's enough to ruin your appetite for birthday cake," Curt said behind her. "That's for sure."

Dory turned to face him. "What happened with you and Jill?"

"I'm too short for her."

That didn't make sense. Gary wasn't much taller. Curt shrugged and smiled but didn't quite look at her. He wasn't telling the truth.

They stood close enough to the French doors that a flash of movement caught Dory's eye and turned her head in time to see Jamie shoot into the ballroom, skidding on the marble floor in his cowboy boots.

He was supposed to be Howdy Doody. The pompadour she'd combed into the front of his red hair with half a can of mousse was falling over his forehead. He'd done exactly what she'd told him not to, the little pain. He'd run all the way from the guesthouse.

"Excuse me," she said to Curt and started toward Jamie.

He was out of breath. That's why she could see his heart pounding in his throat, Dory thought, till she drew close enough to see white lines pinched at the corners of his mouth where she'd drawn dark ones with an eyebrow pencil so he'd look like a wooden puppet with a hinged jaw. What he looked like now was a scared little boy.

And Jamie wasn't afraid of anything.

"Are you okay?" she asked. "You're pale as a ghost."

"I don't feel too good." Jamie swiped at his hair with a shaky hand. "You told me not to run. It made me sick."

He was nervous and jumpy, his eyes darting at the guests turning to look at them. Dory pulled him outside onto the terrace.

"The truth, Jamie." She gripped his arms. "What happened?"

"I'm a dork, okay?" He stuck his chin up but his mouth trembled. "I thought there was somebody following me."

"Did you come up the road or the footpath?"

"The path. I heard noises and it looked like the trees were moving."

"Deer don't usually come this close to the house, but—"

"I mean the trees were *moving*. Like walking along beside me."

Dory pressed her lips to Jamie's forehead. He felt clammy, a bit warm but not warm enough to be running a temperature.

"No fever, so I concur with your diagnosis, doctor. You're a dork."

"Told you," he said and Dory felt him relax, the tension ease out of his thin little arms. "Can I go eat my cheeseburger?"

"Sure." She let him go. "Wallace has it at the soda fountain."

Jamie went inside. Dory went down the terrace steps in the pink slipper socks with nonslip soles she'd put on under her Clarabell shoes to keep them from falling off her feet.

It wasn't unheard of for deer to come this close to the house, but not in spring and sure as heck not in the middle of the day. She followed the flagged walk through the ornamental garden. Where it intersected the gravel path that led to the guesthouse she stopped and eyed the trees.

Maples and other softwoods that had leafed out in the last two days formed a canopy over the path. None of the trees looked like they'd been walking around like the Ents of Middle-earth. She hadn't expected them to; still Dory frowned, remembering the gates standing open in the dark and in the fog.

In spite of his juvenile-hall behavior, Jamie was not given to seeing things. If he said the trees moved, then they moved. She just couldn't figure out why. Not from here, anyway.

Dory picked up a stick and started down the path. It was

mostly shady but the sun splashed in places. Every few yards she gave the split rail fence that held the trees back a good whack, but she didn't flush a darn thing. When she could see the red tile roof of the guesthouse through the trees she stopped and gave the fence one last crack with the stick.

About ten yards in front of her a doe and fawn leaped the fence and skittered away down the path, their white tails flashing. Dory grinned. Okay. So she wasn't Marlin Perkins, but the limbs of the maples quaking behind the doe and her fawn explained the walking trees.

So she thought till a breeze stirred and fluttered something caught on the fence. It looked like a small branch blown off one of the maples. Dory was positive that's all it was, but stepped closer to make certain.

It wasn't a branch. It was a scrap of camouflage material. Snagged on a nailhead on the *inside* of the fence.

Gooseflesh shot through Dory. She wanted to whirl and run—just as Jamie had, she was sure—for the second it took her to reason that the doe and her fawn would've been long gone if there was someone else lurking around. Someone in a camouflage shirt or jacket who had trailed Jamie along the inside of the fence—which would sure as heck make it look like the trees were walking along beside him. Holy crap.

Her fingers trembling inside Clarabell's white gloves, Dory worked the material free of the nail. With her foot she moved a rock against the fence to mark where she'd found it, held the scrap gingerly between two fingers and headed for the guesthouse to put it in a baggie.

What she was going to do with it from there she hadn't a clue.

An-hour. An-hour. He'd-see-her-in-an-hour. An-hour.
Chase stood under the pulsating showerhead in his father's bathroom over the garage, closed his eyes and let the hot spray beat the mantra into his head.
He'd-see-her-in-an-hour. An-hour. An-hour.

If he stayed. Chase turned his shoulders to the massage head and squeezed water out of his eyes with his thumb and forefinger. If he didn't jump into his clothes and grab the first flight back to New York.

Stay or go. He had to decide while he could still think straight. In Jill's presence he couldn't think at all. His brain went to his crotch and stayed there. He hadn't felt like this since he was nineteen, nothing but one giant hormone. It was a total rush—and scary as hell.

He poured shampoo into his hand and scrubbed the Brylcreem hair out of his scalp he'd used to slick back his. He'd asked Jill to dinner again, asked her to wear the white chiffon dress. All afternoon he'd fantasized about unfastening its halter top. He'd either undo the button at the back of her neck tonight or he'd shake her hand and get on a plane.

There was no in between with Jill—there never had been—it was all or nothing.

No gray with her cute as a bug, pain in the butt little sister, either. It was black or white. Pick one. And no apologies accepted.

Chase rinsed his hair and shut off the water, tied a towel around his waist and peered at his face in the mirror. His left eye was still bloodshot. Served him right, he guessed, for all the sponges he'd thrown at her.

He dried his hair, buzzed his razor over his jaw and got dressed. Gray suit, blue shirt and gray and red striped tie. He put his watch on—six forty-five—and picked up his cigarettes. He had time for a smoke on the roof before he picked Jill up.

She was staying at Outlook because Jamie was in quarantine at the guesthouse and Jill couldn't stand him. Normally she liked kids, she said, so long as they were someone else's. Same with him. He didn't especially yearn for offspring so they were in sync on that score.

He and Jill were in sync on a lot of things. He couldn't remember what exactly—he could barely remember his name within ten feet of her—but they'd talked all evening long. You couldn't be enthralled by someone with whom you had nothing in common.

It was nearly dusk. The lights on the wall around the garage roof had come on. Curt sat next to one of them in a brown suit, his tie loose at his collar, his legs stretched out in front of him and his arms folded. He glanced up from his crossed ankles when Chase stepped outside.

"Curt." He pulled the door shut. "Why didn't you knock?"

"I did. You didn't hear me."

"I was in the shower. What are you doing here?"

"You invited me to your dad's party."

"I know I did, but I didn't see you."

"You couldn't see anybody but Jill."

"Treading on your toes, am I?"

"Not at all." Curt stood up and put his hands in his pockets. "Do you know what you're doing, buddy?"

Chase's temper flared. So did his lighter as he lit a cigarette, drew a deep breath to inhale and exhaled slowly. "You mean with Jill."

"At lunch Friday she was queen of the schemers." Curt shrugged. "I'm just wondering what changed your opinion."

Her mouth, her breasts and her wrap-'em-around-me-honey legs, Chase thought, then scowled and pushed Jill's image out of his mind.

"I've gotten to know her better," he said.

"In two days? You work fast." Curt smiled. "So does she."

"Meaning *what,* Congressman?"

"Hey. Calm down." Curt raised a hand. "Watch yourself if she gets near a basket of breadsticks." He twiddled his fingers in the air like he was playing a piccolo. "Puts all kinds of thoughts in a man's head."

The memory of Jill fondling the Stella Doros at dinner last night shifted uncomfortably in Chase's head. "I know what I'm doing."

"Hope so, buddy." Curt moved toward the stairs. "I'm

heading back to Washington tonight. Take care of your-self."

Chase moved to the wall and watched Curt drive away.

He supposed his friend meant well, but what happened—or hadn't happened—between Curt and Jill had nothing to do with him and Jill.

Absolutely nothing.

Operation Cockroach, Phase Three
19:30 Hours
Coordinates: Footbridge over Brush Creek
Country Club Plaza

Jill leaned her elbows on the railing next to Chase and watched him pitch half-dollars into the water. He was just showing off, but if he started pitching fifty-dollar bills she was diving in after them.

He probably thought this was romantic. She thought it was dumb, but he'd wanted to see the new bridge so they'd crossed Ward Parkway after dinner at the Rafael Hotel, holding hands and dodging traffic.

The old footbridge had been torn down with the flood control project that tamed Brush Creek. Which every time it rained hard used to roar like the Colorado River down the middle of Ward Parkway between the north and south-bound lanes and its grassy, tree-lined banks.

The new bridge had a higher arch than the old one. A snazzy rail and carriage lamps were mounted every few feet on black iron posts. Jill had fond memories of the old, unlit bridge where she'd spent many a hot, horny night being fondled by her high school boyfriends. In her opinion the new bridge was a yawn. Just like Chase.

At least he had an edge to him tonight. A glint in his eyes, a clench in his jaw. He scowled when he thought she wasn't looking. It made him only slightly more interesting than Dory when she got wound up and went on and on ad nauseam about interest rates.

If Jill had to bet, she'd bet Chase was royally pissed at someone.

He'd taken his jacket off, laid it over her shoulders to keep her bare back warm and rolled up his cuffs. The light from the closest lamp silvered the hair on his forearms. She liked hairy men. Gary was smooth as an egg. Chase, if she was remembering the right body, had a nice lush thatch of soft, golden chest hair.

The water sliding beneath the bridge flickered with reflections. Jill lifted her gaze past the lights of the Plaza, north toward Westport and stifled a sigh. Gary was less than two miles away and here she was stuck with Studly Dead Bore. The things she did for Dory and the family honor.

Chase tossed his last fifty-cent piece, leaned his elbows on the rail, laced his fingers together and turned his head toward her. "You're an absolute knockout in that dress."

"I'm glad you didn't ask me to wear the wig." She tucked her hand in the curve of his elbow. "It itches like crazy."

He scowled and rubbed the corner of his left eye.

"Stop that." Jill slapped his arm. "You have yet to tell me how your eye got all bloodshot."

"Your sister. She blew the sleeve off a straw right into my eye."

"I'm sure she didn't mean to."

"Oh, she meant to, all right."

"What did you do to her?"

He turned the scowl on Jill. "I told her her costume was cute."

"Chase. For future reference, cute is not a compliment. Cute is an insult. You're lucky it was a straw, not a blow-gun."

"What was I supposed to say to her?" He pushed up on one elbow. "You look ridiculous with that nose and a mop on your head?"

No, stupid! Jill wanted to slap him. *You were supposed*

to say a meteor just fell on my head and made me realize I love you!

She plucked his keys out of the pocket, shrugged out of his coat and threw it at him. She made it off the bridge and across Ward Parkway, stuck the key in the lock of the passenger door of his truck before he caught her by the shoulders and spun her around.

"Don't you *ever* insult Dory again!" Jill pushed the heel of her right hand against his chest. "Do you hear me? Don't you *dare*!"

"Christ, Jill. You're driving me crazy." He pinned her against the truck, pressed his big, hot, hard body against her. "Pick a hotel. Any hotel. The bridal suite. The presidential suite. Whatever you want."

Two dinners, one limo ride. No flowers, no presents, and she was supposed to jump in the sack with him? Dream on! To hell with Dory and the Lambert family honor. She was done with this obnoxious jerk.

"Whatever I want?" Jill held up her left hand and wiggled her naked third finger. "Minimum five carats. Marquise cut, platinum band. Or take me home and don't ever touch me again."

Chase's hands flew off her shoulders, exactly as Jill expected. She smiled. He scowled, stepped back and took her elbow, opened the door and helped her up into the seat.

"Thank you," she said primly and slammed the door in his face.

In the rearview mirror Jill watched Chase walk toward the back of the truck. When he paused at the curb to let a stream of traffic pass, she snatched her cell phone out of her purse and punched Gary's number.

"Don't ever call him on your cell," Dory had cautioned her. "I don't care if it's a life and death emergency, find a pay phone."

On a Sunday night on the Plaza? Fat chance. She was so angry, so disgusted. So aroused thinking about Gary's bald-as-a-cue-ball body she didn't care if Chase heard the call.

"Warm up the futon," she said when Gary answered.

"Jill?" he said sharply. "Are you on your cell phone?"

"I'll meet you at the Happy Spirit in an hour."

"Hang up. *Now*. I'll be ready."

"You always are, baby," Jill purred, pushed END and shivered with anticipation.

Chapter Ten

"Kids playin' paintball," Tom said about the scrap of camouflage. "I've chased 'em out of the fields and the woods along the fences. I've found a couple steers and cows with paint on their hides, too."

"Kids playing paintball," Dory said. "So close to the house?"

Tom shrugged. "Some kids ain't real bright, Miss Dory, or respectful of private property. I'll keep a sharper eye."

"Thanks. And I'd appreciate it if you'd keep this under your hat."

"Meanin' don't tell Miss Ping." Tom smiled. "My lips are sealed."

Eddie was soaping a bay Arab cross-tied in the cement-floored bathing stall. Easter and the Outlook Inn's busy season were only a week away, so Eddie was bringing the horses in for a bath and a refresher course on the lunge line in Mother's riding arena. He gave his sponge to one of his grooms and stepped outside the barn with Dory.

"I haven't seen any of my boys wear anything like this." Eddie gave the plastic-wrapped scrap back to her. "I'm with Tom. It's kids. Some of 'em 'round here got too much money and nothin' to do. They've run the horses a time or two. I've warned 'em and so has the sheriff they could get kicked or bit, but it don't seem to faze 'em."

Dory knew about those incidents. "Have the kids in the neighborhood been sneaking onto Outlook lately?"

"No ma'am. Me or Tom would've told you."

She knew that, too, asked Eddie not to say anything and headed for the greenhouse. Peter tended to overreact, but he knew the grounds around the house better than anyone except Aunt Ping.

The greenhouse smelled heavy on manure thanks to the morning sun beaming through the glass roof. Peter was lugging flats of annuals outside to harden them off. Outlook had about a million flower beds; Peter had about a million flats. Dory carried a few for him.

He frowned when he stopped to examine the piece of green and tan and brown fabric in its baggie. "Show me where you found this."

She led him down the footpath to the rock she'd left as a marker. Peter swung over the fence and disappeared into the trees. He liked order and clear spaces; Aunt Ping preferred *au naturel*. They'd disagreed about the tangle of undergrowth along the footpath more than once.

Dory couldn't see Peter but she could hear him. Every time a twig snapped she started, every time a branch bobbed she shivered remembering the gooseflesh that rushed through her when she'd found the scrap. The frightened look on Jamie's face had kept her awake past midnight checking the locks and wishing Rocky was a Rottweiler.

"No sign of deer. Not on this side of the path." Peter came out of the trees, brushing leaves and plucking stickers off his sleeves. "The weeds don't look like they've been disturbed in years. You know what that, plus a camouflage jacket sounds like, don't you?"

"Yeah, I do." Dory sighed. "Our friends in the orchard."

If you didn't judge by Gary, you'd assume a FBI agent was smart enough to wear camouflage and skilled enough to skulk through the bushes without leaving a trace. But skulking could be risky. If it was a G-man yesterday, he'd been seen or at least sensed by Jamie. What would compel the feds to skulk? The budget cuts? Or had they been skulking all along and this was the first time they'd been detected?

Dory didn't want to think that of Agent Frasier. She used the gold Cross pen he and his then-partner had given her every day. When they'd opened the Outlook Inn, he'd agreed to pull his team back to the orchard. Was this the trade-off for making themselves invisible?

"Maybe I should take a walk in the orchard," Dory said to Peter, "and smell the cherry blossoms."

But first she had to smell pink roses. A billion of them arrived in a humongous bouquet a little after nine, just as Anita was leaving the office to make her Monday morning run to the bank.

Wallace brought the vase into the office and set it on Jill's desk, his expression as solemn as if he carried a funeral wreath.

Jill plucked the card off its clear plastic clip and read: "I'm sorry about last night. I'd like to apologize over dinner. L—Chase."

"L?" Dory asked. "What's that? Love? Like?"

"Lust." Jill frowned. "He got a little carried away last night."

"I don't want to hear about it." Dory held up a hand. "I just want to remind you that the three days you asked for are up tomorrow."

"Why is he still here?" Jill tossed the card on her desk and glared at it. "I told him if he wanted to put his hands on me he'd better put a five-carat marquise diamond with a platinum band on my finger."

"Holy crap, Jill!" Dory cried. "What about Gary?"

"Oh, relax. It worked with Jed Walling. I got a six-thousand-dollar bracelet for the Servants' Fund. Five carats ought to put us at least twenty grand closer to closing the Outlook Inn."

"Twenty thousand is a drop in the bucket," Dory snapped, all the dreams she'd had of Chase putting his hands all over her crashing and burning in her head. "We need twenty million to fund the Outlook Trust."

"*Twenty million?* How much have we got?"

"About five."

"That's *all*?" Jill's jaw dropped. "We've been busting our butts for six years and we only have five lousy million?"

"Six years ago we didn't have five cents. After expenses, salaries, taxes and insurance, an eight hundred-and-thirty-thousand-dollar a year profit is pretty good. We should make a million, maybe a million five this year. If business keeps picking up, next year we could clear close to two."

"It will still take *seven years* to make twenty million dollars!"

"In my original business plan, I calculated it would take ten. We're ahead of my projection." Dory put her hands on her hips. "Did you read the plan? Do you read the profit and loss statements I issue every year?"

"In seven years I'll be forty." Jill glared at her. "Aunt Ping will be almost seventy. She can't do this for seven more years."

"Do you have a better idea?"

Jill opened her mouth, shut it and dropped into her chair. "No."

She sat there for a minute looking stunned, like Chase had in the ballroom on Saturday—smacked with a two-by-four—then she reached for the pile of invitations that had come in the mail while she was in L.A.

Dory watched Jill flip through them and reach for her calendar. The expression on her face was all business, but the wheels in her head were turning. Dory could hear them. They were rusty and they squeaked.

Jill only looked up once, when Gordy, their electronic surveillance expert, arrived in his plumber's disguise to check the phones.

"Isn't he a week early?" Jill asked suspiciously.

"No," Dory said, which was the truth. He was two weeks early.

Anita didn't comment, just glanced at Dory from her PC where she was typing acceptance letters to the applicants they'd approved at the prospective guest committee meeting last Friday.

Dory left the office with Gordy. She didn't usually follow

him on his rounds but she did today. On their way back to
Outlook from the guesthouse, where Esther was sitting
with Jamie and Jamie was in a total snit about it, Dory
showed Gordy the rock and the camouflage scrap.

"This is why you called me last night," he said.

"Yes. Tom and Eddie think it's kids sneaking through the
fence to play paintball. Peter thinks it might be the FBI."

"It's sure not a deer." Gordy gave the scrap back to her.
"Outlook's perimeter is a nightmare, but you know that.
We've talked about it."

"Tell me again how much razor wire costs by the foot."

Dory smiled wryly, making a joke. Gordy smiled back,
kindly.

"Have you hired anybody new lately?"

"How lately? Our last full-time hire was Diego, last
March. He worked for us part-time for two years before
that."

"Want me to nose around? Talk to Tom, Eddie and
Peter?"

"Yes I would, please."

"It probably is just kids, but I'll let you know."

Gordy wasn't a tall man, maybe five seven. He had a little round paunch and a sprinkle of gray in his dark hair
and clipped mustache. He reminded Dory of Daddy, of
how Del Lambert might look these days. The pat on the
arm Gordy gave her as he turned back down the path
toward the greenhouse made Dory's throat swell.

If she could get her hands on her father she'd wring his
neck.

Chase called at two-thirty. Dory bet Anita while Jill was
in the bathroom that he wouldn't call at all, that he'd just
show up.

Anita answered the phone, pushed hold and swiveled her
chair toward Jill. "Chase McKay for you," she said. "Line
one."

She gave Dory a look that said you-owe-me-five-bucks,

took her cigarettes out of her desk and headed for the terrace to smoke.

Jill rolled her eyes at the gargantuan bouquet of pink roses. It was ten times bigger than the arrangement Chase had sent Dory. When Jill reached for the phone, Dory got up to follow Anita.

"Stop right there," Jill said. "I'm doing this for you."

"Don't put this on me." Dory turned around and saw Jill's finger on SPEAKER. "Don't push that button, either. Grinding Chase under your heel was your idea."

"Oh, right. That's why your eyes lit up like it was Christmas." Jill punched SPEAKER, said in her smooth coordinator of public relations voice, "Jill Lambert. How may I help you?"

Dory spun toward the pocket doors. "Do you still love pink roses?" Chase asked and she was caught, trapped by the caress in his voice.

"Yes," Jill replied coolly. "Lucky for you."

"May I take you to dinner? I bought you a present."

"Is it five carats, marquise cut with a platinum band?" Jill asked and Dory held her breath.

"No." Chase chuckled. "But I think you'll like it."

"All right. Pick me up at seven. In a limo or don't bother."

"Yes, ma'am." Dory heard the grin in his voice. "And I promise I will never, ever again so help me God say that your sister looks ridiculous."

Jill gave a startled, strangled gasp. Chase said, "Are you all right?"

Dory shoved the doors open like Aunt Ping had, so hard they cracked like a pistol shot and bounced out of their pockets.

"What was that?" she heard Chase say as she ran out of the office. "Christ, Jill! Have you got me on the speaker?"

Jill wanted Chase tied by his wrists to two of Mother's Arabs and tied by his ankles to two of her saddlebreds. She wanted a riding crop in Dory's hand and then she wanted a gun so she could shoot herself.

It took her five minutes to get Chase off the phone. He yelled at her for being thoughtless and cruel. She yelled back at him that she'd hit SPEAKER by accident. Finally she hung up on him and went tearing out of the office, leaving Anita to cover the phones.

She missed Dory at the guesthouse. Esther said she'd raced upstairs, changed into jeans, her Reeboks and a sweatshirt, grabbed a windbreaker and a ball cap off the hall tree and raced out again. She didn't even check on the monster, and boy, was he pissed because he wasn't the center of Dory's attention for a change. The little shit.

Dory wasn't in the greenhouse or floating facedown in the pool in the pool house. She'd run out of the office without her cell phone or her walkie-talkie and so had Jill. She called Eddie on the house phone. He hadn't seen Dory and neither had Tom. Jill called Anita—no Dory—then she called Diego, told him to bring her car, her cell phone and her walkie-talkie and to be quick about it.

While she waited for him, she called Tom, Eddie and Peter and told them if Dory turned up to let her know ASAP.

"Miss Dory isn't in the house." Diego slid out of her T-bird and held the driver's door for her. "Mr. Wallace had the maids check every room."

"Oh hell. Does Miss Ping realize Dory is missing?"

"No. She and Mrs. Deirdre are playing bridge with Zoe and Felix."

"Thank God." Jill jumped behind the wheel, saw her cell phone and her walkie-talkie in the passenger seat, shut the door and stepped on the gas.

All the golf carts were parked and plugged in, which meant Dory was still on foot. Jill glanced at the dash clock. How far could she have gotten in twenty minutes and where would she go? The Rock Garden? The Rose Garden? The Lily Pond? The Japanese Garden? The Shakespeare Garden? The Poet's Garden with its busts of Keats and Whitman?

Her cell phone rang. Jill grabbed it. "Hello?"

"Where are you?" Chase asked. She heard a jackhammer in the background. Oh goody. He was still at the job site—if God was a woman, his truck would be parked next to a crane with a clumsy operator who'd drop a steel girder on the cab and save her the trouble of killing him. "How did you get this number?"

"Your secretary gave it to me. Have you found Dory?"

"If I had I wouldn't be on my cell phone."

"I'm heading that way to help you look for her."

"She isn't a lost dog, Chase. She's a woman." Pretty, smart, funny, Jill thought, and way too good for you. "I can't find Dory because she doesn't want me to. I can't imagine she'd want you to find her, either."

"You're right. I'm sorry. You aren't thoughtless or cruel. I'm the one who said Dory looked ridiculous. You just pressed SPEAKER accidentally." Chase sighed. "I guess I should cancel the limo."

Jill guessed she should confess. Squashing Chase like a cockroach was the worst idea she'd ever had, but it was all his fault. People born poor were supposed to stay poor. They weren't supposed to end up with millions and offer money to those who were born rich but were now poor. People who desperately needed the money and could never accept it.

It wasn't fair. It just was *not* fair.

"If you want to have dinner with me," Jill said, "I wouldn't."

The orchard was huge, a lot bigger than Dory remembered from her childhood when she'd followed Jill and Chase over here and they'd thrown green apples at her to make her go away.

Where had her head been then? She should've seen the pink roses and "L-Chase" coming when she was eleven years old.

Dory wandered through the cherry trees, the peaches and half of the stooped, gnarled apple trees, following every tractor path she came to in search of a beige sedan with GS plates and two men scrunched in the front seat trying to look invisible. Could she find it? Of course not.

She did find some peace in the shade between the rows of fruit trees and the breeze that sprinkled tiny white blossoms on the bill of her Kansas City Royals baseball cap. The air was still except for the rustle of leaves and the drone of bees. No speakerphones. No born to be rich but now she was poor and mad as hell about it, sister. It was a pleasant, fragrant walk for a couple hours, till she started getting hot and tired.

The windbreaker tied around her waist weighed like a rock. Her head was sweating inside her ball cap. Her nose itched with sunburn.

When she came out of the trees for the umpteenth time by the produce stand, Dory pulled a webbed nylon campstool out from under the counter and unfolded it beneath an elm on the fringe of the orchard.

The surest way to find something, Aunt Ping said, was to stop looking for it. So Dory stopped looking for the FBI and sat down.

It didn't take two minutes for the fed mobile to come rolling out of the orchard. Up the center tractor path, its undercarriage squeaking and the long antenna on the front fender whipping leaves off the trees. Agent Frasier climbed out from behind the wheel, a burly man in a rumpled tan suit with blue eyes, a freckled face and thinning, wiry red hair.

"Miss Lambert." He nodded to her.

"Agent Frasier." Dory stood up, peering through the windshield at the empty front seat. "Where's your partner?"

"Answering a call of nature." He smiled, a twinkle in his eyes. "I told him to watch out for poison ivy, so it'll take him a few minutes."

"New guy, huh?"

"Fresh out of the Academy."

"I found this yesterday." Dory pulled the camouflage scrap out of her pocket and handed it to him. "Caught on a nail in the split rail fence along the footpath between the guesthouse and Outlook. Jamie thought someone was following him. He said the trees looked like they were walking along beside him."

"You were smart to bag it." Frasier plucked a pair of half-lenses out of his breast pocket and held the scrap up to the sun.

He looked it over from both sides, his lips pursed, smoothing it out inside the baggie with his thumb. Dory watched, her throat pounding.

"It wasn't one of my guys." Frasier gave the scrap back to her, took off his glasses and smiled. "I assume that's what you want to hear."

"Yes and no. If it wasn't the FBI, who was it?"

"What do your people say?"

"Kids sneaking through the fence to play paintball."

"You don't believe that or we wouldn't be having this conversation."

"I have to check out all the possibilities."

"You could call the locals, let them have a look-see."

"I could, but if it's only kids I don't want to alarm the guests."

"We would need a court order to hide in the bushes, to keep things neat and legal in case we found something." Frasier grinned. "Uncle Scrooge can't find a judge who'll give him one."

"I keep trying to come up with another name, but you know." Dory shrugged and put the scrap in her pocket. "That one's just so perfect."

"The new guy spilled coffee in his crotch the first time he heard it." Dory laughed. Frasier smiled. "Tell you what. We'll increase our drives around the perimeter. Don't worry. We'll be discreet."

"Thank you, Agent Frasier."

"Take care, Miss Lambert."

He nodded and got in the car, put it in reverse and backed down the tractor path. Dory sighed, took off her cap and wiped the sleeve of her sweatshirt across her sweaty forehead. Since he'd called Marshall Phillips Uncle Scrooge, she doubted the United States attorney would hear about her chat with Agent Frasier.

That was a relief; she'd been worried about Phillips. Every day of her life for the last ten years she'd been worried about Marshall Phillips. She hoped Gary was right about the budget cuts.

Hurry, July. *Hurry.*

Dory didn't look like a lost dog. She looked tired, trudging slump-shouldered along the edge of the front drive.

Chase saw her when he turned the Expedition through the open gates; she was about fifty yards ahead of the truck. She had on jeans, a red sweatshirt, a yellow jacket tied around her and a royal blue ball cap.

He reached for his cell to call Jill, scowled and shut it off, put it in the glove box with the six-carat sapphire bracelet he'd bought her in its black velvet case, and stepped on the gas to rev the engine. Dory heard it, glanced over her shoulder, turned away and kept on trudging.

Chase didn't blame her. He drove up beside her and pushed the button to lower the passenger window. Her face was beet-red and glistening with sweat. "Need a lift?"

"No." She kept walking, didn't even glance at the truck.

Chase stepped on the brake. The Expedition stopped but Dory didn't. He watched her slog on, leaning forward and digging in to climb the first terrace. He could feel the burn in his calves. When she stumbled and almost fell into a bed of jonquils, he took his foot off the brake.

Sped past her, wheeled the nose of the Expedition off the drive into the grass, leaned over the console and shoved the door open, cutting her off and wedging her between the truck and the rock wall of the flower bed. Over the tan leather seat he could only see the top of her head and her brown eyes, wide-open and startled as she swung toward him.

"This is ridiculous. You're falling on your face. Get in."

"I would rather—" Her voice broke and her eyes spilled over. Jesus. She was so exhausted she was crying. She dragged a sleeve across her face and sucked a breath. "I would rather crawl."

"You're pissed at me. I understand that. But you look like you just finished roofing a two-thousand-square-foot house all by yourself. It must be close to eighty degrees. You're in a sweatshirt. The only way you're going to get up the drive on your own is *if* you crawl."

Chase lifted a liter bottle of water from the cup holder. He broke the seal to let her know it was unopened, twisted the cap off and passed it to her. She was smart enough to sip, not guzzle.

"Splash your face," he said. "And the back of your neck."

She did, her hands shaking, and sighed with relief.

"Are you getting in?" Chase asked. "Or making a break for it?"

"I'm getting in." She passed him the bottle, put one foot on the running board so she could reach the strap and swung into the seat like she was Tarzan—make that Jane—swooping through the jungle on a grapevine. It was a nice maneuver, but she couldn't reach the door.

"I'll get it." Chase started to lean across her, but she whipped her head around and stopped him with a glare. "*I* will get it."

She had to hang from the strap again—part squirt, part monkey—but she managed to catch the armrest and haul the heavy door shut.

He flipped the air on high. Her sweat-spiked hair, sticking out in tufts around her ball cap, barely moved in the ice-cold blast. Her nose looked redder than the goofy, round squeak ball she'd had on her face yesterday. She clipped her seat belt and looked straight ahead.

Chase backed the truck out of the grass. The tires had left deep tread marks. If he explained that he'd saved Dory from heatstroke Peter might not kill him. He drove up the first terrace and glanced at her.

"You weren't running around screaming again, were you?"

She turned her head and looked out the side window. Okay. Still on the shit list. She shivered and Chase saw that the neck of her sweatshirt was wet. He turned the fan down. She sneezed.

"God bless you," he said.

She sneezed again, then sniffed. He turned the fan down another notch, nudged the temperature toward warm. She sneezed a third time. He had no Kleenex. A handkerchief was in the back pocket of his jeans but it was probably as dusty a mess as the rest of him.

He'd worked with the framing crew after lunch to let off the head of steam he was building for Jill. Dory chilled easily—her teeth had chattered around the s'mores fire Thursday night—and her nose was sensitive. She'd sneezed like crazy in the apple-wood smoke.

The truck stank of cigarettes. He'd smoked four between the job site and Outlook. He cracked his window to let in some fresh air.

Now that he had Dory he wasn't sure what to do with her, where he should take her—Outlook? The guesthouse?— or where she wanted to go. She didn't tell him, just folded her arms and huddled into them, so Chase decided. He drove past the big house toward the garage. Pink streaks of cloud were swirled together above the flat part of the roof. Chase glanced at the dash clock. Nearly five o'clock.

Except for the greenhouse the garage was the biggest outbuilding on Outlook, constructed of the same rose brick as the house, with room to park twenty cars four-deep behind the white, vinyl-clad steel overhead doors. The sixth door was a service bay with a hydraulic lift.

Diego slept on the ground floor in the assistant chauffeur's quarters. There was a bathroom down there with a shower, his father's office and a tool and parts room.

Above the garage was the apartment where Chase had spent the first nineteen years of his life with his father.

The state champion elm tree, Peter's pride and joy along with the champion burr oak out front, filled most of the lawn next to the garage. It was a monster of a tree, at least two hundred years old, Peter figured. He called it Gramps. Some of the limbs were so thick and hung so low that Peter had fashioned Y-shaped braces to hold them up and keep their weight from pulling the roots out of the ground.

Over the weekend Gramps had leafed out completely. In places, dinner-plate-sized leaves nearly brushed the grass. Chase knew it was there but couldn't see the white bench built around the trunk where Dory used to flop with a book. Crazy Missouri weather. He'd seen his breath Friday morning when he'd toured the job site. Today he'd stripped down to a white T-shirt and sunburned his arms.

He parked the truck near the apartment stairs and turned off the engine. Dory unclipped her seat belt and reached for the door handle. Chase pushed the lock button on the armrest.

"Are you never going to talk to me again?" he asked. She didn't answer and kept her face turned away. "Why? Because I offered you money or because I said you looked ridiculous?"

"I wasn't running around screaming," she said, her voice like stone. "I went for a walk in the orchard."

"If you wanted to smell the cherry blossoms why didn't you send one of the servants to cut you a couple of branches?"

"I don't have servants anymore. I have employees. I don't ask them to do things for me that I can do for myself." She turned her head toward him. "Thank you for the ride. May I have that bottle of water?"

"Sure." Chase was left-handed; he rarely did anything right-handed and apparently Dory remembered. When he reached for the bottle she sprang the lock on the passenger side armrest, popped the door open and bailed out of the truck.

Smart little squirt, but his legs were longer and he was faster. He intercepted her as she came around the back end of the truck. She tried to dodge him, but he caught her by the elbow.

"I did not tell Jill that you look ridiculous," Chase said. "I told her you looked ridiculous in your clown suit."

"You told me I looked cute," Dory snapped and pulled away.

"Okay. Now I'm confused." And he was getting annoyed. "Is cute a compliment or an insult?"

"It might have been a compliment without *squirt* on the end."

"I've always called you squirt."

"And I've always hated it."

"You used to like me."

"Used to," she said curtly. "Don't anymore."

"Because I'm a pompous, arrogant, condescending ass."

"In a nutshell."

"Why are you so angry with me?"

"Because you offered me money and you said I look ridiculous."

"If you were as shallow as Jill, I might believe that."

"If Jill is shallow why are you taking her to dinner in a limo and buying her presents?"

"Is that what this is about? You're pissed 'cause I'm dating Jill?"

"Oh please." She rolled her eyes and turned her head away.

"That *is* what this is about." Hell. He thought he'd killed the last of her crush on him with his ham-handed offer to compensate Miss Ping for the loss of a valuable employee. "I can't help the way I feel, Dory. All I can say is I never meant to hurt you."

"Which time?" She swung a glare on him. "When you tried to bribe me or when you said I looked ridiculous?"

"Will you get off that?" Was she really not getting this? Or was she being deliberately obtuse? "I'm talking about the fact that you've been in love with me your entire life."

Her mouth fell open. She clamped it shut and doubled her fists. "You are pompous, arrogant, condescending and *insane*!"

"Oh, come on. You followed me around like a little dog. If I looked at you cross-eyed you burst into tears."

"You were my hero. I worshipped you!" Her voice throbbed and oh God, he hated himself, felt so sorry for her. "I was also a child."

"Now you're all grown up and all bent out of shape because I don't love you." Chase paused and added as gently as he could, "I love Jill."

"*Oh.*" She sucked a sharp breath. "That's what 'L-Chase' means."

"I don't know what else to call it." But he was sure Curt could come up with another word. "I think I'm going to ask her to marry me."

"Oh—*God*!" Her eyebrows jumped halfway to her hairline and she stumbled a step away from him.

"Jesus, Dory. I'm sorry." He reached for her but she pulled out of his grasp. "I shouldn't have told you."

"Oh *no*! I'm glad you told me!" Her voice warbled and tears flooded her eyes. "Thank you so *much* for telling me. Honestly. Congratulations."

"Dory—" He reached for her again but she ducked under his arm and took off like a shot.

He turned around on one foot and watched her run across the drive and the stretch of lawn on the other side. She slowed to a stiff-legged walk when she reached the pea gravel path. Chase started toward the truck to go after her and drive her to the guesthouse.

There was no wind but something rustled the leaves of the giant elm tree. He glanced at Gramps and saw his father ducking out from under one of the low-hanging branches. A book in one hand, his glasses in the other, a thunderous scowl on his face. Oh, holy shit.

"Proud of yourself?" He bit the words at him. "Feel like a big man?"

"I didn't know you were there, Dad."

"If you'd known would you have spoken differently to Dory?"

"Yes," Chase admitted. "I probably would have."

"That's some comfort. I didn't raise a total son of a bitch."

His father's ears were turning red. He was furious. So was Chase. Furious and mortified, but his father was recovering from a heart attack. He drew a deep breath and checked his temper.

"I'm sorry you overheard, Dad. I know you're fond of Dory."

"You don't know anything. If you did you wouldn't be thinking about asking Jill to marry you. What the hell is that? *Thinking?* If you have to think about asking her, then you shouldn't."

"Jill has obligations here. My business is in New York."

"Do you want to marry her or form a corporation? God almighty! No wonder I don't have grandchildren."

"It's complicated, Dad. I wouldn't expect you to understand."

"Why? Because I don't have a college degree? Because I'm not twenty times richer than Del Lambert? That's part of this. Don't tell me it isn't. She was denied to you once so now you're determined, come hell or high water, to have the boss man's daughter."

"That's enough, Dad. I don't think you should say any more."

"I'm gonna say one more thing." Charles shoved his glasses in his jacket pocket. "If you marry Jill Lambert you're a goddamn fool."

Then he turned on his heel and walked away.

Chapter Eleven

Miss Margaret Lambert
(*My dear darling Aunt Ping*)
Requests the Honor of Your Presence
at the Marriage of her Niece
(*has no idea that this is a stickup, connived by*)
Jillian Laura Drusilla Lambert
(*my not-the-brightest-bulb-in-the-box but crazy like a fox
sister, to get us out of the hotel business*)
To
Chase Malcolm Charles McKay
(*by fleecing this pompous, arrogant, condescending ass out
of twenty million dollars in her prenuptial agreement.*)
On the Afternoon of Saturday, May 8, 2004
(*If Jill doesn't kill him or I don't kill him.*)
The Outlook Inn
(*If Jill has her way soon to be known once more
as Outlook Farm*)
Kansas City, Missouri
(*Which is likely where we'll be tried and sent up
the river for fraud.*)

Exchange of Vows 2 P.M.
(*Wear black. I plan to.*)
Wedding Supper 5 P.M.
(*Bring a raincoat in case a food fight erupts.*)

Dancing 8 P.M.
(*Do NOT dance with the groom!*)
R.S.V.P.
(*English Translation: Please respond. And please come see me in the state penitentiary or the mental ward, wherever I end up when this is over.*)

"This is the invitation you should have sent," Dory said.

She put down the Cross pen she'd written it with, in neat blue-inked letters between the lines of elegantly curved and embossed gold printing, and handed the creamy ivory vellum card to her sister.

Jill sat on Dory's desk waiting for Chase in a white tennis dress that was part Pat Benatar in her slashed and ripped period and part Lil Kim. It didn't have pasties, but it came close.

She read what Dory had written and laughed. "The dimmest bulb in the box. So many people think that of me."

"And so many people," Dory said, "are so wrong."

"You aren't going to end up in a mental ward." Jill put a kiss on the top of her head. "And you aren't going to prison."

"From your lips to God's ears." Dory took back the invitation. "I think I'll send this one to Coop. Kind of a heads-up, keep your calendar open, we might be calling you sort of thing."

"Relax." Jill leaned toward her and lowered her voice. "He signed the prenup. In six months we'll be out of the hotel business."

"You're counting on Chase dumping you. What if he doesn't?"

"He *will*, Dory. He doesn't love me. He wants me. So bad even *I* can taste it." Jill made a face. "Thank God for Listerine."

"Oy vey." Dory slapped her cheek. "I can't believe I agreed to this."

"I caught you," Jill said, "in a weak moment."

Literally, just as Dory had collapsed on her knees, howling in the middle of the pea gravel path. Jill half dragged, half carried her to the guesthouse where Dory threw up in the downstairs bathroom. Jill put her to bed, called her doctor and insisted he come. He did and confirmed that Jamie's pediatrician wasn't kidding when he said even the lightest case of measles could make an adult sicker than a dog.

"But I *had* measles," she'd managed to croak.

"Oh no, Dory," said Deirdre, who'd come over with Aunt Ping to be with Jill when the doctor arrived. "I distinctly remember Drusilla writing that you had chicken pox, not measles, when you were six."

"No, Deirdre," Aunt Ping said. "It was measles."

"I believe you're mistaken, Margaret."

"Deirdre. I was here. I should know."

"Margaret. I vividly recall Drusilla writing it was chicken pox."

The fact that Dory was at that moment hanging over an old plastic dishpan barfing up the rest of her lunch should've settled the argument, but no. The official diagnosis was dehydration and mild heat exhaustion, rubella and one really sunburned nose.

Dory spent the rest of the week in bed, missed the announcement of Jill and Chase's engagement, Aunt Ping's celebratory dinner and the presentation of the eight-carat rock. Fine with her.

Chase sent her yellow roses, yellow gladiolas, yellow every crapping bloom known to man. Dory gave the bouquets to the maids.

Curt sent her a dozen banana popsicles from a swanky ice-cream shop in Washington, D.C., and a card that said, "Caught the creeping crud from your kid? Get well and put the little bugger up for adoption."

It was Saturday, Dory's first day back at her desk. The office was only semi-open on weekends but she had a lot of work to catch up. Her nose was still peeling and she'd eaten the last popsicle last night.

"The fever must've parboiled my brain," she said to Jill. "Are you sure I said 'Go for it' when you told me this insane plan?"

"You were mumbling and mostly incoherent," Jill said with a shrug. "But that's what it sounded like."

"You're lying to me, aren't you?"

"Yes," Jill admitted. "But it's too late to stop the wedding."

"*Au contraire.*" Dory dangled the invitation in front of her. "I could give this to you know who."

Meaning Chase, who stepped into the doorway as if she'd conjured him. The invitation slipped from her fingers and skittered to the floor under her desk. Dory thought seriously about joining it.

Chase carrying his racket and Jill's and both their gym bags, wore white shorts and a white polo shirt with navy piping around the collar. The unbuttoned placket showed a sprig of chest hair. His white crew socks came halfway up a pair of calves a weightlifter would like to have. The sunburn on his arms had faded to a nice, even brown and there was no sign of snakeskin. Greek gods, Dory supposed, didn't peel.

She hadn't seen Chase since he'd told her he loved Jill. He hadn't seen her, either. He didn't see her now. He only saw Jill as she rose off the desk in her is-it-a-bikini-or-is-it-a-bath-towel tennis dress.

"Tell me," he said. "Please tell me that's your wedding dress."

Jill laughed. So did Dory. That's when Chase realized she was there and glanced at her, his eyes a deep, deep blue in his tanned face. He and Jill had been swimming and riding and shooting golf all week. People who didn't have to work could do that sort of thing.

Dory's mouth wanted to quaver but she forced it into a big, cheerful smile. "Hi, Chase. Watch her backhand. It's a killer."

"I'll do that," he said. "How are you?"

"In the pink. Fit as a fiddle. Rarin' to go."

"Why don't you come with us? We're playing at the club. You look like you could use some sun."

Oh, wasn't this sweet. Now he was going to patronize her.

"With this nose?" Dory pointed. "Not a good idea. Besides, I have tons of work. Get out of here, you crazy kids. Go have fun."

Chase scowled. Jill shot her a *watch-it* look, but they went. Dory couldn't decide if she wanted to throw up again or put her head through her computer monitor.

"Tell me again," Chase said, his voice drifting back to her from the foyer. "Who is it we're playing with?"

"Gus and Cydney Monroe," Jill answered. "Georgette Parrish's daughter and her husband. They're both writers. Authors, actually . . ."

And world-class rotten tennis players, Dory added as Jill's voice trailed out of earshot. Cydney was Jill's friend. The Monroes split their time between Kansas City and Crooked Possum, Missouri, in the Ozarks, where Gus had a big place and where he and Cydney were married the first time. They'd gotten married twice. Dory couldn't remember why but she remembered getting lost with Jill trying to find Crooked Possum.

Aunt Ping missed the first ceremony, but made it to the second. They'd all thought it was hilarious that Charles, who had a GPS system in his brain, had gotten totally turned around driving Aunt Ping in the Rolls. They'd ended up in Arkansas where they'd spent the night.

Lost, my foot, Dory thought, and got up to go find Esther.

Jill had a serve like a ballistic missile but absolutely no aim.

Twice she fired rockets over the net at Gus Munroe and hit Chase instead. His left knee was still throbbing from the first hit.

Cydney Monroe could barely see over the net, let alone hit the ball over it. She had curly, silver blond hair, didn't resemble Dory at all except for her brown eyes, but Chase couldn't look at her without thinking about Dory's sick bed pallor and pink-skinned nose.

It was Jill's serve again. When she tossed the ball up, Chase charged the net. If Gus was able to return, Jill would volley and he'd be in position to give the ball a gentle lob toward Cydney. Plus he'd be out of Jill's line of fire.

He never saw the ball. One second he was running toward the net, the next he was on the clay curled in a fetal position, seeing stars and clutching his groin.

"He's all right, Jill. Don't worry, Cydney. He'll be fine," Gus Monroe said. "Go change and we'll meet you for lunch in the dining room."

Chase managed a breath, felt a hand on his shoulder.

"No cup, huh?" Gus asked.

He could only shake his head.

"When are you getting married?"

"A week," Chase squeaked.

"Tough one, brother."

When the stars faded and he could breathe, Gus helped him up and limped him into the locker room. The club trainer suggested a warm shower, maybe a cold pack later and prayer.

Gus had a clean spare jockstrap in his gym bag and gave it to him. "I've played with Jill before," he said and grinned.

Chase said thanks and hobbled off to the shower. His knee was puffing up. He had a knot and a bruise on his thigh where Jill's second serve had nailed him. She'd damn near gelded him with her third.

She hadn't been *aiming* at his balls, had she?

And wreck her honeymoon? That didn't make sense.

She'd let him feel her up a couple times but that was it. She wanted to be a virgin—with him, anyway—on their wedding night, which she wanted to spend at the Outlook Inn in the Honeymoon Suite.

Chase got out of the shower and stood at the mirror ruffling a towel through his wet hair. The lump on the back of his head where Jill beaned him with a golf ball on the fourth hole the other day was nearly gone. The bruise on his ribs from the fall he'd taken off the gentlest saddlebred gelding in the stables had faded from purple to green.

Jill raised hell with Eddie for failing to make sure the cinch was properly tightened. He felt bad about it and apologized later to Eddie. He'd grinned, told Chase not to worry and walked away laughing. Kind of a strange response, but Eddie had an oddball sense of humor.

With the jockstrap he could walk without limping. On their way out of the locker room he thanked Gus again.

When they entered the dining room Jill came running in a blue linen dress and high heels. She threw her arms around him, pressed her breasts against his chest and he would've done anything. Stood naked against a bull's-eye and let her throw knives at him blindfolded.

"Sorry 'bout that last serve," she whispered and touched her tongue to his earlobe. "I'll make it up to you on our wedding night."

Outlook ran like a Swiss watch because of Esther Grant. She supervised the maids, kept each of Outlook's forty rooms white-glove spotless 24/7, took care of the laundry, the dry cleaning, the shopping, and made sure none of the thirty-two bathrooms ever ran short of toilet paper. That in itself was an amazing feat to Dory.

"I'm a triple Virgo," Esther had told her. "I can't help myself."

And she wrote everything down, God love her, in her household ledgers. Recorded everything she did and everything everyone else did on every single day of every single year since she'd come to Outlook in 1968, six years before Dory was born, a year after her husband was listed as missing in Vietnam. He still was and Esther still wore his MIA bracelet. Lt. Matthew Grant, USN, followed by his service number.

The part of her job Esther loved most was caring for the Lambert family china, crystal and silver. To see it all displayed in the china closet, a long, narrow room off the kitchen with four solid walls of built-in shelves with glass doors, drawers and cabinets made Dory think of the treasure chamber in the tomb of an Egyptian pharaoh.

Esther had catalogued every single piece of every china pattern. Over three dozen complete sets that would serve anywhere from twelve to two hundred people. Every place setting of sterling flatware, and there were dozens, every crystal water goblet and champagne flute and every silver serving piece was listed in a massive, red three-ring binder bulging with pages tucked inside clear plastic sheet protectors.

In Outlook's darkest hour, the china closet was their last-ditch way to raise quick cash. An appraiser from Sotheby's New York estimated its contents would bring close to two million dollars at auction.

At the front of the room was a table and chair where Esther sat with the inventory book open in front of her, a pen in her hand and a pad on her knee. She wore her mahogany brown hair, which didn't have a single strand of gray in it, like a girl, shoulder-length and held back by a headband. She glanced up and smiled when Dory stepped into the room.

"Well, you look better than the last time I saw you." Wednesday night, when she'd brought Dory broth and tea and Jell-O for supper.

"I feel better, thanks." She nodded at the inventory book. "Wedding preparations, I take it."

"Miss Ping asked for suggestions on which pieces we should use where and which patterns would be appropriate."

"You're the go-to gal for that." Dory pulled up the ladder that ran on a track around the china closet and sat on one of the rungs. "The wedding will be fun. We haven't had a shindig like this in ages."

"You think Jill marrying Chase will be fun?"

"Well, sure. Why wouldn't I?"

Esther stared at her. Dory held her gaze, her throat

pounding. Her chin was just starting to quiver when Esther shrugged.

"No reason," she said and glanced down at her pad.

Dory sighed, relieved. She hadn't worked at Lambert's long enough to perfect her I'm-a-banker-I-can-look-anybody-in-the-eye-and-lie stare.

"I wonder why Aunt Ping never married."

"Why don't you ask her?"

"I wasn't asking anyone, Esther. I was just wondering."

"If you asked Miss Ping, you wouldn't have to wonder."

Or ask me, said the look Esther shot her, *'cause I ain't sayin' nuttin'.* Which didn't surprise Dory, but she'd felt honor-bound to try a straightforward approach before she resorted to subterfuge.

"Fabulous job on the invitations," she said. "Two hundred printed, addressed and mailed in four days flat. Wow."

"We only have two weeks. It certainly helped that Anita's nephew owns a print shop. Miss Fairview has already returned her RSVP."

"I never saw her crack a smile at Charles' party. Did you?"

"No. I didn't." Esther put down her pad and pen. "Thursday afternoon while Anita was outside having a cigarette, I found Miss Fairview in the office. I asked if I could help her. She didn't answer, just walked past me with her nose in the air."

"What was she doing in the office?"

"Looking through the papers on your desk."

"Really?" Dory blinked, startled. "Were the doors open or shut?"

"Ajar. Anita left them that way so she could hear the phone. She went out on the front steps instead of the terrace to smoke."

"How funny," Dory said, though she didn't think it was funny at all. "In a million years I wouldn't have taken Miss Fairview for a snoop."

"Still waters," Esther said, "run deep."

"Thanks for telling me. If you need a hand with anything, let me know." Dory rose to leave and stopped in the doorway. "When you have a minute, I'd like to take a look at your ledgers. I'm working on projected expenses for next year."

Esther tipped her head. "Didn't I give you last year's copies?"

"If you did, I lost them or Deirdre misfiled them. She means well, but sometimes I wish she wouldn't help when she gets bored."

"You know where the ledgers are." Esther tugged a key ring bracelet off her wrist. It held the small silver key to the barrister's bookcase in her office. "Just put them back in order, please."

"Huh. What d'you know," Dory said. "I did have chicken pox."

And Aunt Ping had fibbed. She hadn't been at Outlook at all. She'd been in Columbia, Missouri, attending the seventeenth reunion of her Stephens College graduating class. Charles had driven her in the Rolls. They'd been gone the whole weekend.

Jamie looked up from his math book. "How do you know that?"

" 'Cause it says so right here." Dory turned the green leather single-entry ledger marked HOUSEHOLD ACCOUNTS, 1980 toward Jamie and pointed at the blue-lined entry.

While he hunched up on his elbows to read it, Dory turned on the lighted ceiling fan above the dining room table and opened the top half of the Dutch door. It was seven-thirty. Still light outside thanks to daylight saving time, but just barely. The sky was nearly the same shade of lavender as the dress Jill had dropped by earlier to pick up. She and Chase were *din*-ing at the club with Cydney and Gus Monroe.

"Not having dinner? You're *din*-ing?" Dory said. "La-de-da."

"What does that mean? Are you jealous?"

"Am I breathing? The last time I was at the club I was eighteen."

"Come with us. You should. Everyone will love seeing you."

Well, this was precious. Now Jill was patronizing her, too.

"No thanks." Dory pointed at her nose. "I look like a leper."

She couldn't care less about *din*-ing at the club. The idea of being able to eat there, being able to afford the dues and all that entailed—that's what she envied, but she didn't dare tell Jill. She'd bump her prenup from twenty million to thirty and call it punitive damages.

She'd felt so noble when she'd worked at Lambert's, when she was rich and didn't have to work. Dory Lambert, great humanitarian, now Dory Lambert, working stiff. Even so, on her deathbed she wouldn't have blessed this idiot scheme. At least Jill admitted it, confessed that she'd shanghaied Chase while Dory was too sick to stop her.

She still could, she supposed—and she was considering it.

Dory sneezed. Peter must've mown the lawn today; the air the fan was pulling in reeked of fresh cut grass. She shut the Dutch door, made sure it was locked and stopped in the kitchen for two bottles of grape soda on her way back to the dining room.

"Why does Esther write everything down?" Jamie asked.

"She can't help herself. She's a triple Virgo."

Dory gave him a coaster and a grape soda and sat down on her right foot in the chair across the table. Jamie cocked his head at her.

"My birthday is December tenth. What does that make me?"

"Sagittarius, the archer. Wonder what Artemis would think of that, since you broke her bow?"

"Diego said the Rolls broke her bow. And Peter said he can fix it."

"He also said lucky for you," Dory reminded him. "Sags

are curious, athletic and bright. On the down side, they tend to be irresponsible, hyperactive and reckless loud-mouths."

Jamie grinned. "You're making that up."

"I am not. Go check it in Jill's *Astrology for Dummies* book."

"Can I live with you after Jill and Chick get married?"

"Chase," Dory said. "Why do you want to live with me?" Her eyes stung and her throat swelled. This was the third time today she'd been on the verge of tears. "I make you behave and learn percentages."

"You don't treat me like I'm a kid. You treat me like a person."

"You're a person who just happens to be a kid. But you *are* a kid, which means you don't get to decide things like that. The adults do."

"Auntie Deirdre and Aunt Ping, which means I can forget it."

"If you went to bed on time, did your homework and stayed out of trouble, I bet they'd at least consider letting you live here."

"So can I?" Jamie's eyes lit up. "Can I come live with you, Dory?"

"You'll have to keep your room clean."

"Jill has one of the maids clean her room. Why can't I?"

"Because the maids have enough to do and because Sister Immaculata would say that hard work is good for your soul."

The light went out of Jamie's eyes. "I don't have a soul."

"Are you cutting catechism class? Everybody has a soul."

"I don't." He ducked his head and plucked at the corner of his math book. "Because of who my father is and what he did."

"Where did you get that numbskull idea?"

Jamie looked at her through his bangs. "The sins of the fathers."

"Are *not* visited upon the children," Dory said vehemently.

"It says so in the Bible. In the Ten Commandments."

"God wasn't talking to *you*, Jamie. He was giving it to the Israelites. They were getting a little wild and crazy. Dancing around and making craven images. Who could blame them? They'd just been released from bondage in Egypt. He was reminding them who's boss, that's all."

"That's not in the Bible, Dory." The corners of Jamie's mouth twitched. "That's in the movie *The Ten Commandments*."

Which Dory owned on DVD and she and Jamie had watched along with *Ben-Hur* over Easter weekend.

"It *is*?" She smacked her cheek and looked thunderstruck.

Jamie laughed, but there was still a cloud in his eyes. Dory reached across the table, twined her fingers in his and squeezed.

"We all love you, squirt. You know that, don't you?"

"Yeah, I know." He wormed his fingers out of hers. "Sometimes I don't know why, that's all. My father stole all that money."

"Do you want to talk about him?"

"*No,*" Jamie said hotly. "I don't even want to think about him."

"Then don't. There's no reason you should. It's over and done with. No one blames you, Jamie. We love you."

"So is it okay if I come and live with you?"

"Absolutely." Dory smiled. "I'd love it."

Jamie grinned, elated, and dove back into his math book.

Jill was ecstatic. The Monroes' son Artie was seven and Cydney liked to be home in time to put him to bed at nine. Yippee! Chase had a headache and a noticeable limp. Double yippee! By eight o'clock, she was free, and the Happy Spirit was open till nine on Saturday.

There was no one in the store but Gary when she pushed

through the door at eight thirty-five. He stood behind the register glaring at her.

"Gary, darling," Jill cooed.

"Go away," he said coldly. "I don't want to see you."

"Let me take my clothes off and I bet you'll want to see me."

She locked the door, flipped the open sign to closed. Gary shot out from behind the counter and ran for the back of the store. Jill heard a slam, dropped her purse in a chair and followed him through the wildly swinging beads. He wasn't in the office. He was in the bathroom. She gripped the knob but it wouldn't turn.

"I'm getting just a little tired of your fragile male ego, Gary," Jill said through the locked door. "You're behaving like a child."

"How could you do this to us? How could you marry McKay?"

"Oh, for heaven's sake! It's not like I'm going to sleep with him!"

"How are you going to avoid it?"

She probably couldn't, totally. She'd have to sleep with Chase once or twice at least. She had to take Dramamine every time she thought of it, but there was no point telling Gary. He was already distraught.

"I'm working on it," Jill said. "I have a plan."

For starters, she'd be a nervous bride, too shy to risk her family hearing her cries of passion on their wedding night. It was thin, but it was the best fallback she could think of if she couldn't put Chase out of commission before the wedding. For the rest of their sure-to-be-brief marriage she'd improvise.

"A plan for every occasion," Gary sneered. "That's you."

"Hey! At least I have one!" Jill smacked her palm against the door. "What's your plan to raise twenty million dollars so I don't have to marry Chase to get us out of the hotel business, which is giving Dory ulcers and making Aunt Ping old before her time? Let's hear it, Mr. FBI guy!"

"We don't *scheme* in the FBI. We *investigate*."

"Then get your ass out of the bathroom and investigate! Go find James Darwood and get our money back so I don't have to do this!"

"Money!" Gary flung the door open. "That's all you care about!"

"You're a fine one to talk, Mr. Double-Dipper! Collecting from the FBI and the salary Dory has to pay you so it doesn't look suspicious!"

"I haven't spent a cent of my Happy Spirit wages!" Gary said indignantly. "Every penny will be returned!"

"Return it now." Jill held her hand out. "I've got a wedding to pay for. I'm not taking one penny more than we need from Chase."

"I can't do that! I'm undercover! I have to turn over my paychecks!"

"Then go find James!" Jill gave him a push in the chest and whirled toward the front door. "Or go screw yourself!"

According to Deirdre, Marilyn hadn't told Jamie much about James, just that Daddy had done something bad and that's why they had to keep moving and couldn't use their real name. When he was eight, Jamie asked Deirdre what Daddy had done that was so bad.

Deirdre told Aunt Ping, who called Gina Vanderpool. Gina came from Vancouver and the three of them, his grandmother and two aunts, sat Jamie down and told him the story. It was Gina who suggested Aunt Ping adopt him so his name could be changed. Just in case. So far as Dory knew, this was only the second time that he'd mentioned James.

At nine o'clock she folded the page of notes she'd taken from Esther's ledgers into her pocket, picked up her keys and the giant metal flashlight she'd borrowed from Peter, locked the door and walked Jamie to Outlook via the pea gravel path that ran along the greensward below the ornamental garden where the few trees were lit by strings of clear, twinkling Christmas lights.

"Why are we taking the long way?" Jamie asked.

"I've been sick." Dory switched on the flashlight. It threw a beam as long and wide as the headlight on a locomotive and weighed enough to knock anyone senseless who might be lurking around in a camouflage jacket with a hole in it. "I need the exercise."

She shooed Jamie into the house through the kitchen, told him to lock the door and beat it. She'd managed to avoid Aunt Ping and Charles today, but she couldn't forever. She hoped she could dodge them till she decided what, if anything, she was going to do about the wedding.

If she blew the whistle now all hell would break loose. Aunt Ping might never forgive Jill. Jill might never forgive her. If she kept quiet, once they were married, Chase would tumble. He was besotted but he wasn't stupid. If Jill could avoid sleeping with him, which she'd told Dory she planned to do—though how she thought she could get away with it Dory didn't know and didn't want to—he'd realize she'd married him for twenty million dollars and all hell would break loose.

Either way, when it was all over she'd never see Chase again.

Dory switched off the giant flashlight and sat in the dark under a clouded half-moon on a bench by the birdbath near Aunt Ping's bedroom window. The one she'd knocked over the night she'd stumbled through the ornamental garden following Jill on her way to meet Chase and change all their lives.

When she'd been too sick to sleep, Dory had lain awake wondering what might've happened differently—maybe some things, maybe none, maybe everything—if Chase had been here when James came to Outlook. Tried to imagine how her life would've turned out if James hadn't stolen thirty-five million dollars from Lambert Securities.

She couldn't see a completely different life for herself, just bits and pieces of one. Like Mother. Over her dead body would she have allowed Jill to marry the chauffeur's son. If Mother hadn't sailed off to the Caribbean and never returned, Dory could've arranged that, no problem. But that's all she could see, just small scenes that were changed. It gave her the weirdest feeling that things were supposed to turn out this way.

And a suspicion that Jill thought, though maybe it was only subconciously, that by marrying Chase she was putting things back the way they belonged, the way they would've been if James hadn't happened.

Jill would deny it. She'd say she was sick of the hotel business, she wanted out and that's all there was to it. But she could be so much like Mother sometimes, so oblivious to the consequences of her actions. Not only for other people, but herself.

Chase thought he loved her. Maybe Jill could ignore that, marry him and fleece him and never look back, but Dory didn't think so. Unless Jill had her fooled and she was truly and utterly Drusilla's daughter. Dory doubted it, but the possibility existed. It worried her and made her squirm with guilt on the bench beside the birdbath.

She'd had a hand in this. She'd told Jill things she'd known darn good and well that she shouldn't. She could've put a stop to Operation Cockroach, but she'd been hurt and angry. Jealous, too, and petty and vindictive. She was not proud of herself. She was appalled. If she tried to fix what she'd done she should start with Chase. Would he believe her or would he think she was just trying to cause trouble to get even?

Dory wouldn't blame him if he did.

She rose off the bench, her notes crackling in her pocket. She was so tired. Lying in bed really took it out of you. That's all she wanted to do, crawl back in bed, but this was the perfect time to check the logbook Charles kept on the Rolls against Esther's ledgers. Chase was out with Jill, and Diego had taken a bunch of the younger maids salsa dancing.

Dory switched on the flashlight and headed for the garage, used her keys and let herself in the door at the foot of the stairs.

Through the half-glass wall on her left she could see the bays and the dark shapes of the cars dimly lit by a row of recessed floodlights in the ceiling along the back wall. Only four these days, the Bentley, the Lincoln limo they'd leased till the Rolls came back from McPherson's, the Ford that van Wallace and Esther shared, though Wallace rarely drove anymore, and a little Ford Escort. Give it another week and the mostly empty bays would be mostly full with guests' vehicles.

Dory turned on another row of backlights—no need to advertise that she was here—looked around and saw that Diego was keeping the garage the way Charles liked it, spotless as a new car showroom. She drew a deep breath just to make sure, but there were no telltale gas or oil fumes, either, to indicate that Diego was sluffing off.

Charles' office was neat as a pin. The logbooks he kept on each car were filed by year. She plucked the Rolls' log for 1980 from a shelf in an oak bookcase, opened it on Charles' rolltop desk, tugged her notes out of her pocket and sat down in his red-padded swivel chair.

He was every bit as anal as Esther. He noted every oil change and lube job, every brake pad or water pump he installed. He even wrote down when he vacuumed the inside of the Rolls and washed the windows. And he recorded every mile he drove, keeping track by the odometer, from Outlook to Daddy or Aunt Ping's destination and back.

She found the trip to Crooked Possum to attend Cydney and Gus Monroe's first wedding in October, the unplanned—or was it?—side trip to Arkansas and seven other weekend out-of-town trips Aunt Ping had taken that year and Esther also documented. All far enough away from Kansas City that no one would notice or care if the chauffeur took off his uniform and the lady of the manse rode up front.

Dory heard a muffled but heavy slam in the driveway and leaped to her feet. She wasn't expecting anyone so she'd left the office door open. Was it Diego—Dory glanced at her watch—at nine-twenty? She'd only turned on the desk lamp. She wasn't sure he'd notice but decided not to risk it and jammed her notes in her pocket. The 1980 log back in its place, she yanked this year's off the shelf, opened it and jumped back into the chair, one foot on the floor to keep it from spinning.

Half a second before Chase appeared in the doorway. Dory nearly swallowed her tonsils. She saw him in the corner of her eye, leaning one shoulder on the jamb, his light blue suit coat hooked over the other by one finger. His tie was loose, his paler blue shirtsleeves rolled up.

"Hi there," he said, his voice neutral.

"Oh—Chase!" She spun the chair around. Since she was expecting Diego her start wasn't totally faked. "Is Jill with you? I can clear out."

"I dropped her off about an hour ago and went for a drive." He pushed off the doorjamb. "Are you looking for something?"

"Found it." Dory held up the logbook marked ROLLS on the spine. "I was going to enter the collision with Artemis but I see Charles beat me to it. Just as well since I can't find a pen."

"Let's see if I remember." Chase crossed the office and leaned over her. The size of him made her feel very small in the big red chair. Dory caught a whiff of his woodsy cologne and something sharper. Alcohol? "Unless Dad has moved things, pens ought to be right here."

He opened the middle drawer and sure enough, there was a plastic tray full of ballpoint pens from gas stations and auto supply stores. Right where they'd always been, which Dory knew as well as Chase.

"What d'you know," she said. "Never thought to look there."

Chase leaned his hip against the desk and looked at her. His eyes narrowed, his lips almost but not quite pursed. "Would you like a Coke?"

"I'd love a Coke."

"Usual place?"

The bench under the elm. That's the only place he could mean.

"Uh—sure," Dory said.

"Cokes still in the fridge?" He pointed his thumb at what Charles called the lobby, the area between his office and the bays.

"Far as I know," Dory replied.

"Go ahead." He tossed his jacket over the filing cabinet. "I'll look."

Dory went, picking up the flashlight and shoving the logbook back on the shelf on her way. She thought about running while she had the chance, but that was chicken. If Chase had something else to tell her, she'd sit and listen and take it like a grown-up 'cause really, what could be worse than hearing him say I don't love you, I love Jill?

The crickets chirping under the elm tree shut up when she ducked under one of the sagging limbs and sat down on the bench, first with her feet on the dew-soaked grass, but that wasn't comfortable. She felt like a shelf sitter, so she scooted her back against the trunk, but that was no good, either. The edge of the bench hit her at midcalf.

Oh, to heck with it. Dory gave up trying to look like anything but what she was, a squirt, and crossed her legs, turned on the flashlight and pointed it away from her. The beam bounced off the dense canopy of leaves and made a nice soft backwash that wouldn't blind anybody.

"Here you go." Chase bent at the waist to clear the tree and hand her a twelve-ounce bottle of Coke. "Where'd you get the searchlight?"

"From Peter. I think I could signal the International Space Station. Want to try? I still remember Morse code from Girl Scouts. "

"Not tonight." He smiled and sat beside her, near enough that Dory could feel the warmth of his body. She scooted away and watched him undo another couple buttons at his collar. "Are you limping?"

"Yeah." He gave a short laugh and pulled his tie off, tossed it on the bench and took a swig of Coke. "I'm limping."

"I told you to watch Jill's backhand."

"You forgot to warn me about her serve."

"Her serve? She has an amazing serve. She's famous for aces."

Chase rubbed his left thigh. "She clocked me with three of them."

"She must've had an off day," Dory said. What was Jill doing? She could knock a squirrel out of a tree with a tennis ball. "It happens."

"I suppose so." Chase shrugged and leaned back against the tree.

He rubbed his shoulders against the trunk like he had an itch. Dory heard bark scrape, thought about offering to scratch it but didn't. Not a good idea to touch something that wasn't hers and never would be. She drew a breath and felt steady inside, almost calm.

Okay. This was good. She was fine. He'd taken off his tie and undone his collar but he was still the expensively tailored ass she despised. If he had another bomb to drop she could take it. Hearing "I don't love you, I love Jill" from the boy she'd loved. The boy in dusty blue jeans and a white T-shirt. That's what had sent her howling to her knees.

Chase turned his head toward her. "So you and the monster are over the measles?"

"Oh, sure. Jamie wasn't sick at all. I, however, prayed to die."

"You thought you'd had measles but you didn't. Is that it?"

"Yes. I could've sworn I did, but Deirdre said Mother wrote her I had chicken pox, not measles. Apparently, she was right."

He took another slug of Coke. "Odd Miss Ping didn't remember."

"Odd but encouraging. It means she's not infallible."

"You're talking to me." Chase smiled. "Are you over being angry or are you going to finish your Coke and belt me with the bottle?"

The backwash of the flashlight beam lit his hair with silver glints, made the fine milled cotton of his shirt shimmer and his eyes look bluer. He had the most beautiful mouth when he smiled.

"I'm not going to belt you and I'm not angry anymore."

"I was unkind to you, Dory, and I'm sorry. I lost my temper."

"I was behaving like an idiot, refusing to get in the truck."

"You weren't thinking straight. You had heatstroke. I didn't. There's no excuse for the way I spoke to you. Well, actually there is, but—" Chase sighed heavily. "I shouldn't talk to you about it."

"Why not? Go ahead. Unless you'd rather talk to your father."

"Not a good idea. He says I'm a goddamn fool if I marry Jill." Chase frowned. "That's another thing I shouldn't have told you."

"I won't tell her. I'm surprised Charles feels that way. He's never said a cross word to me about Jill."

"It isn't Jill. It's me. Dad doesn't believe I love her. He's got it in his head that because she was denied to me once, I'm determined to have the boss man's daughter. That's exactly how he said it." His frown twisted to one side. "And money. He made a few comments about that, too."

"Money?" Dory's voice squeaked. Her brain shot straight to Jill's twenty-million-dollar prenup and froze there. "What money?"

"Mine. McKay Design and Development is worth close to three quarters of a billion dollars."

"I know," she admitted. "I read it in *Fortune* magazine."

"I'm not an idiot. I know Jill's marrying me for my money."

"You *do*?" She blurted, wide-eyed. "I mean—you *what*?"

"Relax, Dory." Chase gave her a brotherly pat on the knee. "I'd be amazed if you hadn't figured it out. So has Curt. So has everybody on the planet, I'm sure. The thing is, I don't care." He took his hand off her knee but Dory could still feel the warmth of his fingers. "Jill could never love a poor man. I know that. If my fortune makes her want me as much as I want her, then I'm fine with it. She'll learn to love me. Seven hundred and fifty million dollars is one hell of an aphrodisiac."

Dory stared at Chase, stunned speechless. What a colossal moron. She could tell him that Gary, the man Jill *did* love, was poor as a church mouse and that he, Mr. Money Bags, was only a means to an end. Maybe he was delusional or maybe he honestly believed Jill could learn to love him. Either way, in a million years he wouldn't believe a squirt.

Chase turned his head against the trunk of the elm and smiled at her. "I sound like a pompous, arrogant ass, don't I?"

"You left out condescending," Dory said and he laughed.

"So you and me." He slapped his thighs. "We're square?"

"We're square," Dory said. *As square as your head,* she thought.

Let the wedding festivities begin. This poor bozo was beyond help.

Chapter Twelve

The Happy Spirit was closed on Sundays. The janitorial service didn't come till four, so Dory had arranged from her sick bed on Friday to meet Gordy at one-thirty.

"Clean as a whistle," he said when he finished sweeping the store. "Figured it would be since it's only been two weeks."

"In light of the latest development I thought it would be smart to check," Dory said and told him Esther had nabbed Miss Fairview in the office. "There was nothing exciting on my desk. Only invoices. I have no idea what she was looking for."

"Maybe she's just nosy or getting a little dotty. But it's odd that she's a frequent guest and you never noticed till now that she's a snoop."

"The guests have free run of Outlook. They've turned up in odd places before. There's usually always someone in the office or someone watching it. Thursday was a fluke. I wouldn't think twice about Miss Fairview if it weren't for the camouflage."

Except Esther had, and Esther didn't know about the scrap.

"I keep trying," Dory said. "But I can't quite picture Miss Fairview in a camouflage jacket. I can't see Diego in one, either."

"I don't care what Frasier says, it could've been the feds.

Could've been kids, too, just like Tom and Eddie said. I didn't find anything else."

"I guess that's what we'll call it, then," Dory replied, though she didn't like it. It just didn't feel right. "Kids playing paintball."

"You know how to do background checks. I taught you," Gordy said. "But I'll run Diego and Miss Fairview myself if you want."

"Yes, I'd like you to." Dory couldn't care less about Miss Fairview, but Diego gave her a pang. "You'll let me know?"

"Absolutely." Gordy said. "You look stressed. Get some rest."

Good idea, Dory thought, so she went home and took a nap.

She woke up at three-thirty, went downstairs and found Peter at the table in the breakfast room drinking coffee and reading the sports section. The Dutch door was open, letting in a breeze scented by the lilac bush at the corner of the back patio.

"So." Peter tossed the newspaper aside. "Am I putting cayenne pepper in Jill's bridal bouquet or not?"

"Not." Dory stifled a yawn, pulled out a chair and sat down. "It isn't her fault that Chase is a moron."

"So how much longer are we going to be in the hotel business?"

That snapped her awake with a startled blink. "I beg your pardon?"

"Oh stop it. Jill wants what's in Chase's pants—his wallet. She hates the Outlook Inn. You know it, I know it. We all know it. Except Miss Ping. She came to the greenhouse to talk about wedding flowers, with orange blossoms dancing in her eyes."

Dory clamped her hand on his wrist. "You can't tell her, Peter."

"Oh lovey, like I would." He raised her hand, kissed it and blinked back tears. "My heart is just shattered for you."

"I'm a big girl, Peter. I'm fine." Once she'd said it a couple hundred times Dory figured she'd believe it. "Chase knows Jill is marrying him for his money but he doesn't care. He thinks she'll learn to love him."

"*Ohhh! My Gawd!*" Peter fell back in his chair laughing.

Dory smiled. Peter had a great chicken cackle laugh. She had time to pour a cup of coffee, lace it with plenty of milk so it wouldn't aggravate her stomach and reheat it in the microwave while he howled.

"Oh my. Oh my, oh my." Peter sighed and wiped his eyes as she sat down again at the table. "He's a complete and *total* moron, isn't he?"

"Looks like it from here." Dory sipped her coffee.

"Then it's just as well," Peter said crisply. "You two would never suit. How long do you think Barbie and Ken will last?"

"Jill thinks he'll dump her in six months."

"No, no, no. It won't take that long. Two weeks, tops."

"Oh c'mon. Chase is too stubborn. Eight or nine months."

"Henry says six weeks." Peter drank his coffee. "We'll see."

"Henry says?" Dory repeated. "Does Eddie have an opinion?"

"I think he's in for three months." Peter tugged a small black notebook out of his overalls and opened it. "Yes. That's right. Three months."

"Let me see that." Dory grabbed the notebook. " 'Eddie—Fifty dollars/three months,' " she read. " 'Diego—Fifty dollars/one month and two days. Esther—Fifty dollars/one week. Wallace—One hundred dollars/three days.' " Dory slapped the notebook shut on the table. "Peter! You're running a pool!"

"Why shouldn't I? This marriage won't last and we all know it."

"But betting on how long it will take to fall apart? Isn't that—"

Hilarious. That's what it was. Dory bit her lip and turned her head away. Wallace—*Wallace!*—bet a hundred dollars it wouldn't take seventy-two hours for Chase and Jill's marriage to collapse. She didn't dare look at Peter, but he darted around the table and grinned at her.

"Go ahead. Laugh," he said. "We couldn't help ourselves any more than Jill can help being an opportunist. She wants Chase's money and he wants to give it to her. Why shouldn't we have a bit of fun with it?"

"It's mean," Dory said, fighting to keep a straight face. "Isn't it?"

"I call it making the best of a bad situation." Peter pulled out a chair, sat down and folded his hands on the table. "We could cry and wail and weep instead and be utterly miserable over something we can't change. That would make us all feel better, I'm sure."

"Okay, okay. I get the point." Dory gave in with a laugh that was only a little bit teary. "Put me down for fifty bucks and eight months."

"That's the spirit." Peter grinned and opened the notebook, fished a pencil stub from his overalls and made the notation. "Since you know the combination to the safe, will you hold the book and the money?"

"Why not?" Dory shrugged. "In for a penny, in for a pound."

Some of the wealthiest people on earth stayed at the Outlook Inn. People with so much money they made Chase look like he was barely scraping by, but they'd never had a real live movie star, his wife and two children as guests. Aunt Ping still wasn't sure that they should.

"I don't know how I let Georgette talk me into this," she said.

It was eight thirty that evening and they were having after-dinner coffee in the breakfast room. Aunt Ping, Jill and Chase, Deirdre and Dory. She thought she knew how Georgette had done it—she'd submitted the application made by Noah Patrick and his wife Lindsay Varner at the prospective guest committee meeting the day after Charles' heart attack.

"I thought we settled this at the last meeting," Jill said.

"Oh, it's quite settled, Jillian. The Patricks are checking in on Wednesday," Aunt Ping replied. "I just don't happen to like it."

"Fine, then," Jill said brightly. "Let's talk about my wedding."

"Oh, let's do!" Deirdre gushed. "I so love weddings!"

Jill shot Chase a dazzling smile. He raised her hand and pressed a fervent kiss to her fingertips. Dory wanted to gag but faked a yawn.

"Is that the time?" She looked at her watch and pushed her chair away from the table. "I have an early morning. Night all."

Dory couldn't get out of the house fast enough. Once she was on the terrace she felt better, calmer, but her face felt hot, which meant she was flushed. If anyone noticed, hopefully they took it for residual sunburn. Better than taking her for a silly little goof who couldn't stand to watch her sister's fiancé kiss her hand.

The scent of peonies drifted out of the garden. Dory wandered down one of the paths to take a closer sniff. It was almost but not quite dark. A few of the ground lights had come on but not the ones around the bench she settled on. She supposed that's why Chase didn't see her when he stepped outside.

She didn't see him, either. She heard the rasp of his lighter and glanced at the terrace. The scowl on his face as he lit a cigarette, the sweep of his gaze past the terrace made her pulse leap. It started to hammer when he moved to the wall no more than thirty feet away from her, his head lifted and turned toward the guesthouse.

Uh. Was he looking for her? Why would he be looking for her?

"Is that the time," he said, a derisive snort in his voice.

Oh. That's why. Dory shrank on the bench.

Chase paced the terrace, smoking and scuffing his left

heel against the flagstones. He came back in her direction with the cigarette in his left hand, his right hand in his pocket, still looking toward the guesthouse. Dory watched him take a last drag, fieldstrip the butt and turn away.

When she heard the French doors shut, she shot off the bench, so eager to be away she took the footpath through the trees rather than the wide open walkway along the greensward to the guesthouse. She'd avoided the footpath for a week but nothing happened, no one had jumped out of the trees. If it was kids playing paintball, she wanted the little bugger with a hole in his camouflage jacket caught so she could give him a piece of her mind.

Which is exactly what Chase looked like he wanted to do—give her a piece of his mind. Why? Because she didn't care to hear the details of this farce of a wedding? Well, tough.

Dory took a bath and put on her pajamas, washed her face and brushed her teeth, turned on her bedside lamp and got into bed with her trusty giant flashlight—just in case it *wasn't* kids playing paintball—a pen, a green highlighter and a ten-page computer printout.

The week's schedule of who was checking in and when, what rooms they'd asked for, any dietary or other special requests; which maids Esther had assigned to which suite, the menus Esme had created. Each guests' transportation needs or other facility requests.

It was the beginning of the Outlook Inn season. Ten- to twelve-hour days with more to do as Esther would say than a one-armed paperhanger. Plus Chase and Jill's wedding on Saturday. I should either clone myself, Dory thought, or shoot myself. When Rocky jumped onto the bed beside her, she smiled at her.

"You would've been proud of me at dinner," she told the cat. "I didn't laugh once when Wallace served me and I didn't spit up in my napkin every time Chase looked at Jill like she was dessert."

Rocky gave her a blasé, I've-heard-it-all-before blink, closed her eyes and started to purr. As quiet as the house was, Dory heard the front door shut as clearly as if she were standing at the bottom of the stairs. Jill, she thought, and tucked the flashlight under her pillow.

"Early night," Dory said, glancing at the clock radio on her nightstand when her sister came into the room. "It's barely ten-thirty."

"It only seems like it ought to be midnight. Thank God Studly Dead Bore had work to do." Jill kicked off her shoes and flopped on her back on the foot of the bed with her arms flung out and turned her head toward Dory.

"Chase is such a schmuck. If he'd just love *you* everything would be perfect."

"Well, he doesn't. He loves you."

"Correction." Jill held up a finger. "He wants me."

"Says you. He says he loves you." Dory tossed the printout aside, folded her knees under the covers and leaned forward on her elbows. "You can't fix things by marrying Chase, Jill. You can't undo James and put everything back the way it was. You know that."

"Want to bet?" Jill sat up and snatched up the printout. "Look at this damn schedule. It has ulcers for you and a nervous breakdown for Aunt Ping written all over it. Twenty million bucks can put a stop to that. All I have to do is marry Chase and stick it out for six months."

"I don't want you to do this for me. Aunt Ping wouldn't, either. We can raise twenty million on our own. I have the plan to do it."

"Your plan will take seven years." Jill moved up the bed and took her hands. "My plan is instant. This time next week we'll have twenty million guaranteed. The only bad part is I may have to let Chase drag me to New York for a while. I can do my job anywhere, he informs me. I told him he could do the same. We're negotiating."

"What about Gary? Is he still threatening to jump off a bridge?"

"I told him to jump or shut up about it."

Poor guy, Dory thought. I know how he feels. "This is going to be a mess," she predicted. "I just know it."

"Think positively. Think about twenty million dollars."
Jill put a kiss on her forehead and grinned. "Think about
all the presents I can buy you with Chase's money before he
dumps me."

The last detail for the wedding was the gowns. Jill had
selected them while Dory was in bed dying of measles; they
only had to be fitted. The seamstress arrived at Outlook at
eight-thirty Monday morning.

"Bride first," Jill said to Dory on her way out of the office. "Maid of honor at nine-thirty sharp. Aunt Ping's sitting room."

"I'll be there." Dory waved. When Jill shut the pocket
doors, she took Peter's black notebook out of her middle
desk drawer and turned her chair toward Anita's desk.
"Fifty bucks and ten days, right?"

"Make it seventy-five," Anita said. "I feel lucky."

Dory made the entry and opened the wall safe behind the
Monet above the fireplace. She zipped Peter's notebook inside a bank bag with the pool money, turned around and
saw Anita looking at her.

"Don't worry. Jill can never remember the combination."

The phone rang. Anita answered it while Dory refilled
her coffee.

"It's Amber from the Happy Spirit," Anita said when she
turned away from the Krups machine. "The door is locked.
She can't get in."

Uh oh, Dory thought, and picked up the phone on her
desk.

"I've tried the front and the back," Amber told her. "I've
been trying for twenty minutes but Gary doesn't answer.
Maybe he overslept."

"I'm sure that's all it is," Dory said. Please God, she
prayed. Please let that be all it is. "I'm on my way."

She hung up the phone and grabbed her purse and her
keys.

"I know what to do," Anita said. "Say nothing."

"I'll call you from the store," Dory said and dashed for the Saturn.

The Happy Spirit was still locked up like Fort Knox and Amber was sitting on the curb when Dory got there. She unlocked the front door at nine-fifteen, left Amber to open the register and headed for the office.

Propped in the middle of Gary's desk was a white envelope with *Jill* scrawled on the front in black ink. Dory ripped it open and read:

> *I've gone to investigate, to find James Darwood so you won't have to marry McKay. So don't. I'll be back before the wedding.*
> *Gary*
> *P.S. I told my boss my grandmother died.*

Dory collapsed with relief in Gary's desk chair. He hadn't jumped off the Paseo Bridge into the Missouri River. She picked up the phone.

"Tell Jill to meet me at the guesthouse," she told Anita. "Tell Aunt Ping the store alarm went kaflooie and I'll be back as soon as I can."

Then she went up front, told Amber the story about Gary's grandmother, offered her a raise and a bonus to be manager till Gary came back. Amber, an accounting student at UMKC, was thrilled. Dory gave her keys to the store and the safe combination, drove back to Outlook, met Jill at the guesthouse and gave her Gary's note.

She read it and moaned in her throat.

"What did you say to him?" Dory asked. "And when did you say it?"

"Saturday night. I told him if he found James and got our money back I wouldn't have to marry Chase." Jill was pale. "What have I done?"

"Maybe nothing," Coop said, when Dory called him from Sister Immaculata's office after her fitting. She trusted Gordy but she wasn't taking any chances about discussing the FBI with the attorney who'd seen them through Outlook's darkest hours. "Gary's note says he'll be back for the wedding. So long as he is, there should be no harm done."

"What if he isn't? He's not exactly James Bond, you know."

"Gary doesn't know anything about where the Bastard Little Prick Squad is or what they're doing. He'll bumble around for a few days and come back with his tail between his legs. You worry too much, Dory."

"You bet I worry. I worry about Marshall Phillips."

"I'll be there for the wedding. If there's a problem, we'll handle it."

Jill didn't want to go to New York. Chase didn't want to stay at Outlook. He couldn't wait to get her away from here, couldn't wait to get his hands on her. He was half-crazy wanting to get his hands on her.

"This is our busiest time of the year," Jill told him. "I absolutely cannot leave Outlook. We need all the hands we can get."

"Forgive me," he'd said. "But do you actually work?"

"You bet I do," she'd said indignantly. "I help Aunt Ping schmooze the guests. If you think that's an easy job, you try it."

Chase thought he'd rather pour concrete. He and Jill had their discussion about New York on Sunday evening. On Monday he hung around to see just exactly what she did that she called work.

She smiled and flirted, and as guests checked in she passed them to Esther to be shown to their rooms. She played golf with an art collector from Boston, showed a racehorse owner from Kentucky the stables. At lunch an heiress from Boca Raton suggested shopping. Jill's eyes lit and she crooked a finger at him to come along with his gold cards.

At dinner Monday evening there were a dozen new faces around the table in the little dining room. Jill reminded Chase of Her Ladyship gliding behind chairs to touch shoulders and smile and chat. She lit cigars for the men in the game room with a saucy wink that made their cheeks flush and Chase's blood boil. She sipped Long Island iced teas with the ladies in the parlor, showed off her engagement ring and shot him smiles that said you'll-get-yours-big-fella.

Her daily routine didn't look that strenuous to Chase. It looked like the life she'd led before the Lambert family went into the hotel business—the life she was gearing up to resume thanks to his money. Which he'd known all along and still it bothered him. He told himself he was just feeling insecure, that once he had Jill in his bed the suspicion that something wasn't quite right would go away.

After dinner Miss Ping played her harp and Deirdre the piano in the music room for anyone who cared to listen. Chase did, hoping his father would wander in, but he didn't. He went to Charles' room afterward and found a DO NOT DISTURB sign on the locked door. He knocked anyway, but his father didn't answer. Chase hadn't seen or talked to him in a week, since Charles told him if he married Jill he was a fool.

He hadn't seen Dory, either, since she'd made that crack about the time. She'd told him they were square but obviously they weren't if she was taking shots. He supposed that's why it ticked him off and why he'd followed her. He hadn't found her last night and he couldn't find her now. The office lights were on, he could see a thin gold line on the floor beneath the pocket doors, but when he tried them, they were locked.

Maybe she'd gone home. Chase walked over to the guesthouse. It was dark and still. No lights on, even around back, but the gardener's cottage was lit up. When he knocked on the door, Henry answered.

"Chase," he said and almost swallowed his black mustache.

"Is it too late to cash my rain check for a nightcap?"

"Uh—no." Henry opened the door wider. "Come in."

He offered him a beer or a margarita. Chase chose the beer and sat down on the couch. It took about ten minutes of awkward small talk and Peter and Henry fidgeting in their matching green recliners for him to realize he was about as welcome as aphids in the greenhouse.

"Okay." Chase put his beer on the coffee table. "What's going on?"

"Going on?" Peter asked. "Going on where?"

"Around here. Wallace called me sir three times today. Esther wouldn't look me in the eye. I asked Esme when was she going to make snickerdoodles again and she handed me the recipe."

Peter looked at Henry. Henry looked at Chase.

"Well," he said. "You *are* marrying Jill on Saturday."

"And that means what? I shouldn't have come over here?"

Henry and Peter stared at their margaritas.

"If Dory wanted to sit in on the poker game Friday night she'd be welcome, wouldn't she?" Chase asked. "But I wouldn't, because I'm marrying Jill? Is that it?"

"That's it," Henry said quickly. "Isn't it, Peter?"

"Precisely." He agreed just as quickly. "You're neither fish nor fowl at the moment. You aren't one of us, you aren't a guest, but you aren't a member of the family yet. No one knows quite what to say to you."

"Uh huh. Back to the poker game," Chase said. "Will I be welcome once Jill and I are married?"

"Um, well." Henry hesitated. "You'll be a member of the family, so I don't know." He looked at Peter. "We'd have to take a vote, wouldn't we?"

"Oh, yes," he agreed staunchly. "We'd have to vote."

"You've already voted." Chase's temper pounded in his temples. "You voted me out and you voted Dory in. She *is* a member of the family. What the hell is this? I lost my chair at the poker table because I got kicked off Outlook?"

"Oh please. None of us cared about that." Peter made a face and plunked his margarita on the table, sloshing frozen tequila over the rim. "We cared about *you,* which you would've known if you'd bothered to send a postcard, but off you went without a backward glance for anyone but your father. We helped raise you, Henry and I. Esme and Esther. Wallace and Tom and Eddie, too. We thought we were your family, but obviously we thought wrong."

"I was angry," Chase said. Long ago the heat had gone out of what he'd felt in the barn that night and the morning after, but it still stung to remember. "And I was ashamed of myself."

"We were proud of you," Henry said. "So proud of all your accomplishments. We would've liked to share them with you, not hear about them secondhand from Charles."

"Every Christmas," Chase reminded him. "Everyone at Outlook gets a Christmas card from me with a check inside."

"Sent by your secretary," Peter said. "A label on the envelope, your name printed by a machine on the inside. Would you like the checks back? We never cashed a single one of them."

"Why not?" Chase made a note to ask Sylvia about this.

"You can't buy affection. You can't pay it off like it's a debt you owe, either. Dory could've walked away with ten million dollars and left all of us unemployed and homeless, but she didn't. Neither did Jill. They cashed their trust funds and gave the money to Miss Ping so she could keep Outlook afloat. They didn't desert us."

"I repaid Miss Ping for my education," Chase said between his teeth. "I sent her a check for seventy-five thousand dollars."

"But you weren't here, were you?" Peter said. "Jill was, selling tomatoes on the side of the road. Dory stayed awake nights till she came up with a way to save us, the Outlook Inn. You never bothered to pick up the phone. Never thought to call any of us and ask how we were getting on. That's what matters. Not money. You lost your chair at the poker table because you walked away and never came back."

Chase was stunned. *You've got me all wrong,* he'd told Dory when she called him a pompous, arrogant, condescending ass. *Oh no,* she'd said. *At last I have you right.* Jesus Christ. Did she? Did Peter?

"If that's your opinion of me," he said. "What was the 'lovely to see you, dear boy, come for a nightcap'?"

"That was two weeks ago," Peter said. "Things have changed."

"Don't bother telling me what things. I think I've got the picture." Chase pushed to his feet. "Thanks for the beer."

Neither Peter or Henry followed him to the door. Chase closed it behind him and drew a breath that didn't quite fill his lungs. It was a warm, starry evening but he felt cold. Nothing like being called a selfish son of a bitch to put a chill in your bones.

Maybe that's why he and Jill seemed to have so much in common, though to hear Peter talk she was Mother Teresa. Or was that Dory?

He went down the steps, following the flagstone walk to the path that ran between the greensward and the garden. Best not tread on the grass and compound his sins. What the hell had he been thinking to ask Peter what was going on? He should've known better; still, this was three times he'd been told he left a lot to be desired as a human being.

He wanted a cigarette but reached for his cell phone and punched Curt's home number in D.C. He answered on the third ring.

"I'm taking a poll," Chase said to him. "Which of the following describes me best? Pompous ass, goddamn fool or selfish son of a bitch?"

"All of the above," Curt said. "Still want me to be your best man?"

"Yeah. See you Friday," Chase said and disconnected.

He wanted to throw the phone but threw his cigarettes and lighter instead. Hurled them across the greensward into the dark. He didn't hear them land, he heard the trickle of a fountain. He'd seen one along here somewhere, shaped like a pagoda, set ten feet or so back from the path in a cluster of ivy tumbling down the slope from the garden. He turned and saw the bench that sat in front of it, half lit by the ground lights, the outline of a small figure sitting on the back.

"Occupied," Dory said and a light the size of a search beacon shot toward the sky. The Paul Bunyan flashlight.

"Did I just walk by you?" he asked.

"Kind of. I saw you coming and hopped up here."

"Nice." Chase flung himself on the bench beside her. She scooted away from him along the back. "Who called you a selfish son of a bitch?"

He pinched the bridge of his nose. His head was pounding. "Peter."

"Getting it from all sides, aren't you?"

Chase dropped his hand and looked at her, perched on the back of the bench like some little wood creature, her dark eyes big and liquid in the bright white beam. "Gimme that," he said and snatched the flashlight.

He used it to search the lawn, found his cigarettes and lit one and walked back to the bench. Dory leaned her elbows on her knees and her chin on her hands watching him. She had on a blue polo shirt, khaki shorts and woven, open-toed sandals. The clear bulbs twinkling in the tree beside the bench gleamed on her shins and her red toenails.

"You could hurt somebody with this thing." Chase switched off the flashlight and gave it to her.

"That's the idea." Dory wiggled her eyebrows. "So watch yourself."

Chase smiled a little, sat down and drew on his cigarette, leaned forward with his forearms on his thighs and flicked ash between his feet.

"Peter gets cranky," she said. "Don't pay attention to him."

"It wasn't just Peter. It was Henry, too."

"Whoa! Tag team. What did you do?"

Chase pushed up on his hands and glanced at Dory. "I walked away from Outlook and never looked back."

She tipped her head at him. "And this was a news flash to you?"

"I don't see it that way." He fell back against the bench

and slapped his thighs. "Why don't I? Am I really a selfish son of a bitch?"

"I don't know." Dory shrugged. She'd dropped one hand off her knee; the other still propped her chin. "Are you?"

"I keep hearing it. Pompous ass. Goddamn fool." He ticked them off on his fingers. "Selfish son of a bitch. All variations on the same theme."

"Don't forget you can't dance to save your butt."

Chase turned his head toward Dory. "You're enjoying this."

"If I thought you were poised on the cusp of an epiphany I wouldn't be." She hopped off the bench and faced him. "But you'll put it in perspective. By morning you'll be your usual self. Sweet dreams."

Dory waggled her fingers and turned away toward the guesthouse, the flashlight swinging in her hand. Chase watched her go, ground out his cigarette and picked up the butt.

"Shit," he said to the wood chips under his feet. "Now I'm shallow."

Tuesday morning the Rolls-Royce came back from McPherson's Body Shop. Chase heard the door lift, picked up the thermos he'd just filled with coffee and headed down the stairs dressed to work with the framing crew again in jeans, work boots and a crappy old shirt.

He designed structures by a rule of three. If three of his associates told him a design sucked he scrapped it. Three people had told him he sucked as a human being. He couldn't scrap himself but maybe he could take a hammer to his head and knock some sense into it.

He stepped into the garage through the open bay door expecting to see Diego, but his father swung out from behind the wheel of the pewter gray Silver Shadow in his uniform. Black suit, white shirt, thin black tie and black dress shoes tied with spaghetti laces and polished to a gleam.

He looked—great. Chase felt a wash of relief and a lump in his throat. His color was good, his eyes bright. Till he reached into the Rolls for his uniform cap, turned around and saw Chase.

"How's she look?" he asked.

"See for yourself." Charles pointed at the flying lady hood ornament and followed Chase around the front of the car.

He dropped to his heels, ran his hand over the fender, squinted at the grille like he knew what the hell he was doing and stood up.

"Looks as good as it ever did," Chase said. "So do you, Dad."

"I saw Woods yesterday." Charles squared his shoulders, expecting an argument, Chase guessed. "I'm cleared for two hours or a hundred miles a day, no freeway or rush-hour driving. And stairs. I can do stairs."

"Great. We'll have a few days to bach it before the wedding."

"I'll stay where I am. I assume you'll be leaving Outlook right after the ceremony?"

"Probably," Chase snapped, stung by the rebuff. "Will that be soon enough for you?"

"It'll be fine." Charles tucked his cap under his arm and turned toward the lobby. "Make sure you run the dishwasher."

Chase trailed him as far as the back bumper of the Rolls, a knot of anger and frustration thumping in his chest. He loved his dad. His dad loved him. How had they gotten to this? Was it Jill? Was it Dory?

"Dad," he said. Charles stopped in the doorway between the bays and the lobby and looked back at him. "Are you coming to the wedding?"

"Of course I am. I was fitted for my tuxedo yesterday. You're a goddamned fool but you're still my son."

Charles scowled and shut the door between them.

Aunt Ping summoned Dory to her suite for tea Tuesday evening.

A fountain of acid shot up her throat when she saw the I

Ching yarrow sticks laid out on the ebony table that Aunt Ping had had made with the sixty-four hexagrams used for divination, inlaid in ivory on the top.

Dory had thrown up for two days straight so she was basically starting over with the Prevacid. Since she'd found Gary's note yesterday her stomach had been a burning pit of fire.

"I received a letter from Sister Immaculata today. You were at the school yesterday, so I assume she told you how much Jamie's math scores and his behavior have improved since he's been back in school."

"Yes, she did," Dory confirmed. Had Sister mentioned in her note that she'd been in her office? "She's very pleased and very encouraged."

"Why were you at the school yesterday?"

"I stop by now and then." Dory shrugged. "Just to say hi and see if Sister has taken me off her Watch List yet."

Aunt Ping smiled. "Jamie has asked Deirdre and me for permission to live with you. He'd like to move in straight after the wedding."

"I told him it would be your decision. I also told him he'd have to behave and do his homework and keep his room clean. He agreed."

"I only have one concern." Aunt Ping put down her cup and saucer. "When you marry, what will become of Jamie?"

"Well, you're hopeful." Dory laughed. "I'm not even dating."

"That will change." Aunt Ping lifted the china server from the lacquered ebony table in front of the embroidered red silk settee where they sat. "I can't imagine you ending up an old maid like me."

"Why did you never marry, Aunt Ping?"

"I chose not to," she said simply.

So the question wasn't a major curveball. She'd probably been asked a million times. Still, a little tremble of the hand as she refilled her teacup would've been nice.

"That's a pretty cryptic answer," Dory said.

"To an impertinent question," Aunt Ping replied and up went the eyebrow. So much for asking, Dory decided. Back to snooping.

"Is it yea or nay on Jamie moving in with me?"

"How does probationary sound?" Aunt Ping replaced the server on its tray and picked up her tea. "Make it clear to Jamie that if he doesn't toe the line he'll be back here sharing a suite with Deirdre."

"Good idea. 'Cause who knows? I could be married next week."

"Not quite so soon, I think. Perhaps six months."

"Now who's being impertinent?" Dory asked. Curiosity and acid reflux were killing her. "Is that why you got out the I Ching?"

"That's one thing I regret." Aunt Ping frowned into her teacup. "You asked me to cast the I Ching when James came and I refused."

"I'd forgotten." Dory had, but she could see herself with the red lacquer box full of yarrow sticks in her hands pleading with Aunt Ping. "It wouldn't have changed anything."

"Since I didn't try," Aunt Ping said, "we'll never know, will we?"

Dory had the Robinson Crusoe dream that night, the one where she saw Daddy wandering the beach in ragged white duck pants. She hadn't had the dream in years. This time she saw Mother sitting offshore in the blue speedboat in the photographs Deirdre had brought with her to Outlook. She was laughing at someone swimming around the boat with a snorkel and a plastic shark fin.

The swimmer surfaced with a big grin and a big splash that soaked Mother. The swimmer was James.

Chapter Thirteen

Aunt Ping rarely hung out in the foyer. She left most of the meet and greet stuff to Jill or Dory, but Wednesday morning Diego carried her pink Louis chair and its matching footstool out of the music room, put it down next to the reservation desk and there she parked herself.

"Aunt Ping," Dory said to her. "The Patricks' reservation is guaranteed through six P.M. I have no idea what time they'll actually arrive."

"That's quite all right." Aunt Ping lifted the leather-bound copy of *War and Peace* in her lap. "I have a book."

She was dressed as Margaret Lambert today: Grandmother's pearls and a Chanel suit in a shade of mauve that made her cheeks look pink.

Was Aunt Ping aiming to impress or intimidate? Dory was aiming to impress. Jill had threatened her with death if she didn't.

"You aren't wearing that, are you?" she'd asked when Dory came into the breakfast room for coffee.

"I thought I was," she said, picking a strand of Rocky's white chest hair off the lapel of her navy pinstripe pantsuit. "What's wrong with it?"

"You look like a funeral director." Jill dragged her away from the coffeepot and back up the stairs to her bedroom. "This is a huge day for the Outlook Inn. Our first big-time celebrities are checking in."

"You don't call the Nobel Prize winner in physics a celebrity?"

"Was he on the cover of *People* magazine as 'The Sexiest Man Alive'?" Jill opened her closet doors and faced her. "No? Well, Noah Patrick was, so you can't dress like a mortician."

"Who cares what I look like? I'll be in the office."

"No you won't. I have a million things to do for this damned wedding on Saturday." Jill tugged a knee-length cinnamon skirt off a hanger. "You'll have to help Esther on the front desk."

"Put that back," Dory said. "I hate panty hose."

"You have great legs." Jill threw the skirt at her. "Show them off."

"Noah Patrick is married. I'm not trying to get a date."

"Not with him, but how about that dishy Adam Haddock?" Jill stepped out of the closet with a beige knit sweater that had three-quarter-length sleeves. "He's a doctor. He told me when I showed him the stables. And he has that sexy Kentucky accent."

"He also has the name of a fish," Dory said. And he wasn't Chase. "He's a horse nut and I'm not. Have you been talking to Aunt Ping?"

"I've been avoiding her, but she keeps giving me these looks." Jill moved to the dresser, opened Dory's scarf drawer and glanced at her. "I think she knows something's up."

"You're imagining things," Dory said.

Oh crap. The I Ching. She didn't know much about it, but it was based on numbers and numbers don't lie. It hadn't occurred to her last night, but it made far more sense for Aunt Ping to be checking out Jill's marriage prospects than hers. Wisely, she hadn't grilled Dory; she knew she'd eat ground glass before she'd give Jill up.

The only person shrewder than Aunt Ping was Georgette Parrish. She came through Outlook's front doors, acknowledging Wallace's half-bow with a nod, just a little shy of eleven. Perfectly coifed and perfectly attired in spring green Armani.

"Peg," she said. "What in hell are you doing sitting out here?"

"Minding my own business in my own house, George," Aunt Ping returned mildly. "What are you doing?"

"Place cards," Georgette replied. "Deirdre and I are writing them out and doing the seating arrangements this morning."

"Lovely." Aunt Ping turned a page in *War and Peace*. "Enjoy."

"You aren't helping?"

"You and Deirdre are the calligraphers. You know everyone who's invited to the wedding as well as I do. I don't see why you need my help."

Aunt Ping arched her eyebrow and went back to her book. Georgette opened her mouth, shut it, and put a hand on her hip.

"I'll tell Deirdre you're here." Dory did, on the house phone, and hung up. Georgette was tapping her foot and Aunt Ping was ignoring her. "Deirdre suggested the library." Dory stepped out from behind the reception desk. "This way."

Like Georgette couldn't find the library blindfolded, but Dory thought it best to get her away from Aunt Ping before one of them blew up. For a second she wasn't sure Georgette would follow her, but she did.

The library was no longer Daddy's private sanctum, so the pocket doors were kept open, the blinds behind the drapes half shut to protect the three thousand leather books on the shelves and the oxblood leather chairs from sun damage. There were three library tables, one of which held a PC with high-speed Internet access for the guests.

In the doorway Georgette caught Dory's arm. "Why is Peg sitting in the foyer?"

"She's waiting for the Patricks to check in."

"Oh, for God's sake," Georgette said disgustedly. "We settled that."

"She says she has no idea how you talked her into allowing show people to stay at Outlook," Dory said and paused.

If she was going to test her theory that if anyone knew *for sure* about Aunt Ping and Charles it was Georgette Parrish, it was now or never. "But I think I do."

Georgette's gaze sharpened and narrowed. "Do you really?"

"You vouched for the Patricks the day after Charles' heart attack."

"And why would that make a difference?" Georgette fired back like a laser and Dory floundered, uncertain what to say.

"Aunt Ping was distracted," Dory said. "That's all I mean."

"I don't think that's at all what you mean." Georgette yanked her into the library, pulled the right-hand door out of its pocket, backed her against it and lowered her voice. "Whatever you think you know, I advise you to keep to yourself. Don't, and you and I will be having another conversation that won't be nearly as pleasant as this one."

"Aunt Ping's been through enough. I just want her to be happy."

"What makes you think she isn't? Because you're miserable?"

"I'm not miserable! Why would I be miserable?"

"Because your sister is marrying the man you love."

"Listen. I had a crush on Chase when I was a kid, but—"

"If you love him, fight for him. Don't let Jill marry Chase. It's just a little too pat and she isn't fooling anyone."

"Oh crap," Dory said. "Does Aunt Ping know?"

"She suspects. I told her she was worrying too much." Georgette took hold of her arms. "It's not too late to call off this wedding.

"Oh! Here you are!" Deirdre popped around the pocket door, her wooden case full of inks and calligraphy pens clutched to her bosom. "Do you have the place cards, Georgette?"

"Right here." She swung away from Dory and smacked the pink leather tote bag hung over her shoulder. "Shall we get started?"

Dory peeled herself off the door and watched Deirdre

and Georgette arrange the pens and the inks on the largest library table, followed by the place cards and a huge sheet of graph paper Georgette unfolded from her tote along with the guest list Anita had typed. Aunt Ping suspected the wedding was a sham, Georgette thought she was a fool and it wasn't even time for lunch.

"Shall I send in a tea tray?" she asked.

"That would be lovely, dear, but don't rush." Deirdre beamed at her. "The Patricks just arrived. They're with Margaret in the foyer."

It was hard to run in heels—damn Jill and this skirt—but Dory managed to make it to the foyer without breaking her neck. If Aunt Ping got up on her Margaret Lambert high horse and screwed this up, Jill would kill *her*, not Aunt Ping. She shot past Wallace at his post by the front door, looking around frantically for a movie star. She didn't see one.

She saw Aunt Ping down on her heels next to a man in jeans, running shoes and a white polo shirt, their heads bent over a cat carrier. A little girl with dark hair squatted between them in print shorts and a tank top with bows on the shoulders. A striking woman with a white streak in the front of her dark hair stood behind them, wrestling with a towheaded toddler to keep him from grabbing the sunglasses stuck on top of the man's blond head.

Who were these people? They weren't the Patricks. Dory had seen pictures of them in magazines and on TV. Lindsay Varner was a blond.

So was the woman Wallace opened the door for, a woman in navy shorts and a flowered camp shirt pulling a small, wheeled suitcase behind her. She was tall and gorgeous and for a second, because she was rattled, Dory thought she was Jill. Till she smiled and shook her head at Wallace when he tried to take the suitcase away from her.

"Thanks, but I can manage," she said. "It's not heavy."

That wasn't Jill's voice—it was Lindsay Varner's. Dory recognized it from *Betwixt and Between,* the TV show she'd been on with her husband, Noah Patrick, when Dory was in junior high school. If this was Lindsay Varner, then the blond guy stooped over the cat carrier with Aunt Ping had to be—holy crap!—Noah Patrick.

Dory wanted to faint. Scream. Crawl in a hole, but she pasted a smile on her face and held her hand out to Lindsay Varner.

"Mrs. Patrick. I'm Dory Lambert. Welcome to the Outlook Inn."

"Hello, Miss Lambert." She had a star-power smile and a cool but firm handshake. "I feel so special being met by a member of the family."

"Call me Dory, please. We do our best to make all our guests feel special." When we aren't busting up fistfights, she thought, or scamming people out of twenty million bucks. "And we are a family operation. Let me introduce you to my aunt, Margaret Lambert."

Dory led Lindsay Varner toward the reception desk. The cluster around the cat carrier included Henry now and had shifted enough that Dory could see Esther standing like a red-faced robot behind the desk, staring at Noah Patrick, and Aunt Ping cradling a sleek, coal black cat with big emerald eyes in her arms.

"That's Pyewacket," Lindsay said. "We didn't realize he'd stowed away in the van till we stopped at a McDonald's about a hundred miles shy of here to buy the kids Happy Meals. Pye loves French fries."

"He won't be a problem," Dory said. "My aunt loves cats."

Aunt Ping was scratching Pyewacket's ears. When he touched his nose to hers, she smiled and laughed.

"He's a beauty," Aunt Ping said. "And such nice manners."

"He's a con artist," Noah Patrick said. Pyewacket the cat turned his head toward him and laid back his ears. "If you don't allow pets, we'll find a kennel for him till we can call home and have someone from Belle Coeur come and get him."

"I won't hear of it." Aunt Ping put the cat back in the carrier, closed the door and rose and offered Noah Patrick her hand. "Pyewacket is most welcome at the Outlook Inn, Mr. Patrick. So are you and your family."

Dory wasn't the only one who mistook Lindsay Varner for Jill.

When Chase came into the little dining room that evening he stopped in the doorway and did a double take. Jill was circulating; Lindsay was seated next to her husband. Chase looked at her, then at Jill, at Lindsay again, shook his head and moved into the room toward Jill.

The hole in her chest where her heart used to be ached as Dory watched him. He wore the blue suit he'd had on Saturday night when they'd sat on the bench under the elm tree. Chase touched Jill's waist. She half turned toward him with a smile.

"Our lovebirds," Deirdre twittered to Adam Haddock, the doctor. "They're getting married on Saturday."

When Jill offered her cheek to Chase for a kiss Dory looked away. Straight at Noah Patrick, seated across the table from her. He winked at her and smiled, a hey-I'm-with-you-babe smile that made Dory flush. Handsome as Chase was, Noah Patrick was the most beautiful man she'd ever seen. Definitely the funniest and probably the kindest.

She'd spent most of the afternoon showing him around Outlook while Lindsay and her cousin, Emma Fairchild, the woman with the white streak in her dark hair, put their kids, daughter Emma and son Ben, down for naps.

"I had no idea this place was a museum," Noah had said to her with an appreciative whistle. "Are you sure it's child-proof?"

"Absolutely. We've never had a problem with juvenile guests."

"How 'bout a two-year-old delinquent who throws tantrums?"

"Worst case, we're insured." Dory laughed. "Wait till you meet Aunt Ping's ward, Jamie. You'll see you have nothing to worry about."

They apprehended Jamie in the pool house.

Peter had yet to transfer the Japanese poi from their winter digs, the giant aquarium near the shallow end of the pool. The cats were not allowed in the pool house, yet Rocky was perched on the lid of the tank, her head hung over the side, her paws batting the glass. The fish shot in crazed, rainbow colored flashes from one end of the tank to the other.

"C'mere, Rocky." The cat gave a yowl of protest as Dory scooped her off the tank. "All right, Jamie. Come out, come out wherever you are."

He dragged himself out from behind a bank of potted ferns, an I'm-busted jut to his chin and a stopwatch in his hand.

"What is this?" Dory asked.

"Fish races," Jamie said, stuffing the stopwatch in his pocket.

"Uh-uh." Dory held out her hand. Jamie heaved an end-of-the-world sigh and gave her the stopwatch. She gave him Rocky. "Take her home and feed her. Tuna, if you please. Before you go, this is Noah Patrick. He and his wife and their two children just checked in."

"Hello, sir," Jamie mumbled and ducked his chin.

"Hey, Jamie." Noah cocked a *May-I?* eyebrow at Dory. She nodded and took Rocky back from Jamie. "Which one's the fastest?"

Jamie glanced up at him through his bangs. "The salmon-colored one with the blue spots on his sides."

"You sure? He looks pretty tired to me." Noah stepped toward the aquarium, bent over and peered through the glass. So did Jamie. The salmon-colored fish was sinking toward the bottom, his gills flapping like mad. "I think you ran him too hard." Noah leaned his hands on his knees and looked at Jamie. "Plus you scared him and you tormented Rocky with a fish he was never gonna get."

"She. Rocky's a she." Jamie blinked innocently at Noah. "I guess it was kinda mean, huh?"

"Do you swim?" Noah asked.

"Yes, sir."

"So do I. Why don't you go put on your trunks, I'll put on mine and I'll chase you from one end of the big pool to the other. How about it?"

"Uh—umm. I've got homework." Jamie turned as red as his hair. "How about if I promise I'll never do this again?"

"Don't tell me." Noah nodded at Dory.

"I'll never race fish again, Dory. Cross my heart." Jamie scooped Rocky out of her arms. "I'll feed her and do my math, okay?"

"Fine," Dory said. "I'll check your homework later."

Jamie clutched Rocky to his chest and fled the pool house. Noah straightened and grinned at her.

"Too smart for his own good," he said.

"Frequently too smart for mine. That was amazing. Thank you. I couldn't decide if I wanted to choke him or drown him."

"I could sort of see that on your face."

Dory raised her crystal water goblet and wondered what Noah had seen just now that made him wink and give her that knowing smile. Did her face really give that much away?

Yikes. If so, she'd have to wear a mask to the wedding.

Dory had legs. Nice legs. Short but nice.

Chase noticed them after dinner when the guests, starry-eyed and gaga over Noah Patrick and his wife, Lindsay Varner, followed them like a pack of enchanted rats from the little dining room to the back parlor where Dory helped Esther hand around cups of coffee or tea.

Shapely calves, racehorse ankles. *Really* nice legs.

"You're ogling the maid of honor." Jill stretched up on her toes and whispered in his ear. "You're supposed to be ogling the bride."

He and Jill stood by the fireplace, in front of French doors that led outside onto a flagged, wedge-shaped terrace between the main house and the north wing. He could see his father's suite, which also had French doors, and the soft glow of lights behind chiffon sheers.

"I'm not ogling. I'm noticing. I've never seen Dory in a skirt."

"You have, too. When she was a kid in her school uniform."

"She didn't have legs." Chase grinned. "She had fat little stumps."

"I won't tell her you said that." Jill put her nose in the air but she smiled. "I should help. I'll bring you a coffee. Don't wander off."

"Not a chance," he said and watched Jill cross the parlor, the hem of her sleeveless peach dress a good two inches above her knees.

Now those were legs. Long, gorgeous legs he couldn't wait to feel tangled with his. Smooth, silky and naked as the rest of her.

Only three more days to wait. Only three more days to put things right with his father. He hadn't seen Charles since Tuesday morning in the garage. Pride went before a fall, but he'd be damned if he'd ask Peter or Henry for tips on how to approach him. He'd taken enough abuse, been given the cold shoulder once too often by the rest of the staff.

At dinner he'd hit Jill up for suggestions. She'd looked at him like he'd dyed his hair purple. "Why are you asking me?"

"You're my fiancée. Who else should I ask?"

"Dory. She hangs out with your father. I don't. Ask her."

Easy to say. He'd been trying for ten minutes to catch her eye, but Dory seemed oblivious. Short as she was, she probably couldn't see him from around Noah Patrick and the horse guy from Kentucky, Dr. Somebody Fish Name. Jill had told him but he hadn't been interested enough to pay attention. The two men seemed to be taking turns making Dory laugh. For some reason, that was annoying the hell out of him.

Chase turned his back on the room and looked out the French doors. He saw dew sparkling on the grass in the ground lights and fireflies winking out of the flower beds.

He'd give just about anything to see his father open the doors of his suite and step out onto the terrace, but all he could see was the reflection of the parlor in the glass panes.

Gus and Cydney Monroe had come for dinner. They were part of the group surrounding the Patricks. Apparently, the four of them were friends. They'd met in some burg town where Lindsay owned a bookstore and Gus—or was it Cydney?—did a book signing. Jill had told him, but again, he hadn't been paying attention.

She brought him his coffee and kissed his cheek. No one noticed. Everyone in the room was talking and laughing. Chase would've thought the "lovebirds" would draw a little attention, but he and Jill stood apart and were pretty much ignored. That annoyed him, too.

A lot of things annoyed him. All week long he'd felt restless and distracted. He got like this when he was working out a design in his head, before he sat down to render it, but there was nothing in his head worth drawing. He wasn't even sure there was a brain up there.

He didn't want to, but he tagged along to the music room with Jill and everyone else for the evening's concert, a lengthy and slumberous piece that sounded like Mozart. He applauded Miss Ping and Deirdre when it finally ended; got up to leave and sat down again when Noah Patrick slid onto the piano bench with Deirdre.

"Do you know this one?" Patrick banged out a couple of chords that made Deirdre laugh. "Oh yes," she said, "I know it."

So did anybody who knew anything about rock and roll—Jerry Lee Lewis' "Great Balls of Fire." Patrick slid off the bench, pulled Dory to her feet and started to dance. Lindsay Varner laughed and clapped.

"Is he a jerk?" Chase muttered to Jill. "Or is it just me?"

"It's just you," she snapped and left him to dance with Gus.

Chase left the music room, turned the corner and walked down the north wing corridor to his father's suite. The damn DO NOT DISTURB sign hung on the knob. He pounded on the door for a good ten minutes but Charles didn't answer.

Okay. That was it. Chase retraced his steps out of the north wing, rounded the corner past the music room and strode down the main corridor of the house to the back parlor. He hadn't seen Miss Fairview at the concert. The back parlor was pretty much her domain.

And there she was, pacing in front of the fireplace with a cell phone to her ear. Chase heard her say something about time—it was the wrong time, not the right time—as he stormed into the parlor. She flipped the phone shut and spun toward him.

"Do you *mind*?" she snapped. "This is a private conversation!"

"Lady, on a cell phone nothing is private." He swept past her, pushed through the French doors and crossed the small terrace.

The lights were still on in his father's suite. Damn stubborn old man. He banged his fist on the French doors till his hand was numb and his father finally realized he wasn't going away. Chase could see him through the chiffon sheers. Watched him slam his book on a table next to his chair and get up. He flung the doors open and scowled at him.

"You don't expect me to give up my life for you, but you expect me to live it to suit you. You don't like that I'm marrying Jill? Tough. I'm a goddamn fool but I'm still your son? Don't do me any favors."

"I don't want to see you make a mistake," Charles said.

"Then send your tuxedo back and go fishing on Saturday."

Chase turned on his heel and walked away, lit a cigarette and tromped all over Peter's precious grass. Tore off his suit coat, ripped off his tie so he could breathe and stalked up the drive. His heart stopped thundering and he'd slowed to a walk by the time he reached the garage.

He'd left the truck parked outside. Somebody had drawn a happy face in the condensation on the back window. It was fresh; the corners of the upturned mouth hadn't started to run yet.

Chase swung toward Gramps the elm tree. The carriage lights at the corners of the garage wall roof made its leaves shimmer a dull silver.

"Dory," he said. "Are you in there?"

"Over here," she said from the stairs.

She flipped on the giant flashlight as he turned around, shooting a stark white beam toward the dark sky. Chase saw her sitting partway up the stairs. She snapped off the light and put the flashlight down. He moved to the stairs, tossed his coat and tie over the railing. "You're the cutest night watchman I've ever seen, but what are you doing here?"

"Jill's looking for you. You didn't answer your cell phone."

"She's not looking for me. She's pissed at me." Chase sat down a step or two below Dory and rubbed his hands over his face. His fingers smelled like tobacco. "She basically called me a jerk."

"That doesn't mean she doesn't want to talk to you."

Chase dropped his hands and scowled at Dory over his shoulder. She was wearing stockings. Her shins glimmered in the carriage lights. She had her knees together but there was a gap between her skirt and her left thigh. If he leaned back on his elbow he could see all the way up.

"Maybe I don't want to talk to her. Did that ever occur to Jill? No?" Chase snorted, swung around and leaned his elbows on his knees. "Why doesn't that surprise me?"

He heard Dory scoot down a step, felt her hand settle on his shoulder. A very small, warm hand. "What's the matter, bro?"

Chase turned his head and cocked an eyebrow at her. "*Bro*?"

"That's what you're going to be come Saturday, isn't it?" Dory moved down one more step and sat beside him. "You aren't mad at Jill."

"I'm sick of being called a jerk." Chase pressed the heels of his hands to his eyes, let them fall and glanced at her. "Am I a jerk?"

"Why do you ask me these things? Am I selfish? Am I a jerk? What am I supposed to say?"

"You're supposed to give it to me straight. Am I a jerk?"

"I can see how the case could be made."

Chase looked at Dory. Her small, earnest face. Heart-shaped, he'd never noticed that before. Her brown eyes soft as velvet in the half-light.

"If anybody has a right to call me a jerk, it's you. But so far you're the only one who hasn't. Why is that?"

"Probably because I don't think you're a jerk."

"The way I beat up on you about Jill, you should."

"Well, I don't, so live with it. Here are the points that could be made in the case for jerkhood. One. You're a man." Chase laughed. Dory grinned, turned sideways on the step to face him. "Two." She counted them off on her fingers. "You're extremely focused. Three. You compartmentalize, which is how you stay so focused, but you don't think of anything or anyone unless it or they are right in front of you."

"Peter jumped me about that. I never write, I never call."

"But you'd be delighted to hear from Peter if he'd called you. That's compartmentalizing. Four. You're very direct. You say exactly what you mean and let the chips fall where they may. That's because you are—five—impatient. You want what you want and you want it *now*."

"I wanted Dad to retire so badly that I rushed it. And I just got impatient again." Chase leaned against the railing and faced her. "I told Dad that if he doesn't like it that I'm marrying Jill he can skip the wedding and go fishing. I meant it. I might not tomorrow, but I do now."

"That's six." Dory held up her thumb. "You're stubborn and hardheaded. So is Charles. He might just go fishing."

"I know. I don't care so long as you don't go with him."

"I'll be there. I have to catch Jill's bouquet." Dory reached for her flashlight, scooted off the steps and brushed the back of her skirt. "Aunt Ping read the I Ching. She says I'm going to be married in six months."

"Who are you going to marry?"

"Beats me. If the I Ching said, Aunt Ping didn't tell me."

"Keep wearing skirts." Chase bent his elbow on the step and gave Dory the once-over. "You won't have any trouble finding a groom."

His father was sitting in the living room above the garage when Chase came down from the loft the next morning. He was wearing his uniform. At the sound of his footsteps on the stairs, Charles stood up, plucked the white handkerchief out of his breast pocket and waved it.

Chase vaulted the scratched-up leather sofa that used to be Del Lambert's and threw his arms around his father. Charles hugged him and backed out of his embrace.

"You're still a damned fool and you're still making a mistake." He used the handkerchief to blow his nose and stuffed it in his pants pocket. "That's the last time I'll say it. I can have one highball a day. Pick me up at seven and we'll go have a drink to celebrate your marriage."

The phone on her nightstand woke Dory at 6:12 A.M.

"Sorry to call so early," Gordy said. "I'm on my way out of town."

"It's okay." Dory kicked off the covers, blinked to wake up and swept her hair out of her face. "My alarm's about to go off anyway."

"Diego is clean, but I hit a snag with Miss Fairview. In May of 1998 she flew to London. From there she supposedly embarked on a train tour of Europe. She was stamped in and out of every country on the Continent. Problem is I can't find her registered at any hotel anywhere in Europe from May 15 through August 18 when she boarded the Concorde in Paris and flew back to New York."

Dory was wide awake now. "Could she have stayed with friends?"

"That's probably exactly what she did. I'll have to dig deeper to verify it and I won't be able to till Monday, maybe Tuesday. Depends on how long this out of town thing takes. Any more kids playing paintball?"

"Not that anyone has told me. Thanks, Gordy. Safe trip."

Dory shut off her alarm and brushed her teeth. Made her bed and got dressed in the navy pinstripe pantsuit Jill had rejected yesterday, went downstairs and pushed the red button on the coffeemaker.

Miss Fairview was as forthcoming as a clam, but Dory still couldn't picture her in camouflage. She couldn't picture her with friends, either, but she could be Queen Elizabeth's bosom bud for all Dory knew. Miss Fairview was old money. If you weren't worth at least ten million, your function in life was to serve those who were. She'd hardly confide in anyone named Lambert, no matter how rich they used to be.

Dory ate a carton of blueberry yogurt and drank a cup of coffee, poured another into an insulated mug, clipped her walkie-talkie to her waistband and headed for the garage. Chase's truck was gone and she was glad. She'd lain awake for almost an hour smiling at the ceiling because he'd said she should keep wearing skirts. How dumb was that?

Diego was barely out of bed. Dory handed him the insulated mug and told him Esther had found Miss Fairview snooping in the office.

"Is she loony tunes?" He took a slug of coffee. "Or just nosy?"

"I don't know. Do you think you could keep an eye on her?"

"Just call me Homez." Diego grinned. "Sherlock Homez."

At ten o'clock Anita went outside to smoke. When the pocket doors closed behind her, Jill swiveled her chair toward Dory's desk.

"It's Thursday," she said. "Where is Gary?"

"I don't know." Dory looked up at the Excel spreadsheet on her monitor. "I've been trying not to think about that."

"He said he'd be back before the wedding." Jill's eyes filled and she plucked a Kleenex out of the box on her desk. "What if he isn't?"

"You aren't counting on Gary to find James so you don't have to marry Chase, are you?"

"Oh, hell no." She wiped her nose. "I just miss him so much."

This wasn't good. Jill was in tears because she hadn't seen Gary in five days. How was she going to survive not seeing him for six months? Providing that's all the time it took Chase to dump her.

"Gary loves you, Jill. He'll be back."

"Why hasn't he called?"

"He can't. He's undercover."

"I *hate* this!" Jill crushed the Kleenex in her fist. "We should've gone out and found James ourselves!"

"Jill, honey," Dory reminded her, "the Bastard Little Prick Squad has been looking for James for ten years."

"They're men," she said disgustedly. "Men can't find their socks."

The intercom on Dory's desk phone buzzed.

"Lovey," Peter said. "Do you still have that scrap you found?"

Dory's pulse jumped. "Yes."

"Bring it. I'm in the greenhouse."

Peter met her at the door, pulled her inside and flipped the lock. He wasn't wearing his work gloves, but a pair of disposable vinyl ones.

"Oh crap," Dory said. "What is it?"

"I turned the compost pile this morning." Peter led her down the long rows of plants and into his workroom. "I found that."

He nodded at a camouflage jacket laid out on one of the rough wooden potting benches. It was filthy and wrinkled and it reeked of decomposing vegetation. Peter handed her a pair of disposable gloves.

"It's torn and there's a hole in the right sleeve," he said.

Dory put on the gloves and took the scrap out of its Ziploc bag. Peter smoothed the sleeve and flattened the edges of the tear. The scrap fit into the hole as neatly as a jigsaw puzzle piece. Dory's stomach turned. She put the scrap back in its baggie, the baggie in her pocket.

"I found the scrap two weeks ago, on Charles' birthday. When did you last turn the compost heap?"

"Three weeks. The jacket came up on my second full pitchfork."

"So it probably went in after you turned it," Dory said and Peter nodded. She scraped mud off the label with her gloved thumbnail. "Men's large. Doesn't look like a kid playing paintball. Unless this belongs to somebody's daddy or older brother."

"I suppose it could," Peter said. "But I think it's more likely that whoever threw it in the compost heap knew you'd found the scrap. Otherwise, why dispose of the jacket?"

"I want to know *who* disposed of it," Dory said. "Do you have a big plastic bag and a safe place to keep this or should I put it in the safe?"

"Don't tell me you're going to show this to Agent Frasier. I'm with Gordy. It makes more sense for the FBI to be creeping around Outlook."

"I don't know what I'm going to do," Dory said. "I'll take a Prevacid and think about it."

Which she did on her way to Jamie's school and the telephone in Sister Immaculata's office.

"The jacket is a mess," she told Coop. "It has gunk all over it and a couple spots where the fabric has already started to break down. Peter's compost heap should be declared a toxic waste dump."

"Then it's doubtful it will tell us much. The scrap might. If you like, I'll bring them back to New York and run them through a lab."

"I'd like that, thanks. If the FBI *is* lurking in the bushes, I couldn't figure out how I was going to get the jacket off Outlook to have it tested."

"I agree this is suspicious, but is it a threat?" Coop asked. "Jamie saw the person who was wearing the camouflage jacket. The question is what was that person doing? Spying on Jamie? Unlikely. Spying on all of you? Infinitely more probable than kids playing paintball. It points to the FBI and backs Gary's claim that Marsh is running out of time and getting desperate. But there's another possibility. That Jamie came across a burglar who was casing Outlook with the intention of robbing it."

"Why would a thief throw his jacket in the compost heap?"

"If Jamie saw him, he saw Jamie. He was probably expecting the police. He got rid of the jacket because Jamie could identify it."

"I never thought of that. It's so simple and so *not* sinister." Relief so intense it made her dizzy swept through Dory. "You're a genius, Coop."

"I know." He chuckled. "That's why I make the big bucks."

Chapter Fourteen

The world was a wonderful place. A fabulous place. Dory was so relieved and so happy to be relieved she wanted to sing. Unfortunately she couldn't carry a tune with a wheelbarrow.

Ah, but she could dance, which was more than Chase could do, and Jamie had surprised a burglar! Woo-hoo!

Her sister was marrying the man she loved. Boo-hoo, sob, sob. The FBI could be snooping around Outlook, too—but they weren't! Ha-ha!

"If you don't stop grinning—" Jill threatened Dory's beaming reflection in the trifold mirror the seamstress had set up in the sitting room of Aunt Ping's suite. "—I'm going to strangle you with this veil."

"Be my guest," Dory said cheerfully.

Jill burst into tears. It was eleven A.M. Friday morning. This was the final fitting of her wedding gown; the fifth time today she'd broken down.

The seamstress stuck her head around the doorframe and smiled.

"All brides cry," she said and popped back into the bedroom where Aunt Ping and Deirdre were trying on their dresses.

"Never mind." The bride sucked back a sob. "I'll strangle her."

"You can't keep doing this." Dory stepped up on the seamstress's stool, offered Jill a tissue and put her hands on her shoulders. "You have to get a grip on yourself or you have to cancel the wedding."

"Over Gary's dead body!" Jill snatched the tissue. "If he doesn't make it back here in the next twenty-four hours I will *kill* him!"

She let out another wail. Dory reached for another tissue.

"Jillian." Aunt Ping appeared in the doorway. "Are you all right?"

"She's fine," Dory said to her over Jill's shoulder. "All brides cry."

Aunt Ping didn't say anything. She raised her eyebrow, but turned away and went back into the bedroom.

"Okay." Jill drew a deep breath through her nose. "I can do this."

"You can still get cold feet," Dory said. "It's not too late."

"Stop saying that!" Jill shuddered at her reflection and turned her back to the mirror. "Unzip me. I hate this damn dress."

No, Dory thought, *you hate that you're wearing it for the wrong man.* The dress was gorgeous. A strapless, ivory satin tube with a detachable train. She'd look like a Q-tip in it but Jill was stunning. The tears clinging to her lashes only made her eyes look more like sapphires.

"I don't know why you're so happy," Jill complained as she wiggled out of the gown. "You keep saying this will be a disaster."

"It's gonna be, but why should I be miserable?" Dory took the dress from her and put it back on its padded hanger. "I tried everything I could think of to talk you out of it. My conscience is clear."

Except for one teensy little thing—the fifty-dollar bet that Jill's marriage to Chase would fall apart in eight months. The pool had made her laugh when she'd desperately needed something to be funny, but now she felt like a gawker in the middle of a crowd laying wagers on whether the guy on the twenty-story ledge was going to jump.

Once the fittings were finished, Jill left to have a manicure and a facial—like she needed one. Dory went to the office and opened the safe.

She left her money in the pot but drew a line through her name in Peter's notebook. Then she sighed, smiled and felt ever so much better.

By five-thirty when the wedding rehearsal started, Jill had pulled herself together. She was calm and composed, but her eyes looked funny. Overly bright like she was about to cry again.

Dory pulled her aside under the rose silk canopy erected over the terrace, from which Jill would make her entrance into the ballroom for the ceremony. She went up on her toes and peered at her sister's eyes.

"Have you been drinking?" Dory hissed at her.

"No, goofy." Jill pushed her away. "Georgette gave me a Valium."

"Then *don't* drink," Dory warned, but Jill ignored her.

It was Chase's fault. He popped a magnum of champagne when the rehearsal ended. Jill swigged two glasses like they were shots of tequila and started to wobble on the two-inch heels that matched her yellow linen sheath. By the grin on his face as he caught her by the elbow, Dory guessed Chase thought his bride was just tipsy.

"Whoa," Curt said behind her. "She's swacked already."

"Jill gets loopy on aspirin." Dory turned to face him. "A well-meaning friend gave her a Valium."

"She'll regret that in the morning. So will the friend when Jill sobers up." Curt grinned. "Dance with me later?"

Was this the groom the I Ching had seen for her? She'd forgiven Curt for Jill months ago. He was kind and funny and his brain was definitely in his head, not his pants. But he wasn't Chase.

"Absolutely." Dory smiled. "I'll see you after dinner."

"I'll find you." Curt gave her elbow a squeeze and turned away.

He had a nice touch, warm and gentle, but there was no zing in it, no clear-to-the-bone sizzle like she felt at the slight brush of Chase's hand. Dory watched Curt follow the wedding party out of the ballroom toward the little dining room where they would eat a catered dinner with the rest of Outlook's guests. Jill was supposed to hostess the meal. Dory hoped Chase could keep her from falling off her chair.

She hurried toward the kitchen, into the china closet where Aunt Ping and Deirdre had already changed into their black tuxedos and were helping Jamie fasten his red cummerbund.

"Hurry, Dory," Aunt Ping said. "They're seated and waiting for us."

Chase had never seen anyone get looped on two glasses of Dom Pérignon. At least Jill was a happy drunk, giggling and saying "Whoops!" every five seconds. He had no idea why.

Curt sat on Jill's other side. Every now and then he'd grab Jill's arm to keep her from sliding under the table. Chase signaled the waiter and ordered coffee.

"Night off," was all she'd said when he'd asked where Wallace and the maids who helped him serve were.

The java did the trick. Jill stopped slurring her words.

"What time is it?" Jill grabbed his right wrist and glanced at his Rolex. "Oops. Gotta go. I'll be back."

She aimed a kiss at his jaw that didn't quite connect and slipped out of her chair. She hadn't kissed him on the lips in a week. Not once had she voluntarily opened her mouth. He practically had to pry her jaws apart. Chase thought about that for a nanosecond and went after her.

In the corridor he caught a glimpse of her yellow dress as she pushed through the servants' door at the far end. She wouldn't meet a boyfriend in the kitchen, would she? Better than a bedroom, he supposed.

He pushed through the door maybe five seconds behind Jill but couldn't find her. He looked in the family kitchen and breakfast room; she wasn't in Esme's kitchen or the pantry, either. Where was she?

As he passed it, Chase happened to glance up the service hall that connected the kitchen to the grand dining room. A flash of something caught the corner of his eye. He backed up and took a better look. Through the porthole in the service door at the end of the hall he saw the huge crystal chandeliers in the grand dining room ablaze with light.

What was this? He turned up the hall, looked through the porthole and couldn't believe what he was seeing.

The Outlook servants, his father among them. All wearing their best clothes, seated at the football field–length table. Miss Ping, Deirdre, Jamie and Dory, dressed in black tuxedos, serving them wedges of chocolate torte on Outlook's best china. A pattern Chase knew was priceless. He'd accidentally brushed a cup off Esme's counter when he was ten. His father had thrown his back out diving to catch it before it hit the floor.

Jill was speaking but the door was soundproof. Chase nudged it open just enough that he could hear what she was saying.

" . . . so I wish you'd all stop looking like you want to crawl under the table and enjoy this, our gift to you, for all you've done and all you do for us. We couldn't think of a better way to show you how much we appreciate you, how much we rely on you, and how much we love you."

Miss Ping stood like a dutiful servant behind his father's chair. When Jill said, "how much we love you," Miss Ping laid just the fingertips of her left hand on his shoulder. Only for a second, barely more than a heartbeat. Chase doubted anyone else saw. He wasn't even sure he'd seen it.

"I've come to ask a favor," Jill said. "Tomorrow I'm being married. Would you, Wallace, and you, Charles, Peter, Henry, Eddie and Tom. Would you do me the honor of walking me down the aisle?"

Chase saw his father's chin tremble, Peter and Henry throw their arms around each other and Eddie rub his nose.

Tom cleared his throat. Only Wallace kept his composure. He rose from his chair and bowed.

"Miss Jillian," he said. "The honor will be ours."

Dory applauded. So did everyone else, except Esther. She was weeping into her napkin. Chase eased the door shut.

For the past two weeks every person at that table had busted their butt getting Outlook ready for this wedding, his wedding. His and Jill's. He should've thought of doing something like this, but he hadn't.

Compartmentalized was just a fancy word for self-absorbed.

The worst thing Chase could've done was go back to the little dining room and the Dom Pérignon, but what the hell. He couldn't dance; he might as well drink.

Maybe fifteen minutes later, Dory came in. She'd changed her tux for a flirty celery green skirt, a sweater with short sleeves and a scooped neck that just showed her collarbone.

"This evening we're hosting a party to honor our staff," she announced to the guests. "Our wonderful employees, who make your stay at the Outlook Inn as relaxed and easy as being at home. We'd like to invite all of you to join us if you're so inclined. Just follow me."

She held her hand out and smiled at Curt. He damn near broke his neck getting out of his chair and around the table.

"Let's go, princess." Noah Patrick pulled his wife to her feet. "I've never met a party I didn't like."

Lindsay Varner laughed. Most everyone at the table laughed, too, and followed Mr. and Mrs. Movie Star out of the dining room. Chase didn't think Noah Patrick was all that funny. He thought he was obnoxious and annoying, but he tagged along, hoping to find Jill.

Torches lit the path from the terrace, through the ornamental garden and down the steps past the pool to a lawn tent the size of a circus big top with the sides tied back. Chase saw tables of food and beverages, small bistro-style tables and chairs, a live band with big amps, drums, guitars and an organ set up in one corner—and Jill on the dance floor laid over the grass boogying away with Diego.

She hadn't come to collect her fiancé for the party. Imagine that.

All week long she'd been moody. Sweet and affectionate one minute, sharp and snippy the next. He supposed that's why his mind leaped to a boyfriend, why he wondered, as he watched Jill laugh at something Diego said, if it wasn't stretching credulity just a bit too far to believe that he'd stepped back into her life at a moment when she was unattached. A woman as beautiful and desirable as Jill Lambert?

Then there was the matter of where they were going to live. They'd had a heated discussion about it just before the rehearsal, when he'd gifted his bride with first-class tickets to Maui. Jill squealed with delight, then glared when she read New York as the return destination.

"A week in Maui is doable. New York is *not,*" she'd said. "This is our busiest time of year. I told you that. I thought you planned to stay at Outlook as long as it took you to convince Charles to retire."

"Dad refuses to retire so there's no reason for me to stay."

"You have the money so you call the shots?" She'd parked a hand on her hip, her eyes spitting blue fire. "Is that how it's gonna be?"

"My business is in New York. Besides, you won't need to work."

"I told you I couldn't leave Outlook. Weren't you listening? Or do you only hear what dovetails with what you want? I agreed to marry you, not give up my life for you. Change the tickets."

"Where do we live, Jill? Where?" He'd spread his hands. "You told me Outlook is booked solid for the season."

"The north wing isn't. We left it open in case Charles needed it through the summer. The suite he has adjoins another one with an extra bedroom. We can combine the two. It's all arranged with Aunt Ping."

"When were you going to tell me?" He'd bitten back his temper. "You remember me, don't you? Your about-to-be *husband*?"

"I didn't? Are you sure? I could've sworn I did."

"Jill. Would I have put New York as our return if you had?"

"Oh. I guess not. I guess I forgot to tell you. I've had so much on my mind. I mean, with the wedding." Her bottom lip quavered and the fire in her eyes dissolved into tears. "Oh, Chase. I'm so *sorry*."

She slipped her arms around his neck, pressed her hips against his, her breasts to his chest and he would've pitched a tent in the middle of the cow pasture if that's where she wanted to live.

She'd manipulated him, pure and simple. Used her body to diffuse his temper. He couldn't have cared less at the time. Now it irritated the hell out of him. And he couldn't shake the thought of a boyfriend. Obviously, it was the champagne. He hadn't drunk enough of it yet.

He should march down there and reclaim his fiancée. If he wasn't so certain he wouldn't be welcome, so positive he'd blow up if Peter or Wallace or Esme snubbed him, he would have. Instead he parked himself and his new best friend Dom Pérignon on the wall that held back the bottom terrace of the garden, well away from the flare of the torches.

"Hey, Chet. Would you move it to the right about a foot?"

The voice belonged to Jamie. Who else would call him Chet? But it took Chase a second over the organ music thumping out of the tent—"Light My Fire" by the Doors—to pinpoint it. He glanced over his shoulder at Jamie, peering at him from a clump of hostas on the other side of the wall, his face a pale oval in the ground lights.

"What are you doing back there?"

"The girl in the pink dress? She's looking for me."

Chase glanced at the tent, at a spot near the edge of the dance floor where a little girl with a pink bow in her dark hair stood on her white patent leather tiptoes peering around the grown-ups.

"Looks a little young for you. Who is she?"

"Emma Patrick. She's seven. Her mom lets her come to parties all the time, but she has to be in bed by nine o'clock."

"She's cute. Why are you hiding in the bushes?"

"She told me she's gonna marry me when she grows up."

Chase looked at his watch. "It's eight forty-five. You've got fifteen minutes, Jimbo."

Jamie grinned. "Is that champagne you're drinking?"

"Yes." He took a pull on the bottle. "And no, you can't have any."

"Something keeps trying to crawl up my pants." Jamie swatted at his left leg. "Do you think she'll see me if I come up there with you?"

"Doubt it. The ground lights are pretty dim over here."

Jamie swung up on the wall, took off his shoes and his socks and shook them out, put them on and swiped his hair out of his eyes.

"Why are you marrying Jill?"

Chase looked at him sideways. "How old are you?"

"I'll be eleven in December."

"In two years you'll know why. Be patient, grasshopper."

"Will you give me a job this summer?"

"No." Chase took another swig of Dom Pérignon and watched Jill lead Henry out onto the dance floor. "You're not old enough."

"Okay. Then give me fifty bucks and I won't let the ring fall off the pillow on my way up the aisle tomorrow."

Chase scowled. "Whose idea was it to make you ring bearer?"

"Aunt Ping's. The offer is a job or fifty bucks. Take your pick."

"That's not an offer. That's extortion."

"C'mon. You can afford it. Besides, you owe Dory."

"I *owe* Dory?" Chase raised an eyebrow. "For what?"

"Leading her on. Esme says so. Till Jill came home, then you dropped her like a hot rock. Esther said the hot rock part. You give me fifty bucks, I'll take Dory some place nice to cheer her up and you'll be off the hook. You'll have to drive us, 'cause I don't have a license."

"You've probably heard this before, but you're a scary kid."

"Dory says I'm a person who just happens to be a kid."

"Does Dory think I led her on?"

"I don't know." Jamie shrugged. "I asked her if she liked you and she said yes 'cause she's known you all her life. I guess she didn't know you very well, though, huh?"

Could he sink any lower than this? The Bad Seed thought he was a louse. Esme thought he'd led Dory on. Esther thought he'd dropped her like a hot rock. What had he done to give them that impression? He'd hung out with Dory his first night at Outlook. He'd taken her for a drink on Friday, sent her flowers on Saturday.

Chase squirmed on the wall. Okay. He could see how Esme and Esther thought he'd led her on. He could see how Dory might think it, too, and recalled the look on her face when he told her he loved Jill. He hadn't meant to woo her; he'd meant to use her to further his case with his father. All the while knowing, yet conveniently forgetting, that she'd been nuts about him her entire life. Lucky Esme had a recipe card, not a steak knife in her hand when he'd asked about snickerdoodles.

No wonder they'd kicked him out of the poker game. His father's fury. Wallace calling him "sir." Peter and Henry treating him like a leper. It made sense. Why hadn't they simply said, "Look. We think you're pond scum 'cause you jerked Dory around." He could've . . . could've what? Told them they had him all wrong? Hell. Even Dory didn't believe that.

"Jill and I will be in Maui next week." Chase drew a money clip out of his pocket and peeled off two fifties.

"You pick a night when we get back and I'll be your chauffeur."

Jamie reached for the bills. Chase held on to them.

"The extra fifty is to make sure you *don't* drop the ring."

"I won't." Jamie grinned. "Promise."

The wind gusted as he stood up and pocketed the money. The torches flared just as little Emma Patrick turned in their direction.

"Jamie!" she yelled. "Come dance with me!"

"Crap," Jamie said. "I'm gone."

He shot away up the terrace steps as Lindsay Varner stepped out of the crowd on the dance floor, her golden hair lit by the bright tent lights. She wore a blue dress, Jill a yellow one. Chase knew that, yet for an instant he thought it was Jill laying a hand on Emma's shoulder. It was probably the distance, the darkness, maybe the Dom Pérignon, still this was twice he'd mistaken Noah Patrick's wife for his fiancée.

Chase took a swig of champagne, lit a cigarette. Watched Jill dance with Peter, Dory dance with Curt, and remembered the lawn parties Del and Her Ladyship used to throw. He'd hang out on the garage roof parapet and watch the Lamberts live their lives in small pieces.

He'd wonder what they did when he couldn't see them. Tried to imagine what it would be like to live in a house like Outlook. How people who had all the money in the world spent their days, what they thought about, what they ate, what problems they could possibly have.

Dory had tried to tell him—the same problems everybody did—but he hadn't listened. How ironic was that? She had the insider's view he'd always yearned for and he'd blown her off 'cause she was just a kid. He hadn't thought he was envious of the Lamberts then. Now he wasn't sure. If he'd only been curious, why hadn't he listened to Dory?

It reminded him of what his father had said, of what he'd implied—that by marrying Jill he was playing one up on Del Lambert. He didn't think so, but what the hell did he

know? He'd been a jerk for thirty-five years and hadn't realized it till today.

Chase lifted the Dom Pérignon bottle, scowled at it and
set it aside.

"Not so fast." Dory sat down beside him, bumping him
with her shoulder as her foot slipped in the grass. "Pass
that over here."

"Where'd you come from?" Chase gave her the bottle.
He could see the shine in her eyes as the torches flared
again and the gleam of her hair, dark as a raven's wing. "A
minute ago you were dancing."

"Bathroom break." She wiped the bottle with the hem of
her sweater, drank and wiped it again. "What'er you doing
over here?"

He took the champagne and a good long pull. "Getting
drunk."

"You should be down there dancing with Jill."

"Why? So you can laugh at me?" He smiled to let her
know he was teasing. "I can't dance to save my butt, according to you."

"Oh, what do I know." She grinned and reached for the
bottle.

With her arm raised and her head tipped back to drink,
the neckline of her sweater slipped. He couldn't see cleavage, just the hollow of her throat and collarbone. She had
bones like a bird. Tiny and fragile.

"You know a lot," Chase said. "You always have."

"Oh no. The person who knows a lot is Aunt Ping."
Dory wiped the bottle and passed it. "In just the last two
weeks I've discovered that she knows tons of stuff I had no
idea she knows. She amazes me daily."

Chase thought of Miss Ping's hand on his father's shoulder. He still wasn't sure he'd seen it or what it signified. The
wind lifted again. Not enough to gutter the torches, just
enough to blow away the smoke from his cigarette as he
rubbed it out, and lift the scent of roses and peonies—or
was it Dory's perfume?—to his nose.

"It wasn't Miss Ping's idea to serve dinner to the staff," Chase said, guessing out loud. "It was yours, wasn't it?"

Dory blinked at him, surprised. "Did Jill tell you?"

"I followed her. I watched through the door and wished I'd thought of it." He raised the bottle and drank the last of the Dom Pérignon. "I felt like an ass. A pompous, arrogant, condescending ass."

"I wish I'd never said that." Dory tipped her head at him and frowned. "You're not okay, are you?"

"Hell no, I'm not okay. You drank all my champagne." He wanted to scowl but smiled. Wanted to tell her he was beginning to think his father was right—he was making a huge mistake—only he couldn't. She was Jill's sister, for God's sake. "I need another bottle."

"Chase." Dory grabbed the lapels of his gray jacket as he started to rise and yanked him back down. He pitched toward her off balance and landed on the wall with his arm half encircling her, his weight braced on the heel of his hand. "I was angry when I called you those names. I didn't mean them. Peter and Henry didn't mean what they said, either. You're taking all these hurt feelings and out-of-joint noses way too seriously."

"Am I? My own father thinks I'm a goddamn fool." She uncurled her fingers from his lapels, pressing them with her palms to smooth them. He could almost feel the sympathy oozing out of her pores. A wry, is-that-a-kick-in-the-head-or-what smile lifted one side of his mouth. She started to smile back at him, then blinked and jerked her hands away. Like she'd just realized where they were. On his chest, where they'd felt pretty damn nice. A soothing, gentle, there-there touch.

"So you're sitting here feeling sorry for yourself. Is that it?"

"No. I'm sitting here wondering why Jill thinks we need a suite with an extra bedroom. Got any ideas?"

"*Me?*" Dory pressed a hand to her throat, the same squeak in her voice he'd heard when he told her he knew Jill was marrying him for his money. "How would I know?"

"Jill told me when we get back from Maui we'll take over the suite Dad has now and the one next to it. The one with the extra bedroom." Chase paused. "Jill said she'd talked to you and it was all arranged."

"Oh. That suite." Dory nodded. "I'm with you now."

The hell she was. She was with Jill. Naturally. They were sisters.

"So why do you think she wants an extra bedroom?"

"Simple. For the closet space." Dory hopped to her feet and grinned at him, twitched her shoulders and snapped her fingers to the music spilling out of the tent. "Want to dance?"

"What the hell? Why the hell not?"

"That's the spirit." Dory pulled him off the wall. "Come on, bro."

Chase let her drag him across the lawn. Out of the dark where the grass sparkled with dew into the bright glare of the tent, her hand hardly bigger than a child's, wrapped around the first two fingers of his left hand. He had no idea why it depressed him to hear Dory call him bro.

He almost said forget it, almost pulled away as Dory wove them a path through the crowd on the fake parquet dance floor. Then he caught sight of Jill by the refreshment table with his father. Charles was smiling, his hand cupping her elbow.

Chase tensed, ready to scowl as they glanced in his direction and saw him with Dory, but his father waved and Jill blew a kiss. The brilliant smile that lit his bride's face pierced the cloud of doubt hanging over him. Closet space. Of course. It made perfect sense. He hadn't seen Jill wear the same pair of shoes twice in the last two weeks.

He smiled, his heart light, and blew a kiss back to her.

The music stopped and so did Dory. She turned to face him, her head and one eyebrow cocked, a teasing twinkle in her brown eyes.

"All better now?" she asked.

The band began "Love Me Tender" by Elvis. A break for Chase. A challenge for Dory. Her nose only came to the middle button of his shirt.

He bent his knees and grinned at her. "Want to stand on my feet?"

"Just dance, King Kong." She made a ha-ha face and laid her palm on his lapel. No way could she reach his shoulder. "And don't step on my feet. I need them to walk up the aisle tomorrow."

He made a curled lip, ha-ha face back at her and Dory laughed.

She was amazingly easy to dance with, a little bit of nothing to steer around the floor, nimble enough to keep away from his big, no-rhythm feet, the whole time beaming a happy, shining eyed smile up at him that gave him a deep, sudden rush of affection for her.

When the song ended, Chase impulsively caught her hand against his chest and held it there. Such a small hand, such a sweet, funny, pretty little woman with her lustrous dark hair and big luminous eyes.

"We're square, aren't we, Dory?"

"Yes, Chase." She laughed with a roll of her eyes. "We're square."

"Good." He let go of her hand and slipped his arms around her.

He meant the hug to be quick and brotherly, just a squeeze to let her know he cared about her. He expected it to feel like hugging Esme or Esther, like hugging the sister he'd never had. He didn't expect it to feel like he was hugging a woman, slim yet soft and curved in all the right places, the scent of her hair and her skin, like roses and peonies to fill his head, or the sizzle of male-female awareness that shot through him.

Chase let her go and backed away, but it was still there, a low heated thrum sliding through him and settling in places it shouldn't unless he was holding Jill. His fiancée, Dory's sister, the woman who this time tomorrow would be his wife. Deprivation. That's what it was. That's *all* it was. His lust meter was spinning around the dial out of control.

Dory smiled at him but it was shaky, quivery at the

edges, her eyes overbright like she was trying to be the brave little soldier and not cry. Oh hell. He'd done it *again*. Thought only of himself.

"Dory," he said, his voice about an octave deeper than usual. He reached for her but she skittered away, said, "Thanks for the dance, bro," and vanished into the crowd.

Chapter Fifteen

Overnight Dory made medical history—her heart grew back.

She knew it was there when she woke up Saturday morning, on Jill's wedding day, and felt it aching and weeping in her chest.

If only Chase had kept his hands off her she'd have been fine. Well, not fine, but at least she wouldn't have this sobbing, throbbing thing to drag around. She wanted to punch Chase in the eye.

Her brand-new heart weighed like lead but she managed to lug it, along with her bouquet, all the long way up the aisle in the ballroom. She could feel Chase watching her but kept her head down like a good little maid of honor, took her place to the right of Father Murphy and caught Jamie's hand in her clammy-with-nerves fingers.

Poor Jill. She looked so beautiful in the ivory dress with her poufy veil. Her entrance, beginning with Eddie who passed her to Tom, Tom who passed her to Henry, Henry to Peter, Peter to Wallace and Wallace to Charles, who gave her to Chase, reduced Aunt Ping to hiccupping tears.

Dory almost cried, too, thinking of Daddy. Wishing he were here so she could hit him over the head with the bouquet of pink (*blech*) roses Peter had created for her to carry.

When Father Murphy got to the "speak now or forever hold your peace" part of the ceremony, Dory held her breath. Hoping, praying the ballroom doors would crash open and she'd hear Gary's high, piping voice shout, "Stop the wedding! Stop the wedding!"

But of course that didn't happen. Gary didn't come bursting in on a white horse dragging James by a rope. Chase didn't push Jill away and say, "Wait! I'm marrying the wrong woman! Dory! My darling! Be mine!"

She expected her heart to explode when Father Murphy pronounced Chase and Jill man and wife but it didn't. It locked her gaze on Chase, made her watch as he lifted Jill's veil. The smile on her sister's face was so brilliantly look-how-happy-I-am that Dory feared every one of the two hundred people in the room would know it was fake.

Chase kissed Jill and that was it. They were married. Mr. and Mrs. Chase McKay. And Dory still had a heart.

A heart that wrenched and sobbed and wailed all the way down the aisle behind Chase and Jill, its keening so loud she could barely hear the joyous notes of the recessional soaring out of the piano where Deirdre sat playing and weeping. Bless Curt, who held on to her and kept her from falling on her knees and howling again.

This was her punishment. God hadn't struck her dead for aiding and abetting Jill in her lunatic plan. He'd given her back her heart instead. Clever deity, God. Dory figured it was the least she deserved.

Something was wrong but Chase couldn't put his finger on what.

The icy kiss from Jill when he'd lifted her veil? No. They were both so stiff with nerves he imagined his lips felt like stone. A certain part of his anatomy should be stiff, should have turned to stone now that Jill was his but it hadn't. He hoped that was just nerves.

The heartbroken sobbing Jill did on Miss Ping's neck when the last guest passed through the receiving line? That made him scowl till Dory patted his arm and said, "Don't take it personally, bro. All brides cry."

The "bro" bugged him, but it always had, so it wasn't that.

The shudder that rippled through his bride when he took her in his arms for their first dance as man and wife he blamed on her paper-thin dress and the air-conditioning in the ballroom set on polar digits.

Wedding etiquette called upon him to dance with the maid of honor. Holding Dory felt warm and soft—holding Jill felt cold and frigid, like dancing with an icicle and just plain damned not right.

"Congrats, bro." Dory knuckled him in the shoulder and he gritted his teeth. "You did it. You got the girl. The one you always wanted."

Did I? Chase wondered, gazing down at the isn't-this-fun smile on her upturned face. If Jill was the girl he'd always wanted why did Dory's mouth look so delectable? Why did he suddenly want to kiss her? Because he never had? Why did he feel the urge to sweep her off her feet, throw her in the Expedition and get them both the hell out of here?

"Ow! You stepped on my foot!" Dory jumped away from him, then leaned closer and peered at his face. "Hey, bro. Are you okay?"

"Don't call me bro," Chase growled.

"Oooh, touchy," she taunted and laughed at him.

He needed a cigarette, maybe a chat with his buddy Dom Pérignon, but first he had to dance with Miss Ping. Then Deirdre, then Jill again. She was still stiff and he wasn't.

This was not good. This was not good at all.

"Four generations of Lambert brides have used this to cut their wedding cake." Aunt Ping offered Jill an ornate sterling silver knife with a long satin ribbon tied to the handle. "You are the fifth."

"How lovely. Aunt Ping, thank you."

Jill took the knife, touched a finger to the blade. It was as dull as her bridegroom. Damn. A trip to the ER for stitches was brilliant. She'd been willing to trade blood and a scar for drugs to knock her out and postpone her wedding night, but she'd be lucky if this thing cut the cake.

She and Aunt Ping were in the kitchen. Jill looked over the top of her perfectly coiffed head into the china closet, wondering if there was something sharper in there—say, a sterling silver chainsaw—and how she could talk Aunt Ping out of it.

"Jillian," she said worriedly. "Are you happy?"

Jill kissed her cheek. "I'm delirious."

Hey. Maybe that would work. If she held her breath till she passed out, Chase would rush her to the hospital. If she begged, maybe they'd admit her for observation.

"*Voilà!*" Esme called out and Jill turned toward her wedding cake, bumping toward her over the brick floor on a pink damask-covered cart.

The cake was a five-layer marvel of yellow lilies and pink roses twined with green leaves and vines on frothy white frosting. On the top tier a tiny blond bride stood next to a tiny blond groom. It was supposed to be her and Chase. *But it should be Gary and me!* Jill wanted to wail.

"Oh, Esme." She sniffed back tears. "It's beautiful."

"A true work of art, Esme. We'll be along shortly." Aunt Ping waited till she was out of earshot with the cake, then took Jill by the arms. "The cake has more color than you do. What on earth is going on?"

"Nothing," Jill lied as sincerely as she could. "I'm just nervous."

Oh, this was awful. Aunt Ping loved her and she was lying to her.

Jill loved Esme and Esme loved her. But Esme loved Chase, too. Jill didn't believe he loved her, no matter how many times he said it, but what if he did? What if she broke his heart? Would Esme and Esther still love her? And Wallace? Peter and Henry, Tom and Eddie and—oh God—Charles. Would they forgive her when she had the money to close the Outlook Inn or would they despise her for hurting Chase?

And Aunt Ping. What would she say?

The brooch Chase had given her before the ceremony glittered on her bosom next to her corsage of pink rosebuds. He'd given Deirdre a brooch, too, a lovely emerald crescent, and Dory a gold bracelet with three rubies. He'd grinned like a little boy, so pleased with himself, when they'd kissed his cheek and thanked him after the receiving line in the little dining room.

Oh God. Dory was right. This was going to be a disaster.

"Listen to me, Jill." Aunt Ping took her firmly by the arms. "If there's a problem, if there's something wrong between you and Chase, tell me now and we'll go to Father Murphy right this second."

She meant for an annulment and, oh God, was it tempting. But an annulment wouldn't net them twenty million dollars. Not with that pesky little annulment clause in the prenuptial agreement.

"Aunt Ping, please. Don't worry. Everything is fine."

"All right, Jillian." She sighed. "Let's go cut the cake."

Okay. He was going to try this again. One more dance with Jill before they cut the cake and headed upstairs to the Honeymoon Suite.

Chase spoke to the orchestra leader, asked for something slow and romantic to put the bride in the mood. The groom, too, but he didn't say that. The maestro winked and told him not to worry. When he led Jill onto the floor, the orchestra played "I'm in the Mood for Love."

He felt loose since he'd had a cigarette and bourbon in the billiard room. Jill wasn't stiff—neither was he, which was starting to worry him—but at least she wasn't an icicle because she'd been outside with Dory.

He'd met them at the French doors when they came inside, Jill flushed and bright-eyed, Dory's dark hair mussed. She'd smiled at him and ducked away, sweeping her hair back into its smooth curve around her ears. She missed a spot that he'd wanted to brush into place with his fingers. He'd scowled instead, shoved his hands into his pockets and headed straight for the bandleader.

The violins swelled on the chorus. Chase spread his hand on Jill's bare back under her veil. He'd had a hell of a time sleeping for the past two weeks, picturing her naked, imagining the feel of her skin. It was soft as mink. She twitched away from his fingertips on her shoulder blade.

"It's humid outside and I saw lightning. I think it's going to rain."

"I love to sleep in the rain." Chase drew her closer, felt the press of her breasts against his chest but no answering leap of desire. "But I don't think we'll be doing much sleeping tonight."

"I won't if it starts thundering and lightning. I'm terrified of thunderstorms. Did I tell you that? No? Well, I am. They scare me to death. The only place I feel safe is under the bed, so if it starts crashing and booming that's where I'll be. Under the bed."

"Is that so?" Chase said. Her eyes were huge and she'd rattled that off about thunderstorms in less time than it took him to light a cigarette.

"You're welcome to join me. We can hold hands." She shrugged a gorgeous, bare shoulder that he had absolutely no desire to kiss. "Or something."

"Why don't we wait and see what comes up?"

Christ. Something better come up. He brushed the nape of her neck, trying to get himself going. Jill shrugged him off. Three days ago she would've purred something like, "Naughty boy. Hands to yourself."

He knew she wasn't in love with him but he'd thought she at least wanted him. He'd wanted her from the moment she'd tried to tip him for delivering flowers to Dory. How could he not want her now? He'd married her, she was his. It didn't make sense. Was he that nervous? Was she?

"Jill," he said. "Why do you want a suite with an extra bedroom?"

"Are you serious?" She gave him a *duh* look. "For the closet space."

He should feel better hearing the same thing from Jill that he'd heard from Dory, but he didn't. He felt confused and suspicious. When "I'm in the Mood" ended, Chase escorted Jill to the cake table. The wedding guests gathered to watch. He looked for Dory but didn't see her. He saw his father trying not to scowl and Miss Ping, teary-eyed and beaming, as he wrapped his fingers around Jill's on the handle of a silver knife tied with ribbons and they cut the first slice.

Jill piled a fork with cake and shoved it in his mouth. He damn near choked and grabbed a flute of champagne. The guests thought it was hilarious. Chase thought his bride was trying to strangle him.

He saw Dory then with a basket over her arm, passing out tiny bottles of bubbles. Curt followed her, showing the guests how to unfold the wands inside and blowing bubbles at Dory, ending each blow with a smack like a kiss. Dory laughed. Chase scowled and drank another flute of champagne. What was wrong with him? Curt was his best friend.

When he and Jill left the ballroom, most of the guests trailed behind them blowing bubbles on their fairy-sized wands. Jamie danced ahead of them with a wicked grin and a plastic bubble gun that shot softball-sized bubbles. The Bad Seed was having a hell of a lot more fun at this wedding than he was.

As they passed through the foyer and made the turn toward the stairs, Chase saw a flicker of lightning through the tall windows beside the front doors. He heard a rumble of thunder, slipped an arm around Jill and felt her shiver. Was it him or was it the thunder?

Since they weren't going away, only upstairs, they stopped on the gallery so Jill could throw her bouquet and he could throw her garter.

His bride made a show of it, shimmying her skirt up and laughing at the wolf whistles. Chase slid the ribbon-threaded bit of satin past her knee and down her silken calf, reaching in his head for the fantasy of her long, shapely legs wrapped around his naked waist, but it wasn't there.

The two flutes of champagne on top of the bourbon hit him as he straightened up with the garter. His head spun and his world with it. For a split second he could've sworn

Jill's eyes were brown, then he shook himself and blinked and they were blue again, as blue as the sapphire tennis bracelet he'd given her.

Jill turned her back to the stairs and pitched her bouquet over her shoulder. Chase watched it sail, saw Dory put a hand on Deirdre's shoulder and jump. She caught the bouquet of pink roses and lilies in midair with a squeal of delight that made him want to bash his head against a wall. When he threw Jill's garter and Curt caught it, Chase wanted to bash *his* head against a wall.

This was insane, nuts. What was his problem? What the hell was wrong with him? Chase scooped Jill into his arms and started up the stairs toward the Honeymoon Suite. He glanced over his shoulder, saw his so-called best friend plant a good-catch kiss on Dory and knew exactly what his problem was, precisely what he'd done.

He'd married the wrong sister.

The most requested room at the Outlook Inn is the Honeymoon Suite, Chase recalled from the article in *Condé Nast Traveller* as he carried Jill along the second floor corridor. *Miss Lambert asked us not to photograph or describe it in this article. We agreed, but take our word for it—it would be worth a trip up the aisle to spend a night in this room.*

Maybe so, Chase thought. If you married the right woman.

He rounded the corner at the far, far end of the corridor, stopped outside the double doors of the Honeymoon Suite, leaned forward so Jill could push them open, and carried her over the threshold.

He'd dreamed of this moment, fantasized tossing her on the bed with her head thrown back and laughing and flinging himself on top of her. His, all his, at last. He felt Jill tense in his arms, set her gently on her feet and stepped away from her. She blinked at him, surprised, as if being thrown on the bed was exactly what she'd expected.

She was still as beautiful as she'd ever been. Stunning face, succulent mouth, lay-it-down-on-the-bed-and-give-it-to-me body and he didn't want it. Not any of it. He didn't want her.

"I'm glad that's over." Jill sighed. "Aren't you?"

"Glad doesn't even come close."

Chase turned away from her. The longer he looked at Jill the more he wanted to run downstairs, grab Dory and kiss her and make sure he'd married the wrong sister. Not that it would change anything. Right or wrong, for better or worse, he'd taken vows and married Jill.

His father warned him, told him if he had to think about marrying Jill he shouldn't. He should've corrected the old man right there, told him the only reason he'd said *thinking* was to soften the blow for Dory.

He'd stopped thinking the second he'd laid eyes on Jill. When she'd wiggled her finger, said minimum five carats, marquise cut, platinum band or don't ever touch me again, he couldn't buy a ring fast enough.

How had he forgotten the lesson of Del Lambert's life? Never lead with your heart, never let a woman influence your decisions and never, ever let your dick call the shots. That's exactly what he'd done and look where he was—in the Honeymoon Suite with the wrong woman.

Hey! said a voice in his head. *Don't blame this on me!*

Chase figured it was the bourbon and the champagne talking. He ignored the voice, turned again and surveyed the Honeymoon Suite.

It was large enough to impress, yet small enough to feel intimate. Two people focused on each other didn't need a soccer field. Someone clever enough to know that had designed the room around a bed so big it made the California king in his bedroom in New York look like a toddler bed. It was set up on a dais and covered by a quilted ivory silk coverlet scattered with cushions in every color.

"That's some bed," Chase said.

"Look at this," Jill said, a quick-over-here, look-anywhere-but-at-the-bed clip in her voice. She waded across the plush ivory carpet, the pile so deep it swallowed her three-inch heels, and opened the top of a hand-painted distressed armoire. A light came on and a cloud of condensation rolled out. "It's a fridge. Clever, eh?"

"Extremely," Chase said. "Now about this bed—"

"You have to see the his-and-hers bathrooms." She grabbed his wrist and towed him across the room, opened a door with a cloisonné cake top figure of a groom on it and gave him a shove. "Take the tour."

Chase made sure a second before she slammed the door in his face that the lock was on the inside. What the hell was she doing? He'd give her a minute, take the tour as she'd suggested and then go find out.

There was plenty of room to wander in, between the bathroom and the adjacent dressing room. The suitcase he'd packed for Maui was here and the couple changes of clothes he'd brought up to the house earlier. He imagined he had Henry to thank for hanging them up. Chase got rid of his tie, hung the jacket of his tux on the back of a leather valet chair, removed his cuff links and rolled up his sleeves.

In the bathroom everything was rose-veined marble, the walls, the floor, the double-sink vanity. The shower was the size of a car wash bay, very high-tech with jets everywhere. Chase could envision sexual water aerobics on the long, curved benches, but not with Jill. He used the toilet and washed, played with the towel warmer, then went to find her.

A very feminine vanity table sat near French doors draped with ivory chiffon sheers. Jill sat on a rose velvet bench taking the pins out of her hair. She'd kicked off her shoes and flung her veil over a pink art deco chair. She twisted around when she saw him in the trifold mirror.

"One more time," Chase said. "About this bed."

Jill sprang to her feet. "Would you undo me, please?"

"In a minute." He mounted the marble dais steps and tapped the solid base beneath the bed with the toe of his shoe. "It's on a pedestal. Where are you going to hide if it rains?"

"In the bathroom." She turned her back to him and

lifted her hair, unwinding from its curls in long corkscrews, off her neck. "Would you?"

Her dress closed with a row of ivory buttons. Itsy-bitty devils tucked in tiny ivory loops. His fingers should be thick and clumsy with desire but they weren't. He should want to rip the dress off her but he didn't. He sat on the bench and freed the buttons one by one. As skittish as Jill had been about the bed, it surprised him that she'd asked him to undo her, that she stood patiently between his knees.

From the corner of his eye he saw a flash of lightning outside the French doors. A second later thunder rattled the panes. Jill didn't flinch, didn't shiver, didn't cower. She wasn't afraid of him, which was good, and he'd bet she wasn't afraid of thunderstorms, either.

It was time to find out what was going on in his bride's head.

Chase undid the last button and curved his hands around her hips. Jill didn't pull away but she stiffened. He didn't.

"I think it's time for bed," he said. "Don't you?"

She hesitated for a moment, then turned between his legs, holding the bodice of her dress up with one arm pressed to her midriff.

"I need a bath. It'll relax me and put me in the mood."

"Can I wash your back?"

"Naughty boy." She lowered her lashes and her voice to a sultry purr. Jill the tease was back. "That's peeking."

Chase slid his hands around her waist. "Kiss first?"

"Just one." She leaned forward with her mouth drawn in a bow.

He expected the dry peck she usually gave him when he asked for a kiss. He got a wet, open-mouth lip lock, her tongue and a nip on his bottom lip. Three days ago he would've needed the jaws of life to get a kiss like this out of Jill. Chase was so startled he bit his tongue as she broke the kiss, smiled at him and ran a finger over his bottom lip.

"Turn down the bed. I won't be long."

"Take your time. We've got all night."

"Mmmm." She traced his lip again and gave him a slow, sexy wink.

Then she sashayed into the bathroom with her dress falling open, the soft light of the vanity lamps shimmering on the long, sleek line of her back. She shut the door between them but didn't lock it. Chase sat on the bench staring at the cloisonné bride, his heart thudding.

Christ. Now what?

He pushed to his feet and paced the room while he listened to the tub fill. When he passed the double doors that led into the corridor, his gaze caught on the ornate brass handles. If he hurried he might be able to make it downstairs and plant one on Dory before Jill finished her bath. Oh, that was a great idea. Where the hell had it come from?

You're the one with the Phi Beta Kappa key, said a voice in his head. *Not me. If you don't want my input, just say so.*

"I don't want your input," Chase said and went back to pacing.

Which part of himself was he telling to butt out? The reckless part? The impulsive part? He'd never listen to either one of them again, so help him God. They'd gotten him into this until-death-do-us-part-or-the-lawyers-get-into-it mess.

Lawyers didn't scare him. Dory scared him. If he'd confused lust with love and Dory was truly the one—and how in hell was he going to determine that while he was married to her sister?—what would she do when he told her he'd made a terrible mistake? After he'd patted her on the head and told her to buzz off like he'd used to when she was a kid? How could she believe him? How could she ever trust him?

"Cha-*ase,*" Jill sang out of the bathroom. "Are you naked?"

"Uh, no," he answered. "I'm waiting for you to undress me."

"Chase. If I come out of here and you're not naked," Jill called playfully, "I'm going to be very disappointed."

"You aren't coming out *now,* are you?"

"Nooo. I'm just turning on the Jacuzzi." He heard the motor kick over, the thrum of the jets and Jill's throaty, breathy, *"Ooohh!"*

Then she started to sing "I'm in the Mood for Love."

He had two choices. Cut and run or strip and get in bed. One was impulsive, the other reckless. He wasn't sure which was which.

Let me clear that up for you, said the voice in his head. *Reckless is the guy on my left. Impulsive is the guy on my right.*

"Huh?" Chase said out loud, thoroughly confused.

Reckless is a little on the plump side. Impulsive hangs just a tad lower. You getting my drift here?

He hadn't had too much to drink. He hadn't had nearly enough.

Chase leaped up the dais steps, snatched the magnum of Dom Pérignon chilling in an ice-filled sterling silver bucket beside the bed and drank about a third of it. Closed his eyes and felt the fiery rush of the wine through his bloodstream, heard the thudding of his heart, the pounding in his ears, but no more from the voice.

"Thank God." He sighed and sat on the side of the bed.

We have a name for you, the voice said, *if you'd care to hear it.*

"No!" he shouted. "I would not!"

"Chase?" Jill called and the Jacuzzi switched off. " 'No' what?"

"Don't come out yet! I'm fixing us a drink. Fire up those jets."

"Are you naked yet?"

"No. I spilled ice cubes. I'm cleaning them up."

"Well, hurry up. My nipples are turning into raisins."

"Right with you!" Chase called.

It was the golf ball in the head. That's what this was. He still had a goose egg, a sore spot, probably a concussion. That's all this was. He couldn't possibly be sitting here having a conversation with his—

Don't even, the voice cut in, *call me Dick.*

"Okay," Chase said, low enough that Jill wouldn't hear. "What should I call you?"

Oh. I don't know. I kind of like Dom.

He was right. Thank God. It was only the booze talking.

"Ready or not!" Jill called. "I'm coming out on the count of five!"

"Make it ten and I'll be ready!"

Speak for yourself, said the voice.

"I already did." Chase scowled. "I said 'I do.'"

He couldn't up and say I don't. Not after he'd pushed and forced this wedding through as quickly as possible. What made him think he'd made a mistake and married the wrong sister, anyway? Because he'd seen Curt kiss Dory and wanted to deck him?

The bottom line was, he was married. The best thing he could do for Dory—and it was high time he thought about *her* feelings for a change—was call it brotherly concern and let it go.

And he wasn't the only one who'd said "I do." So had Jill. He knew she didn't love him. He'd thought she at least wanted him, but apparently he'd thought wrong. So she had to hop in the Jacuzzi and let the jets have their way with her. At least she was trying. Could he do less?

Let's see how far you get without me and Reckless and Impulsive.

"Shut up." Chase swept the accent cushions off the bed and flung back the ivory silk coverlet. "I'm through talking to lunatic body parts."

He peeled off his shirt, shucked his trousers and his socks, saw the bathroom door handle turn and jumped under the sheet, shoved the bed pillows behind him and held his breath as the door opened and there was Jill. His bride, his wife, in a pretty peach nightie with a ribbon threaded through the scooped neckline, the pleated hem flirting around her knees. He let his breath go in a sigh of relief that she wasn't nude.

She came up the steps and blinked. "Where's my drink?"

"Forgot the glasses." Chase sprang off the bed and the

dais, crossed the room and turned around. "Uh. Where are the glasses?"

"In the fridge, chilling." Jill sat down on the bed and watched him walk back to her. "You aren't naked."

"Neither are you." Chase lifted the Dom Pérignon out of its bucket and swung onto the bed, filled the frosted flutes and gave one to Jill. She raised an eyebrow at the already open bottle. "You started without me."

"I had a nip. To us," he said and raised his glass.

"To us." Jill tossed back the champagne like it was a shot with a beer and held out her glass for a refill.

She knocked back two more before he finished his first. She'd done the same thing before the rehearsal dinner. He could tell her it wouldn't work, that she was risking strange voices, but hey, what did he know. He was the guy sitting in bed with a gorgeous woman and a limp dick.

"Okay. Ready." She set her glass on the low pier built around the bed and turned toward him. "Where do you want me?"

How 'bout New Jersey? said the voice in his head.

"You aren't helping," Chase snapped.

Jill blinked at him. "What?"

"How about on my lap?" Chase slapped his thighs.

"Swell," Jill said. God, I hope so, Chase thought, catching her by the waist as she lifted her nightie and straddled him, wiggled around a little and frowned at him. "You aren't ready."

"I will be in a minute." He pulled her closer. "Kiss me."

Jill drew a breath and pressed her mouth against his, her lips cool and shivery. She cupped his face, Chase angled his head and parted her teeth with his tongue. Jill jerked away.

"Do you have erectile dysfunction?"

"Do I have what? Oh. Am I impotent? No." He smiled, trying to make a joke and lighten the mood. "Are you?"

"No. I don't have a dick." Jill wiggled around some more. "And right now I'd say you don't have much of one, either."

Chase felt his face flame. "I should've joined you in the Jacuzzi."

"Let's try this." She closed her eyes, lifted his hands and clapped them over her breasts. "Does that help?"

The round, perfect orbs he'd dreamed about filled Chase's hands and his head full of Dory. Laughing in the dark last night and guzzling champagne with him straight from the bottle. Her goofy flashlight and her claim that she could contact the International Space Station. The code names she made up to befuddle the FBI. Running around the trees in the park screaming. Shooting a straw wrapper in his eye. Staggering up the drive on the verge of heat-stroke rather than get in the truck with him. Knuckling him in the arm and congratulating him for getting the girl.

The girl he'd always wanted. Until now, when she was his at last.

Not so fast, said the voice in his head. *She's really stacked. Let's have a feel. I might be able to get up for this.*

At last his cock stirred, and Jill was trying. Holding her breath, but she was trying. Chase squeezed gently, swept his fingers over her peach silk-covered breasts. Nope. Not there. Maybe over here . . .

"What *are* you doing?" Jill snapped, her eyes squeezed shut.

"Looking for your raisins."

"Oh, for God's sake." She gripped his face, clamped her mouth over his and sucked like a plunger, his tongue and the breath right out of him. Chase clutched her hips and hung on, felt her shudder, heard her whimper a pulse beat before she tore her mouth away and flung herself, sobbing, off his lap. "I can't do this! I thought I could but *I can't!*"

What the hell? Chase touched his lip and tasted blood. He shook his head to clear the ring in his ears, turned and saw Jill crawling away from him, crying like her heart would break.

"Jill. Honey." He rolled on his side and laid his hand on her back. "It's okay if you're not ready."

"I will *never* be ready!" She turned on her knees, sat back on her heels and sobbed, her eyes streaming tears.

"I'm sorry, Chase. You deserve a reward for putting up with all my crap and I thought I could do this. I really did. Close my eyes and pretend you're Gary but *I can't!*"

She wailed again and buried her face in her hands.

"Gary?" It took a second to place the name. "*Gary!*" He pushed up on his arm. "You mean that nutcase from the Happy Spirit?"

"He's not a nut." Jill's head snapped up. "He's an undercover FBI agent. Marshall Phillips thinks we're contacting Dad and Mother through the Happy Spirit." Jill sniffed and wiped her eyes with the hem of her nightie. "The goddamn FBI is everywhere. They monitor our cell phones and walkie-talkies. They're even in the fucking orchard."

"Diego told me about the orchard. Marshall Phillips introduced himself to me when I met Curt at the federal courthouse for lunch."

"But how did he—" Jill's wet, red eyes narrowed and she smacked a fist against her knee. "The FBI followed you from Outlook."

"Phillips wanted me to be his new best friend and snoop on you and Dory and Miss Ping. I told him to go find James Darwood."

"Gary went to find James!" Jill sobbed again. "I haven't heard from him in a week! I don't know where he is and I'm worried sick!"

"Dory told me Miss Ping has detectives looking for James. Why did Gary join the hunt?"

"Oh, what the hell. You might as well know it all." Jill looked at him through tear-spiked lashes, her eyes like drowned sapphires. "I told Gary if he didn't want me to marry you, he should go find James so Marshall Phillips would unfreeze our money so we'd be rich again and we could close the Outlook Inn. Nice, huh?"

"I see." Chase felt like he'd swallowed a snowball. "You married me for my money. Is that it? No other reason?"

"I'm so sorry, Chase. I know you love me, but I love Gary."

"How much money do you need?"

"Twenty million dollars."

"That's what you asked for in your prenuptial agreement."

"That's how much we need to fund the trust Dory set up to keep Outlook running forever, so future generations of Lamberts won't have to worry about losing it."

"Why didn't you just ask me? I would've written you a check."

"Would you?" Jill raised an eyebrow. "If I'd said no when you asked me to dinner? If I'd told you I have a boyfriend?"

"Well. Maybe not. But I would've written Miss Ping a check."

"She'd strangle herself with one of her scarves before she asked you for money. I thought about asking you, but then it would've been a loan. A loan has to be repaid and then we'd never get out of the hotel business. Thank God, Dory thought of the Outlook Inn because it saved us, but I *hate* it and I don't know how much more Aunt Ping can take."

"Do you think Gary has a prayer of finding James Darwood?"

"No. The Bastard Little Prick Squad has been looking for him for ten years." Jill balled her hands into fists on her knees. "Gary says the funding for this investigation, for keeping the FBI up our butts will likely be cut in July, but that won't affect Daddy and Mother. Until James is caught, they're fugitives. If they come home, they're convicts."

If he told Jill that hearing she didn't love him made him the happiest man in the world because he'd finally realized he loved Dory, Chase was positive she'd kill him. After all her machinations and the stress she was under worrying about Gary, there wasn't a jury who'd convict her.

"This is all my doing." Jill laid her fingertips on his knee. "Aunt Ping doesn't have a clue and Dory did her best to talk me out of it. Please don't blame them. If you want to hate someone, hate me."

"I don't hate you, Jill." Chase lifted her hand and gave it a gentle squeeze. "I feel like a damn fool, but that's on me."

"No, it is *not*!" She snatched her hand back. "This whole mess is *my* fault! I threw myself at you and you got sent away. I threw myself at James and he got even. It's my fault that we're poor. My fault that Daddy and Mother can't come home. My fault—"

"Whoa, Jill. Stop." Chase took her by the shoulders. Her voice was breathy, on the verge of hyperventilating. "You didn't hold a gun to my head. I asked you to marry me and I rushed this wedding because I was hot to have you. I suspected you had a boyfriend. If I'd confronted you, it might've changed things, but I doubt it. I'm stubborn. I think I know everything and I was determined to have you."

"You're being awfully nice to me," Jill said, her mouth trembling.

"I'm being honest. So are you. We both thought we'd gotten what we wanted. I'd say that makes us a couple of prime fools."

"I was thinking shallow and self-centered."

"That, too." Chase laughed and hugged her impulsively. She laid her head on his shoulder and sighed. "We may not want each other, but we deserve each other, don't we?"

"No argument there, but that doesn't mean we're stuck with each other. Unless you want to stay married to me."

"I don't." Jill raised her head. "I just want twenty million dollars and a graceful way out of this for both of us."

"I'll give you the twenty million," Chase said. "*Give*, not loan."

He'd give every cent he had if he could close his eyes, open them and see Dory sitting beside him in a peach nightie. Jill's face lit with a teary smile that made her eyes sparkle.

"The graceful exit." Chase leaned back against the pillows and rubbed his chin. "Could take some thought."

"So start thinking." Jill sat up beside him and reached for the champagne. "We've got all night and nothing else to do."

Chapter Sixteen

That pizza-loving, baseball cap–wearing mouse Chuck E. Cheese grinned at Dory from his picture on the wall. Jamie sat on her right stuffing his mouth like a chipmunk with pepperoni pizza because Deirdre wasn't here to make him use a fork; Curt was across the table from her swirling the ice cubes in his glass, Jill's garter on his right wrist.

Goofy music blared. Lights flashed on pinball machines. Kids ran and shrieked. The floor under the table felt sticky, but at least her feet reached the floor. It was the perfect end to the weirdest day of Dory's life.

Coming here was Jamie's idea. When Wallace's substitute for the day closed Outlook's front doors behind the last of the wedding guests, Jamie had fished two fifty-dollar bills out of his pocket.

"How 'bout pizza?" he'd said. "I'm buying."

At that moment, if Jamie had been Attila the Hun asking if she'd like to go pillage and burn a few villages she would've said, "Just a minute. I'll get my purse." Anything to stop thinking and worrying and grieving about Jill upstairs in the Honeymoon Suite with Chase.

Jamie wiped his mouth with a greasy napkin and turned toward Dory on the picnic table–style bench. "Are you having fun?"

"I'm having a ball, squirt. This was a great idea."

Jamie beamed. "Let me get you a refill." He picked up

Dory's empty glass, slid off the bench and headed for the beverage bar.

"That kid's a hoot," Curt said. "Where'd he get a hundred bucks?"

"Chase paid him off to make sure he didn't drop the ring."

"He'd do well in politics."

"Or banking," Dory said and Curt laughed.

Now that she had on jeans and a red cotton sweater she finally felt warm. Her maid of honor gown was pretty but thin as tissue paper. Her nothing-but-gold-straps sandals were cute but killer. In socks and Reeboks her feet were so happy her toes wiggled, but her newborn, freshly broken heart ached in her chest.

Curt had changed his tuxedo for jeans and a sweatshirt he had in his car. Dory hadn't seen him this dressed down since he'd won his election to Congress. He snapped the garter on his wrist and grinned.

"When d'you want to get married? I'm free Tuesday." Dory laughed. He smiled. "You've got your eye on Jamie for Lambert's, don't you?"

"Shhh." She pressed a finger to her lips. "He thinks I want him to be an astronaut."

"You're dying to see a Lambert in your father's office. Why not you? Cliff Niles told me today he's thinking about retiring."

"I worked in the mail room." Dory laughed to hide the pang just thinking about Lambert's gave her. "Besides, I'm in the hotel business."

"For another nanosecond, maybe. Soon as Jill has Chase where she wants him—" Curt glanced at his watch. "—and I'll bet she's had him there at least twice by now, you'll be out of the hotel business."

"Did you talk to Peter today?"

"He asked me to dance, but I declined."

"Seriously, Curt. Where did you get that idea?"

"Out of my head. Anyone who knows Jill knows she despises the Outlook Inn. Anyone who knows Chase knows he's got the bucks to shut it down and dump you all back into the lap of luxury."

"You make it sound like that's why Jill married him."

"It isn't?" Curt said and Dory glared at him. "I'm not going to put it up on a billboard, Dory. It's just what I think. So do a lot of people."

Dory hunched toward him over the table. "Who thinks it?"

"Everybody I know who knows Chase and Jill. Everybody I talked to at the reception."

"Who, Curt? Give me names."

He reeled off a dozen names, most of them sons, nephews or sons-in-law of Aunt Ping's friends. Aye-yi-yi. If one of them made a comment to their parental units, it could easily get back to Aunt Ping, who already suspected there was something not quite right about Jill and Chase getting married in the blink of an eye.

Jill hadn't seen this coming. Neither had Dory, but she should have. What did people love to do? Especially people with bags of money and nothing better to do? They loved to talk. The wild stories that spread through Aunt Ping's circle when James knocked over Lambert Securities flitted briefly through Dory's head and made her wince.

"What are these people saying?" Dory asked Curt.

"Why do you want to know?"

So I can figure a way to spin it before Aunt Ping hears it, Dory started to say, but stopped herself. Too many people thought they knew Jill's true motives and too many people were right. She could've told Chase or Aunt Ping what Jill was up to and stopped her, but she'd been angry and jealous so she'd kept her mouth shut. It was the worst choice she could've made and there was only one way to fix it— tell the truth. To Aunt Ping, at least. It was too late to tell Chase anything but good-bye.

"Just curious." Dory shrugged at Curt.

She wasn't sure he believed her, but Jamie came back with her Coke and a pocketful of tokens and dragged her away to play Skee-Ball.

He was the Tiger Woods of Skee-Ball, rarely missed sinking the ball, usually in the hundred points slot. The machine Jamie played spit out tickets till he had enough to "buy" Dory a stuffed Chuck E. Cheese.

"Here you go," he said and gave it to her with a red-faced shrug.

"Jamie." Dory wanted to kiss him, settled for a smile that wouldn't embarrass him and blinked back tears. "Thank you."

Thunder clapped and a few raindrops splatted Dory on the head when they left the restaurant—the storm she'd seen flickering in the sky when she and Jill were out on the terrace. Jamie held the Styrofoam box with their leftover pizza in it over his head. Dory tucked the stuffed mouse that meant more to her than the ruby bracelet from Chase under her sweater, took Curt's hand and dashed for the car.

After so long without rain—Dory couldn't remember how long—she cracked her window and breathed the smell of damp pavement and wet grass. By the time they reached Outlook the rain had stopped, the lightning had faded; the thunder had rolled away like a bowling ball.

Diego buzzed Curt's cranberry red Toyota Camry through the gates. On the intercom he told Dory Mr. Wallace had gone to bed, that Miss Ping and Mrs. Deirdre were having cocoa in the breakfast room.

Curt wound the Toyota up the drive, the blacktop glistening with rainbows through the steam rising in the headlights. The grass sparkled and the trees dripped. Outlook seemed half asleep, exhausted after its busy day. The outside security lights gleamed on the darkened first floor windows like lamp glow shining on a sleeper's closed eyelids.

"Dude." Jamie stuck his left hand between the front bucket seats when Curt stopped the car under the portico. "Thanks for driving."

"Dude." Curt slapped Jamie's palm. "You're welcome."

"I'll be in, in a second," Dory said to Jamie in the rearview mirror.

He picked up the pizza box and reached for the door

handle. "You don't have to kiss him," Jamie told her. "I said thank you."

"*Jam-ie,*" Dory said and he opened the door.

"Okay. I'm going."

Jamie skipped up the brick steps and crossed the porch. Diego opened the door and Dory raised a hand to him. He nodded, shut the door and she turned sideways in her seat to look at Curt.

"So Jamie's your new roommate?" he asked.

"Yep. He and Diego finished moving him into the guest-house this morning. You've never seen a ten-year-old with so much stuff."

"You looked really pretty today, Dory."

"Thank you. You looked very handsome in your tux."

"Big as the wedding cake was, I think they could've just stood you and me up on the top of it."

Dory laughed. Curt leaned over the console and kissed her. He had a nice mouth, warm, firm lips. But he wasn't Chase.

He drew away and smiled at her. "I'm not the one, am I?"

"I don't know, Curt." Dory sighed. "You're an awfully nice one."

"I'm heading back to Washington. Can I call you?"

"Sure. Can I call you?"

"Absolutely." Curt grinned. "Do you have my numbers?"

"Jill does in her Rolodex. I'll filch your card and put it in mine."

"Great. G'night, Dory."

"Good night, Curt."

She got out of the car, walked up the steps and waved good-bye to him from the porch. When she turned around, Diego opened the door. He still wore his tuxedo pants; his white sleeves rolled up his brown forearms. The toes of his Cuban-heeled half boots glittered in the backwash of the foyer chandelier, a massive acorn shape dripping with prisms.

"How'd it go today, Mr. Homez?" Dory kept her voice

low as she stepped inside and Diego shut the door and tripped the locks.

"Snoop Dog was good as gold," he said, referring to Miss Fairview by the code name Dory let him choose when she'd asked him to keep an eye on Outlook's most frequent guest. "She never went no place she wasn't supposed to be."

"Great. Want some pizza?" Dory retrieved the fanny pack with her cell phone and walkie-talkie from the sideboard. She'd felt half naked at Chuck E. Cheese's without them. "We've got sausage and pepperoni."

"Lead me to it." Diego grinned and followed her down the corridor.

He was the only member of the staff who would enter the family quarters unafraid and unintimidated. The others wouldn't push through the green door unless summoned if their lives depended on it. Oh the times, Dory thought, they were a-changing.

Aunt Ping and Deirdre sat at the oak table. They still wore their wedding finery but they'd kicked off their shoes and propped their stockinged feet on the chair between them. Jamie sat on the other side of the table cutting a slice of cold pepperoni with a knife and fork on a bone china plate, a cocoa mustache on his top lip.

"Diego." Deirdre smiled delightedly. "Come join us."

"Any sausage left, Mrs. Deirdre?"

"Two slices. Just for you. Cocoa? Would you like some, Dory?"

"Just cocoa, please. Thank you."

Deirdre rose to fetch extra mugs. Aunt Ping swung her feet to the floor and Dory dropped into the chair beside her.

"How's Charles?" she asked. "Did he survive all the excitement?"

"Yes, though he was very tired," Aunt Ping replied. She looked so exhausted her eyes were puffy. "I offered him a guest room, but no. He insisted on returning to his quarters."

"How about lunch after mass tomorrow? You and me

and Deirdre." Why not, Dory decided. Kill two birds with one stone.

Aunt Ping pursed her lips, considering. Dory squeezed her hand.

"Come on. Live dangerously. I've been driving you to church since Charles got sick and I haven't killed you yet."

"I would *adore* lunch," Deirdre chimed in. "I'll go if Margaret won't."

Enthusiasm from Deirdre was all it took to persuade Aunt Ping.

"As it happens," she said, her eyebrow sliding up, "Margaret would be enchanted to go for lunch after mass."

"Oh *man*." Jamie groaned. "Do I have to go?"

"To lunch, no," Dory said. "To bed, yes. It's almost ten-thirty so finish up and rinse your dishes."

Jamie rinsed Dory's cup, too, and kissed Aunt Ping and Deirdre good night. So did Dory, giving Deirdre a thank-you, you-sweet, sly-boots wink, and headed for the guest-house with Chuck E. and Jamie.

They crossed the terrace, wet and shiny in the dark, and went down the steps to the better-lit pea gravel path that ran between the lowest terraced level of the garden and the greensward. The windows in Charles' apartment glowed with light and Dory smiled. Except for Jamie, Jill and Chase, everyone was back where he or she had started.

"Why do we have to go the long way?" Jamie scuffed his feet in a puddled patch of gravel and swiped his hair out of his eyes.

" 'Cause I don't want to fall on my face in the dark on the footpath." Dory hooked an arm around his neck, rubbed Chuck E. in his nose and piped in a falsetto voice, "Me neither, squirt."

He giggled and tried to break free. Dory pulled him closer, tighter.

If she hadn't, the dark figure that burst out of the garden would've scooped Jamie up and been gone with him in a flash across the greensward. Dory barely saw him leap the bench she'd been sitting on when Chase had walked by her, had half a second to scream before he hit her with his shoulder and clamped a hand too strong to belong to a woman on her arm. He wrenched her elbow, shoved her so hard she fell, grabbed Jamie by the front of his sweatshirt and tried to swing him off his feet.

He wants Jamie! Dory's mind cried in horror.

"Jamie, *run!*" she screamed, scrambling in the gravel to get up.

Jamie didn't. He grabbed the man's wrists, fighting and twisting to keep him off balance, hollering his head off like they'd taught him to do in school if he was ever attacked. *Thank you, Sister Immaculata!*

Dory made it to her feet clutching Chuck E., jumped on the man in the ski mask pulled over his face and started whaling him with her stuffed mouse. He jabbed her with an elbow, caught her in the cheek and sent her spinning toward the ground, seeing stars and grabbing for the fanny pack that wasn't there. She had a clear picture of it hung over the back of Deirdre's chair before she hit the gravel and skidded on her chin.

She pushed up on her hands and rolled, sensed rather than saw Diego vault over her and fling himself at the man who had his hands clamped on Jamie. All three of them went down with a thud. Diego came up first on his knees, fists swinging and swearing in Spanish, the man kicking at Jamie, who was stuck like a burr to his left knee and trying to bite.

"Jamie, *no!*" Dory grabbed him and pulled him off, which gave the man a foot to plant in Diego's chest and send him sprawling on his back.

Then he wheeled to his feet running, half falling on his hands, off the path and across the greensward, shadowed by the cloud-draped moon and the mist rising from the wet grass. Diego sprang up on his feet to follow, but Dory clawed a handful of his shirt and held him back.

"No, Diego. He's gone," she panted, out of breath. "Let him go."

Jamie threw his arms around her and sobbed. Dory held

him, felt him shiver and his teeth chatter against her shoulder, heard an engine fire somewhere off in the dark. In the mist, it was hard to tell just where.

"Sounds like an ATV," Diego said. He sucked a deep breath, swept her fanny pack off the ground and held it up to her. "You forgot your walkie-talkie, Miss Dory."

Diego wanted to call the police from the guesthouse. Dory said no.

"I don't want to alarm the guests," she said, her jaw throbbing and cracking with each word. "Or disrupt Jill's wedding night."

"At least let me bring Miss Ping and Mrs. Deirdre."

"No, Diego. They've gone to bed. Leave them be."

He said something in Spanish that sounded like he was clearing his throat and slammed out the door. Dory locked it behind him and threw the deadbolt, hooked the double chains on the Dutch door, made sure all the windows were locked and turned on every light in the house.

Then she shagged Jamie upstairs and into the shower, told him to put on his pajamas and stay in his room and wait for her. She ran a bath and sank into it, forgot about her scraped-raw chin and covered her face with her hands, threw her head back against her bath pillow and squeezed her eyes shut on stinging hot tears.

Flashes of the attack jerked behind her eyelids. She tried to hold them steady so she could examine them for clues to identify the man who had come after Jamie, but the images wouldn't hold still, they kept jumping away. Her left shoulder and her wrenched elbow stabbed her with hot needles every time she moved her arm.

Dory fumbled for the soap with her right hand, opened her eyes and saw Rocky perched on the edge of the tub. The tuxedo cat tipped her head to one side and made a soundless "Meeew." Dory touched noses with her, heard the purr in her velvety white chest and felt calmer.

She finished her bath, brushed mud and pea gravel off Chuck E. and propped him on her bed, put on her pj's and went to get Jamie. He was sitting on his bed waiting for her, just as she'd asked.

"Now comes the fun part," Dory said. "Now we get to play doctor."

Jamie jumped off the bed, clinging to her hand like he hadn't since he was six years old. Rocky padded downstairs with them and into the half bath. Jamie sat on the closed toilet lid and let Dory clean his skinned elbow and knuckles with cotton balls and hydrogen peroxide. She didn't have to fake the hopping, hissing, yelling dance she did to make him laugh, to chase the chalky pale, wide-eyed terror from his face when she let him press a soaked cotton ball to her chin.

"Hey, Dory." Jamie peered at her while she flapped her hands in front of her face to dry her chin. "You're gonna have a black eye."

"Think Aunt Ping will believe I ran into a door?"

"You aren't gonna tell her somebody jumped us?"

Us. Thank God he thinks it was us.

"Did you see how tired she looks?" Dory asked and Jamie nodded. "She's still worried about Charles. Do we want to tell her and start her worrying about something like this happening to one of the guests?"

"Where'd that creep come from?" Jamie pressed his palms together between his knees and shivered. "How did he get onto Outlook?"

Under the cover of the wedding, in all the commotion and comings and goings of two hundred people. Just like he'd slipped onto Outlook and into the trees along the footpath on Charles' birthday to try to grab Jamie the first time. This time he was smarter. This time he'd waited till dark.

"Outlook has about a billion miles of open fence line, Jamie, and the world is full of nuts. Come on. We need more cocoa."

Dory needed to keep busy so her hands wouldn't shake. She got out the Hershey's and made cocoa from scratch. While Jamie stirred, she tossed marshmallows left over from the s'mores in super-size mugs, made cinnamon toast and looked at the Kliban Cat clock on the wall.

Quarter past eleven. She'd last seen the time on the dash clock in Curt's car. He'd dropped them off at nine forty-five, an hour and a half that seemed like five minutes ago. Or ten lifetimes. Dory couldn't decide.

When the toast was ready, they sat at the breakfast room table. Rocky jumped into Jill's chair and licked cinnamon and sugar off Jamie's fingers. He was pale anyway, because he was a redhead, but his face had enough color now that his freckles didn't look like dots of red ink.

When the doorbell rang Dory jumped. Jamie spun out of his chair and went with her to the front door. So did Rocky, jumping up on the fourth step behind them as Dory flipped on the outside light. When she and Jamie stood on their toes to peer through the small window, she realized her right eye was swelling.

Agent Frasier stood on the front stoop with Diego.

"Hey," Jamie said. "It's the fat guy who hangs out in the orchard."

"His name is Agent Frasier, Jamie." Dory opened the door. "Hello, Agent Frasier. Should I start the coffee? Is Marshall Phillips on his way?"

"No, Miss Lambert. He's not on his way. Officially, I'm not even here." The shoulders of Agent Frasier's gray suit glistened in the drizzle misting around the porch light. He nodded at Diego, who lifted his chin defiantly. "Mr. Rivera thought I could persuade you to call the police."

"Since you're here." Dory backed away. "I suppose you can try."

Agent Frasier had barely stepped over the threshold when his beeper went off. He plucked it off his belt, glanced at it, then at Dory.

"I'll be back, Miss Lambert. Mr. Rivera, would you come with me?"

"Sí," Diego said and turned down the steps with him. He did that when he was angry or upset, slipped back into Spanish.

Dory watched them push through the gate in the patio wall, swing into the tan fed mobile and drive away with only the parking lights on.

Jamie slipped his hand into hers. "Do you think they caught him?"

"I hope so." Dory squeezed his fingers and started to shut the door. It was about time the Lambert luck changed.

"Wait!" Peter called to her. "It's us!"

She swung the door wider and saw Peter and Henry in their pj's, bathrobes and red rubber galoshes. Peter held a green and white striped golf umbrella over their heads. Henry carried a wicker basket.

"Oh lovey." Peter collapsed the umbrella on the stoop. "That eye."

"Diego called us," Henry said. "On the walkie-talkie."

"Before or after he went into the orchard for Agent Frasier?"

"On the way." Peter fished in Henry's basket and slapped a bag of frozen peas in her hand. "Put that on your eye and don't fuss at Diego. I would've done the same thing if you'd told me not to call the police."

"Come help me in the kitchen, Jamie." Henry took him by the arm. "We're going to make a poultice for Dory's eye."

Peter forced Dory onto the couch, put a cushion behind her head and the bag of peas over her eye. It stung for a second, then the cold leeched the throb out of her cheekbone and she sighed. Rocky jumped on her stomach and started to purr.

Peter sat on the coffee table in yellow silk pajamas, bent his elbows on his knees and asked quietly, "What happened?"

Dory told him, keeping her voice low. "He kept pushing me off, knocking me down. He didn't want me. He wanted Jamie."

"Kidnapping, do you think?" Peter asked and she shook her head. "If it wasn't, then there's a pervert loose. Maybe I *should* call the cops."

"I'll get the phone." Peter went for the cordless on the desk by the stairs, veered left when the bell rang and opened the door on Charles in his rain-spotted navy poplin jacket. "Is she all right?"

"Oh for heaven's sake!" Dory took the bag of peas off her face, sat up and glared at Peter with her one good eye. "Who did *you* call?"

"Just me and Tom and Eddie," Charles said. "I called Coop on the house phone. He'll be here."

"Great! Make piña coladas and let's have a party!" Dory fell back on the couch and clapped the peas over her nose. Hopefully, they were still cold enough to freeze the tears in her eyes. Being brave for Jamie was all she could handle. She did not need an audience.

The couch cushion dipped beside her, the bag lifted from her eyes. Charles leaned toward her, his voice low. "We got him. Jamie should be out of earshot when Agent Frasier comes to tell you about it."

"I'll see to it," Peter said and hurried off into the kitchen. He challenged Jamie to a football duel. Clever man.

"Dory." Jamie huffed into the living room. "Peter thinks he can take me at NFL football. Can we go up to my room so I can kick his butt?"

"Sure," she said. Peter winked and trailed Jamie upstairs.

"Who caught him?" Dory asked Charles. "How?"

"I got the Rolls out and drove the roads. Tom and Eddie roused their boys, fired up the tractors, saddled the horses and split the fields between them. Wish I could say we made a daring capture." Charles smiled. "Truth is, the scum who attacked you overturned the ATV he was on and broke an ankle. Eddie found him crawling for the fence."

"Was anybody on our side hurt?"

"No. But if Eddie had seen this—" Charles tipped her face up without touching the scrape on her chin. "—the bastard would've had more to worry about than a broken ankle."

He put a kiss on her forehead that made her tears spill over.

"Don't make her cry. Not with that eye." Henry put a tray on the coffee table, tugged the dish towel off the shoulder of his green satin pajamas and swatted Charles with it. "Get up and let me in there."

"In a second," Charles said to Henry. "One more thing," he said to Dory. "The idea was to trap or flush this guy. We had to get ourselves out there and cover as much territory as quickly as possible. I needed another driver. I couldn't wake Wallace, and he doesn't move that fast anymore. So I called Chase."

"Oh no." The images that the trip to Chuck E. Cheese's had erased from Dory's head, of what *might* be going on in the Honeymoon Suite, came flooding back with a flush. "If Jill's awake, she'll wake Aunt Ping and—"

"Chase said Jill didn't wake up." Charles rose to make room for Henry. "He made it out of the house without disturbing anyone."

While Henry bathed her cheek with a cotton ball dipped in distilled witch hazel to stop the swelling, Charles took the peas to the freezer. Dory's pulse jumped when the bell rang but it was Coop, not Chase. He came toward the couch in khaki pants and a beige sweater and sat down on the table, a sympathetic furrow on his forehead.

"You should see the other guy," Dory said and Coop smiled. "I'm sorry Charles dragged you out of bed."

"He was absolutely right to wake me. You shouldn't so much as nod to Agent Frasier without me being present."

"I'm responsible for the feds. I wouldn't let Diego call the police."

"That was foolish," Coop said sternly. "This isn't kids playing paintball or Jamie surprising a burglar. Where is Jamie, by the way?"

"Upstairs with Peter playing whatever."

"Somewhere else would be better." Coop looked at Charles.

"I could take him with me to put the Rolls up," he said to Dory. "He loves to monkey around in the garage."

She nodded and Charles turned up the stairs. Coop's cell phone rang. He got up and went into the kitchen. Henry gave her a bowl full of shredded raw potatoes.

"Press some to your cheek," he said. "Odd, I know, but my mother swore by raw potatoes to take the discoloration out of a black eye."

Jamie came pelting downstairs in jeans and sneakers, tugging a sweatshirt over his head. Peter and Charles came behind him.

"I knew it would be cool living with you." Jamie dropped to his knees beside the couch. "No way would Aunt Ping or Auntie Deirdre let me go hang in the garage with Charles this late at night."

"I probably won't very often. Enjoy it."

"Your eye is swollen. Does it hurt?"

"Not too much. Have fun, squirt."

Jamie and Charles went out the front door, Peter into the kitchen. Dory gingerly pressed shredded potatoes to her cheek. She heard Coop end his call and ask about coffee, listened to cabinet doors open and close, water run and deep male voices.

Every sound, every noise made her nerves jump. When she thought she'd scream if these people didn't get out of her house, a boom of thunder rattled the windows and the bell rang. Henry rushed through the living room and opened the door for Agent Frasier. He stepped inside in a wet tan trench coat.

"It's pouring," he said to Henry, who took the coat and hung it over the newel post. To Dory he said, "Where's Jamie?"

"Elsewhere," she said and Agent Frasier nodded. "Good."

Coop brought him a cup of coffee and introduced himself. Peter brought a dining room chair so Frasier could sit near Dory and another one for Coop. He and Henry sat on either side of her on the couch.

"The man who attacked you is in custody," Frasier said. "When your groom found him, I called in the local boys. Diego got the best look at him, so he's on his way to the station to give his statement. Chase McKay is driving him. I got you a pass for tonight, but tomorrow a Kansas City police detective will be out to talk to you and Jamie."

"Thank you," Dory said. She'd been foolish to think she could keep this from Aunt Ping. Her eye would give it away in a flash.

"You owe Diego for coming to get me," Frasier said. "I think this character might've been able to stonewall the local guys, but my big shiny FBI badge scared the crap out of him. He couldn't talk fast enough. You aren't going to like what he had to say, but you need to hear it."

"I assume," Coop said, "that what you're about to tell Miss Lambert you'll also have to report to Marshall Phillips."

"Yes, I'll tell him, but I don't expect him to do anything about it," Agent Frasier said to Coop. "I've been down this road with Mr. Phillips. He doesn't care to hear anything from my team that doesn't drive a nail in Del Lambert's coffin. Since what I'm about to say doesn't, he'll likely tell me to write a report, which he'll file and never read. I wouldn't be concerned about the United States attorney sticking his nose into this."

"I see." Coop frowned. "I appreciate your candor."

Poor Coop. When Dory called him after Gary confessed to Jill, Coop claimed that the judge who'd denied Phillips' request for a phone tap on the Happy Spirit was wrong to call it a vendetta. He'd maintained that his old friend wasn't vindictive but a dedicated public servant.

"Do you want to know this low-life's name?" Frasier asked Dory.

"No. I don't want it in my head. Just tell me why he came after Jamie. He *was* after Jamie, wasn't he?"

"Yes. The boy was the target. That's how this sterling individual makes his living. By grabbing kids from parents in ugly custody battles."

"Why did he come after Jamie?" Dory asked. She had a roaring headache. Maybe that's why she wasn't grasping what Agent Frasier was saying. "Jamie's mother is dead.

His maternal grandmother is Aunt Ping's dearest friend. Gina Vanderpool suggested that Aunt Ping adopt Jamie. He spends two months every summer with his grandparents in Vancouver. Gina Vanderpool has no reason to do something like this."

"I didn't say it was the Vanderpools, Miss Lambert."

"Then who—?" A rush of horror flooded through Dory, every hair on her body stood on end. "Oh God. No. Not *James*."

"That's how it looks to me," Agent Frasier said. "I'd say James Darwood found out he has a son."

Chapter Seventeen

The scumbag named Wally Stark wasn't supposed to keep Jamie. He was supposed to grab him and deliver him to a slimeball registered under the name Joe Bauer at a Super 8 Motel near Kansas City International Airport.

Three unmarked KCMO Police cars rolled into the parking lot at 12:43 A.M. Two detectives presented their credentials to the night manager, who told them Joe Bauer checked out at twelve-fifteen, paid his bill in cash and wished him a good night.

"Joe Bauer is a phony name," Chase told Charles. "No one matching the description the manager gave the cops boarded any of the red-eye flights out of KCI. He got in his car, drove away and disappeared."

It was four minutes past three according to the Valvoline Motor Oil clock on the paneled wall of his father's office. Charles sat at his desk in his robe and slippers, Chase in a molded plastic chair from the lobby.

Diego leaned on a wooden table that held Charles' coffeemaker. He'd taken a shower, washed the mud and pea gravel out of his brown, almost black hair and put on jeans and a sweatshirt.

"Medium height, sandy hair, blue eyes." Charles shook his head. "That's not James unless he dyed his hair and walked on his knees."

"In cases like this, the cops said it's usually one of the

parents. They were careful *not* to say for sure that it was Darwood."

"Least they were careful." Charles snorted. "Agent Frasier told Dory it *had* to be James. Scared the living hell out of her, Peter said."

"Darwood abandoned Marilyn before she knew she was pregnant, didn't he?" Chase asked.

"That's what she told Deirdre." Charles scowled. "But if Marilyn didn't tell James, then how did he find out about Jamie?"

"Who says he has? Not the cops," Chase reminded him. "They say it's possible that Stark and Bauer cooked this up as a simple kidnapping and ransom. When Stark didn't make the rendezvous at the motel, Bauer figured something had gone wrong and took off. If that's all this is, then Agent Frasier made a knee-jerk assumption based on Stark's record and shot his mouth off when he should have kept it shut."

"For Dory, Miss Ping and Deirdre's sake, I hope the police are right." Charles rose and pushed in his chair. "Thank you for your help, son. You should go back to your bride and I should go to bed."

When Charles left the office, Diego pushed off the table. "Do you think it was just a kidnapping and ransom?"

"No," Chase said. "I don't think Dad will, either, in the morning. But hopefully he'll be able to sleep the rest of the night."

"Maybe I know how this James guy found out about Jamie," Diego said. "Maybe Miss Dory does, too. I'm not sure she'll tell that detective we talked to when he comes to see her tomorrow, but I figure if I tell you, you'll be able to convince her that she should tell the cops."

"I can't promise," Chase said. "But I'll do my damnedest."

"Okay." Diego nodded. "Esther caught Miss Fairview in the office snooping around Miss Dory's desk. Esther told her and Miss Dory asked me to watch Miss Fairview. Keep an eye on where she goes and what she does."

"When did Dory ask you to watch Miss Fairview?"

"Early Thursday morning. She came down here to the garage."

The night before, Wednesday, when Chase stormed through the back parlor to bang on the terrace doors of his father's suite, he'd overheard Miss Fairview on her cell phone. She'd said something about time. It was the wrong time, not the right time. For what? Kidnapping Jamie?

"You're the man, Diego." Chase clapped him on the arm. "You saved Jamie from God knows what."

"Don't give me a medal," Diego said. "He's such a little shit I thought about letting the guy have him."

"But you didn't. Get some sleep."

"You, too, Mr. Chase," Diego said as he left the office.

Oh, yeah. He was a member of the family now.

He had a wife he didn't want. A wife he should go back to in case she woke up, but as much champagne as Jill had swilled while they'd sat side by side in the giant bed trying to figure out how to gracefully get rid of each other, Chase doubted she'd crack an eye before noon.

He stepped outside into the dark and the mist that had settled in behind the rain, shut the door and leaned against the garage, the rough brick scraping his scalp. What a day. Chase rubbed his hands over his face and exhaled a deep breath. What a night.

He wanted to see Dory. Not to tell her that he was an idiot and he'd married the wrong sister, just to see her. His father and Diego both told him she was all right, but he wanted to see for himself. Make sure before he went back to the Honeymoon Suite to grab as much sleep as he could before Jill woke up and he had to tell her what had happened.

Chase pushed off the garage, zipped the maroon and navy McKay Design and Development jacket he'd thrown on with jeans and a gray sweater on his way out and headed for the pea gravel path. He wanted to see where Dory was attacked. Diego told him by the bench in front of the pagoda fountain. The bench Dory was sitting on Monday night when he'd thrown his cigarettes on the greensward and used her giant flashlight to find them, when he'd noticed how luminous her eyes looked in the dark and that she painted her toenails red.

The night she'd told him he was shallow.

The path drained well enough that only a few puddles stood between the garage and the guesthouse, one smack in front of the bench. Mist hung in the ground lights, but Chase could make out slurred footprints and smeared skid marks in the muddy gravel.

The terrace above the bench was too steep, Chase decided. Stark hadn't used the fountain for cover. He'd lurked up top in the ornamental garden, watching and waiting. He'd followed Dory and Jamie partway down the flagged steps, then cut across the terrace and used the back of the bench as a springboard to leap out at them.

Jamie had fought Stark, Diego said. So had Dory. Chase clenched his fists, his heart pounding. He still had the cold, hard ball in his gut that he'd swallowed when his father told him Dory had been attacked.

Why was he doing this, imagining how Stark had done it, how he'd set it up? Because he hadn't been here to take the elbow in the face for Dory that Diego had witnessed? Because he'd been too damn dumb to realize on Monday how adorable she was, how funny, how smart and how well she knew him? Better than he knew himself, that was for sure.

Standing here choking on guilt and stupidity wouldn't help Dory. Or Jamie. The kid was a royal pain, but he was just a kid. He could be at serious risk from the man who had contributed the sperm that conceived him. The son of a bitch who schemed and plotted for six years to screw the Lamberts because he thought they'd screwed him.

If Darwood wanted Jamie, Chase thought he knew why—so he could screw the Lamberts one more time. If Darwood *was* behind this, if he wanted Jamie that badly, he had to be stopped. To be stopped, he had to be found. Chase had no idea how to locate a man who had vanished without a trace. He'd have to polish up his Phi Beta Kappa key and think about it. He turned from the bench toward the guesthouse.

With the exception of Jamie's bedroom, every light in the place was on, which didn't surprise Chase. He'd sleep with the lights on, too. Plus Peter and Henry could still be awake. His father told him they were sleeping over to keep an eye on Jamie and Dory.

Pots of dripping wet white geraniums stood on the steps. Chase bumped one, shaking rain on his shoe, and knocked quietly on the door. If Dory was asleep, he didn't want to wake her with the bell.

I don't want to talk to her. I don't want to upset her. In his head, Chase ran through what he'd say to Peter. *I don't want to lead her on or drop her like a hot rock. I just want to look at her for a minute.*

It was Peter he expected to answer his knock. He never imagined it would be Dory, but Dory opened the door. Dory in pink and blue check pajamas and a yellow bathrobe, holding a bag of frozen peas over her right eye. Chase wanted to sweep her into his arms, but just smiled.

She pressed a finger to her lips and he nodded. Stepped inside and stepped aside. Dory shut the door and motioned for him to follow her.

Henry and Peter were dead to the world in their pajamas on the living room couch, Peter's head on one arm, Henry's on the other. The black and white cat curled in a ball on the middle cushion where their feet met and tangled together.

Dory led him through a sunken dining room, a breakfast room and kitchen. Past a laundry room where an electric dryer tumbled and down three more steps into a room behind the stairs. The walls were stone like the fireplace. A computer sat on a mahogany desk. The carpet was paprika, the furniture, two oversize chairs with a square upholstered ottoman between them, sage green. Hickory ladder shelves leaned against the walls. Aha. He'd found the designer of the Happy Spirit.

And his heart in the tiny woman plopping cross-legged

into one of the chairs with a scraped chin and a bag of frozen peas over her eye.

"We can talk in here and not wake Peter and Henry," Dory said.

Chase took off his jacket and hung it on the back of the desk chair. "Why aren't you in bed?"

"I could ask you the same question." She grinned, or tried to, and ended up wincing. Chase gripped the chair till the urge to beat Wally Stark to a pulp passed, then walked toward Dory. "How's your eye?"

"Let's just say I'll be doing my Jack Nicholson impersonation for the next week or so."

There was a tray on the ottoman, a bottle of witch hazel and cotton balls on the tray, as well as a small bowl floating a facecloth in a couple of inches of water and another bowl covered with plastic wrap.

"What's this?" Chase lifted the tray from the ottoman and put it on the table next to Dory's chair.

"In the covered bowl? Shredded raw potatoes, which Henry swears will take the bruise out of a black eye," she said. "I've been sitting here all night with peas in one hand and potatoes in the other. I'm so hungry I could eat my bathrobe."

Chase sat on the ottoman. He spread his hands on the big stuffed arms of the chair, leaned forward and pressed a chaste, brotherly kiss to her forehead. The left side of his mouth brushed the cold bag of peas. He leaned back and watched a single giant tear fill Dory's left eye.

"Potatoes in one hand, peas in the other, and your head full of bad dreams," he said to her. "I'll stay so you can sleep. I won't let anything like this happen to you ever again."

The tear rolled out of her eye. Chase caught it with his thumb.

"You shouldn't be here," Dory said. "You should be with Jill."

"She drank a magnum of Dom Pérignon. She won't miss me."

Chase raised his hand. Dory drew back in the chair, a glitter of reproach in her eyes. He'd made so many mistakes with her, missed so many cues. There was no missing this one. She didn't want him to touch her. That's all he wanted to do, but he laid his hand back on the chair.

"I know you mean well, Chase." Another tear filled Dory's eye. "But it's very hard for me to be with you right now. I wish you'd leave."

"Why? So you can go back to ducking and dodging me? I spent my first week at Outlook trying to find you. At the time I was too dense to figure out what that meant. I might have, but then Jill showed up and launched Operation Cockroach and I was a goner."

Dory blinked the tear out of her eye. "Uh—what?"

"Operation Cockroach. Grind Chase McKay under my heel because he hurt my baby sister. Jill had a lot to say once she'd put away a magnum of champagne. We had a long talk. That's all we did. We talked till she passed out."

"So you dropped by to what?" Dory asked. "Blacken my other eye?"

"I came to make sure you're all right." His hands felt clammy on the chair arms, his pulse thudded in his ears. What the hell, Chase decided. He'd come this far. "And to ask you to wait for me."

"You're leaving. I knew it." She slid the bag of peas over both her eyes and held it there. "I knew you would. I don't blame you."

"Dory. I'm not leaving." He moved his grip farther up the chair arms and pulled himself closer to her. "Do you love me?"

The bag dropped in her lap and Chase sucked his teeth. Jesus. The bruise covered her cheekbone. Her right eye was swollen almost shut, her left one wide open with shock.

"You married my sister today. How can you ask me that?"

"Jill doesn't want me. She wants twenty million dollars for the Outlook Trust. She doesn't love me. She told me about Gary."

Dory's mouth fell open. "*All* about Gary?"

"He's a FBI agent. He went to find James Darwood so she wouldn't have to marry me for my money. Did she leave anything out?"

"No. Those are the high points." Dory shrank in the chair, her shoulders slumped, her chin starting to quiver. "I can't believe she did this. I can't *believe* Jill dragged all of us through this wedding and then poured her heart out to you as soon as you carried her over the threshold!"

Dory grabbed the bag of peas. Chase thought she meant to hit him with it and ducked, but she threw it across the room. It smacked into the stone wall, split and scattered half-thawed peas. Dory winced, clutched the right side of her head and said, "Ow," in a small, broken voice.

Then she started to cry, which had to hurt like hell with that eye. It hurt him, knowing he was part of why she wept. Her last cue was don't touch me, but when her swollen, bruised eye squeezed out a tiny tear Chase couldn't stand it. He scooped her out of the chair.

"No," she mewled, trying to twist away from him. "*No.*"

"Just for a minute. Just till you stop crying."

"Okay," she sniffled and curled in his lap. "Just for a minute."

A minute, hell. For the rest of their lives if he could keep his cool and not blow this. Chase tucked the top of Dory's head under his chin. Her bathrobe was a big, bulky terry-cloth blanket. Wasn't much to feel underneath, which was just as well. Not a good time for the lust meter to spin into the red zone. He wrapped his arms around her, snuggled her against him and felt her choke back a sob.

"I never cry," she told him. "It's just been a really bad day."

"I'm glad it's over." He touched his lips to her hair. It was thick and soft and smelled like the peonies that were in bloom all over Outlook. It must be her shampoo. "How's Jamie?"

"Charles took him up to the garage and let him touch all of his tools. He was in high alt. He went right to sleep."

Dory sucked a shaky breath. "The FBI thinks James hired that creep to grab Jamie."

"The cops aren't sure. Least that's what they told Diego and me."

"I have no idea how I'm going to tell Aunt Ping."

"You don't have to tackle her alone. I spoke to the police and briefly with Agent Frasier. I'll back you up."

"If you'd just tell Jill I'd be grateful."

"You don't want to break it to her?"

"No. At the moment I just want to break her neck."

"Dory. Jill isn't entirely to blame for the wedding. So am I."

She sat up in his lap and blinked at him like an owl. Her right eye was completely closed, the left one puffed up from crying.

"If you're not leaving, why did you ask me to wait for you?" She asked. "What *exactly* do want me to wait for?"

"This," he said and kissed her.

Her mouth was so close he barely had to move his head to catch her lips. They were cool but soft and they parted for him, which sent the lust meter spinning way past red but Chase held himself back, kept the kiss as gentle as he could so he wouldn't hurt her. He'd hurt her enough.

He'd absolutely, positively married the wrong sister. Jill's kiss had never penetrated past his physical senses. Dory's kiss burst in his heart, bloomed like a sweet little flower meant to open only for him. No matter what came out of her mouth when he let her go, she loved him. He felt it in the shiver of her lips, the flutter of her breath.

Chase broke the kiss. Dory stared at him. He smiled.

"I married your sister today, but I love you. I know that makes me an imbecile. You can tell me you never want to see me again, toss me off Outlook on my stupid, sorry ass and I'll go, but I love you. I realized it when you caught Jill's bouquet. I had a hunch before that, but I didn't connect the dots. I don't always—I compartmentalize—but I put it together when you caught Jill's flowers. The thought of you marrying someone else made me want to bash my head against the wall."

"How ironic," Dory said. "I was just thinking of doing that."

She slid out of his lap and plunked into the chair, her legs and her arms crossed. She was royally pissed, but she loved him. So long as he knew that, he could sit here and take whatever she had to dish out.

"You told me you love Jill. Now you say you love me. You're sitting in my house, married to my sister. You *kissed* me. This afternoon you kissed Jill and carried her upstairs to the Honeymoon Suite. Why on earth should I believe you?"

"I can't think of a single reason, but I can show you one."

Chase held his hand out to her, palm up. Dory turned her head to the left so she could see him better. She was wary but she was considering. When she sighed and laid her fingertips on his, Chase went down on his knees and pressed her hand to his chest, held it there and felt his heart pound like a sledge beneath her palm and his.

"I've kissed a lot of women, but my heart never did this, never tried to jump out of my chest. I don't recall this happening before, either."

Chase raised her hand and curved her fingers around his jaw, let her feel the muscle jump at her touch, turned his head and brushed his lips against her palm. So small and soft, his mouth shivered. He felt his breath catch—hers, too—pressed her hand to his chest and thanked his heart for its set-me-free gallop against Dory's tiny hand.

"You have no reason to believe me, every reason to doubt me. Why should you trust me? All I've ever done is hurt you. I don't know why you talk to me. I don't know why you let me in. I don't deserve you. Believe me. I know I don't deserve you, but I love you." Chase raised his right hand. "And I promise, swear to God. I will never, ever again call you squirt."

She laughed, then she cried, grabbed a handful of tissues

out of a box beside the tray and pressed them to her face, sucked a shuddery breath and looked at him with her red, puffy, tear-sparkled left eye.

"Are you a dream? Did I get hit so hard I'm in a coma?"

"I'm real," Chase said. "I'm here. I'm yours if you'll have me."

Dory scooted to the edge of the chair. He expected her to slap him; he ached for her to put her arms around him. Instead, she laid her palm on his chest, her small hand probing like the room was dark and she was feeling her way. Chase drew a breath to fill his lungs, felt her hand curve around the rise of his chest. Her lips made a moue. Her fingertip touched his flat but hard nipple and made the muscle underneath flex. She snatched her hand away and looked up at him.

"Are you sure you love me, Chase?"

"Yes." What a thing to hear, are you sure, but with his track record he didn't blame her. "I'm positive. I love you."

"I've dreamed about this. All my life I've dreamed about this moment." Her voice warbled and she blinked back tears. "I thought I'd die when you lifted Jill's veil and kissed her."

"Dory." Chase felt his heart twist. "Sweetheart—"

"I'm not finished." She flung up a hand as he reached for her. "I didn't die, but if you aren't absolutely certain that you love me, *you* will. Slowly and painfully. I'm forever or I'm not at all."

"Forever is exactly what I had in mind." Chase tried a smile. Dory arched an eyebrow. "I'd give every dime I have if I could turn the clock back twenty-four hours, but I can't. All I can say is I'm sorry I hurt you. I will never hurt you again or give you a reason to doubt me. I don't expect you to take my word for it. Just give me a chance to prove it."

She pursed her lips for a second, then shrugged and said, "Okay."

"Okay?" Chase laughed, relieved that he'd gotten this far and she hadn't killed him. "That's all I get? Okay?"

Dory tipped her head at him. "What do you want?"

"You. Naked. A ring right here." He sucked the third finger of her left hand into his mouth, watched Dory's breath catch and her lips part. Her finger tasted starchy, like raw potatoes. He ran his tongue around the knuckle, let her finger go. "A ring I put there. What d'you say?"

"Are you asking me to marry you?"

"I'm on my knees, aren't I?"

"You're also my sister's husband."

"In name only, I swear to God. A small stumbling block that I intend to sweep from our path as soon as humanly possible."

"How?" Dory crossed her arms. "When?"

"Jill konked in the middle of hammering out our graceful exit strategy, but it will likely be an annulment. The marriage wasn't consummated so it should be fairly straightforward."

"Chase." Dory sighed irritably. "Haven't you figured out yet that nothing, and I mean *nothing,* is ever straightforward with Jill?"

"Don't worry." He cupped her elbows. "I'll call Coop Junior tomorrow. Get him started so he'll be ready to go Monday morning."

"How is an attorney going to help with Father Murphy? Or Aunt Ping? She cried through the whole wedding. I have no idea how I'm going to tell her that Jill's marriage is kaput already."

Dory's eyes, even her swollen, bruised right eye, looked huge in her small, heart-shaped face. She was pale, so exhausted her left eye looked black and blue underneath where it was still puffy from crying.

"You aren't going to tell her anything. Jill will or I will." He slid his hands under Dory. "You are going to bed."

"Hey! Put me down! Not so fast! We've got to get this stuff settled!"

Dory tried to twist away, but that's all she could do. He had the advantage of size and strength and leverage. She hooked her legs around his waist to help him balance her weight as he stood up, but jammed her arms together. She looked like a mad little bird with its wings folded.

"Are you giving me directions to your bedroom?" Chase asked. "Or am I going to stand here and hold you while you sleep?"

"Tell me first what Coop Junior is going to do."

"He's going to transfer twenty million dollars to the Outlook Trust."

Her arms sprang apart so suddenly she almost fell. Chase shifted his grip and caught her. She clutched the front of his sweater, pulled herself up and looked at him nose to nose.

"Why would you do that? Is Jill blackmailing you?"

"Jill wouldn't do a thing like that."

"Oh yes, she would," Dory said, in a trust me tone of voice. "In a heartbeat if she thought it would get us out of the hotel business."

Chase frowned. "You're really angry with her."

"Angry doesn't even come close. I can forgive the disaster of this wedding, but if goading Gary till he went tearing off to find James brings Marshall Phillips down on our necks, Esme had better hide the knives."

"Didn't Jill tell you that the funds to keep the FBI poking around Outlook will likely dry up in July?"

"Gary told me. The day I went to the Happy Spirit to fire him and I *stupidly* let him talk me out of it." For a second Chase thought Dory was going to beat her head against his shoulder. "When he left to find James he told the FBI his grandmother died. That was a week ago. How long do you think it will be till Marshall Phillips comes looking for him?"

"Agent Frasier seems like a nice guy. Won't he cover for Gary?"

"Gary doesn't report to Frasier. He reports to Uncle Scrooge."

"Oh," Chase said. Oh hell, he thought. He'd call Coop Junior in the morning. After lunch, he'd invite Coop Senior for a game of nine ball in the billiard room and a long talk about Phillips and James Darwood. Oh, yes. And Miss Fairview, too.

"Jill thinks the entire mess of our lives is all her fault," Dory said. "For the past ten years I've been telling her no, but I think I'm starting to come around on that. She's beginning to remind me of Mother."

"No one is that self-absorbed. Jill seems genuinely concerned about the strain the Outlook Inn puts on Miss Ping."

"So am I," Dory snapped. "But I wouldn't dream of hatching a plan to marry you and screw you out of twenty million dollars."

"Are you sure? I'd be glad to lie down for that one."

"Chase." Dory flushed, then glared at him. "I'm trying to stay mad."

"Why? Is anger going to change Jill? Bring Gary back?"

"You're awfully happy for a man who just got scammed."

"Why wouldn't I be happy? I've got what I want. You."

"You don't have to put twenty million in the Outlook Trust to keep me. I would've been happy to spend my life washing cars with you."

Chase had a flash of Dory in the driveway, on her pudgy, skinned-up knees, diligently scrubbing tar off the wheel covers on the Rolls. The delight in her eyes when he stood beside her, holding the chamois under her hand with his, showing her how to buff the hood.

"Kiss me," he said and she did, hooking her arm around his neck.

There it was, that sweet little flower bursting inside him, in his heart where it had always been, just waiting for him to find it. He swept his arms around Dory, buried his face in the curve of her neck and inhaled the scent of her. Peonies, the white ones she'd used to pluck off the bushes and stick in her Coke bottle when they finished washing the cars.

"Chase? You're trembling." Dory braced her hands on his shoulders, pushed back and tipped her head to the left. "Are you *crying*?"

"Men don't cry, sweetheart." He laughed, heard the tears in it and blinked like crazy. "We just get something in our eye."

"Really? Well, whatever it is, it's wet and dripping off your chin."

He sat down in the chair he'd plucked her out of with her straddling his lap on her knees and nuzzled his face between her breasts, small and round and perfect. He felt her suck in her breath, her lips in his hair, her fingers feathering the back of his neck. He gripped her waist and sat her down on his thighs.

"I was thinking about peonies." Chase told her what he'd remembered and she laughed, turned herself around on his lap and leaned her left cheek against his shoulder. "Ah, the peonies. Mother threw them away, but Aunt Ping would change the water in the Coke bottle every day and keep them on her little Chinese desk till the last petal fell off."

"She gave me a tin of Esme's snickerdoodles the day I left Outlook." Chase rubbed his cheek in Dory's hair, like silk against the stubble on his jaw, and wrapped his arms around her. "Inside there was an envelope with twenty brand-new one-hundred-dollar bills."

Chase told her he'd invested the money, how he'd started McKay Design and Development. Dory told him about Jill flashing the FBI in her underwear and Deirdre bringing Jamie to Outlook.

"If I had a buck for every sponge you threw at me we wouldn't have had a thing to worry about when Uncle Scrooge froze Daddy's assets."

"Oh, come on. I didn't throw that many."

"Oh, come on. You did, too. I stopped counting at twelve million, six hundred and seventy-four thousand, nine hundred and sixty-two."

Chase threw his head back and laughed, grinned down at Dory, her face tipped up against his shoulder. "Is it time to settle up?"

"Yep." She puckered her lips and pointed at her chin. "Right here."

"I always pay my debts." He cupped her face with one hand and covered her mouth. Gave her a little nip, a little suck, a just-wait-till-you're-mine flick of his tongue, then drew away. Her left eye was bleary with fatigue, a loopy smile curved her Bing cherry lips. "You have the most beautiful mouth. I knew you'd be a dreamy kisser."

"Baby, you have got to go to bed." Chase touched his lips to her hairline. "Your one poor little eye can hardly stay open."

"Why can't I stay here with you? Are you like one giant cramp?"

"Uh, no." Chase pressed her hand to his rigid fly. In his head Dom sang "I'm in the Mood for Love." Dory grinned. "I could wake up for this."

"You're not in any shape for wild animals in the jungle sex." Chase bared his teeth and growled in his throat. Dory's eye went as big as a saucer. "You're right. I should go to sleep now. G'night."

She ducked her head and tucked it against his shoulder. Chase managed not to laugh, drew her bathrobe around her and folded her in his arms. That wasn't at all what he had in mind. Not for their first time, anyway, but it worked. She was out like a light in seconds.

He leaned his cheek on her head and shut his eyes, heard a stir of movement and glanced at the doorway where Jamie stood in blue pj's.

"What are you doing here?" he asked.

"Looking out for Dory," Chase said.

"Cool." He yawned and turned away. " 'Bout time."

Chapter Eighteen

The woman he loved snored. Like a kitten curled up with a warm belly after nursing, but still, she snored. Chase had never used the word *precious* to describe anything in his life, but precious was the only word he could think of to describe the way Dory snored.

Once she was good and asleep he carried her upstairs. She'd told him about the pizza foray. That's how he found her room, by the stuffed Chuck E. Cheese on the double bed.

Someone had turned back the spread and piled the pillows against the headboard. Henry, he thought, as he laid Dory down, covered her, and dumped himself in a wing chair that sat in the corner by the bathroom door. He swung the rectangular ottoman that matched the chair lengthwise and almost had room to stretch out his legs.

He nodded off, envisioning how he'd tell the kids he'd discovered Mommy snored but he'd married her anyway. The kids he never thought he'd wanted but could see as he drifted off to sleep, whooping and running up Outlook's rose brick front steps to visit Great Aunt Ping. A girl with Dory's dark hair and a towheaded boy. Under his arm he carried a redheaded hellion who looked frighteningly like Jamie, which was genetically impossible, but that's what dreams were, impossibilities.

Things you never wanted or realized you wanted till you thought you'd blown your chance to have them. Sometimes in life you got as lucky as you did in dreams. In his, Dory struggled up the steps to catch the dark-haired girl and the towheaded boy, waddling like a duck because she was pregnant. Holy God. *Again?* Chase woke up with a giant erection and a sleepy grin on his face.

He slid out of the chair, planning to drop to his knees beside the bed, press Dory's hand to his fly and say, "Look what I have for you," but the bed was empty, the covers thrown back, the sheets cool. She must've gotten up with the chickens, Chase thought, and glanced at his watch.

Hell. It was almost eleven o'clock. He could've sworn he'd just fallen asleep. He used Dory's bathroom and washed, found mouthwash in the medicine cabinet and gargled, ran his damp fingers through his hair, opened the bedroom door and headed downstairs.

The smell of sausage and French toast hit him halfway across the living room. His stomach growled and his pulse kicked. He looked like hell, whiskered and rumpled, but Dory loved him. She wouldn't care how he looked. A few more strides to the kitchen and he could wrap his arms around her and never let her go.

She wasn't in the kitchen. Peter and Henry and Jamie were in the kitchen in their pajamas.

Jamie in blue ones was making toast, Peter in yellow silk, garnishing bowls of fruit with mint sprigs. Henry in green satin manned an electric griddle, spatula in hand to turn the French toast. All three of them looked at Chase when he came through the breakfast room.

Jamie gave him a freckled, just-point-me-and-I'll-wreak-havoc grin. Peter and Henry stared down their noses at him, their nostrils pinched with reproach and disapproval. First thing in the morning. Jesus.

"I love Dory," Chase said. "I'm going to marry her. I should've married her yesterday but I screwed up, okay? Jill wants twenty million bucks, which I'm going to put into the Outlook Trust. Enough?"

Apparently not. Peter and Henry's noses pinched even tighter.

"All Jill and I did was talk. I slept in the chair in Dory's room."

"Dear boy!" Peter tossed mint sprigs into the air.

"Oh, happy day!" Henry waved his spatula.

He and Peter embraced, then swept Chase into a hug and clung to his chest. Jamie wormed between them and grabbed the front of Chase's sweater to get his attention.

"Dory's a package deal," he said belligerently. "I come with her."

"I know." Chase scowled. "Have you considered military school?"

Jamie blanched. Chase grinned. "Relax. I'm kidding, squirt."

"Dory calls me that, too," he said and rolled his eyes.

"So where is she?" Chase asked. "Where's Dory?"

"Upstairs asleep," Henry said. "Isn't she?"

"No. I thought she was down here."

"Jamie," Peter said. "You were the first one up."

"I haven't seen her." He shrugged. "I thought she was sleeping."

Chase had a flash of the Honeymoon Suite. Jill sprawled on her back. Arms and legs flailing. Dory pressing a pillow over her face.

"I'll bet she's up at the house talking to Miss Ping," he said, edging toward the door. "I'll go see."

"Dear boy," Peter said. "Miss Ping, Deirdre and Miss Fairview left in the Rolls with your father to attend mass half an hour ago."

"Then she's probably in her office." Chase shrugged. "I'll find her."

He smiled and turned out of the kitchen, strolled through the house, out the front door, shut it behind him and broke into a run.

Two things Miss Fairview never missed at Outlook: meals and the Sunday morning drive to mass in the Rolls.

Dory stood on the balcony off Miss Fairview's room—her bedroom when she was a child—with high-power binoculars she'd found sitting in plain sight on a shelf in one of the built-in bookcases. She raised them gingerly to her sore, still-a-bit-puffy black eye and fiddled with the focus.

"*Whoa,*" she said in amazement.

These babies made the binoculars she and Jill had used to spy on Chase look like the toilet paper tubes Jamie used to duct-tape together when he was five and played African safari in the garden.

"*Dory!*" Chase shouted from below, startling her so badly she bumped the right eyepiece against her cheekbone.

Pain zipped up her sinus, two tiny white stars danced in her vision. She almost dropped the binoculars and cried, "Ow!"

"What," Chase shouted, "are you doing up there?"

Dory put a hand over her throbbing right eye and peered over the parapet. Chase stood on the terrace wall in his creased jeans and sleep-wrinkled gray sweater scowling at her like a thunderhead. Her heart soared—he loved her. Her stomach sank—he'd caught her.

"In the vernacular of the detective novel," Dory called to him, "I'm tossing Miss Fairview's room!"

"*Stay right there!*" Chase pointed at her and jumped off the wall.

Dory watched him hurry across the terrace and disappear beneath the balcony. When she heard the ballroom French doors shut, she raised the binoculars and made a sweep of the grounds. Yee-*hah.*

If she and Jill had had these puppies they could've counted the hairs on Chase's chest. Soon, hopefully, she'd be able to do that herself, let her little fingers pluck them, one by one. The feel she'd had of his chest last night made her stomach flutter and the binoculars wobble.

Dory drew a breath to steady them and played with the focus. Now she could see cracks in the mortar between the bricks in the garage wall, bees swinging from purple coneflowers in the garden. And through a break in the trees that lined the footpath where the creep who'd jumped them last night had hidden on Charles' birthday—a crystal clear, close-up view of Jamie's bedroom window.

Gooseflesh crawled through Dory. The drapes were open, the blind up. Jamie's desk sat smack in the middle of the window. She could read the title of his math book, see eraser shavings he'd scooped into a pile. The wrinkles in the sheets on his unmade bed, yesterday's socks on the closet floor, the royal blue and gold bands around the elastic tops.

"Thank God. I think," Chase said behind her. "At least you're not murdering Jill in her sleep."

"That's next on my to-do list." Dory turned around and saw Chase standing between the French doors, his hands spread on the frame. "I'll bet you'd like to know why I'm snooping around Miss Fairview's room."

"I know why. Diego told me last night." Chase pushed out of the doorway onto the balcony. "What are you looking at?"

"I found these on one of the bookshelves." Dory handed him the binoculars. "Aim them at the guesthouse and see for yourself."

He did, frowned, then bent his knees and said, "Jamie's bedroom." Chase lowered the binoculars. "This doesn't mean she stands out here spying on Jamie. It doesn't mean she doesn't, either."

"On your father's birthday," Dory began and told Chase about the walking trees. "How did the creep know where to wait for Jamie if someone at Outlook didn't tell him he'd be coming to the party from the guesthouse?"

"Stark *could* have just picked a lucky hiding place," Chase said.

"Is that his name?" Dory asked. Chase nodded. She frowned and rubbed her arms. "I didn't want to know his name."

"Sorry, sweetheart." Chase cupped the back of her head, tipped her face up and kissed her, a long, full tongue kiss that left her clinging to his arm to stay on her feet. He raised his head, his eyes about four shades bluer than usual. "Wild animals in the jungle sex. Don't forget."

"I'll make a note," she said weakly. "What was my name?"

"Dory Lambert." Chase grinned. "Soon to be Dory Lambert McKay."

"You have no idea what my middle name is, do you?"

He shook his head. "Not a clue."

"I'm not going to tell you till we apply for the marriage license."

"Are you looking for something in particular?" Chase nodded at Miss Fairview's room.

The sun slanting across the balcony hit his face just the right way and lit the golden stubble on his jaw. Dory could still feel the sting of his whiskers, a little flicker of the thrill that coursed through her when he'd rubbed his nose between her breasts. He looked like a man who'd slept in a chair, which he had, and still he was so handsome and she loved him so much that her day-old heart staggered. "Something that links Miss Fairview to James." Dory stepped back inside and Chase followed her. "Don't ask me what, 'cause I haven't the foggiest."

"Where were these?" Chase raised the binoculars.

"Third shelf." Dory nodded at the bookcase on the right side of the marble fireplace. "Next to a copy of *The Secret of the Old Clock*."

"Nancy Drew." Chase put the binoculars next to the book. "Don't tell me. This is who you wanted to be when you grew up."

"I wanted to be president of Lambert Bank and Trust." Dory waved her hand. "This was my room when I was a kid. That's the entire Nancy Drew series. They were Aunt Ping's when she was a girl."

"Nice bed." Chase gave the mahogany four-poster the once-over and leered. "Is this where you used to have erotic dreams about me?"

"No. That bed spontaneously combusted. Which reminds me. I assume the honeymoon trip to Maui is cancelled?"

"Jill can take the tickets and go if she wants. I'm staying here."

"Good answer. Where are you going to sleep?"

"Good question. Can I book a room?"

"I think we can squeeze you in. What time is it?"

Chase glanced at his watch. "Eleven forty-five. The next time you break and enter you might want to wear a watch."

"I'm not breaking and entering. I'm the innkeeper. I have every right to enter a room if I suspect there's something funny going on." Dory sighed and turned a circle, looking around her old room. "Mass ends at noon. I've got half an hour to find something funny."

"There may be nothing to find. Where have you looked?"

"Everywhere. In the closet. Her suitcases and hatboxes, the pockets of her clothes. Every drawer and shelf in the bathroom and in here."

"The books?" Chase pulled Nancy Drew number four off the shelf, *The Mystery at Lilac Inn*. "Could something be stuck between the pages?"

"I didn't check the books. That seemed a little *too* Nancy Drew. Plus the maids dust and rotate the books. Esther's a stickler for musty books, but what the heck." Dory shrugged. "I've looked everywhere else."

"Look again. You might've missed something. I'll do the books."

Dory went back to the Chippendale dresser where she'd started her search. She didn't look at her face in the mirror. She'd seen it earlier when she'd brushed her teeth. Her eye wasn't as purple as she'd expected—maybe Henry's remedies worked—but that one peek was plenty. Instead she watched Chase put number four back on the shelf and take down number five, *The Secret of Shadow Ranch*. People would talk when he annulled his marriage to Jill—if she didn't simplify things and just drown Jill in the bathtub—but Dory didn't care. Aunt Ping might be scandalized. Maybe not, if you considered Charles, but even Aunt Ping's disapproval didn't faze her. Chase was hers. He loved her. So long as she—

"Aha!" he said and Dory spun away from the mirror. "What?"

"A Juicy Fruit wrapper." Chase held up a yellow, tri-folded paper rectangle. "I used to chew this stuff like crazy when I couldn't smoke."

"I know. That's yours. I used to pick them up behind you."

"Oh honey." He raised an eyebrow. "You had it bad."

"I still got it bad," she said cheerfully. "Do you know a cure?"

"Wild animals in the jungle sex."

Dory laughed. Chase grinned and slid *The Secret of Shadow Ranch* between number four and number six, *The Secret of Red Gate Farm*. He'd always been a quiet, thoughtful person, not humorless, just serious. She'd never seen Chase smile and laugh and grin so much. He must be really happy. He must truly love her.

Could that be the reason he was smiling and laughing? Could that be why? Because she loved him? Did she make him that happy? *He loves me. Chase McKay loves me.* The wonder of it swept her with joy, rushed tears to her eyes she could barely keep back. Happy tears, Cydney Monroe called them. She should know. Jill's friend cried at the drop of a leaf.

Dory turned to the dresser. In the mirror she watched Chase move to the bookcase on the other side of the marble-fronted fireplace where leather-bound, gilt-stamped adult books lined the shelves. She opened a top drawer, started to lift a folded stack of lace-trimmed hankies and glanced at herself in the mirror, at Chase lifting a book off a shelf, shut the drawer and turned around.

"There's nothing to find or I would've found it by now," she said. "We should go before Miss Fairview comes back."

Chase smiled. "Conscience kicking in?"

"Yes, finally. So what if Esther found Miss Fairview in

my office? She's cranky and crabby, but that doesn't mean she's spying for James."

"Doesn't mean she isn't," Chase said. "What about the binoculars?"

"Hardly incriminating. Jill and I used to swipe Daddy's field glasses so we could watch you smoke on the garage roof."

"You vixen." Chase put the book he held back on the shelf, looked at the one next to it, laid his finger on the spine and grinned over his shoulder. "Dory Whatever-Your-Middle-Name-Is Lambert. *Lady Chatterley's Lover.* I'm shocked."

"That's not my book. I've never read it." Dory went to the French doors to make sure they were latched. "If it belongs to Aunt Ping, you'll find a Chinese silk-screen bookplate on the inside cover."

"Let's find out." He wagged his eyebrows and took the book down.

Across the room Dory heard something go *clunk,* turned and saw the uh-oh look on Chase's face. A sliver of gooseflesh slid up her spine.

"What is it?" she asked.

"Not a real book, that's what. It's hollow but it's not empty."

Dory flew across the room. Chase met her at the small writing desk that matched the Chippendale dresser, put the imposter *Lady Chatterley's Lover* on the polished surface and opened the fake cover.

Inside were two hardly-more-than-palm-size gizmos. Silver or stainless steel, one with a grilled front. The other looked like a cigarette lighter with a tiny, dark plastic eye. A lens, Dory realized, and felt her knees turn to water.

"This is Spy Store stuff." Chase picked up the devices and looked them over. "This," he said of the one with the grill, "looks like a micro-recorder. This—" He held up the lighter. "—I think is a camera."

"There's an envelope, too." Dory peeled it off the bottom of the box. White, about the size of a greeting card, with something inside.

Photographs of Jamie. Four-by-six-inch snapshots. Jamie leaving for school in the van with Diego, his backpack over his shoulder. In the music room with Deirdre, taking his piano lesson. Cutting wheelies in a golf cart by the clubhouse. On his knees in canvas gloves with Aunt Ping in the garden. Hanging over one of the white-railed fences with Tom, looking at something in the pasture, probably the steers.

The shot that nearly stopped Dory's heart showed her and Jamie walking along the pea gravel path, laughing and swinging hands. It was taken from the side, at an angle, like the photographer had been hiding in the garden. Say, behind the bench in front of the pagoda fountain.

"Look at this," she said and passed the photo to Chase. He gave it a nanosecond's glance that made his jaw clench and his nostrils flare. "Okay. That's it. This is more than enough. I'm calling the police."

"Do *please,* Mr. McKay," Miss Fairview said haughtily from the doorway. "How *dare* you rifle my things! *Miss Lambert!* I am *shocked!*"

Miss Fairview stood clutching the ornate brass door handle Dory hadn't heard click open over the pounding of her heart. When she swung away from the desk, a pale wash of shock took some of the high, indignant color out of Miss Fairview's face.

"Good heavens," she said. "What happened to you?"

"Jamie and I were attacked last night, walking from Outlook to the guesthouse. Right here." Dory snatched the photo of her and Jamie from Chase. "Right where you took this picture for James Darwood."

"Dear lord," Miss Fairview said and fainted in the doorway.

"I wasn't destitute, but my funds were shrinking when I met James Darwood," Miss Fairview said. "I was staying with a friend in Milan. James told me his name was Peter Dawson. This was June of 1998."

Dory caught Coop's eye. He leaned on the mantel in the back parlor, on the opposite side of the fireplace from Miss Fairview, who sat in her favorite upholstered chintz armchair. Once they'd revived her and while they waited for Detective Emerson of the KCMO Police Department to arrive—the detective who had taken Diego's statement— Dory told Coop that Gordy had tracked Miss Fairview by her passport that summer, touring Europe by train from May through August.

Coop nodded to her, then glanced at Miss Fairview, twisting between her hands one of the hankies Dory had found in her top drawer.

"My friend and I were having coffee in a café. James introduced himself. He was very charming and, I thought, as American as I am. I have friends in London, but I heard not a hint of an accent in his speech. He told us he was traveling on an inheritance from his grandmother. She'd been killed, he said, in a boating accident in Aruba with her husband, who was a viscount. He told us her name was Diana."

That gave Dory the willies. The morning he'd left Outlook, James had leaned over her, sitting with Tobias on the white iron bench on the front porch and said, "I hate my mother." The memory made her shiver.

"Diana is James' mother," Deirdre said faintly. "My cousin."

Aunt Ping sat beside Deirdre on a striped settee nearest the chintz chair. Her gaze never left Miss Fairview but she squeezed Deirdre's hand.

Detective Emerson sat on a matching settee across a marble-topped table. He reminded Dory of Gary. Slight and sandy-haired with gold wire-framed glasses. He glanced up from the spiral pad on his knee.

"Heard from your cousin lately?" he asked Deirdre.

"Not since she ran away to Aruba with the viscount."

"Most con artists mix fact with fiction," Coop said. "Verisimilitude is their stock in trade. By using real names there's less chance they'll trip themselves up and get caught in a lie."

Deirdre gave him a grateful smile. Detective Emerson looked like he wanted to say something to Coop—butt out. He wasn't thrilled to have an audience, but Miss Fairview insisted that everyone hear what she had to say—Aunt Ping and Deirdre, Coop and Chase and Dory.

It was one-thirty. The guests were at lunch in the little dining room under Wallace and Esther's watchful eyes. Henry was manning the concierge desk, Diego the front door. Peter had put Jamie to work in the greenhouse, his penance for Artemis, to keep him away from Outlook.

"James claimed that he missed his grandmother," Miss Fairview continued. "He said I reminded him of her. Since I have no family, I was flattered. He escorted my friend and me to places we didn't feel comfortable on our own. We became quite close. I confided to him that I was beginning to worry I might outlive my money. James suggested an investment, which earned me several thousand dollars in just a few weeks. I was so grateful. I would've done anything for him."

"When did he ask you—" Detective Emerson glanced at his notes. "—to look in on his son now and then?"

"The night before I left Milan he told me he'd discovered he had a son from what he called an indiscretion. The boy's mother had died and he'd been sent to relatives in Kansas City who owned a hotel. James offered to cover my expenses and pay me a yearly retainer if I would provide periodic reports on the boy's welfare. The amount took my breath away. I asked why he didn't visit the child. He told me he'd been rebuffed by the relatives."

"Did he say," Deirdre asked, "how he'd found out he had a son?"

"I didn't ask then. I did later, but he refused to tell me. I accepted his offer and came to Outlook the first time in October of 1998."

"That's true," Dory said to Detective Emerson. "I keep files on all our regular guests. Check-in and check-out dates, which room they occupy, meal and laundry preferences, any special needs, transportation requirements, pretty much everything. I can give you a printout."

"I'll let you know," Emerson replied. "Now, Miss Fairview—"

"Miss Lambert." Miss Fairview looked at Dory. Her pale green eyes glittered and her thin mouth trembled. "I'm so dreadfully sorry that you were hurt. I had no idea James intended to kidnap Jamie. I would never have helped him if I'd thought for a second he meant to harm anyone."

"Wally Stark is the man who blackened Miss Lambert's eye," Detective Emerson said. "He was hired to grab Jamie Lambert by a guy named Joe Bauer, who took off when Stark didn't show with the kid. I have a description of Bauer. Would you describe James Darwood?"

Miss Fairview rose to her feet and looked at Chase. "Would you stand for me please, Mr. McKay?"

"Sure." Chase stretched out of the leather chair he'd moved next to the settee where Aunt Ping sat with Deirdre. Dory scooted out of the way on the ottoman she'd drawn up at his feet. "I'm six four if that helps."

"It does, thank you." Miss Fairview sat down. "James is six feet two inches tall. Very slim. Brown hair, blue eyes. He has the most amazing eyelashes I've ever seen on a man. He's quite good-looking. He reminded me very much of—" Miss Fairview faltered. "Oh, what *is* his name? The British pop singer. The band with the insect name."

"Paul McCartney," Dory said, remembering when Marilyn shoved her face in the pillow for saying James didn't look like Sir Paul.

"Yes, that's it. Paul McCartney. That's who James resembles."

"That's not Bauer," Emerson said. "I'll run Peter Dawson by Stark, but I'll bet it doesn't ring a bell. When did you last see James Darwood?"

"Two months ago, in March. We met in the Caymans. His hair was very light. I believe it was natural, not dyed. I recall thinking he must've arrived well before me and spent time on the beach."

"Why did you meet him?" Detective Emerson wrote while he talked.

"I needed a rest, James said. He was concerned for me. Ha," Miss Fairview said bitterly. "He knew he was losing control of me. For the past year, he's been very demanding. On this trip, he wanted me to ascertain Jamie's schedule. His *precise* schedule. Exactly when he left for school, arrived home and the travel time between. He suggested I purchase a stopwatch, rent a car and follow Diego in the van. When I refused, he cajoled me down to the Caymans."

Miss Fairview pressed her hankie to her nose with a shaky hand. Dory looked at Aunt Ping, saw a furrow of sympathy creasing her brow.

When James highjacked Lambert Securities, she'd had Aunt Ping. Aunt Ping had her and Jill. Wallace and Esme and Esther, Peter and Henry, Tom and Eddie. And Charles. None of them had faced destitution alone. Even Daddy and Mother had each other. Miss Fairview had no one, poor thing. Dory let go of her anger and felt her stomach stop shooting needles of acid. She'd forgotten to take her Prevacid. Again.

"How did he contact you, Miss Fairview?" Emerson asked.

"He gave me a cell phone before I came to Outlook the first time. I'm to keep it charged and turned on at all times. I have no telephone number for him, cellular or otherwise. I send photographs of Jamie and my reports, as he calls them, though I simply write down what I observe, like diary entries, to a post office box in Key West, Florida."

"How do you contact him?" Emerson asked.

"Through the post office box."

"What did he say when you met him in the Cayman Islands?"

"He apologized for alarming me and assured me that he meant no harm. He'd simply thought, since the family refused to receive him, that perhaps he could arrange to meet Jamie somewhere off Outlook. I was not reassured, though

I believe I convinced him." Miss Fairview sniffed and dabbed her nose again. "I wish I'd had the courage to go to the authorities on my own. I'm so relieved that I've been discovered."

"When did you figure out Peter Dawson was James Darwood?"

"Quite early on, during my fourth visit to Outlook. Bit by bit I overheard what had befallen the Lambert family, did some research on my own and surmised that the man I knew as Peter Dawson must be James Darwood. I was appalled that I'd become the pawn of such a person. I'm ashamed that my fear of poverty kept me under his sway. I thought of confronting him but he was beginning to frighten me. I considered confessing to you, Miss Lambert." Miss Fairview looked squarely at Aunt Ping. "So many times, but I feared I'd be arrested and prosecuted as an accessory to his original crime."

Aunt Ping's eyebrow went up. "And now?"

"He's threatening a child. His own son. He's a monster. I will gladly do whatever I can to help apprehend him before I'm taken into custody." Miss Fairview turned her trembling chin on Detective Emerson. "Do you think that might be possible, young man?"

"Unless you've been pilfering the silver and Miss Lambert wants to prosecute I have nothing to hold you on. If your story doesn't check out, that could change. If I can link you to Stark, it will definitely change."

Dory thought she could tell by the expression on Emerson's face, part pity, part what-a-waste-of-time-this-was, that he didn't expect it. Neither did she, but she glanced at Coop for confirmation. He nodded.

"That's all for now, Miss Fairview." Emerson turned a fresh page in his notebook, stood up and handed her his card. "I have to ask you not to leave town. If you change hotels, call me at this number."

"Miss Fairview," Aunt Ping said, "will be staying at Outlook."

*   *   *

Jill lay unmoving on her back in the middle of the humongous bed in the Honeymoon Suite. Tangled in the sheet, arms and legs spread, a pillow over her face.

For a second Chase thought Dory had beaten him up here, then Jill moaned and he grinned. Hung over as hell. He pushed the trolley Esme had loaded with coffee, orange juice, croissants and aspirin into the room and eased the doors shut with hardly a click.

"Chase?" Jill whispered from under the pillow, her voice a hoarse croak. "Is the undertaker with you?"

"You aren't going to die, Jill. I brought coffee." Chase pushed the trolley toward the bed. "Have you stopped throwing up?"

"Hours ago. You left me here to die. Where have you been?"

"Have some coffee and a shower first."

"Maybe in a couple days."

Chase hung Jill's bathrobe over the towel rack, put the sunglasses she'd packed for Maui on the sink and took her a wet facecloth for her eyes. He walked her into the bathroom and sat her down on the toilet lid, cranked on the shower and shut the door with the cloisonné bride on it behind him as she started screaming.

He pushed the trolley onto the balcony, poured himself a cup of coffee and sat on the balustrade to light a cigarette. The rush from the nicotine made his head spin like it had when he'd kissed Dory. She tasted better than Marlboros. Long term she was healthier, too, though he'd nearly had a stroke when he'd seen her on Miss Fairview's balcony.

In the parlor he'd almost been able to see the synapses firing in her head as she listened to Darwood's accomplice spill her guts. His beloved was hatching something in that quick little mind of hers. Chase had no idea what, but he'd keep an eye on Dory. He would've tied her to her bed if he'd thought she intended to search Miss Fairview's room.

What a thing that was, to have Darwood's spy under all their noses all this time. The day Esther caught Miss Fairview in the office was one of the days she'd wanted to confess. She'd seen Anita head outside to smoke and nipped into the office hoping to catch Dory alone.

When Detective Emerson left with Dory to talk to Jamie, Chase asked Miss Fairview if she'd been talking to Darwood on her cell phone the night he'd stormed through the parlor. Yes, she'd said. Just thinking about it made Chase gnash his teeth. So near and yet still no one could find James Darwood.

He wasn't a phantom. Miss Fairview had been with him in the Caymans two months ago. He hadn't changed his appearance, other than his hair was sun-bleached. Arrogant son of a bitch. 'Course it had been ten years. Did Darwood think the FBI had given up finding him? Or did he know they'd never really looked because he'd so cleverly and equally pointed the finger at Del and Drusilla Lambert?

He was smart enough to stay off U.S. soil; that's why he'd enlisted Miss Fairview, to be his eyes and ears at Outlook. He had nerve and incredible patience. He'd spent six years planning the Lambert Securities theft, another six years so far on Miss Fairview. Not to mention a boatload of money. She'd told Emerson that Darwood had become very demanding in the last year. Was he finally running out of patience?

Chase figured James would give up on Jamie rather than risk being caught. So the big question was how badly did he want Jamie? How much longer would he wait, how far would he go before he gave up and slipped away?

If Darwood thought he was losing control of Miss Fairview the answer was not much farther and not for much longer. The window for nailing him could already be closing. Chase thought it might be, and if he thought it, more than likely so did Dory.

The sun had swung over the roof. A giant oak growing on the edge of the ornamental garden soared above the house and cast the balcony of the Honeymoon Suite in deep shade. Jill crept through the French doors, moving like her ankles were broken, a towel on her head, her shades on her nose, her robe tightly belted. She eased onto a chaise beneath the overhang of the big oak, leaned her head gingerly against the cushions.

"You are a shitty husband," she rasped. "As soon as I can move without my head falling off I'm going to kill you."

"Drink this." Chase wrapped her shaky hands around a cup of coffee. "Eat and take the aspirin." He laid a napkin with a croissant and two Bayer tabs on her pink terrycloth-wrapped abdomen. "It's three o'clock. You need to make an appearance before Miss Ping thinks I killed you."

Jill shot her chin up and winced. "You didn't *tell* her, did you?"

"No. You get to do that." Chase went back to the wall, lit another cigarette and glanced over his right shoulder.

He couldn't see much of the grounds. The Honeymoon Suite was directly above Miss Ping's rooms in the south wing, built at a bent elbow angle to the rest of the house. He couldn't watch for Dory coming back from the greenhouse. He'd just have to trust her not to do anything else in the vernacular of the detective novel till he could catch up with her.

"I'm finished," Jill snarled. "Where did you go? Hot date?"

"I wish." Chase put out his cigarette, went to the chaise and sat down beside Jill. "I went to help Dad and Eddie and Tom catch the creep who tried to abduct Jamie last night. Dory was with him. Diego ran the guy off. Dory's okay, but she has a black eye."

A tear slid out from under Jill's sunglasses. "Did you get him?"

"Eddie did. The cops arrested him." Chase told her the rest of it, about Miss Fairview and James Darwood. He didn't think it was possible, but Jill's face turned paler and every inch of her started to quiver.

"Get me off this damn chaise! Help me get dressed! God-damn it, Chase!" She caught a sob in her throat and threw a fist at him that bounced off. "Why in *hell* didn't you wake me?"

"I'd given you up for dead." He swooped her off the chaise and carried her inside toward the bed.

"No, no, no! The bathroom!" Jill plucked off her shades, moaned and clapped a hand over her eyes. "*I can't see!* Where's my underwear?"

Chase dumped her on the toilet, crying and ripping the towel off her head, went into the bride's closet and rummaged in her suitcase till he found a lacy red bra and panties. He took them to Jill with a pair of white crop pants and a sleeveless white eyelet blouse.

"You moron!" she shrieked. "I can't wear red under white!"

He went back to the closet and the suitcase for white underwear. The phone rang on his way to the bathroom. Chase threw the undies at Jill, slammed the door and jumped for the phone.

"You sound winded," Dory said. "What kind of shape is she in?"

"Sick as a dog." Chase sucked a breath. "And hysterical."

"*Chase! Get in here! I can't find the hooks on this fucking bra!*"

"I heard that," Dory said. "Get her dressed. Help her if you have to, but get her down here as fast as you can. Eddie just caught Gary trying to sneak onto Outlook."

Chapter Nineteen

It was a miracle Gary made it to the house alive.

He had sense enough to hide when he saw the fed mobile coming up the hill from the bridge to cruise the back fence line. Unfortunately, he'd been raised in Chevy Chase, Maryland. When he stepped out from behind the man-size roll of hay he'd dived behind to escape the sharp eyes of his fellow G-men, Bruno was there. All sixteen hundred, heavily muscled, ebony black pounds of Bruno, Tom's prize Angus bull.

"My God, oh my God," Gary sobbed in Dory's arms. "I had no idea an animal with testicles that *huge* could run so fast!"

"I know." Dory rocked and shushed him. "It's okay. It's over now."

That's what Gary had thought when he slid headfirst under the bottom rail of Bruno's paddock and missed being trampled to death by inches. Till he heard a piercing scream and saw a giant red horse—a feisty but tiny bay Arab mare, barely fourteen and a half hands—flying at him with flared nostrils, bared teeth and a crazy man—Eddie—leaning out of the saddle trying to knock his head off with a riding crop.

Gary ran for his life—"Straight into another pack of those fucking black cows!"—but as every cop knows, you can't outrun the radio.

When the steers stampeded, the mare shied and Eddie

lost Gary in the melee of curly black beef, so he jumped on the walkie-talkie. Gary barely made it to the next enclosure when a four-by-four pickup driven by Tom came jolting at him over the ruts in the pasture and he had to run again.

When Aunt Ping heard the APB, she raced for the blue golf cart, Henry for the white one. Deirdre and Miss Fairview flew up to her balcony and the high-power binoculars. Once he'd evaded Bruno and Eddie and Tom, Gary had cleared the farm. But by then Charles was out in the Rolls and Diego in the Bentley, both of the big, powerful cars prowling the roads like panthers, so he had to sneak through the shrubbery.

Detective Emerson had just left when Eddie raised the alarm. Peter fired up the lawn tractor, Dory and Jamie hopped in the tool trailer and they joined the hunt. Almost on two wheels, Peter's little tractor careened through the fork in the pea gravel path that led to the greenhouse.

"There!" Jamie cried, pointing. "There he is!"

"Wait a minute." Dory went up on her knees to see over Jamie's shoulder. "That looks like—*Gary*!" She shouted, and again, *"Gary!"*

He couldn't hear her over the tractor engine—or maybe it was the thunder of the bay Arab mare flying behind him across the greensward, on his tail again. When Gary sprinted across the pea gravel path and leaped for the flagstone steps that led up through the garden to the terrace and the house, Dory expected Eddie to rein the mare in, but the horse jumped the path and sprang up the steps behind Gary.

Because he was looking over his shoulder at the mare, Gary didn't see the Olympic-size marble pool at the top of the steps. He raced across the flagged apron and plunged into the water—his arms and legs still pumping to run— and landed on Noah Patrick, who was minding his own business swimming laps till Gary caromed on top of him.

Noah came up almost instantly, saw Gary sinking, sucked a breath and went down for him. He hauled Gary to the surface and towed him, flailing and choking, toward the edge of the pool where the Arab mare, named Spitfire because that's what she was, screamed and danced on the apron, her neck curled and her tail flagged. For his trouble, Noah got an elbow in the face from Gary as Eddie pulled him out of the water.

So now Gary was soaked and sobbing on Dory's shoulder, Noah Patrick was sitting on a stool beside Gary in Esme's kitchen, drying out with a T-shirt on over his trunks, a towel around his neck and a bag of frozen peas pressed to his blackening left eye.

"Are you going to sue us?" Dory asked him.

"Not you, cutie." Noah smiled. "I'm gonna find Lindsay so she can kiss my boo-boo. Take care of that eye of yours."

"I'll send a shredded potato up to your room. It really helps."

"Thanks. Let me know how it comes out with Eliot Ness."

"*Hey.*" Gary raised his head from Dory's shoulder and glared.

"How did you get into the FBI if you can't swim?" Noah asked him.

"My uncle is a senator."

"Unc wasn't much help at the bottom of the pool, was he?" Noah slid off the stool. "I've got two words for you, pal—swimming lessons."

When he left the kitchen, Gary looked mournfully at Dory.

"Big surprise, but I flunked the obstacle course at Quantico."

"You passed the one today with flying colors. What I want to know is why, Gary? Why didn't you go back to your apartment?"

"Marshall Phillips left a million messages on my cell phone. I didn't want him to find me till I had a chance to tell Jill what I've discovered, but I'm too late." Dory heard a sob in Gary's sigh. "She's left already with McKay, hasn't she? Probably on some big fancy honeymoon, right?"

"Wrong. Jill said 'I do' but she didn't. She couldn't. She loves you." Dory lifted a towel off the counter and laid it around his shoulders. "She confessed to Chase and they're getting an annulment."

"I've got to see her! Where is she?" Gary jumped to his feet, slipped and almost fell in his sodden, squeaky track shoes. "I've got to see her!"

"Not so fast. Jill will be down in a few minutes." If Chase doesn't throttle her, Dory thought. She caught the towel and held Gary still. "You've got to see Aunt Ping, but not like this. Henry is bringing you clothes."

"I can't see Miss Lambert!" Gary blanched. "She hates the FBI! She'll hate me when she finds out I've been under-cover all this time!"

"You should've thought of that *before* you tried to sneak onto Outlook in broad daylight and sent everybody to their battle stations."

"I didn't know that would happen, that some clown tried to kidnap Jamie." Gary dropped his voice. "Are you sure Jill wasn't behind it?"

"Get in there." Dory shoved him into the china closet and turned to meet Henry, coming through the back door with a pair of his navy blue trousers, underwear, socks and a plaid shirt.

"I think these will fit." Henry passed the clothes to Gary. "We haven't found your glasses yet, but we're still looking. Hopefully, they weren't sucked into the pool filter."

"Thanks," Gary said to Henry. "I appreciate it."

"Change," Dory said and shut the door on him. She wished Gary *could* change—into Eliot Ness or Luke Sky-walker. Heck. At this point she'd settle for Darth Vader. No, wait. That was Marshall Phillips. At last she'd found another name for him besides Uncle Scrooge.

"That's the man Jill loves?" Henry's eyebrows lifted. "And he's an undercover FBI agent?"

"Yep." Dory nodded. That's all she'd had time to tell Eddie, once she and Peter and Jamie came tearing up the steps to the pool, to keep him from calling 911. "It boggles my mind, too."

"Ah, but Chase loves *you*. He told us this morning." Henry beamed and plucked a clothes brush from his pocket, ever the valet, and swept the grass and hay and dirt she'd picked up from Gary off her jeans and sage green sweater. "We can't wait to dance at your wedding."

"Neither can I." Dory grinned. Wow, she thought. Chase must love me. He's telling people. She was so happy she almost wiggled.

She ought to be worried, possibly she should be terrified. James was trying to kidnap Jamie, Marshall Phillips was on the hunt and the jig was up with Aunt Ping. When Noah finished CPR on Gary, Dory raised Aunt Ping on the walkie-talkie. False alarm, she'd said. Ha, ha. The intruder was only Gary, the manager of the Happy Spirit.

"Hooey," Aunt Ping said sharply, her voice crackling with static. "I'll receive him—whoever he is—in the breakfast room in half an hour. Make sure you and Jillian are present as well. Mama San One, out."

When he came out of the china closet in Henry's clothes, which weren't a bad fit except around the waist, Gary had more color than when he'd gone in. Good, Dory thought, he wasn't borderline in shock anymore, then she covered her right eye and squinted at him.

"Gary?" she said. "Are you sunburned?"

"With my skin tone it doesn't take long to fry in the Caribbean."

Dory's pulse jumped. "Have you been to the Cayman Islands?"

"I've been everywhere in the freaking Caribbean." Gary rubbed the towel through his hair and hung it around his shoulders. "I think I may have found James Darwood."

"The Bastard Little Prick Squad has been looking for Darwood all over the planet. Jill told me," Gary explained to Aunt Ping, Deirdre and Coop. "So my starting premise was what if he never left the Caribbean? Or if he did, not for long. He kept coming back because the Caribbean is his base of operations."

Deirdre looked startled, Coop thunderstruck, as if the possibility had never dawned on him. It hadn't occurred to Dory. She felt like she ought to be wearing a T-shirt that said SLAP ME AND CALL ME STUPID.

When Gary said he thought he'd found James, Dory dragged him into the breakfast room, pushed him into a chair at the oak table and said, "Talk." Coop had smoothed the way by explaining to Aunt Ping that Gary was an FBI agent, working undercover at the Happy Spirit.

When Gary said, "What if he never left the Caribbean?" Aunt Ping looked ill, as if she were trying *not* to think about how many hundreds of thousands of dollars she'd spent looking everywhere *but* the Caribbean for James. Then she drew a breath, her composure recovered.

"Oftentimes it was thin and sketchy," she said to Gary. "Nonetheless, the detectives I hired followed the trail James left."

"Maybe they followed a trail left by someone Darwood paid to make the trail. Someone who looks enough like him to pass for him. I read the case file before I left. It didn't give me much to go on—Mr. Phillips has always been more focused on arresting your brother than James Darwood—so I went by what Jill could remember, which wasn't much. We only talked about the case once."

Uh huh, Dory thought. Jill told her they'd never discussed Daddy and Mother. She'd figured it for a lie when it fell out of Jill's mouth.

"Jill couldn't remember much, but she did recall Buenos Aires in January of 1996 and Singapore in June of 1998, when Jamie came to Outlook and you realized he could speak French, so what I did—"

"Miss Fairview met James in Milan in June of 1998," Dory cut in. "Only he told her his name was Peter Dawson. No way could James have been in Milan and Singapore at the same time."

"Peter Dawson?" Gary's head snapped toward her. "I

ran across that name in Guatemala, Costa Rica and Belize. Couple other places, too, but I'll have to look up where and when in my notes."

"Please do," Aunt Ping said. "We'll wait."

"I don't have them on me." Gary flushed. "I stashed my carry-on in a big pile of straw out in the field where I came through the fence."

Aunt Ping looked puzzled until Dory said, "Bruno's paddock."

She nodded, her mouth twitching, and said to Henry, who had followed Dory and Gary into the breakfast room, "Would you ring Tom and ask him to look through Bruno's hay for a suitcase?"

"Yes, Miss Ping." Henry nodded and turned toward the kitchen.

"How many false identities," Coop asked Gary, "were you able to tie to James Darwood in the Caribbean?"

"Three, primarily. Peter Dawson was the one that kept coming up the most in the past five years. How many was he using?"

Coop deferred to Aunt Ping. She said, "Nearly two dozen."

"Yow," Gary said. "Top notch IDs don't come cheap."

"He did steal thirty-five million dollars," Aunt Ping said dryly.

"Beyond Singapore and Milan in June of 1998," Coop said, "how many instances of James being in the Caribbean and somewhere else at the same time were you able to establish?"

"Under two different names in the last five years, sixteen."

"So in essence what you did," Aunt Ping said, "was backtrack."

"Yes, ma'am. That's what an investigator does when he hits a dead end. He goes back to the beginning—which in this case is Belize, where Darwood picked up the money—and he starts over."

"The detectives I employ have backtracked at least half a

dozen times. How do you account for your success and their failure?"

"Frankly, I think I got lucky," Gary said and Dory had a glimmer of what Jill saw in him: honesty and humility. "I dug up the right detail at the right time, talked to the right guy in the right place. Two dozen false IDs. No matter how many times you backtrack that's like trying to follow a spiderweb. Pluck the wrong strand and it disintegrates in your fingers. I *think* Darwood set up all those bogus IDs to keep the cops and your guys chasing the wrong threads."

"I'd like to see your notes," Coop said to Gary. "With your permission, Margaret," he said to Aunt Ping, "I'd like to let this young man have a look at the latest reports from the Bastard Little Prick Squad."

"Perhaps. Just a moment, please." Aunt Ping raised her eyebrow at Gary. "What *is* your real name, young man?"

"Gary Sanders, Miss Lambert. I didn't lie about my name."

"Do you plan to return to your position with the FBI?"

"After this, ma'am, I doubt they'll want me."

"You trespassed on my property. You crossed Bruno's paddock, outran a horse, a pickup truck, and nearly drowned, simply to bring me this information? Or is there another reason you risked life and limb?"

"There is, ma'am," Gary said. "May I show you?"

Aunt Ping nodded. "Please do."

When Gary stood and bent to roll up his pant leg, Dory shot off the stool she'd brought in from the kitchen. "Uh, Gary—"

"Be quiet, Dory," Aunt Ping said and swung the eyebrow on her.

Gary lifted his left foot in Henry's clean sock onto the oak table and showed Aunt Ping the tattoo Dory had discovered on his calf the day she'd gone to the Happy Spirit to rescue Gary from Chase. A red heart with JILL stitched in flowery script. Aunt Ping's eyebrow didn't budge.

"I'm in love with Jill. She loves me. I want to marry her."

"You are aware that yesterday she married Chase McKay?"

"That's why I went to find Darwood. So Mr. Phillips could arrest him and unfreeze your assets so Jill wouldn't have to marry McKay for the twenty million bucks Dory said you need to close the Outlook Inn."

Aunt Ping's gaze lifted from Gary's calf and settled on Dory. She looked shot through the heart, like she had on that long ago Palm Sunday when Deirdre came to Outlook with snapshots of Daddy's speedboat.

By the heat flushing up her throat, Dory figured her face was vermilion. She was a dead woman standing. She hoped Aunt Ping would let her live long enough to kill Jill. This wasn't her mess, but she was going to pay for it because she'd known about it and hadn't stopped it and because Jill wasn't here to face the music.

"I'm sorry beyond words, Aunt Ping," Dory said. "I wish I'd told you. I did try to stop Jill, but truthfully, I didn't try very hard. That's no excuse. I should've told you. I should've tried harder. I—"

"Oh, shut up!" The green door from the corridor flew open, cracked into the wall like a gunshot and Dory heard a strangled *"Aagh!"* Then Jill reeled into the room clutching her head, a pair of sunglasses crooked on her nose. "It's just a *tad* too late to apologize, don't you *think*?"

"Jill! Darling!" Gary swung his left foot off the table, hopped on his right toward her, off balance but recovering till he bumped into his chair.

Jill could've caught him, but she stepped back. Gary fell flat with his arms open to embrace her.

"That's how I feel, like I ran face-first into a brick floor," she said to the back of his head. "I had the worst night of my life, no thanks to you."

Then she stepped over him and faced Aunt Ping across the oak table, weaving on her feet, her hair a half-dry mess of corkscrews. Dory had never seen her sister look so awful. Or frankly, enjoyed it more.

"You know how I hate the hotel business," Jill said to

Aunt Ping, her voice raw, like her throat was sore. "Chase wanted me, I wanted his money so I married him. All Dory did was tell me how much we needed for the trust so we can close the Outlook Inn. That's *all* she did. This isn't her fault. It's my fault. Blame me."

"Jillian," Aunt Ping said. "If you intend to marry Gary, don't you think you should help him off the floor?"

His father was sitting on the garage roof, his glasses and a book, his walkie-talkie and binoculars on a TV tray beside him. The shotgun Chase hadn't seen him touch since they'd gone rabbit hunting when he was twelve lay across the arms of his aluminum lawn chair.

"When's the last time you fired that thing?" Chase asked when he reached the top of the stairs.

"It's only buckshot." Charles stood the gun on its stock in the corner of the wall. "I don't want to kill anybody. Just scare 'em off."

"Eddie isn't armed, is he?"

"Hell, no." Charles grinned. "He's just out riding the range."

As he was leaving the house, Chase had caught Dory hurrying from the breakfast room to Miss Ping's suite, where Jill could lie down. She'd told him briefly about Gary, Darwood and the Caribbean. "I haven't found you a room yet, but I will," she'd said. If all else failed, Chase figured there was always the couch in her living room.

"Till Darwood is caught, private security might not be a bad idea." He sat down on the wall near his father. "If Miss Ping's interested, I'll call the company who's handling the security on the Summit Crest site."

He'd called Coop Junior after he'd taken a shower in the Honeymoon Suite, which was blissfully quiet once he'd pushed Jill out the door. He'd called Sylvia to let her know he hadn't fallen off the planet, checked in with his Summit Crest foreman and considered flopping on the giant bed for five minutes' shut-eye. He had a crick in his neck from sleeping in the chair.

"After all this time," his father said, "you think Darwood is finally going to be caught?"

"Yes, I do. He wants Jamie badly enough that he's shown too much of his hand to Miss Fairview." Besides which, Chase thought, he had enough money to buy an army and invade the Caribbean.

"I just heard Wallace on the walkie-talkie," Charles said. "Do you have any idea why Father Murphy is here again so soon?"

"That's why I came," Chase said. "So you could say I told you so."

"That doesn't bring me joy." Charles scowled. "What happened?"

"I married the wrong sister."

"When did you come to that realization?"

"Before, Dad, *before*." His father flushed and Chase laughed. He was tired, he was happy and Dory loved him. "Father Murphy is here to help Jill arrange her annulment."

Charles' scowl lifted a bit. "What about the right sister?"

"I'm the luckiest moron on the planet. She loves me. She's agreed to marry me. Mr. I Know Everything now realizes he doesn't know shit."

"Am I finally going to have grandchildren?"

"I'll ask the Little Boss. How many do you want?"

"Will I have to move to New York to see them?"

"Take a ride with me." Chase rose off the wall, took his keys out of his pocket. Charles picked up his walkie-talkie. "Where are we going?"

"Do you want to ruin the surprise? Is that it?"

"Okay." Charles headed for the stairs. "I'm getting in the truck."

Chase had found the spot he was looking for in the dark and the rain, while he and his father drove the farthest reaches of Outlook in search of Wally Stark. By the time he found it again, the sun had swung way to the west and lit the Expedition's windshield with a silver glare. He had to squint to see the crescent of trees that had caught his attention when he'd swept it in the dark with the truck's spotlight.

"Here we are." Chase parked the Expedition, got out with his father and walked to the edge of the road. "What do you think?"

"What do I think of what? There's nothing here."

"Not yet. If Miss Ping approves, there will be."

Chase forgot sometimes that other people didn't have AutoCAD in their heads. He laid an arm on his father's shoulders and traced his index finger along the rise of ground in front of the trees.

"I want to build a house right here. I've been drawing it in my head all day. Once Darwood is caught, the Lamberts can come home. I figure Dory will want to be as far away from her mother as possible."

His father didn't say anything. He just stared at the bare sweep of spring green pasture. This wasn't the reaction Chase had expected.

"Actually, I've got plans for two houses. One for me and Dory and the kids. The other one for you." Chase moved his index finger to the right. "A ranch. No stairs. An attached garage, big as you want. Plenty of room for the Rolls if Miss Ping doesn't care where you park it."

Charles turned to face him. "What about New York?"

"Forget about New York." He took his father by the shoulders. "You're here. Dory is here. I'm home, Dad. I'm staying."

When Father Murphy arrived, Aunt Ping dismissed Dory. She was so grateful she almost ran out of the south wing. Whatever cockamamie story Jill had concocted to tell their priest, Dory did not want to hear.

She went to the office and brought up the occupancy chart on her PC. She tried to focus on where she was going to put Chase and Gary, but her brain kept coming back to Marshall Phillips; kept sticking on the million messages he'd left on Gary's cell phone.

Tom had rescued Gary's carry-on from Bruno's hay and Peter had fished his glasses out of the pool with only a bent earpiece.

"Dumb luck triumphs again," Gary said with a grin.

"You should get another tattoo," Dory told him and Gary laughed. He'd thought she was kidding.

Aunt Ping gave her blessing to sharing the Bastard Little Prick Squad files, Gary unpacked his steno pad and went upstairs with Coop to compare notes in his room. Dory had two seconds to ask Coop, "What about Uncle Scrooge?" He'd patted her arm and told her not to worry.

What else was she supposed to do? Plan her wedding? Nope. Her fiancé was married. Sit on Miss Fairview and her direct cell phone line to James? Nope. Deirdre had that watch. Patrol the grounds? Negatory. Tom and Eddie and Peter and Charles had that covered.

"What do you think your father will say?" she'd asked Chase when she'd run into him in the corridor on her way to Aunt Ping's suite.

"About me and Jill? What can he say? I'm a pompous, arrogant, goddamn fool?" Chase shrugged. "I've heard it all before."

Seeing Chase had lifted her spirits, but now she was sinking into fret and stew mode and she didn't like it. Had she become as obsessed with Marshall Phillips as he was with her father?

That was scary. Hopefully, it was just the headache she'd had since Stark hit her in the face that was making her think bleak thoughts. Even her computer glasses didn't help. Dory took them off, put her elbows on her desk and carefully covered her eyes with her hands.

The whole right side of her face throbbed. She kept getting little tingles like needle pricks in her cheekbone. Henry told her that was a good sign; it meant the bruise was already starting to heel. Yippee.

Dory felt tears in her eyes. She wanted Chase to kiss her boo-boo. A few dozen other things while he was at it and like magic, felt Chase's lips touch her forehead. He'd kissed her only half a dozen times, but already she knew the feel of his mouth. She uncovered her eyes and smiled at him, leaning over the front of her desk on his spread hands. She drew a breath to sigh and smelled earth and grass and fresh air.

"You reek of the great outdoors," she said. "Where've you been?"

"I went for a drive with Dad." Chase leaned closer, the rub of his lips in her hair and the murmur in his voice making her shiver. "Be nice to me and I might take you for a ride later."

"Let me see how fast I can find you a room."

"Forget it. I'll bunk with Dad." Chase laughed, took her hands and lifted her out of her chair. "He wants grandkids, by the way."

"Whoa. Back up the truck." Dory resisted the tug Chase gave her to pull her around the desk. "What did you tell Charles?"

"Everything. He's delighted. He wants to know how many grandkids he gets. I told him I'd ask the Little Boss and get back to him."

"Who's the Little Boss?" Dory pressed a hand to her throat. "Me?"

"It won't be me." Chase grinned. "I'll be the guy wearing the T-shirt that says HE WHO MUST OBEY."

"I get a big picture of that." Dory laughed. Chase pulled her around the desk, into a kiss he had to bend nearly double to plant on her mouth and left her knees melting like Jell-O at a picnic. "I didn't have a chance to talk to Aunt Ping. I hope Charles can keep his lip zipped."

"He will. Come on. It's Al Fresco Night and I'm starving."

One Sunday a month from May through September when the weather was nice, Al Fresco Night gave Esme a break. Little bistro tables were set out on the terrace, gourmet boxed meals were delivered and Wallace poured from a case of the Happy Spirit's best wine.

Candles danced on the tables covered with yellow cloths,

their edges fluttering in a light breeze that mixed the scents from the garden with tubs of flowers from the greenhouse. Deirdre sat with Miss Fairview, the direct cell phone to James on the table. Dory didn't see Gary or Coop, who was smart enough to keep Gary out of sight. Aunt Ping sat with Jill and Father Murphy, who rose and gestured toward Chase when he came outside through the ballroom French doors with Dory.

"There's my summons," Chase said to her from the side of his mouth as he raised a hand to Father Murphy. "See you later. I love you."

A thrill shot through Dory. Just like that, I love you. Like he'd said it to her a billion times already. How cool was that? Dory sat on the wall at the far end of the terrace away from the guests and hugged herself.

When Chase sat down beside Father Murphy, Jill got up from the table. Aunt Ping had given her a clip for her hair. She came toward Dory in her sunglasses, doing a little dance step that Father Murphy didn't see, sat down beside her and bumped Dory with her shoulder.

"Mission accomplished. Are you proud of me?"

"I think you're proud enough for both of us."

"Was that a shot? What's wrong with you?"

"This for starters." Dory pointed at her black eye. "Then there's Gary. How long, do you think, before Marshall Phillips comes to Outlook to find him?"

"Why would he come here? Gary isn't wearing a homing device."

"We own the Happy Spirit, Jill. Where do you think Phillips will come when he visits the store and Amber says she hasn't seen Gary?"

"Oh," she said in a small voice. "I didn't think of that."

"I'm sure it was the first thing Aunt Ping thought of when she found out Gary is FBI. I just hope Phillips doesn't come with a search warrant. If he does and he finds Gary . . ."

Dory didn't say it. She didn't even want to think it.

"Why can't we just hide Gary?" Jill said.

"And ask everyone on Outlook who's seen him to lie to the FBI?"

"Good point." Jill tapped the perfectly French manicured nail of her index finger on her chin. "Don't worry. I'll think of something."

"Do us all a favor, Jill. *Don't* think." Dory pushed off the wall. "If you feel a thought coming on, go hide till it gives up looking for you."

"Don't I get any points for Gary finding James?"

"James isn't found yet. Gary narrowed the search, that's all."

"Why are you so angry with me?"

"I'm scared. James hired an extremely bad man to steal Jamie. He tore him right out of my grasp. If Diego hadn't followed us—"

"Don't think about it. I'm sorry." Jill jumped up and hugged her. "I was afraid you'd be mad because I spilled the beans to Chase."

"I *was* mad. I was *furious*. Then I thought, wait a minute. What if I'd been stuck in the Honeymoon Suite with Gary? I would've done anything, said anything to get the hell out of there."

"All *right*." Jill pushed her away, laughing. "We're even."

"Not quite." Dory grinned. "You're still married to my fiancé."

Jill lifted her sunglasses and said, "Huh?"

Uh oh, Dory thought. "Nothing," she said and turned away.

"Hold it." Jill spun her around by the arm. "Do you mean *Chase*?"

"Uh, yes. He realized he loves me when I caught your bouquet."

"He *what*?" Jill jammed her shades on the top of her head, gasped and pinched her nose. When she opened her eyes, they flared like blue white coals. "After all the hell I went through? All the lousy, boring dates? All the—" She broke off and blinked. "What am I saying? This is perfect!"

"No, Jill. It's not perfect. Perfect would be no wedding, no Operation Cockroach, no screw Chase out of twenty million—"

"Okay, so it's not perfect. It's fabulous! The man of your dreams!" Jill hugged her and held her at arm's length, her eyes shining with happy tears. "We have to start right now planning your wedding."

"I think we should at least wait till Father Murphy leaves."

"Don't worry about Father Murphy. He's had two glasses of wine."

"Shouldn't we plan your wedding to Gary first?"

"I've had my fill of weddings. Gary and I will go to City Hall." Jill tugged her down off the wall. "First, your dress. An A-line, I think."

Wallace appeared between the French doors. He caught Dory's eye and nodded. "Be right back," she told Jill and crossed the terrace.

"Tom for you, Miss Dory," Wallace said. "On the house phone."

"Thank you, Wallace." The house phone meant ordinary, mundane, everyday stuff. Dory sighed with relief and took the call in the kitchen.

"Me and Marjorie got the grandkids," Tom said. "Seth and Joey. Thought Jamie might like to sleep over. I know it's Sunday, but I figured it might be good if he wasn't where he's supposed to be tonight."

"It's not only good, it's brilliant. Thank you for thinking of it, Tom. I'll bring Jamie down in the next hour or so. Will that be all right?"

"Be just fine, Miss Dory. We'll have the popcorn ready."

"I knew it would be totally cool living with you." Jamie did an excited fidget in the passenger seat of the Saturn, his Spider-Man backpack between his knees. "No way would Aunt Ping or Auntie Deirdre let me sleep over on Sunday night."

"It's been a wild weekend. Time for some R & R." Dory

smiled at him and steered the Saturn around the curve past the barns that led to the stone and stucco farm manager's cottage. "I might let you stay home from school tomorrow. How 'bout that?"

Jamie grinned. "You rock, Dory."

"I wish, squirt." She laughed and flicked the lights on high beam.

The shadows of the trees lining the road were too close, too dark. Her hands were damp on the steering wheel. It made her so angry to feel threatened on Outlook. She was glad Tom had suggested this. Jamie would have a ball eating junk food and playing video games with Seth and Joey. She didn't have to be brave. She could go home and cry in the bathtub, put on her jammies, take Rocky to bed with her and hide.

The porch light was on, Tom and Marjorie in the swing by the door. Seth and Joey waited on the steps for Jamie. They ran down the walk to meet him when the Saturn pulled up, ten- and eight-year-old towheaded brothers; Seth had brown eyes, Joey blue.

Shades of Charles' grandchildren to be, Dory wondered, as she got out of the car to smile at the boys and say thank you to Tom and Marjorie. They invited her to stay awhile, but it was getting darker and she was getting jumpier. When Jamie went inside with Seth and Joey, Dory told Tom she was keeping Jamie home from school.

"Think that's smart. I'll fetch him home to you in the morning."

Dory's faithful little green Saturn brought her home safe and sound to the guesthouse. She'd left every light on, stayed in the car with the engine in gear and the doors locked till the overhead door came down.

"Idiot," she muttered and turned the car off, took her key out of the ignition and walked through the breezeway into the kitchen.

A yellow rose that hadn't been there when she left stood in a crystal vase on the counter. Dory picked up the white card propped against it and read "Please note that this rose is *not* pink," and laughed.

"Peter let me in," Chase said from behind her. "Hope you don't mind."

Dory turned, saw him leaning in the doorway between the kitchen and the hallway in a loosely knotted blue silk robe that showed most of his blond-haired chest and legs almost as long as she was tall.

Dory whistled. "You have the most beautiful feet I've ever seen."

"Do you want me now?" Chase asked. "Or do you want to wait until we're married? Or at least till I'm not married to Jill?"

"That's a trick question, right? I've been waiting all my life, Chase."

He crooked his index finger. "Then c'mere."

Dory went, a full body flush surging through her. He didn't touch her, just bent his head and kissed her, rubbed his nose against hers and nuzzled her ear. "Where do you want me?"

"Is right here, right now too forward?"

"Not a bit." Chase smiled. "But I've got a better idea."

He swung her into his arms, carried her up the stairs and into her bathroom. Three candles burned on the corners of the tub, another yellow rose stood in a vase. He'd already spread the white looped bathmat on the floor and laid a pile of towels next to the tub. Chase put her down.

"Five minutes. Then I'll be back to give you a bath."

He left and shut the door. Dory opened it. Chase leaned against the doorframe on his spread hands smiling. Waiting for her.

"Could you make that fifteen? I've got a few things to do."

"I'm really good at shaving." He rubbed his knuckles under his chin. "Years of practice."

The thought of Chase stroking a razor up her legs made Dory feel faint. "It'll be a lot quicker if I do it."

He bent his head and kissed her. "Hurry."

"Fast as I can. I'll call you when I'm in the tub. Okay?"

He kissed her again, said "Hu*rry*," again, this time with a growl.

Dory shut the door and leaned against it. Chase loved her. He wanted to bathe her, wanted to run his big, soapy hands all over her body. Her stomach quivered and her breath caught. She hoped he knew CPR. She wasn't sure how much her baby heart could take.

A naked blade in a shaky hand spelled blood, so Dory turned on the overhead light, undressed and used her cordless electric razor, started the water and added bubbles. While the tub filled, she washed her face, brushed her teeth, used the toilet and flushed, turned off the light and the water in the tub, slipped into it and drew a breath.

"Okay," she called. "I'm ready."

"Good timing." Chase came through the door. "Me, too."

Neck deep in bubbles, Dory turned her head on her bath pillow and watched him roll up his sleeves, bare the long, muscled forearms that used to make her whimper when they'd washed the Rolls. He dropped to his knees, reached across her for the soap and lathered his hands.

"Where do you want me to start?"

"Right here." Dory put her soapy finger on her lips.

Chase leaned down to kiss her, sliding his hands into the water, beneath her and around her. His fingers felt like silk, his mouth like fire.

When his hands cupped her breasts she sucked in her breath and his tongue, arched up so she could breathe, felt his thumb and index finger close around her right nipple and forgot about air, about first-time modesty and being shy, wrapped her arms around his neck, let her wet fingers slide into his hair and pulled him tighter, closer.

He tore his mouth away from hers, spread his hands on her back, on her shoulder blades to hold her up and suckled her breast, swirling his tongue around her nipple. Dory arched her head back and cried out.

"Sorry," he murmured, moving his mouth to her lips to kiss her. "I'll slow down. I didn't mean to go this fast."

"Don't slow down." Dory drew in a shaky breath, her whole body quivering. "You aren't hurting me. I just don't want to get ahead of you."

"You won't, don't worry." He eased her onto the bath pillow and soaped his hands again, his elbows leaning on the edge of the tub; his gaze sliding down her body, only half covered by bubbles now. Dory could hear them hiss and pop and scooped handfuls over her breasts. Chase blew them away. His breath made her nipples peak and Dory sigh.

"I have no idea—" He gripped the tub with his soapy hands, his voice an octave deeper than usual. "—what made me think I could do this."

"Let me help you." Dory raised her left knee and her leg out of the water, her pointed toes dripping bubbles. Chase cradled her foot in his right hand, rubbed his left thumb across the base of her toes.

"Red toenails." He smiled and massaged her foot. "That's the first girly thing I noticed about you. Your red toenails."

He raised her foot and sucked her big toe into his mouth. Dory moaned and almost slipped under the water. Chase brought her up with his mouth over hers, his left hand sliding up her calf, past her knee, up her thigh. Dory parted her lips for his tongue, her legs for his hand, felt his finger stroke between her folds and Chase groan against her mouth.

"Oh God," he rasped in her ear. "You're slick."

"I love you," Dory murmured and nuzzled his jaw.

"I think you're clean." He drew his hand away and leaned back on his elbows, his pulse jumping in his throat. "What d'you think?"

"I think if you don't get me out of this tub, I'm pulling you in."

Chase grinned and shucked his robe, the hair on his chest shimmering like gold in the candlelight. He leaned into the tub, elbow deep, looped an arm behind her, lifted her and pressed her wet breasts to his chest. Hair tangled around her nipples, his tongue tangled in her mouth and he scooped her out of the tub, dripping water and bubbles.

He sat back on his heels and laid her in his lap, holding her with his mouth and his right arm, rubbing water and soap off her breasts with his left. Dory put her arm around his neck, shivering with damp and want, rolled toward him on his thighs and felt his penis hard and hot and throbbing against her belly.

"Oh, Chase." She broke the kiss and whimpered. "Hurry."

He draped a towel over her and stood her up. Dory's head spun at the change in altitude. She closed her eyes as he carried her to the bed and laid her on the turned-back sheets, cool against her wet shoulders. Dory fluttered her eyes open, saw candles lit on the bed tables, Chase sitting beside her on his folded right leg, his left foot on the floor.

"Oh my," she breathed and brushed his penis with her fingertips.

He dipped his chin and watched her, smiled when she moaned, closed his eyes when she wrapped her hand around him and squeezed.

"Careful," he whispered. "I've never been this ready in my life."

"Neither have I," Dory murmured, letting go of him and smiling when he opened his eyes.

"Do you think you can take me?"

"Oh yes," she breathed and touched him again, lightly.

"Do you want me to use a condom?"

"No." Dory opened her legs for him, held her arms up to enfold him. "I just want you to kiss me when I climax."

"Oh God." Chase closed his eyes for a second, drew a breath that flared his nostrils and slipped into her arms, between her hips, his weight on his knees and his elbows. "Don't let me hurt you. Stop me."

"Chase." Dory wrapped her arms around him. "Make love to me."

He pushed and she felt the head of his penis, the quiver in his muscles. He was going slowly, trying not to hurt her. He was killing her with trying not to hurt her. Dory opened her legs wider, drew him deeper. Chase stroked, pushed farther, spreading her hips, filling her with heat.

"Oh yes," she breathed and arched her back. "Oh, Chase. Get ready with that kiss."

"Oh God, Dory." He stroked again, pushed deeper. "Already?"

"I love you." She gripped his hips and looked up at his face, his deep, deep blue eyes, his heart thudding in his throat. "I've been waiting for this all my life."

"Okay, baby." Chase bent his head and kissed her. "Here it is."

He went up on his hands and pushed all the way inside her. So hot, so hard, so *huge*. Dory wanted to scream he felt so good, so big inside her, but she clamped her throat shut, terrified to make a sound for fear Chase would withdraw and she'd die of unrequited lust.

"Dory? Are you okay?" He looked down at her, the muscles in his arms quivering. "You just went really still on me."

"I'm afraid to move. I'm afraid to breathe. You aren't hurting me. You feel—" She made a tentative wiggle, felt him pulse and almost swooned. "*Ohhh*. So wonderful I want to scream."

Chase groaned in his throat, said "Scream," and drove into her.

Hard enough to push her back on the pillows, twice, three times, thrusting deeper, long, hard strokes that made her head spin, arched her back to lift her pelvis to meet him. The boy she'd loved all her life, a big, strong, beautiful man, all silver and shadows in the candlelight, lifting one hand to caress her breasts while he plunged deeper and sweeter and faster inside her, making her rock and buck and—

Chase caught her scream and her climax with his mouth, gave her his tongue to suck while the orgasm spiraled through her and he came right behind her, shuddering against her, pulsing inside her, sighing as he settled on top of her, his heart pounding against her breasts, his nose nuzzling her ear, his hips still pushing against hers.

Dory wrapped her arms around him, her legs around his waist. Well, sort of around his waist. He chuckled, reached behind him and cupped her thigh, gave her a boost so her heel at least cleared his hip.

"Tiny everywhere." Chase kissed her ear. "Except where it counts."

"Big everywhere." Dory kissed his jaw. "Especially where it counts."

He sighed and nestled into the pillow beside her. "Too heavy?"

"Not so far. You'll hear it if my ribs crack."

Chase chuckled and slipped a little inside her. "I love you, Dory."

She sighed happily. "Now the experience is complete."

"I hope our kids come out with your wit. I'm not that funny."

"Oh, how can you say that? I laughed myself silly watching you make a fool out of yourself over Jill."

"Don't remind me." Chase groaned, bent his arm over her breasts and covered his eyes. "I wussed out on telling Jill I love you. I need to do that, let her punch me or slap me and get it over with."

"No you don't. I did it for you."

"Do I need to wear body armor?"

"She only wanted to kill you for ten seconds. Now she's thrilled beyond measure and planning my wedding for me."

"Excellent. Now you'll have more time to spend on your back letting me impregnate you."

"If I may say—" Dory turned her head and looked at Chase, his face half buried in the pillow beside her, his sweat-spiked hair sticking out above his ear. "—your eagerness for children surprises me."

"Surprises me, too." He pushed up on his elbow. "While

I was delusional I thought, great, Jill doesn't want kids any more than I do. But I had a dream last night, right over there." Chase nodded at the wing chair in the corner by the bathroom. "I saw you and me and two of the cutest little kids walking up the front steps of Outlook. Well, we were walking. You were waddling 'cause you were pregnant." Chase grinned. "Again."

"Three kids, huh? Well. Sister Immaculata will love you. She's been worried that enrollment is down."

"Actually, there were three kids in my dream, plus you were pregnant, but one looked like Jamie. I figure he was the nightmare part."

Dory laughed. "How do you account for this change of heart?"

"I don't know." Chase smiled, spread his hands on her belly and teased little circles with his fingers that made her quiver. "Must be love."

"You think?" Dory asked softly and lifted her mouth for a kiss. The phone rang and she sighed. "I should answer that. It could be Tom. He and Marjorie have Jamie for the night." Chase nodded. She rolled toward the nightstand, lifted the receiver and said, "Hello?"

"Dory? Is that you?" It was a man's voice, deep and quivering with emotion. "My dearest Dory. My darling girl. It's me. It's Daddy."

Chapter Twenty

All the times she'd dreamed this, imagined picking up the phone and hearing Daddy's voice. That some pervert would choose this moment to strike, to kill the joy of listening to Chase tell her about their dream children infuriated Dory, made her think of James and Miss Fairview, made her wonder if there was another spy at Outlook.

"Whoever you are, you are sick." She rolled up on the side of the bed, switched on the lamp and pressed the record feature on the answering machine. "You need help. How dare you pretend—"

"Dory dearest. It's me. Truly." The man's voice broke, like he was fighting tears. Oh, he was good.

"You are *twisted*. Who put you up to this?"

Dory felt Chase spring off the bed. He came around in front of her, a worried scowl on his face. She mouthed "Cell phone 911." Chase nodded, wheeled toward the wing chair and grabbed his jeans.

"Listen to me, Dory," the man pleaded. "Your first pay packet from Lambert's was sixty-seven dollars and eighty-three cents. I loaned you twenty for carfare and lunches. You repaid me with eight percent interest. Twenty-one dollars and sixty cents even. Do you remember?"

Like it was yesterday. Daddy flashing the money at Mother and proudly proclaiming, "Look here, Drusilla. We've raised a banker!"

"Daddy?" Tears flooded Dory's eyes, closed her throat

and nearly choked her. She could barely see Chase, her eyes were so full, but she shook her head and her hand at him. *No. Wait.*

"Dory." Her father sobbed her name. She thought her heart would tear itself in two. She'd never heard her father cry. "Dory, darling."

"Daddy, is something wrong? Is Mother all right?"

It was the only thing Dory could think of, the only scenario she could imagine that would make her father risk a phone call.

"She's fine, darling. Gordy is spinning his finger around like he's a helicopter, which means he wants me to speed this up."

"Gordy!" Dory cried, so surprised her mouth fell open.

"Yes, dear one. I've done all I can from this distance to help you."

"Oh, Daddy." Dory remembered her fury over his speedboat and clapped a hand over her mouth to keep back a sob. She looked at Chase, saw him smile and toss his jeans and his cell phone on the chair.

"I'm going to put Gordy on in a moment. He has my complete trust. Will you give him yours? Will you do what he asks?"

"Daddy, yes. Of course I will. What's happened?"

"The most amazing and ironic thing. Isla Rica has a new resident. He purchased the villa next door. Your mother and I have been living here as Roger and Priscilla Davenport. Bertie suggested it. The name Lambert was rather notorious. That's who he thinks we are, our new neighbor. He thinks we're Roger and Priscilla. You'll never guess who he is, darling. In a million years you'll never guess, but it's *him,* Dory. The bastard little prick. He's surfaced at last, just over the back fence."

"*James?*" Dory's heart nearly stopped. "Daddy! Has he seen you?"

"No, but I saw *him,* the rotten little bastard. I was on the veranda, having my whiskey sour. I dashed inside and rang Gordy. This was Thursday last. I haven't put a toe out the door since, nor have I told your mother. I'm slipping her Valium. I can't for much longer, obviously, nor can we stay shut in. It will rouse suspicions. Time is of the essence."

"Yes, Daddy. I understand." Dory's mind was racing, her heart pumping like mad to keep up. "What do you want me to do?"

"That's my girl." Her father's voice thickened. "My clever girl. I'm putting Gordy on. The whirlybird is spinning like crazy. I love you, dearest. Ping and Jilly, too. You'll tell them for me, yes?"

"Yes, I'll tell them. I love you, Daddy." Dory swept her tears away, drew a breath to clear her head so she could focus and think.

She glanced up, saw Chase coming out of the bathroom with her yellow robe and realized she was trembling. He sat beside her, draped the robe and his arm around her and pressed a kiss to her temple. She had a moment to savor the press of his lips before Gordy came on the line.

"Hey, kiddo. Ready for your marching orders?"

"In a minute. I need to tell you a couple of things."

As quickly as she could, Dory told Gordy about Miss Fairview. How many times Gary had run across the name Peter Dawson in the Caribbean, about Wally Stark trying to abduct Jamie, and Joe Bauer, the guy who had disappeared from the motel. "Somehow James found out about Jamie and he wants him. That frightens me, Gordy."

"Don't worry. James isn't going to get his hands on Jamie. James is going to jail. He's using the name Peter Dawson here on Isla Rica. Be sure you tell Gary. He wasn't my first choice, but we need a fed to make the arrest. Tell Gary to bring everything he's got on Peter Dawson with him. And tell him not to forget his handcuffs."

"Got it. Where do you want Gary and his handcuffs?"

"Cancún. We can't touch James on Isla Rica. I want Gary in Cancún ASAP. I want you there, too, Dory. And I want Jamie. I need a surefire bait to lure James off the island."

"*Gordy!* No! I won't put Jamie in danger. Think of another way."

"We've been trying, your father and I. Jill was the best we could come up with. Jamie is better. You think he'll be in harm's way in Cancún and he's not at Outlook? Where did Stark come to get him? Bauer got away. He could be planning another grab. Jamie won't be completely safe until James is behind bars."

"You're right. I know you're right. You've never steered me wrong. It's just—" She was trembling again, and now she had gooseflesh. Dory sighed, drew a shaky breath. "It scares me, that's all."

"I won't let anything happen to Jamie. He doesn't have to do anything. He just has to be in Cancún. Tell him it's a vacation. Make it look like one. Bring Jill. If you've got a boyfriend, bring him. Got a pencil?"

"One second." Dory fumbled for a notepad and pen out of her nightstand drawer. "Okay."

"Here's where I want you to stay in Cancún." Gordy gave her the name of a hotel. "Bring a beach umbrella. I'll see to it that James knows his son is within reach. Tell Miss Lambert. If Marshall Phillips isn't hunting Gary yet, he will be. She needs to be ready. If Fairview hears from Darwood I want to know about it. You've got my cell phone. Get to Cancún as fast as you can and call me when you get there."

The line went dead. The record light on the answering machine stopped flashing. A rush of gooseflesh flooded Dory's entire body. Chase pressed another kiss to her temple and chuckled.

"Good news, I take it?"

Dory moved the answering machine into the living room. Half an hour later she hit PLAY and let Jill and Gary, Deirdre and Coop and Aunt Ping listen to her conversation with Daddy and Gordy. Chase heard it while they'd dressed, made her bed and blew out the candles.

Jill managed not to cry till the end. Then she wailed, "Oh Daddy!," flung herself in Gary's arms and sobbed.

Aunt Ping didn't weep. She smiled, then she sighed. So deeply Dory wasn't sure she intended to draw another breath, but she did.

"How perfectly poetic," she said.

Dory perched on the desk on the staircase wall. Chase leaned against it beside her. She pressed STOP, then just to be on the safe side, DELETE. She didn't need to save the message. She'd be seeing Daddy soon.

"Dory." Deirdre sat red-eyed on the couch, a handkerchief twisted between her hands. "Will you ring Margaret and me when it's done? When it's over, when James is no longer a threat to Jamie."

"Yes, Aunt Deirdre. The second Gary cuffs him." Dory smiled at her, then looked at Coop. "Did you know about Gordy?"

"No, but I'd like to meet him. He sounds very efficient."

"He sounds ex-military. He looked it, too, when he came into the Happy Spirit." Gary unwound himself from Jill. "I've met a few guys like him in the Bureau. They don't screw around."

"Then we shouldn't, either," Chase said. "Transportation to Cancún is on me. I'll charter a jet. I travel with my passport. Is everybody else's up to date?"

"Chase," Aunt Ping said, "that's very kind of you."

"Not at all, Miss Ping. It's the least I can do."

Dory blinked at him. "Are you coming along?"

"Try going without me." He bent his head and kissed her, then looked at Aunt Ping. "In case you're wondering, I'm the boyfriend."

"I assumed so," she said dryly, a sparkle in her eyes.

"Chase has the transportation. Gary has the handcuffs," Coop said. "That leaves Marsh to you and me, Margaret."

"I think we can handle him," Aunt Ping said, her eyebrow lifting.

"I should be gone before he gets here," Gary said. "Like now."

"Oh Gary, *no*," Jill said petulantly. "Not again."

"I'll be waiting for you in Cancún," Gary told her. "Dory. You've got a copy machine, don't you?"

Darth Vader, AKA Uncle Scrooge, arrived at Outlook at nine-thirty Monday morning without the Storm Troopers. A black SUV wound up the terraces and stopped beneath the front portico. Marshall Phillips sprang out of the passenger door.

"Here he comes." Coop lifted one of the sheers on the library windows. "Agent Frasier is with him."

Poor man, Dory thought. She sat next to Jill at one of the library tables, across from Chase, who was supposedly reading the newspaper. Aunt Ping presided in her pink Louis chair on one side of the fireplace as Margaret Lambert, in orchid Chanel and Great-grandmother Lambert's pearls. Deirdre sat with her in the rose brocade wing chair.

Diego manned the pocket doors. He opened them for the United States attorney and Agent Frasier, shut them and stood back against the wall. Uncle Scrooge had lost a lot of hair on top since Dory had seen him.

"Good morning, Miss Lambert." Phillips nodded to her.

"Mr. Phillips." Aunt Ping inclined her chin. "May I offer you coffee?"

"Thank you, no. I have only one question. Where is Gary Sanders?"

"I have no idea. I saw him last yesterday evening." Aunt Ping picked up the manila folder in her lap. "He left this for you."

"I hope that's his resignation."

"It's information, Mr. Phillips, regarding the whereabouts of James Darwood. You recall the name. My brother's nephew, the man who stole thirty-five million dollars from Lambert Securities. The person you have steadfastly refused to pursue and apprehend. Gary believes he's found James. He thought you might like to know so that you can arrest him."

"At the moment, Miss Lambert, the only person I want to arrest is Gary Sanders. Or perhaps *you,* young lady." Uncle Scrooge swung toward Jill, who quailed and clutched

Dory's hand under the table. "You're his little shackup, aren't you?"

"Back off, Phillips." Chase pushed to his feet, the picture of affronted manhood. "Jill is my wife. We were married on Saturday."

"How convenient." Phillips wheeled toward Coop. "Aren't you past the age of cheap theatrics *yet?*"

"You should take the folder, Marsh," Coop said calmly. "Gary's information is good and it's current."

"If you know where he is, Coop, this is the time to tell me."

"At this precise moment? I have no clue where Gary is."

"Parsing words, are we? All right. Parse this." Uncle Scrooge faced Aunt Ping, a vein in his temple pulsing. "I could have a court order and be back here within an hour. At which time, I'm sure you'd be delighted to produce Gary Sanders just to make me look like a damned fool."

"I don't see the need," Aunt Ping said, her eyebrow fully arched.

"Twenty-four hours, Miss Lambert." Marshall Phillips looked at his watch. "If Gary Sanders doesn't turn himself in to me by nine-fifty A.M. tomorrow, I will be back with a court order and I will take your precious Outlook apart brick by brick. Good day."

Agent Frasier looked like he wanted to trip Uncle Scrooge. He shot Dory a *sorry* smile, followed Phillips out of the library and drove him away in the black SUV.

At eleven-ten A.M. two more nondescript sedans with GS plates rolled into the orchard to join Agent Frasier's tan fed mobile. By eleven thirty there was another listening post established and two nimble FBI agents straddling stout limbs high up in the hardwood trees at the edges of the orchard, watching Outlook through high-power binoculars.

At eleven forty-five, Eddie swung out of the bay Arab mare's saddle under the front portico and caught her bridle.

"There's six of 'em total in the three cars. I didn't see

Agent Frasier," he told Dory. "Got four of my boys watching the tractor paths."

"Stay off the radios until we know if this is going to work."

"They know to do that, miss. Don't you worry."

Eddie mounted Spitfire and rode off to watch the watchers. Dory went up the steps and into the foyer.

"Wallace," she said to the butler at his post, "call Charles on the house phone. Tell him five minutes. Esther," she said to the housekeeper at the reception desk, "time to ring Room Twelve."

"Yes, Miss Dory," they both said.

Anita was at her desk. She turned away from her PC when Dory came into the office and nodded at the green canvas tote on Dory's desk.

"Passports are in there. Yours, Jill's and Jamie's. Cash, credit cards, Blue Cross cards. Miss Ping's written permission to seek medical treatment for Jamie if the little goof catches a jellyfish on the beach. Earplugs for the plane and your Prevacid."

"Anita." Dory kissed her cheek. "You're a jewel beyond price."

"That's what your father used to say. Amber called. The FBI just left the Happy Spirit. They took the hard drive from Gary's computer. Can you believe they gave her a receipt?"

"Nothing surprises me anymore. Hold down the fort."

Dory picked up the tote and went back to the foyer, in time to see Lindsay Varner come down the stairs in a big-brimmed hat, sunglasses and a hot pink capri set that belonged to Jill. Noah Patrick followed her carrying Jill's red wheeled carry-on and makeup case.

"Whoa," Dory said to Lindsay. "You look enough like Jill trying to keep a low profile, to *pass* for Jill trying to keep a low profile."

Lindsay laughed. "That's the whole idea, isn't it?"

"Thank you so much for doing this, Mrs. Patrick."

"Oh no, thank you. I need an afternoon away from the kids and I have never been chauffeured in a Rolls-Royce."

Wallace appeared beside Dory and nodded to Noah. "May I, sir?"

"Knock yourself out." He gave Wallace the luggage and lifted the sunglasses off his wife's nose. "Lead 'em on a merry chase, princess."

"The merriest." She kissed him back and said to Dory, "Ready."

The Rolls pulled up under the portico. Charles popped the trunk lid and came around the passenger side in his uniform. Wallace flung Outlook's front doors wide open, stepped aside and bowed.

Lindsay hurried down the steps. Dory followed her onto the porch to make it look good. Lindsay ducked into the Rolls; Charles shut the door, took the bags from Wallace and stowed them in the trunk, paused at the driver's door and looked at Dory over the silver-gray roof.

"You and Chase get that bastard James," he said to her. "I'll take these FBI boys for a ride they won't forget."

The Rolls purred away down the drive. Dory went back inside and paced. Henry came up from the concierge desk and stood with Esther and Wallace at his post. Anita came out of the office with an unlit cigarette. Noah Patrick slouched against the giant palm tree in its tub.

"Chill, cutie," he said to her. "It'll work."

When her walkie-talkie went off, Dory's heart leaped and she dashed outside where the reception was better. "Mama San Three."

"Man-O'-War, little mama." Eddie's laugh crackled. "They're gone. All three cars, two agents apiece, the guys in the trees. Peeled outa here right behind the Rolls. Coast is clear."

"Yes!" Dory made a fist, pumped her right arm and whirled, saw Wallace on the porch with Henry and Esther and Noah. And Chase, coming toward her down the steps, grinning.

"They bought it!" She squealed and jumped. He caught

her around the waist; she looped her arms around his neck. "You are brilliant!"

"If you want to build a house, first you clear the site." He kissed her, put her down and reached for his cell phone. "I'll call the helicopter down. Diego's out back in the truck. He has the luggage and Jill and Jamie. Get your stuff. We have to go."

When the Expedition turned in to the parking lot adjacent to the golf course, where the helicopter would set down, Aunt Ping and Deirdre came out of the clubhouse to see them off. Jamie was so excited he could hardly hold still for them to kiss and hug him.

Chase held on to him by the straps of his Spider-Man backpack as the helicopter came in, whipping the trees and plucking at Aunt Ping's scarves. She caught one before it blew away, tied it around Dory's neck and kissed her between the eyes.

"For luck," she said and Dory hugged her. "We'll bring Daddy home with us. Put his chair back in the library."

The hotel in Cancún was fabulous: open to the beach with tile and stucco in the Mayan motif. White hot sand blazed against blue sky and bluer water everywhere Dory turned.

Chase had reserved a suite with two bedrooms joined by a sitting room with a flat-screen TV, every electronic gizmo imaginable, a wet bar, a fireplace, opulent bathrooms and beds—oh my, the beds.

Dory gazed at a California king swept with silk and scattered with suggestively shaped pillows and whimpered. Jill gave the bed the once-over and quivered.

"Enjoy your room, ladies." Chase winked at Dory from the threshold and pulled the double doors shut with a click.

"No!" Jill gave a strangled cry and spun toward Dory. "Why does he get to decide the sleeping arrangements?"

"Simple." Dory tossed a pillow at her shaped like a giant cupcake with a cherry on top or a 42D-size breast. "He's picking up the tab."

"Just wait till I'm rich again," Jill muttered.

Dory called Gordy's cell phone. "We're here."

"Good. I'll be there in forty-five minutes. We'll have dinner."

Dory passed the word to Chase, Diego, Jamie and Gary, who'd been waiting for them in the lobby when they checked in. She and Jill had time for a quick shower and a change into something cooler: a tropical print sarong for Jill; for Dory, a yellow sundress with tiny white flowers, a flirty skirt and white sandals with tiny heels that showed her red toenails. When she came out of the bedroom, Chase's gaze went straight to her legs. The smile he gave her made her stomach flutter.

Gordy met them in the lobby. Dory introduced him to Chase, Diego and Jamie. She'd told Jamie that Gordy was a friend of Aunt Ping.

"What kind of friend?" Jamie asked. "A boyfriend?"

Gordy smiled. "I think she's a little old for a boyfriend, don't you?"

"I won't tell her you said that. Or Charles, either."

Chase's eyebrows shot up. Gordy guffawed. Jill's jaw nearly hit the floor. Gary flushed and Diego looked at the ceiling.

"Oh, Jamie." Dory laughed, hooked him around the neck from behind and knuckled him in the head. "You little kidder. Who's hungry?"

Then she caught his elbow and towed him toward the restaurant adjacent to the lobby. "What'd I say?" he asked puzzledly.

"Later, squirt. We'll talk about it later."

After dinner they adjourned to the open-air bar. The sand glowed orange in the twilight. The surf slipped and murmured up the beach. The palm frond thatch rustled in the breeze. Dory smelled salt and jungle. A barman lit torches along the walkway and Diego took Jamie on a coconut hunt while Gordy outlined his plan to catch James.

"We'll take him on the beach. Right here, behind the hotel." Gordy cocked his thumb over his shoulder. "He'll feel safe in the open with lots of people around. I'll go next door in the morning and borrow a cup of sugar, chat him up, tell him about the nice young woman I met at the hotel. Dory Lambert from Kansas City, come to bake on the beach with her ten-year-old nephew Jamie. When he heads for the quay and his launch, I'll be on him like a chicken on a June bug. I'll call you on your cell phone, Dory. It's twenty minutes by boat from Isla Rica."

"So you want Jamie and me on the beach tomorrow," she said. "With the umbrella you told me to bring."

"From ten o'clock on. What color is the umbrella?"

"Purple with white polka dots. My suit is teal, two-piece. My cover-up is white. Jamie's trunks are green and yellow."

"Pick your spot. Keep Jamie by the water as much as you can. The surf makes the footing shift and I want Darwood off balance. Keep Jamie close, but don't hover. Don't look for James, especially after I call you. And don't look for me. Just trust that I'll be two steps behind him."

"Where do you want us?" Chase stretched his arm along the back of Dory's chair. The warmth of his skin made her realize that even in the midseventy-degree air she was chilled.

"Gary, I want you closest to Dory. When I take Darwood down—I'm not going to shoot him, I'm going to tackle him so he can't run—I want to see your badge under his nose and hear you singing Miranda before his back hits the sand. Chase, you and Diego take the flanks. Dory is the pepper, Gary is the salt." Gordy placed the salt shaker behind and a little to the right of the pepper. "My napkin is the water." He traced two lines with his fingers from the salt shaker to the edge of the napkin. "Put yourselves somewhere in here. If James bolts, you can cut him off and run him down before he clears the beach."

"What do you want me to do?" Jill asked.

Gordy said, "You wear bikinis, don't you?"

Jill said, "Duh."

"Then you're a problem. I don't want Darwood to decide he's got time for you before he makes a grab for Jamie.

Stay here in the bar. Pick a stool that gives you a clear view of Dory's umbrella. If I give you this sign—" Gordy raised his arm over his head and made a bent elbow wave. "—get hotel security down here on the double."

Jill put a hand on her hip. "I'm the *lookout*? That's all I get to do?"

Gordy shrugged. "It's the only job I've got left."

"Hey, Dory!" Jamie hollered, trotting up the walkway with an armful of coconuts. "We hit the jackpot!"

Diego followed, grinning and picking up the coconuts he dropped.

Gordy turned toward Dory. "Diego. He pulled Stark off Jamie?"

"He's the Cisco Kid." Dory smiled. "He deserved a trip to Cancún."

While they waited for the elevator in the lobby, Gordy pulled Dory aside. "I can't guarantee Darwood will take the bait tomorrow. He may think about it. I'll try to speed him up, tell him you're about to leave."

Dory's stomach sank but she smiled. "Thanks for the heads-up."

"One more thing." Gordy touched her elbow. "If this goes south it's okay to scream. In fact, I want you to scream. Scream your head off."

In the elevator, she stood in front of Chase. As the car opened on their floor, he murmured in her ear, "Balcony," and Dory nodded. She assumed he meant once Jill was asleep.

Jamie almost nodded off brushing his teeth, but Dory thought Jill would never go to sleep. She tossed and turned and thrashed.

"Who does Gordy think he is?" Jill bitched. "James Bond? Where did Daddy find him, anyway?"

"I don't know." Dory sighed. *Go to sleep!* "I'm just glad he did."

"Look out," Jill muttered into her pillow and finally fell asleep.

When she started breathing through her mouth, Dory

slipped out of the bedroom, through the sitting room and onto the balcony. Chase leaning on his elbows on the railing in the dark turned his head and smiled at her, his hair and his white T-shirt lit by moonlight.

Dory hadn't bothered with a robe. Chase hadn't bothered with pants, just boxers and his T-shirt. She slipped up beside him, wrapped her hands around the curve of his elbow and leaned her cheek against his arm. He kissed the top of her head and nuzzled her hair.

"Are we just going to stand here?" she whispered.

"I think we'd better. I've got a problem you can't help me with."

"Wanna bet?" Dory steered him backward toward a wooden deck chair on the far wall of the enclosed balcony. "How quiet can you be?"

"I'm not the screamer." He grinned, his teeth a white flash.

"I can be quiet as a mouse." Dory pushed him into the chair and straddled him, felt how hard he was and shivered. "Mmmm."

Chase slid his hands inside her nightie, cupped her breasts, teased her nipples between his thumbs and forefingers and kissed her. He didn't make a sound; neither did Dory. He raised his hips; she lowered his boxers and guided him inside her. Chase gripped her hips and rocked her from side to side. Oh, it was bliss. He caught her climax in a kiss, wrapped his arms around her and held her.

"How scared are you?" he murmured into her hair.

"Pretty darned if you want the truth, but not for me."

"Do you think you should tell Jamie what's going on?"

"I don't want to. If this goes the way Gordy has it planned, he won't even realize what's happening." Dory rested her forehead against his. "Jamie told me he doesn't have a soul because of what his father did."

"Oh hell," Chase said. "Don't tell him."

At ten o'clock Tuesday, Dory and Jamie were on the beach.

On their way they made a pass through the gift shop. Dory bought a book and a boogie board for Jamie. He helped her put up her umbrella and unfold her beach chair, let her smear him up with sunblock, then he went tearing away and flopped into the surf on his board.

Dory draped Aunt Ping's pink and orange silk Hermès scarf around her neck and leaned back in her beach chair. She wanted desperately to know where Chase and Diego and Gary were, but she kept her nose in her book, though she never read a word.

Her heart shot into her throat when her cell phone rang at ten minutes past eleven. It wasn't Gordy; it was Aunt Ping.

"James just rang Miss Fairview to confirm that you and Jamie are in Cancún," she said, a faint tremor in her voice. "He asked when you were returning. She told him she didn't know. I hope that was all right."

"Me, too." Dory's stomach clenched. "Thanks, Aunt Ping."

She put the phone down and pressed her hands to her face. She had sweat on her upper lip but her fingers felt like ice. Oh crap. Had they blown this already? There was only one way to find out—wait.

At twelve-fifteen she and Jamie went up to the bar and ate lunch with Jill. Chicken salad sandwiches and Cokes.

"Where's Diego and Gary and Chet?" Jamie asked.

"Chase. I don't know." Dory shrugged. "They can't be far."

After lunch she made Jamie sit for thirty minutes on the towel beside her chair. Then she hosed him down with sunblock again.

"Okay, squirt." She gave him a swat on the butt. "Have fun."

Jamie grabbed his board and made a beeline for the water. Dory leaned back in her chair and opened her book. A woman came around the umbrella and dropped onto the beach towel beside her. A woman in an ugly purple and yellow Muumuu split to the knee on the sides and a frumpy straw hat pulled over a red scarf tied around her hair.

"Who do you think you're going to fool in that getup?" Dory asked.

"Your so-called bodyguards for starters." Jill took off her shades. "I walked down here without Gary or Chase or Diego batting an eye."

"That's reassuring." Dory laid her book aside and turned toward her. "You know you aren't supposed to be here."

"I bit off two fingernails this morning watching you sit out here all by yourself. To hell with Gordy. He's not keeping me out of this," Jill said fiercely. "I've got a couple things I'd like to say to James."

"So do I. Just wait till he's handcuffed, okay?"

When Dory's cell phone rang, they both almost jumped off the beach towel. It was Gordy. "We're on our way," was all he said.

"Oh boy." She drew a shaky breath and looked at Jill. "Here we go."

"Call Chase." Jill put on her shades. "I'll watch Jamie."

Dory speed-dialed Chase, her heart banging. "James took the bait," she told him. "He's coming in."

"We'll be ready," Chase said. "I love you. Take care of yourself."

Dory put the cell phone on the towel where she could see the clock, and squinted down the beach. She could just see the quay where James would have to moor his launch. It was twenty minutes by boat from Isla Rica. The quay looked to be a five-minute walk from the beach.

It was twenty past one. By two o'clock James ought to be here.

At ten minutes till two, Dory heard footsteps squishing toward her through the sand and glanced up. A huge shadow loomed beyond the curve of the umbrella. Before she could grab Jill, who hadn't taken her eyes off Jamie, Agent Frasier plopped down on the towel in front of them.

"Well." He grinned. "Fancy meeting the two of you here."

He wore khaki shorts, a lavender Hawaiian shirt, white Gilligan hat and boat shoes with no socks. His ginger-haired legs were pale and speckled with spider veins.

"Agent Frasier," Dory said, stunned. "What are you doing here?"

"I'd ask you the same question, but I think I know the answer." He glanced at Jill. "That was Lindsay Varner in the Rolls, wasn't it?"

"Scram, G-man," Jill snapped. "We're trying to catch a thief here."

"That's what I thought. That's why I came."

"Sweet of you, but bug off," Jill said. "You no more look like a tourist than I look like an old frump. We don't need you. We've got Gary."

"Lord help us," Agent Frasier said, but he got to his feet. "I'll be around if you need me. Just yell."

He lumbered away and Jill sighed with relief. So did Dory. The clock on her cell phone said it was one fifty-five.

"That was too close. James could be here any sec—"

"Dory." Jill's fingers clamped like a manacle on her wrist. "Look."

Jill was staring, white-faced. Dory turned her head to the right and saw James. He hadn't changed a bit in ten years. He still looked like Sir Paul out for an amble on the beach. He was about thirty yards away, strolling toward them with his hands in the pockets of his white pants, cuffs rolled, a black ball cap on his head.

"Don't stare." Dory shoved her book at Jill and snatched up the bottle of sunblock. "Don't even look at him."

Jill ripped the book open and buried her nose in it. Dory squirted sunblock in her hand and stuck her right leg out. She counted to ten, wiped her hand on the towel and glanced up to see where James was just as he turned his head in her direction and saw her.

She knew he saw her—he was barely twenty yards away—but did he recognize her? Did he recognize Jill? Dory didn't blink; she didn't breathe. Jill didn't move. James swung his head away. Dory ducked her chin, raised her eyes and watched him over the rims of her sunglasses.

He looked at her and Jill again, slowed his pace and stared at them, dropped his hands out of his pockets, and glanced at the water, at Jamie skimming toward him on the crest of a two-foot wave. All he had to do was turn and pluck Jamie off the boogie board. When James turned, Dory shot to her feet.

He would not touch Jamie—he would *not*!

And he didn't. The wave petered out ten feet shy of the beach and dumped Jamie into the surf, rolling him away from James, out of his reach. James made a dive for him that came up empty, then waded into the surf, groping for Jamie under the surface of the water.

"Where's Gary?" Jill was on her feet beside her. "Where's Gordy?"

Jamie surfaced about fifteen yards away from James, shaking his head and spewing water. James spun in the surf, saw him and smiled.

"Find Gary." Dory shoved Jill and broke toward the water. "*Jamie!*" she shrieked, running as fast as she could. "*Jam-ee!*"

He didn't hear her. He drew a breath and dived in search of his board, but James swung around, weaving in the knee-high water and saw her pelting toward him. His eyes widened and then Gordy hit him from behind, lassoing him around the knees. Dory skidded to a stop in the sand, watching James stagger and pinwheel his arms to keep his balance. He might've managed it if Chase, Diego, Gary and Agent Frasier hadn't come crashing into the surf all at once.

Chase caught a fistful of James' sodden white shirt and smashed his left fist in his face. Dory grinned as James went down, limp as a dead fish. Gordy came up beside him, choking on salt water, and caught James by his right arm. Diego took James' left arm; Gary and Frasier his legs and they carried James up the beach. Chase followed them, shaking his hand. Jill met them and fell into step beside

Gary, her arm looped around his waist. Dory couldn't tell if she was laughing or crying.

"Hey, Dory," Jamie said and she nearly jumped out of her white cover-up. She spun toward him, wet and sunburned beside her, his boogie board under his arm. "What's with that dude?"

"Dude?" Dory said. "What dude?"

"The dude Diego and Gary and Gordy and—" Jamie broke off and blinked. "Hey. Is that the fat FBI guy from the orchard?"

"In Cancún? I don't think so. Didn't you see what happened?"

"No. I was looking for my board. Didn't you see?"

"Nope. I didn't see a thing." *Thank you, God,* Dory sent up a prayer. "I've had enough of the beach for one day. How 'bout a Coke?"

Jamie helped her collapse the umbrella. While he shook sand off the towel and folded it, Dory stuffed her book and the sunblock in her fishnet tote, stood up and saw Jill coming toward them, her hat and her scarf in her hand and a dazzling, sparkly-eyed smile on her face. Jamie didn't see her till he rose to his feet with the towel. Before he could open his mouth to scream, Jill scooped him into a hug and kissed him.

"Come on, monster. I'm buying you ice cream." She hooked an arm around Jamie's neck and said to Dory, "It's your turn."

Jill nodded at the low wall that separated the beach from the road, picked up the umbrella and drew a shocked Jamie toward the bar.

James sat on the wall, surrounded by Chase, Diego, Gordy, Agent Frasier and Gary. His hands were cuffed behind him, his right eye was turning black from Chase's fist. He was soaked and he was finished. His hair was still long, a scraggly, sand-caked mess. When Dory stopped in front of him, Chase slid up behind her and put his hand on her shoulder.

"Hello, pug." James squinted at her with his one good eye. "Clever little mutt, aren't you?"

"A lot cleverer than you. Your new neighbors on Isla Rica? Roger and Priscilla Davenport? Their real names are Del and Drusilla Lambert."

James stared at her for a moment, then said, "Bugger."

"Now we're even." Dory took off her sunglasses, pointed at her still black eye and smiled at him. "Good-*bye*, bastard little prick."

Epilogue

Mr. and Mrs. Del Lambert
(*My dear darling Daddy and my dim-witted Mother, who
nearly cost Aunt Ping her Outlook*)
Request the Honor of Your Presence at the Marriage of
their Daughter
(*and was horrified that Jill had married Chase till Jill ex-
plained they were getting an annulment so Chase could
marry me.*)
Dory Drusilla Diana Lambert
(*At which point Mother said, "Oh. Well, that's all right,
then."*)
To
Chase Malcolm Charles McKay
(*The best darned architect in the country but still the
chauffeur's son as far as Mother is concerned.*)
On the Afternoon of Saturday, September 4
(*Also the day of the Annual Labor Day Picnic for Lambert employees, which is only fitting since I'm now vice
president of operations.*)
Outlook Farm, Kansas City, Missouri
(*Known as the Outlook Inn until July 31, when its doors
closed forever.*)

Exchange of Vows 2 P.M.
(*I vow not to choke Mother so long as Daddy gets her off
Outlook ASAP*)

Wedding Supper 5 P.M.
(*Hot dogs, beans and barbecue on the lawn*)
Dancing 7 P.M.
(*Do NOT dance with the groom!*)
RSVP
(*No. This does not spell déjà vu.*)

"This is the invitation we should have sent." Dory tugged the ivory vellum card out of the back pocket of her jeans and handed it to Chase.

She'd written between the lines with the gold pen that Agent Frasier gave her when she'd received her MBA. While Chase read the invitation, Dory brushed sawdust off her hands, plucked the bandana Chase had given her out of her front pocket and sneezed.

She sat beside him on the open edge of the roughed-in, plywood-floored second story of the house he was building for them on Outlook. It made her feel giddy to sit up here forty feet off the ground, almost as giddy as realizing that this time tomorrow she'd be Dory Lambert McKay.

It was going to be a wonderful house. Her very own. She was thirty-one and she'd never had a home of her own. Chase had let her help him design it. She'd sat in his lap at his drawing board, told him what she wanted and where she wanted it. He'd insisted that she sit in his lap.

"Isn't this awkward for you?" she'd said.

"You bet." He'd grinned. "But when you get in my way I get to feel you up."

The best part of the house? It was way, way, *way* far away from the big house. A precaution in case Mother changed her mind about returning from Isla Rica, which she claimed to love dearly and miss terribly.

Daddy and Mother had returned to Outlook two weeks after James' capture, once Coop made sure the coast was legally clear for them to do so. Aunt Ping met them in the front drive under the portico. She'd embraced Daddy, turned to Mother and said:

"I suffered you under my roof for thirty years. No more.

You may stay in the guesthouse. I will allow you to attend Dory's wedding. Jill's, if she has one. Beyond that, be grateful I let you through the front gates."

Two days of tears from Mother and begging from Daddy later—to which Aunt Ping turned a deaf ear—Mother decided she couldn't bear to leave her dear little villa on Isla Rica. Where she could be Queen Bee of all she surveyed without interference. Dory would've danced a jig if only she wasn't taking Daddy with her.

"It's not forever, darling," he told her. "We'll be popping back for holidays and board meetings."

"The day she was named vice president of operations, Lambert's board of directors voted to reinstate Daddy as chairman. Even Mother had shed a few tears of joy.

Chase finished reading, threw his head back and laughed, pulled her into a one-armed embrace and kissed her on the mouth. Oh. He had the most beautiful mouth. A quiver of lust shivered through Dory. Chase chuckled and rubbed his lips on her temple.

"Down girl," he murmured. "It's only twenty-four more hours."

Dory looked up at him and wrinkled her nose. "Your taking a shot at chastity before the wedding idea sucks."

"You say that now." Chase kissed her lightly. "Wait'll you see what two weeks of celibacy gets you."

"What's that?" Dory asked.

Chase grinned. "Wild animals in the jungle sex."

"I keep hearing about that but I have yet to see it."

"Yeah? Well, tomorrow night you *get* it."

"Hey Chet!" Jamie hollered from below. "What is this thing?"

Chase looked down at him, standing on the makeshift ramp that led up to the gaping hole where the front doors would be. So did Dory and felt her heart seize at the nail gun in Jamie's hands.

"Put it down, Jimbo," Chase said. "Put it down and back away."

Jamie rolled his eyes. "I just want to know what it is."

"Put it down, back away, and I'll tell you."

"Jeez criminy." Jamie put the nail gun down on the ply-wood floor, walked down the ramp and held his hands up. "How's this?"

"Stay right there." Chase pulled Dory to her feet, led her out of Jamie's bedroom and down the roughed-in steps, picked up the gun and said, "It's a nail gun."

"I *knew* it!" Jamie smacked a fist against his thigh. "Will you teach me to use it?"

"Next weekend. It's getting late," Chase said and it was, the setting sun sliding long, golden, almost-autumn beams through the four by fours of the framed-in house. "Where are the safety goggles I gave you?"

"On my bike," Jamie said and nodded at the goggles hung over the handlebars of the silver and black BMX bike leaning against a tree.

"No goggles, no gun, so don't lose 'em," Chase said and put a kiss on Dory's forehead. "I'll put my tools away, then we'll go."

"Ready when you are." She turned and watched him stride away through the house, tall and handsome and hers. She was getting used to his tailored suits and shirts, but this was how she loved Chase best and always would, in jeans and a white T-shirt.

"Gag puke," Jamie said. "You're gonna drool in a minute."

"Hey, squirt." Dory threw her balled-up bandana at him. He caught it and tossed it back with a grin. "Want to put your bike in the truck?"

"Nah. I'll ride back." Jamie pulled his bike off the tree and hopped on, braced his feet on the ground and squinted up at the house. "I wish Chet would hurry up with this place. Auntie Deirdre is driving me nuts."

"Patience, squirt." Dory wrapped her fingers around the handlebars. "Daddy and Mother will be gone on Monday. When Chase and I get back from Tahiti, the three of us can move into the guesthouse."

"Uncle Del is nice," Jamie said. "But I won't miss *her*."

Neither would Deirdre. In response to the umpteenth note Mother sent up to Outlook claiming how she'd wept every day in Isla Rica over the loss of her dear sister, Deirdre had written:

"May I remind you that you have a cousin? One with whom you have so much in common. I have heard from Diana and enclose her address in Aruba. Do let her share the details of how she abandoned Jamie and me in London. I'm sure she'll be delighted to hear how you turned the both of us away from your door on Isla Rica. Have a lovely catch-up, you two, and trouble me no more."

Deirdre had let her read the note. Dory gave her a high five. Aunt Ping gave Deirdre a check for eight million, three hundred and twelve thousand dollars, her initial investment in the Outlook Inn, two weeks after Daddy's assets were unfrozen and he repaid Aunt Ping the fortune she'd spent to bail out Lambert Securities. Deirdre had waived interest.

"Don't be ridiculous, Margaret," she'd said. "You gave Jamie and me a home when we had nowhere else to go."

"This is still your home, Deirdre," Aunt Ping replied. "Outlook will always be your home."

They'd hugged and cried and kissed each other on the cheek.

Dory's eyes filled remembering how sweet it was to see her dear Aunt Deirdre and her beloved Aunt Ping wrapped in each other's arms. Happy tears for them and sad tears for her stupid, silly mother who would never in a hundred million years get it.

Jamie cocked his head at her. "Are you crying?"

"No." Dory wiped her lashes. "I've got sawdust in my eyes."

"Yeah, right." Jamie grinned. "Jill says all brides cry."

"If you see Jill, don't tell her where I am."

Jamie shuddered. "Can you make her stop kissing me every time she sees me? It's weird. Ever since—" He broke off and ducked his head.

"Cancún? Do you wish I'd told you what was going on?"

"No!" Jamie's chin shot up and he said again, vehemently, "*No*. I'm glad you didn't tell me. It's just—he won't ever get out of jail, will he?"

"Not for a long, long time. He's in for attempted kidnapping as well as fraud. If he ever *does* get out, he'll be deported on the spot."

It was the last thing Marshall Phillips told them before he resigned as United States attorney and moved to Arizona. Coop had flown in from New York for that party. He was flying in tonight to attend Dory's wedding.

Jamie swung off his bike, let it fall to the ground and threw his arms around her. He was shivering like a little monkey, the way he'd used to when he was small. Dory wrapped her arms around him.

"'Member when Auntie Deirdre and I came to Outlook and you said no one would ever love me like my mummy but you promised you'd try?"

"Yes, Jamie." She stroked his hair. "I remember."

"You kept your promise. So I promise I won't drop the rings."

Dory laughed, blinked back tears, cupped his devilish, freckled face in her hands and gave him a smacking kiss on the lips.

"*Yech!*" Jamie dragged the sleeve of his Spider-Man sweatshirt over his mouth but he grinned as he yanked his bike up and hopped on. "For *free* I promise I won't drop the rings."

"Go, home, squirt." Dory laughed.

She couldn't swat him so she threw her balled-up bandana at him again. Jamie caught it, threw it back and rode away down the road to Outlook, grinning at her over his shoulder and waving. Dory waved till he was out of sight, then she buried her face in the bandana and sobbed.

She didn't hear Chase come up behind her, but she felt his hands on her shoulders, let him turn her around and wrap her in his warm, strong arms.

"All brides cry," he said gently and Dory knew he'd heard every word, which only made her cry harder. "Don't you want to save some of those tears for tomorrow?"

"The happiest day of my life?" Dory wiped her eyes with the last dry inch of the bandana. "Why would I cry? I plan to laugh myself silly."

"C'mon, Mrs. Almost McKay." Chase put his arm around her and drew her toward the burgundy red Expedition. "Let's go grab a burger."

He didn't have to, she had climbing into the behemoth truck down to a science, but Chase helped her up into the passenger seat. Dory belted herself in, turned on the radio and bounced and jiggled to a Beach Boys' song on the oldies station.

Chase grinned at her. "Show-off."

The road made a wide, tree-shaded curve about thirty yards from its juncture with the South Drive. The sun slanted in a vivid blaze past the reddening maples that overhung the road, turning the truck's windshield silver with glare. As silver as the Rolls-Royce purring past the juncture and sweeping away along the South Drive.

"What the—?" Chase stepped on the brake, turned his head and watched the Rolls glide out of sight. "Where the hell is Dad going?"

"Did he see us?" Dory asked.

"Not with the sun at this angle. He would've honked the horn."

"Then I think I know where he's going. And he's not alone."

Chase glanced at her and blinked. "You're kidding."

"Let's find out. Follow that Rolls."

Dory directed him to the walking trail that sliced through the trees, ran parallel with the bridle path in places and skirted the green on the sixth hole of the golf course. They left the truck on the road and followed the trail to the Lily Pond, where the willows lining the banks dipped their long, yellowing fronds into the green water.

The big oak Dory hid behind the day Aunt Ping ran away

from the prospective guest committee meeting dropped mottled gold leaves on their heads as she and Chase leaned past the gnarled trunk. Aunt Ping sat on the bench with Charles' arm around her and her head on his shoulder. When she raised her face, he kissed her on the mouth.

"I'll be damned," Chase whispered in Dory's ear. He didn't say anything else till they were back in the truck. "How'd you find out?"

"I followed Aunt Ping once," Dory told him. "Are you shocked?"

"No. I'm amazed I never saw it before." He shook his head and smiled at her. "Now I know why Dad ixnayed the house I wanted to build him next door to ours. Why didn't you tell me?"

"I wasn't completely sure that I wasn't crazy," she said, and told him while he drove them back to Outlook how she'd snooped through Esther's household ledgers and the logbooks Charles kept on the Rolls.

Chase parked in front of the garage, came around the truck and lifted her down from the seat. "Promise me something, sweet stuff."

"Keep calling me sweet stuff and I'll promise you anything."

"Promise me you won't do anything else ever again in the vernacular of the detective novel."

"Cross my heart." Dory stretched up on her toes for a kiss. "My snooping and sleuthing days are officially over."

The look on Jill's face, when she caught Dory trying to sneak into the house through Esme's kitchen, said her life could be over. Since her courthouse wedding to Gary a month ago, she'd turned into the wedding planner from hell.

"Look at your nails!" Jill howled and grabbed her right hand. "Don't hold dinner, Esme. We're off for an emergency manicure."

She ignored Dory when she said Chase was taking her for a burger and hauled her upstairs to the room that had recently been Miss Fairview's. While Dory changed, Jill speed-dialed Chase on his cell.

"You were a shitty husband, now you're a shitty fiancé!" She yelled at him. "Forget the burger! Dory has to have another manicure!"

Dory didn't want another manicure, but Dory got one at Jill's ultra-exclusive and obnoxiously expensive salon on the Plaza. She got a facial she didn't want, either, and a body wax, too.

"You'll thank me the day after tomorrow," Jill said with a smile. "And if you don't, Chase will."

The maniacal gleam was gone from her sapphire eyes. For the most part, Jill was blissfully happy being married to Gary. He was blissfully happy married to Jill and practicing law. Not to mention that he'd been as glad to see the last of the FBI as the Bureau was to see the last of him.

No burger with Chase, but Jill bought Dory dinner.

"I just love having this back," she said and kissed her platinum American Express card.

"Don't forget the Matron of Honor," Dory told her on their way to the car. "Your job tomorrow is to keep Mother away from me."

"That's me." Jill slung an arm around her neck and kissed the top of her head. "Still the lookout."

Aunt Ping and Deirdre helped her dress for her wedding. Deirdre smoothed her hair into place and seated her headdress and veil. Aunt Ping fastened Great-grandmother Lambert's pearls around her throat, laid her hands on Dory's shoulders and smiled at her in the mirror of her dressing table.

"You're the most beautiful bride I've ever seen," she said. "And I love you with all my heart."

Except for the part that belongs to Charles, Dory thought. She laid her hand over Aunt Ping's on her shoulder and smiled. "I love you, too."

At two o'clock, Daddy walked her down the aisle formed by chairs in the ballroom. Chase waited for her in a midnight blue Armani tux she knew he'd had to have tailored to fit his shoulders. When he took her hand from Daddy, she murmured to him, "It's déjà vu all over again."

He was still trying not to laugh when Father Murphy pronounced them man and wife and he raised her veil to kiss her. When the receiving line ended, Chase handed Jamie a one hundred-dollar bill.

"What's this?" he asked. "I said I wouldn't drop the rings for free."

"That's so you'll lose the bubble blaster gun."

"You got it, Chet." Jamie grinned.

First, Dory danced with her husband, then Daddy, then Curt.

"Always the groomsman, never the groom." He grinned at her. "But we're still friends, right?"

"Always. But you'll never be Chase's best man ever again."

While Chase danced with Esme and Esther and Aunt Ping and Deirdre, Dory shared a glass of champagne with Coop on the terrace.

"Been a while since we did this." Coop smiled and lifted his flute. "Congratulations, Dory."

"Thanks, Coop." She kissed his cheek. "If you'd like to submit a bill for all your pro bono work, feel free. My husband is loaded."

Next Dory danced with Gordy and Agent Frasier. He'd retired two weeks after Marshall Phillips resigned. Dory and Chase had attended his retirement party, met his wife and his grandkids.

"I'm glad your parents are home. Too bad they aren't staying."

"Oh, no. It's a good thing," Dory assured him. "As soon as my mother leaves for Isla Rica I'm sure I'll stop grinding my teeth again."

He laughed and so did Dory. She laughed when she danced with Charles and Tom and Eddie and Peter and Henry, managed to compose herself while Wallace waltzed her around the ballroom, then she started to laugh again just because she was so happy she could hardly stand it.

When her feet had had enough dancing, Chase loaded her into the blue golf cart and whisked them down to the picnic, where all of Lambert Bank and Trust's six hundred and thirty-seven employees cheered them and applauded. Anita sat with them at a picnic table and ate hot dogs.

"I've been boning up on my shorthand," she told Dory. "I'll be ready to go when you start October first, madam vice president."

Dory kissed her. "I'll have the best secretary in the whole bank."

When it got dark, they had fireworks. Chase put his arm around her and whispered in her ear, "This is nothin'. Wait'll I get you upstairs."

He kissed her and topped her glass with Dom Pérignon.

By the time she threw her bouquet, Dory was half-loaded. Deirdre caught the gorgeous yellow roses Peter had made for her. Her aunt stood next to Gordy and blushed like a girl. He grinned and darn near hurt himself catching her garter.

"That's it. We're done," Chase said and swept her into his arms.

He ran all the way to the Honeymoon Suite.

"I guess you know the way," Dory said and laughed.

Chase laughed, too. He kicked the doors open, rushed across the room and threw her on the bed, whirled and kicked the doors shut, turned the locks and spun around, his eyes deep, dark navy. He ripped off his tie, shucked off his tuxedo jacket and kicked off his shoes and jumped on the bed beside her.

"Missed me!" Dory crowed and rolled away from him, shrieking with laughter and tangling herself in her veil.

She'd never been so happy or had so much fun in her life. She was sure she would again, every day for the rest of her life from now on. She rolled onto her stomach, so twisted up in her veil she couldn't move.

"Chase?" She tried to lift her head but couldn't. "I'm stuck."

"So I see." He chuckled. "How bad do you want out?"

"How bad do you want in?"

"Pretty bad." He leaned over her and nuzzled the back of her neck. "Let me see if I can find the end of this thing."

He did finally and unwound her, pulled her up into his arms and kissed her. "Ready for wild animals in the jungle sex?"

"Past ready," Dory said, quivering all over.

Chase went up on his knees, gripped the front of his shirt and ripped it open, peeled it off and tossed it. Then he closed his fingers on the bodice of the gown Daddy had paid six thousand dollars for and split it right down the middle. Dory shrieked with laughter. Her underwear came off in shreds, then his pants and his boxers.

He slid between her legs, wrapped them around his waist and Dory stopped laughing. She put her arms around Chase's neck and kissed him a zillion times, while he made love to her in an amazing array of positions that left her head spinning and her body throbbing for more. He caught her last climax in a kiss, then tucked the two of them under the covers, cuddled her against his chest, wrapped his arms around her and kissed her hair.

"Lemme know when you're ready for more."

"Oh boy." Dory sighed. "Am I glad I talked Jill out of hanging a trapeze in here."

Chase laughed, kissed her and cradled her face in his hands. "I'm having a lot more fun than I did the first time I was in this room."

"Of course you are, darling." Dory kissed his chin. "That's because this time you married the right sister."

Pillow Talk

SUBSCRIBE TO THE **FREE** PILLOW TALK
E-NEWSLETTER—AND RECEIVE ALL THESE
FABULOUS ONLINE FEATURES DIRECTLY IN
YOUR E-MAIL INBOX EACH MONTH:

- Exclusive essays and other features by
  major romance writers like
  Suzanne Brockmann, Julie Garwood,
  Kristin Hannah, and Linda Howard

- Exciting behind-the-scenes news from
  our romance editors

- Special offers, including promotions to win
  signed romance novels and other prizes

- Author tour information

- Announcements about the newest books on sale

- A Pillow Talk readers forum, featuring
  feedback from romance fans...like you!

Two easy ways to subscribe:
Go to www.ballantinebooks.com/PillowTalk
or send a blank e-mail to
sub_PillowTalk@info.randomhouse.com

Pillow Talk—
the romance e-newsletter brought to you by Ballantine Books